POSTAL™

CREATED BY MATT HAWKINS

VOLUME 5

PUBLISHED BY TOP COW PRODUCTIONS, INC.
LOS ANGELES

POSTAL

CREATED BY MATT HAWKINS

BRYAN HILL
WRITER

ISAAC GOODHART
ARTIST

K. MICHAEL RUSSELL
COLORIST

TROY PETERI
LETTERER

**ELENA SALCEDO &
MATT HAWKINS**
EDITORS

COVER ART FOR THIS EDITION BY
ISAAC GOODHART

ORIGINAL EDITIONS EDITED BY
**ASHLEY VICTORIA ROBINSON
& RYAN CADY**

BOOK DESIGN & LAYOUT BY
CAREY HALL

To find the comic shop
nearest you, call:
1-888-COMICBOOK

Want more info? Check out:
www.topcow.com
for news & exclusive Top Cow merchandise!

For Top Cow Productions, Inc.
For Top Cow Productions, Inc.
Marc Silvestri - CEO
Matt Hawkins - President & COO
Elena Salcedo - Vice President of Operations
Henry Barajas - Director of Operations
Vincent Valentine - Production Manager
Dylan Gray - Marketing Director

IMAGE COMICS, INC.
Robert Kirkman—Chief Operating Officer
Erik Larsen—Chief Financial Officer
Todd McFarlane—President
Marc Silvestri—Chief Executive Officer
Jim Valentino—Vice-President

Eric Stephenson—Publisher
Corey Murphy—Director of Sales
Jeff Boison—Director of Publishing Planning & Book Trade Sales
Chris Ross—Director of Digital Sales
Jeff Stang—Director of Specialty Sales
Kat Salazar—Director of PR & Marketing
Branwyn Bigglestone—Controller
Sue Korpela—Accounts Manager
Drew Gill—Art Director
Brett Warnock—Production Manager
Leigh Thomas—Print Manager
Tricia Ramos—Traffic Manager
Briah Skelly—Publicist
Aly Hoffman—Events & Conventions Coordinator
Sasha Head—Sales & Marketing Production Designer
David Brothers—Branding Manager
Melissa Gifford—Content Manager
Drew Fitzgerald—Publicity Assistant
Vincent Kukua—Production Artist
Erika Schnatz—Production Artist
Ryan Brewer—Production Artist
Shanna Matuszak—Production Artist
Carey Hall—Production Artist
Esther Kim—Direct Market Sales Representative
Emilio Bautista—Digital Sales Representative
Leanna Caunter—Accounting Assistant
Chloe Ramos-Peterson—Library Market Sales Representative
Marla Eizik—Administrative Assistant
IMAGECOMICS.COM

POSTAL VOLUME 5 TRADE PAPERBACK.

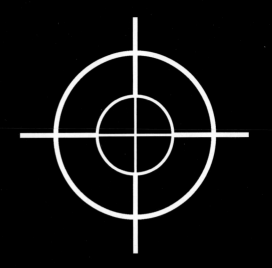

POSTAL

THE STORY SO FAR…

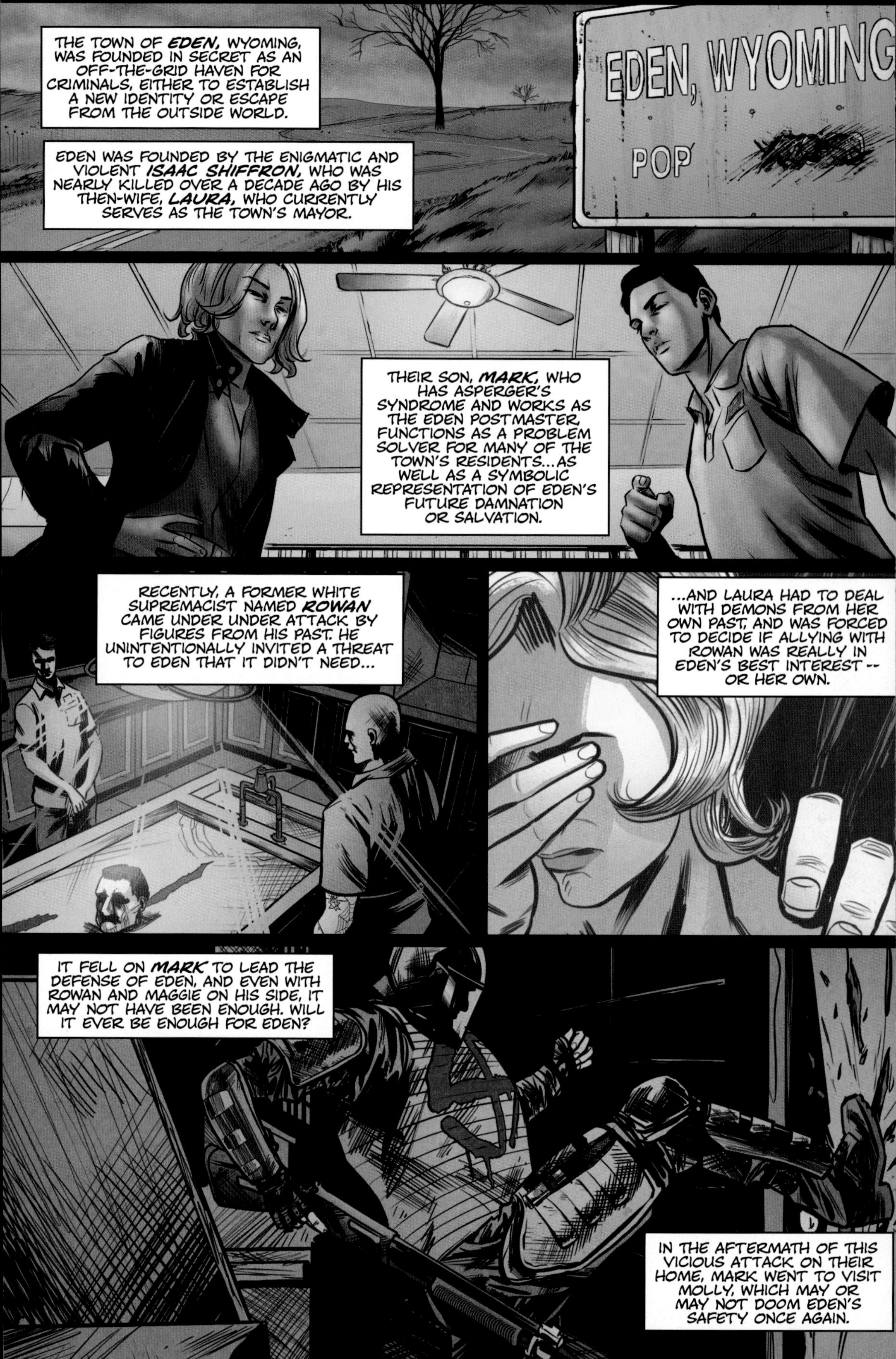
THE TOWN OF EDEN, WYOMING, WAS FOUNDED IN SECRET AS AN OFF-THE-GRID HAVEN FOR CRIMINALS, EITHER TO ESTABLISH A NEW IDENTITY OR ESCAPE FROM THE OUTSIDE WORLD.
EDEN, WYOMING
POP
EDEN WAS FOUNDED BY THE ENIGMATIC AND VIOLENT ISAAC SHIFFRON, WHO WAS NEARLY KILLED OVER A DECADE AGO BY HIS THEN-WIFE, LAURA, WHO CURRENTLY SERVES AS THE TOWN'S MAYOR.
THEIR SON, MARK, WHO HAS ASPERGER'S SYNDROME AND WORKS AS THE EDEN POSTMASTER, FUNCTIONS AS A PROBLEM SOLVER FOR MANY OF THE TOWN'S RESIDENTS...AS WELL AS A SYMBOLIC REPRESENTATION OF EDEN'S FUTURE DAMNATION OR SALVATION.
RECENTLY, A FORMER WHITE SUPREMACIST NAMED ROWAN CAME UNDER UNDER ATTACK BY FIGURES FROM HIS PAST. HE UNINTENTIONALLY INVITED A THREAT TO EDEN THAT IT DIDN'T NEED...
...AND LAURA HAD TO DEAL WITH DEMONS FROM HER OWN PAST, AND WAS FORCED TO DECIDE IF ALLYING WITH ROWAN WAS REALLY IN EDEN'S BEST INTEREST -- OR HER OWN.
IT FELL ON MARK TO LEAD THE DEFENSE OF EDEN, AND EVEN WITH ROWAN AND MAGGIE ON HIS SIDE, IT MAY NOT HAVE BEEN ENOUGH. WILL IT EVER BE ENOUGH FOR EDEN?
IN THE AFTERMATH OF THIS VICIOUS ATTACK ON THEIR HOME, MARK WENT TO VISIT MOLLY, WHICH MAY OR MAY NOT DOOM EDEN'S SAFETY ONCE AGAIN.

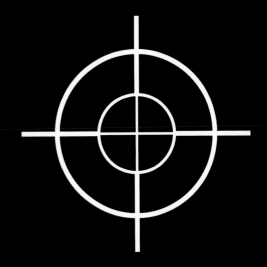

Chapter 17

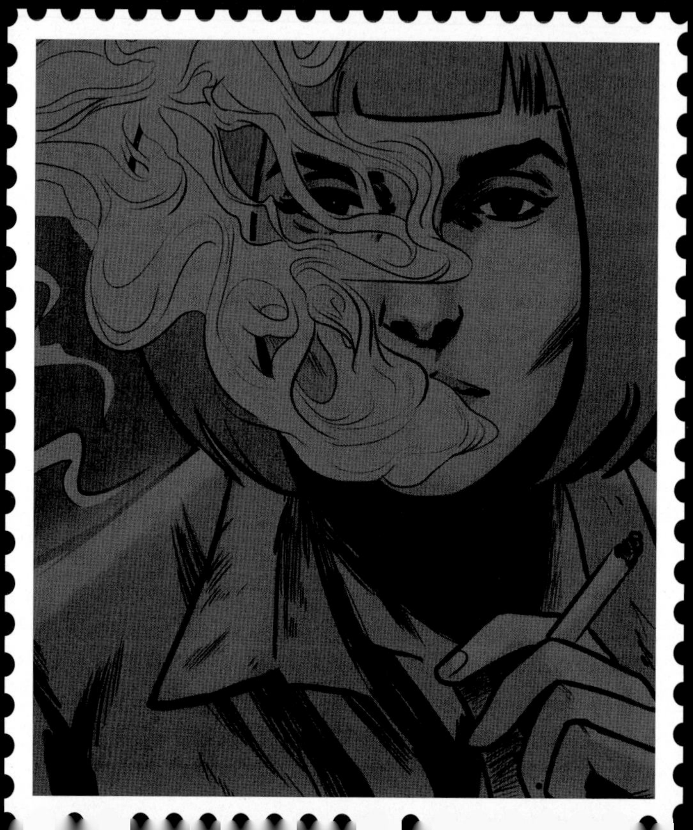

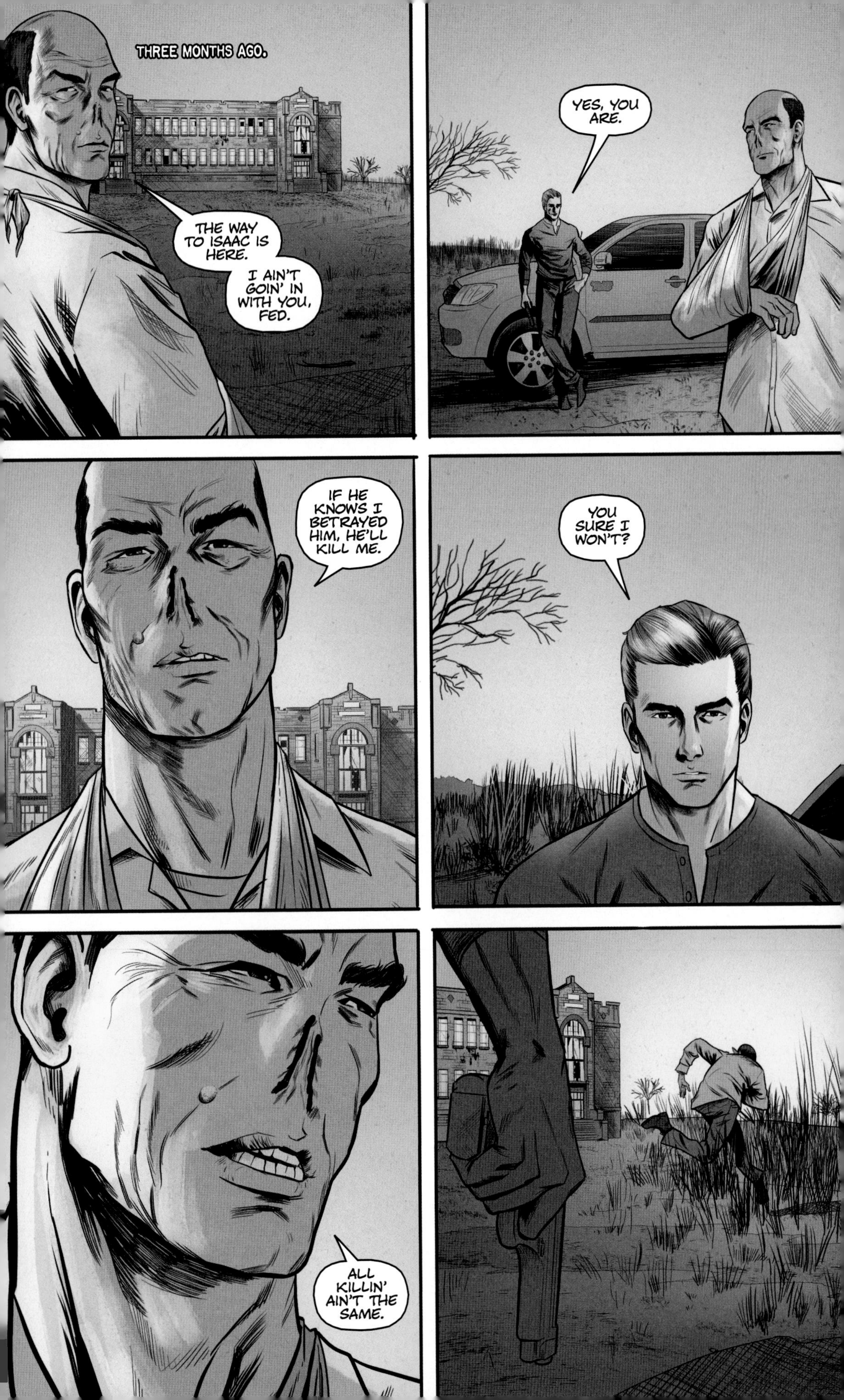

THREE MONTHS AGO.
THE WAY TO ISAAC IS HERE.
I AIN'T GOIN' IN WITH YOU, FED.
YES, YOU ARE.
IF HE KNOWS I BETRAYED HIM, HE'LL KILL ME.
YOU SURE I WON'T?
ALL KILLIN' AIN'T THE SAME.

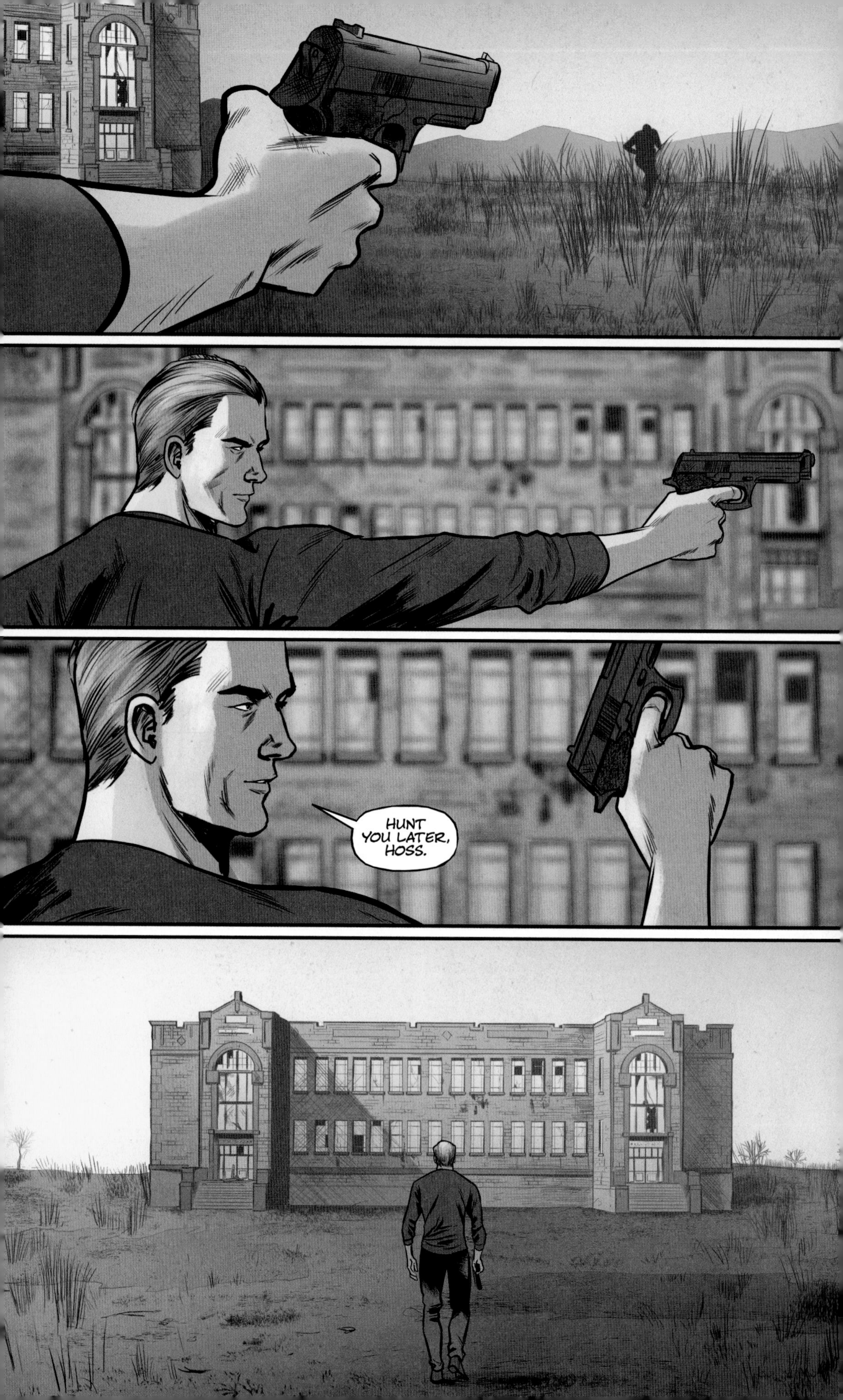
HUNT YOU LATER, HOSS.

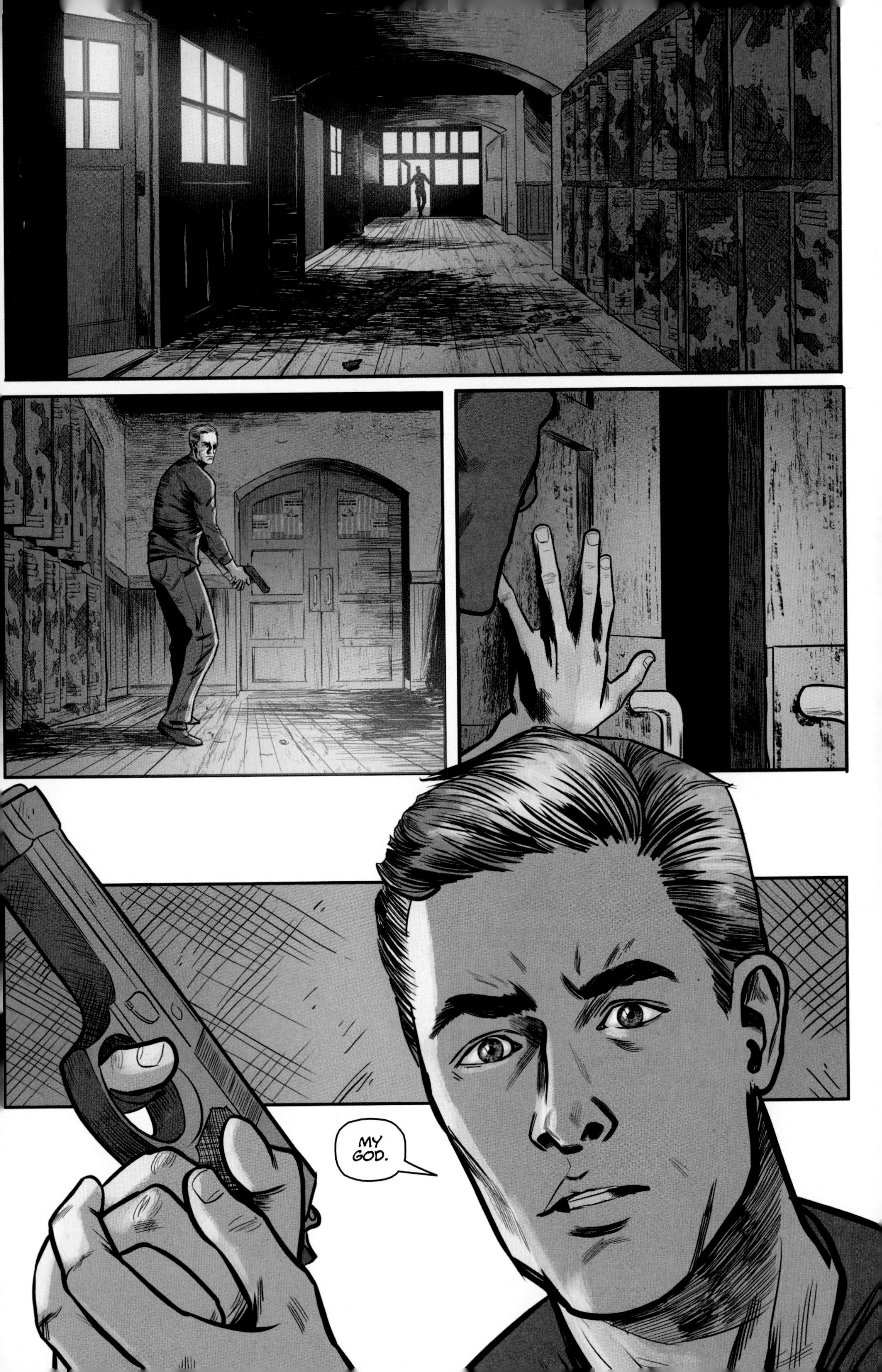
MY GOD.

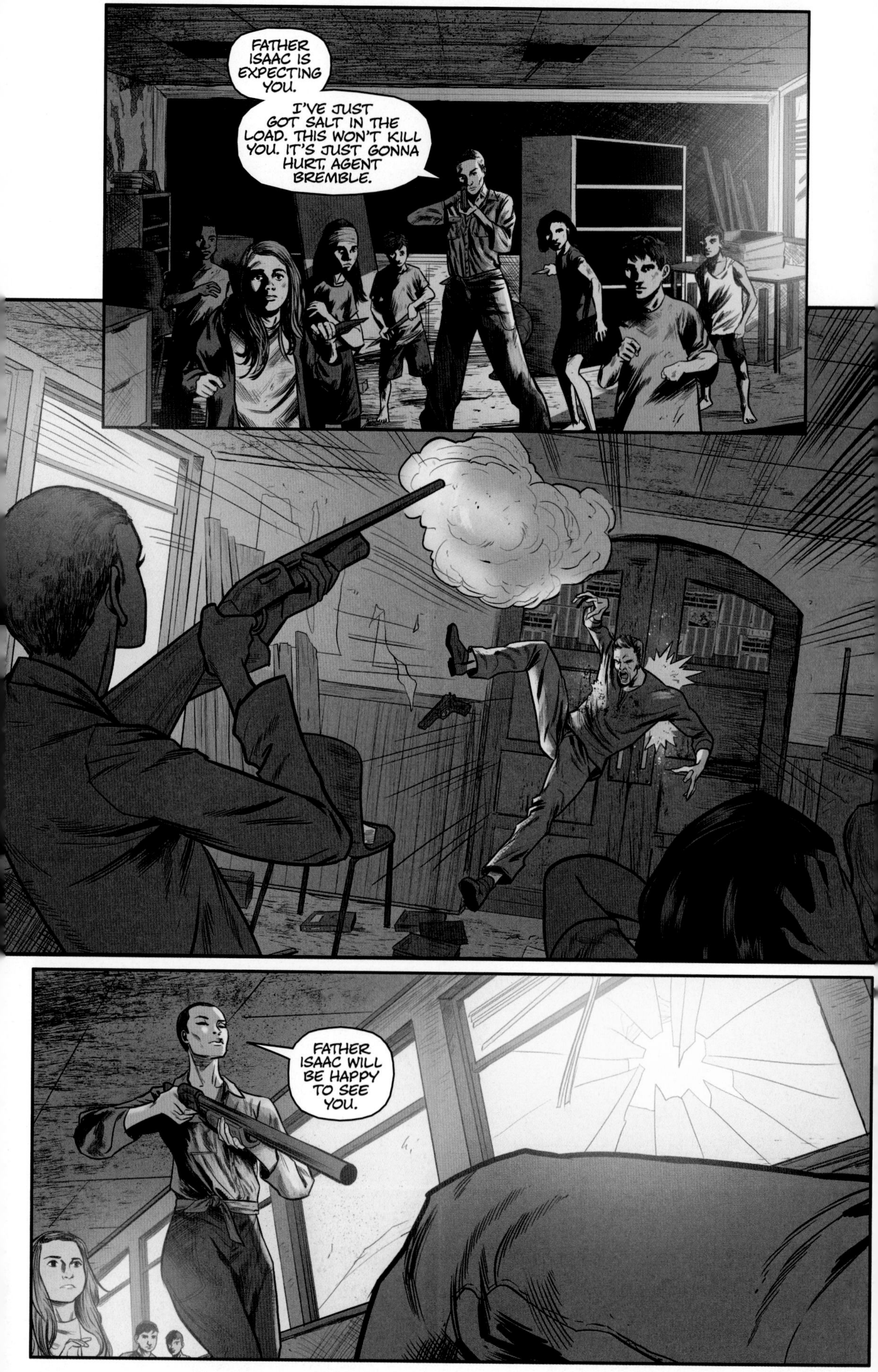
FATHER ISAAC IS EXPECTING YOU.
I'VE JUST GOT SALT IN THE LOAD. THIS WON'T KILL YOU. IT'S JUST GONNA HURT, AGENT BREMBLE.
FATHER ISAAC WILL BE HAPPY TO SEE YOU.

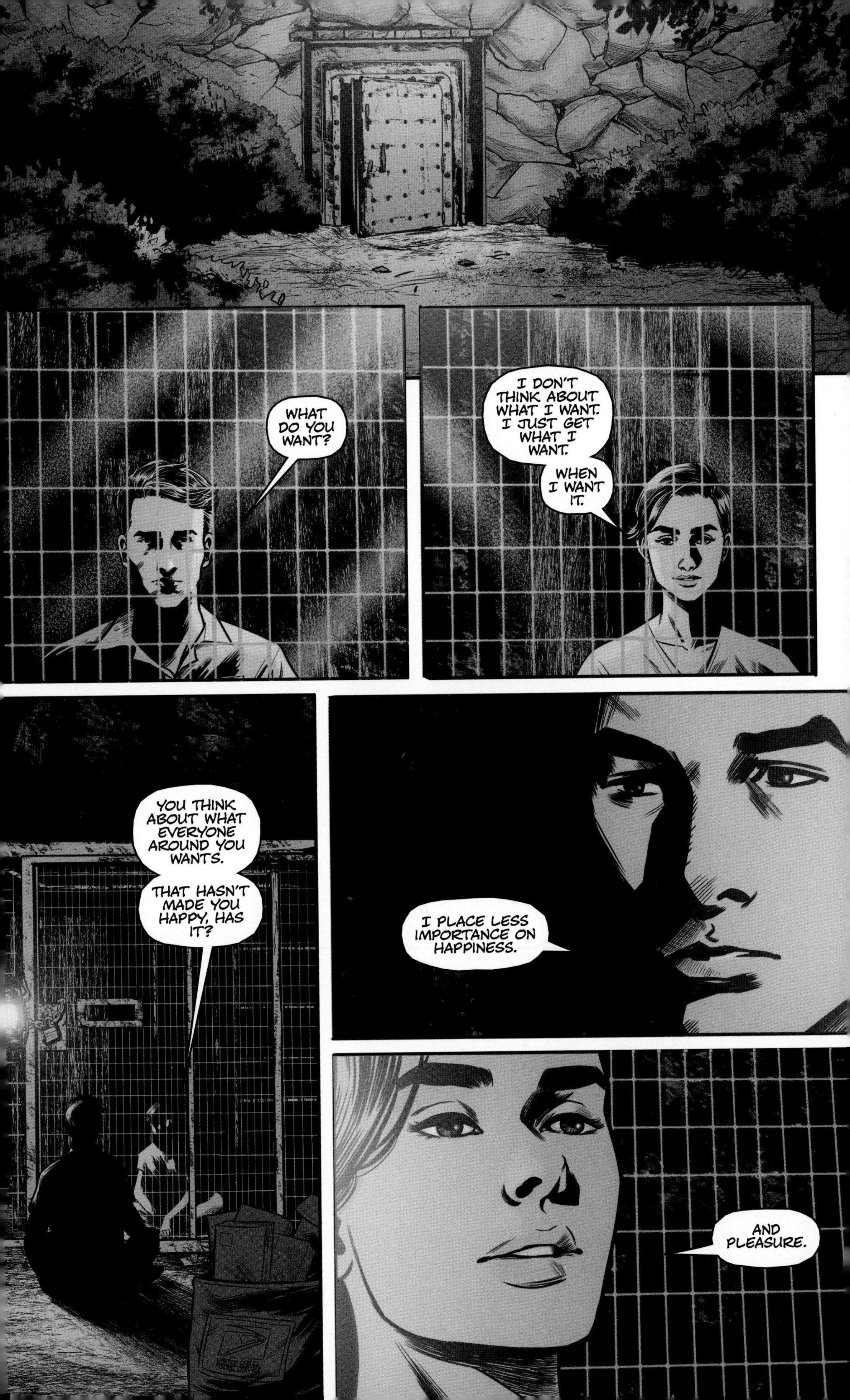
WHAT DO YOU WANT?
I DON'T THINK ABOUT WHAT I WANT. I JUST GET WHAT I WANT.
WHEN I WANT IT.
YOU THINK ABOUT WHAT EVERYONE AROUND YOU WANTS.
THAT HASN'T MADE YOU HAPPY, HAS IT?
I PLACE LESS IMPORTANCE ON HAPPINESS.
AND PLEASURE.

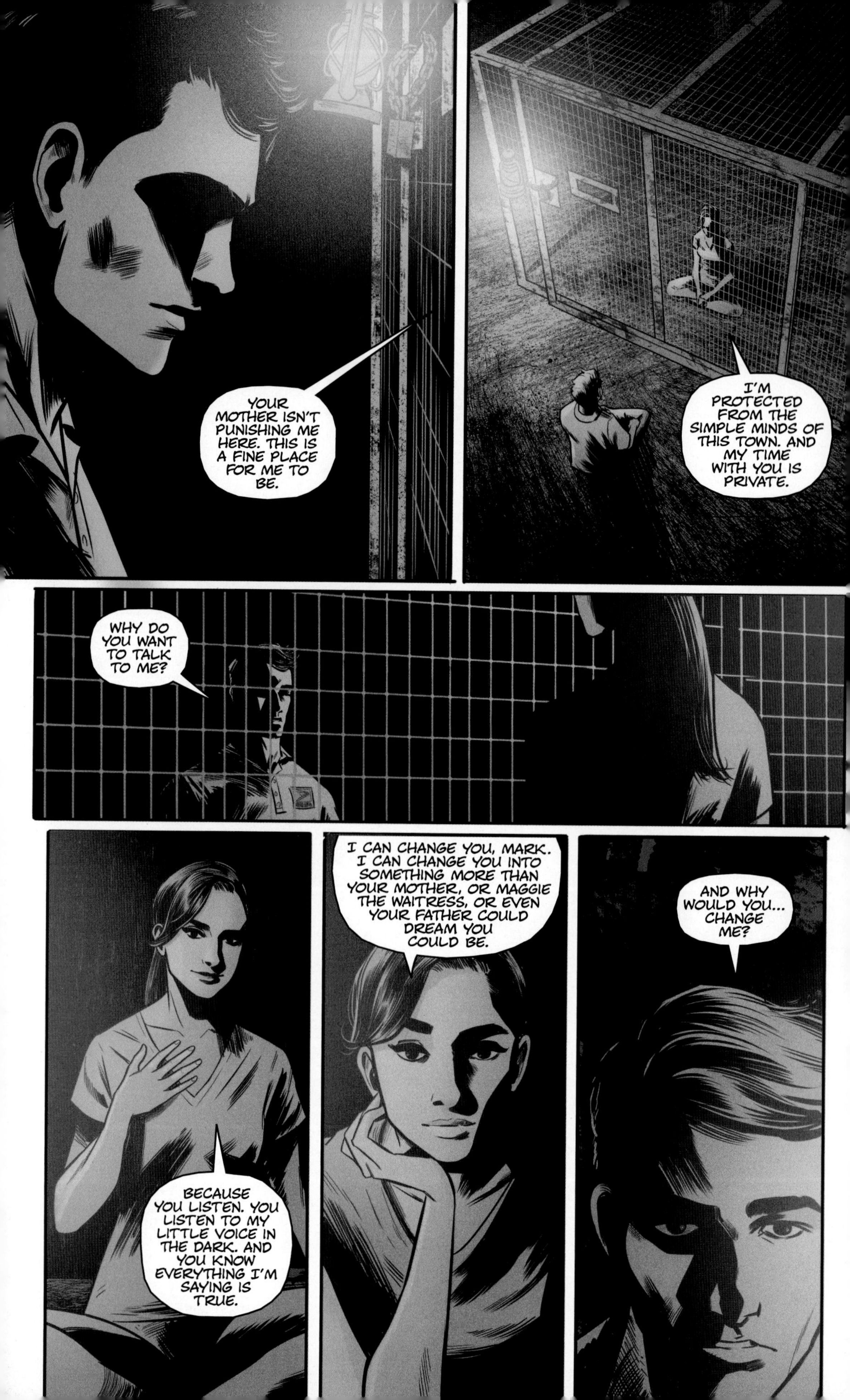

YOUR MOTHER ISN'T PUNISHING ME HERE. THIS IS A FINE PLACE FOR ME TO BE.
I'M PROTECTED FROM THE SIMPLE MINDS OF THIS TOWN. AND MY TIME WITH YOU IS PRIVATE.
WHY DO YOU WANT TO TALK TO ME?
BECAUSE YOU LISTEN. YOU LISTEN TO MY LITTLE VOICE IN THE DARK. AND YOU KNOW EVERYTHING I'M SAYING IS TRUE.
I CAN CHANGE YOU, MARK. I CAN CHANGE YOU INTO SOMETHING MORE THAN YOUR MOTHER, OR MAGGIE THE WAITRESS, OR EVEN YOUR FATHER COULD DREAM YOU COULD BE.
AND WHY WOULD YOU... CHANGE ME?

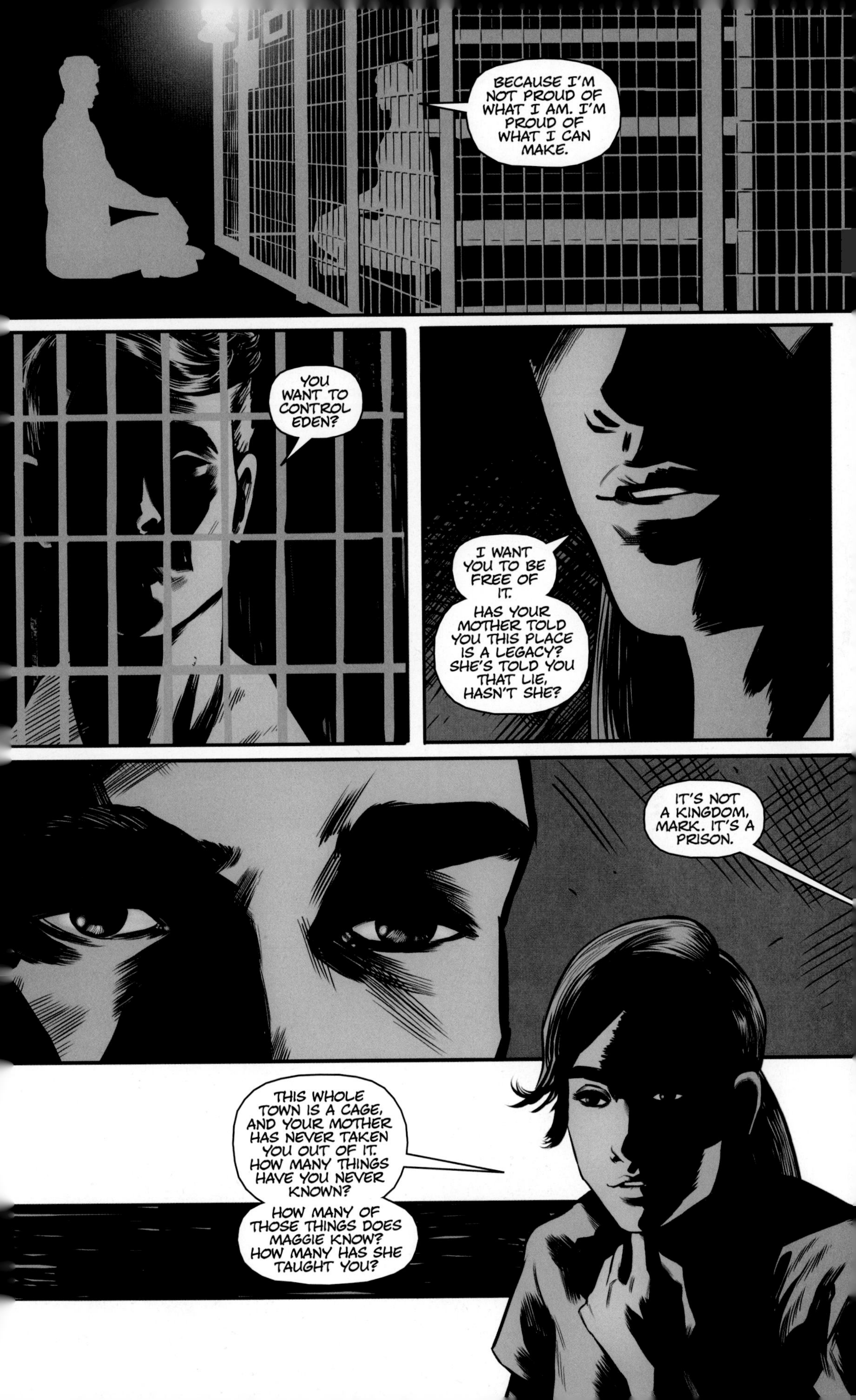
BECAUSE I'M NOT PROUD OF WHAT I AM. I'M PROUD OF WHAT I CAN MAKE.
YOU WANT TO CONTROL EDEN?
I WANT YOU TO BE FREE OF IT.
HAS YOUR MOTHER TOLD YOU THIS PLACE IS A LEGACY? SHE'S TOLD YOU THAT LIE, HASN'T SHE?
IT'S NOT A KINGDOM, MARK. IT'S A PRISON.
THIS WHOLE TOWN IS A CAGE, AND YOUR MOTHER HAS NEVER TAKEN YOU OUT OF IT. HOW MANY THINGS HAVE YOU NEVER KNOWN?
HOW MANY OF THOSE THINGS DOES MAGGIE KNOW? HOW MANY HAS SHE TAUGHT YOU?

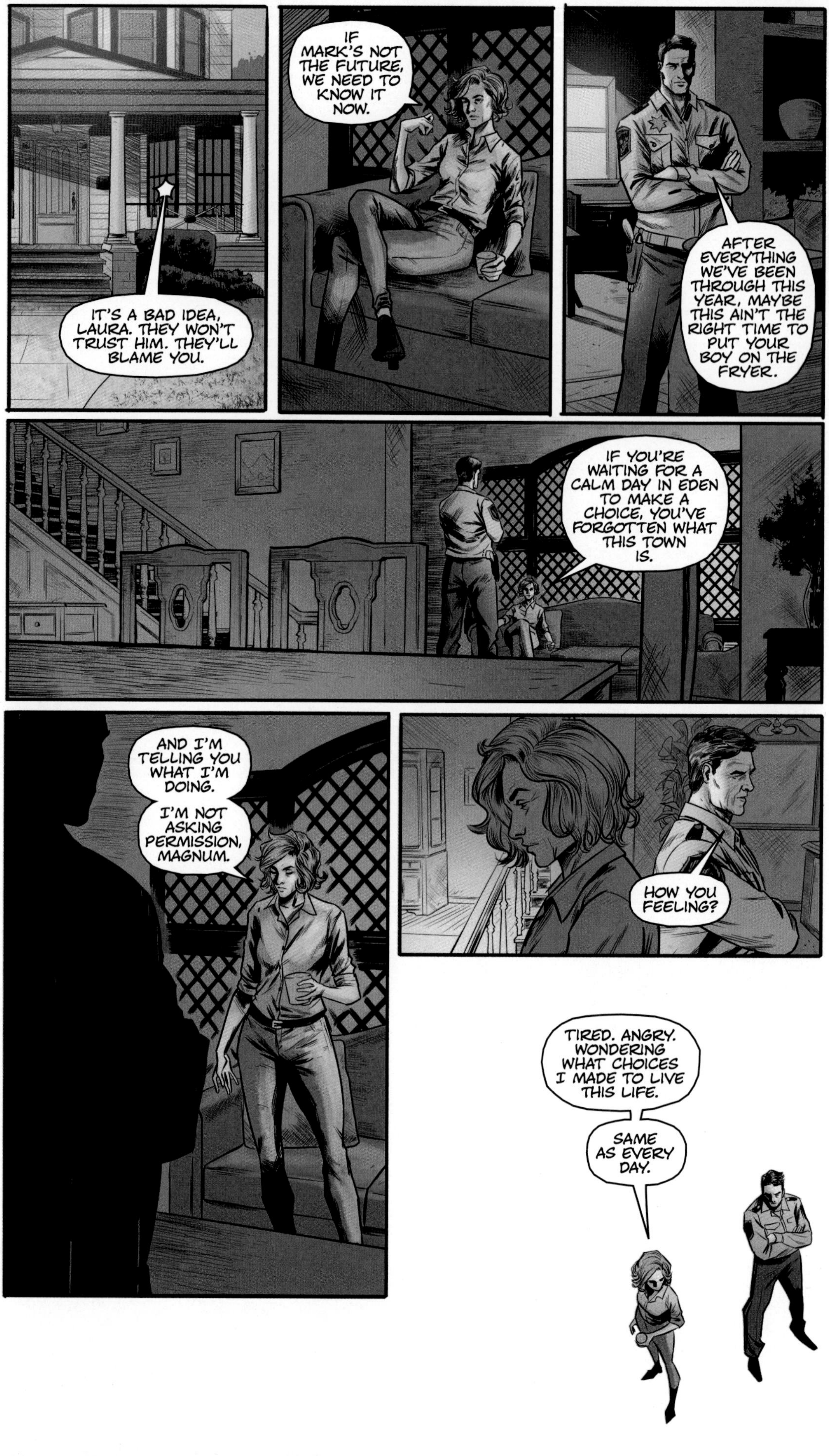
IT'S A BAD IDEA, LAURA. THEY WON'T TRUST HIM. THEY'LL BLAME YOU.
IF MARK'S NOT THE FUTURE, WE NEED TO KNOW IT NOW.
AFTER EVERYTHING WE'VE BEEN THROUGH THIS YEAR, MAYBE THIS AIN'T THE RIGHT TIME TO PUT YOUR BOY ON THE FRYER.
IF YOU'RE WAITING FOR A CALM DAY IN EDEN TO MAKE A CHOICE, YOU'VE FORGOTTEN WHAT THIS TOWN IS.
AND I'M TELLING YOU WHAT I'M DOING.
I'M NOT ASKING PERMISSION, MAGNUM.
HOW YOU FEELING?
TIRED. ANGRY. WONDERING WHAT CHOICES I MADE TO LIVE THIS LIFE.
SAME AS EVERY DAY.

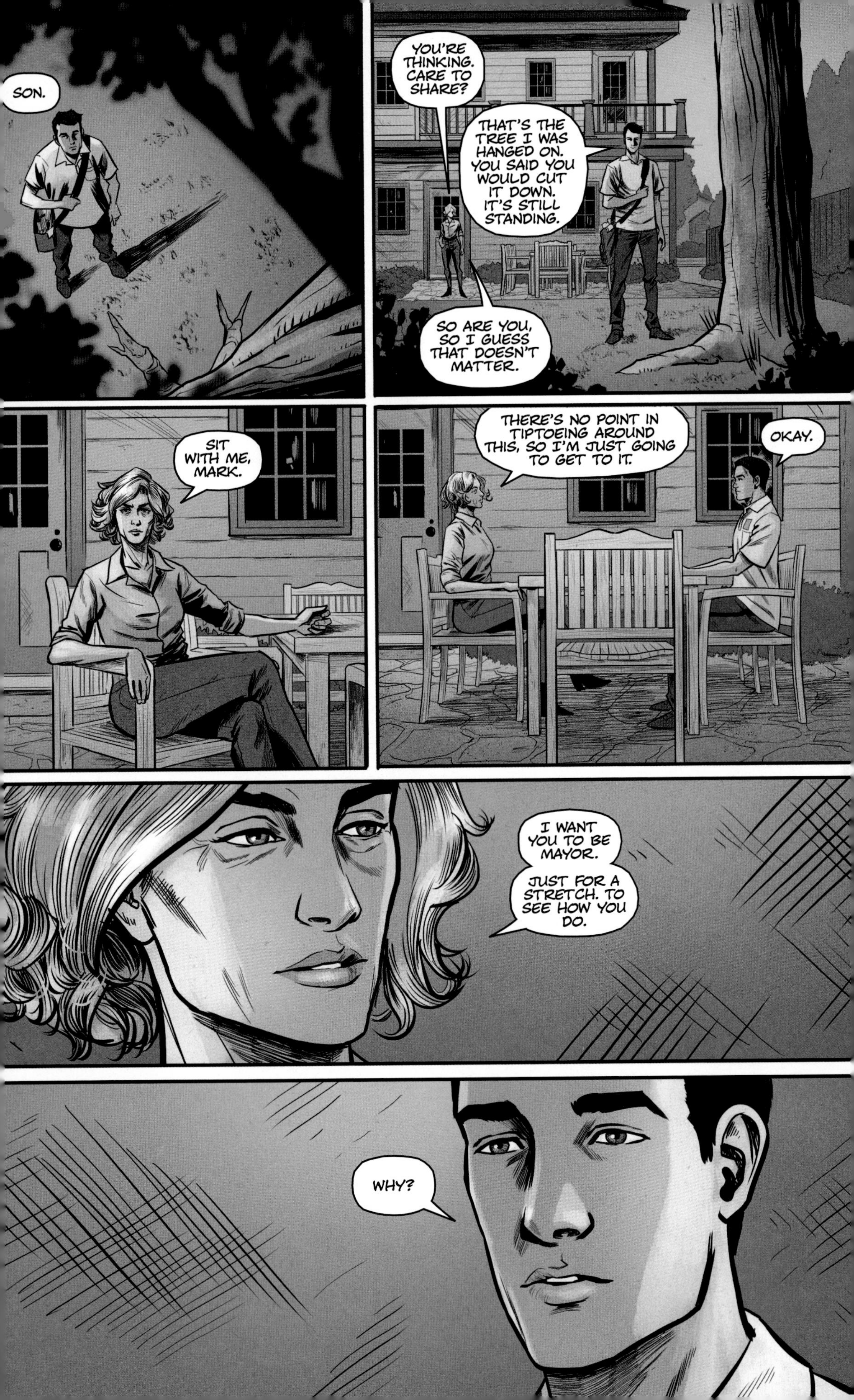
SON.
YOU'RE THINKING. CARE TO SHARE?
THAT'S THE TREE I WAS HANGED ON. YOU SAID YOU WOULD CUT IT DOWN. IT'S STILL STANDING.
SO ARE YOU, SO I GUESS THAT DOESN'T MATTER.
SIT WITH ME, MARK.
THERE'S NO POINT IN TIPTOEING AROUND THIS, SO I'M JUST GOING TO GET TO IT.
OKAY.
I WANT YOU TO BE MAYOR.
JUST FOR A STRETCH. TO SEE HOW YOU DO.
WHY?

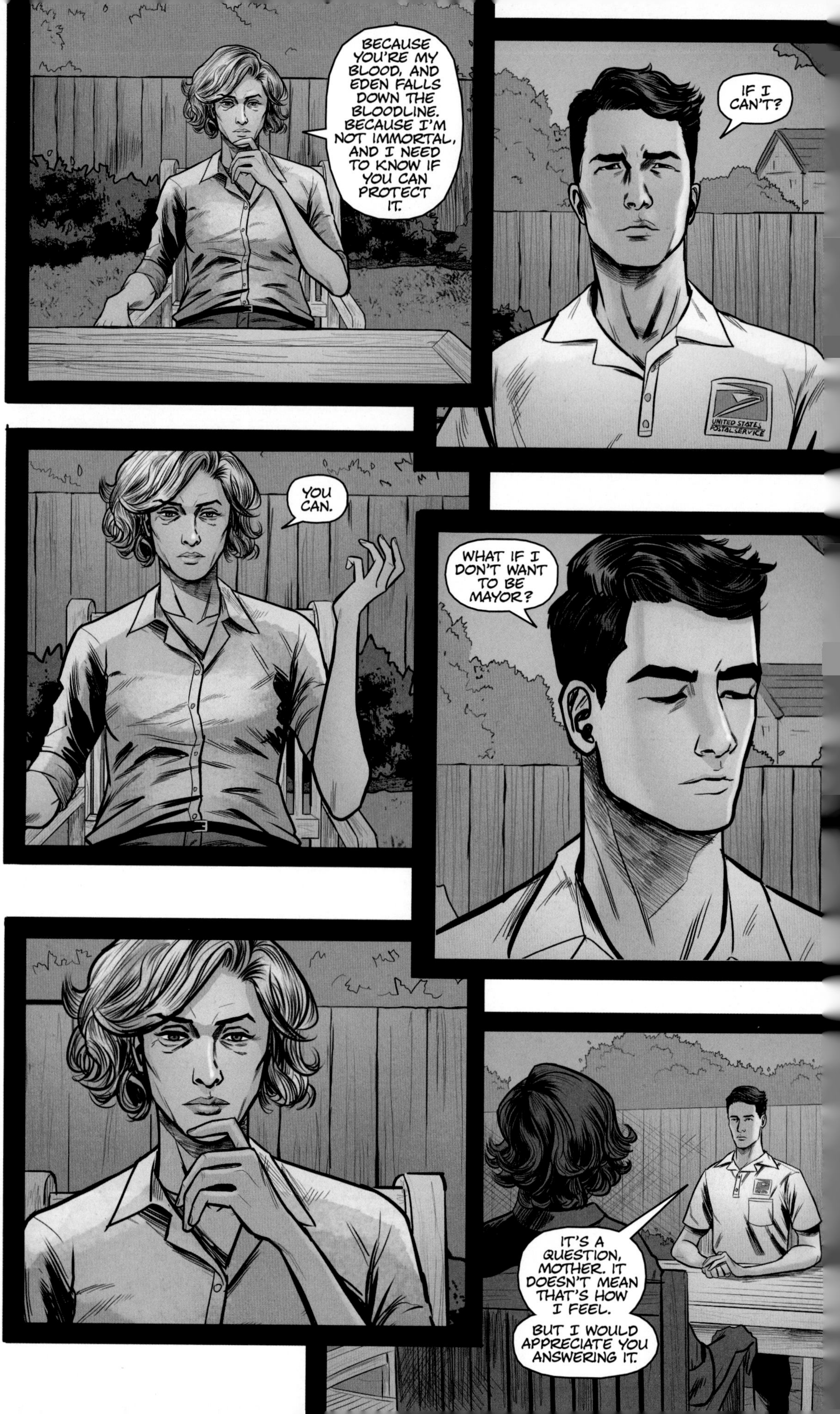
BECAUSE YOU'RE MY BLOOD, AND EDEN FALLS DOWN THE BLOODLINE. BECAUSE I'M NOT IMMORTAL, AND I NEED TO KNOW IF YOU CAN PROTECT IT.
IF I CAN'T?
UNITED STATES POSTAL SERVICE
YOU CAN.
WHAT IF I DON'T WANT TO BE MAYOR?
IT'S A QUESTION, MOTHER. IT DOESN'T MEAN THAT'S HOW I FEEL.
BUT I WOULD APPRECIATE YOU ANSWERING IT.

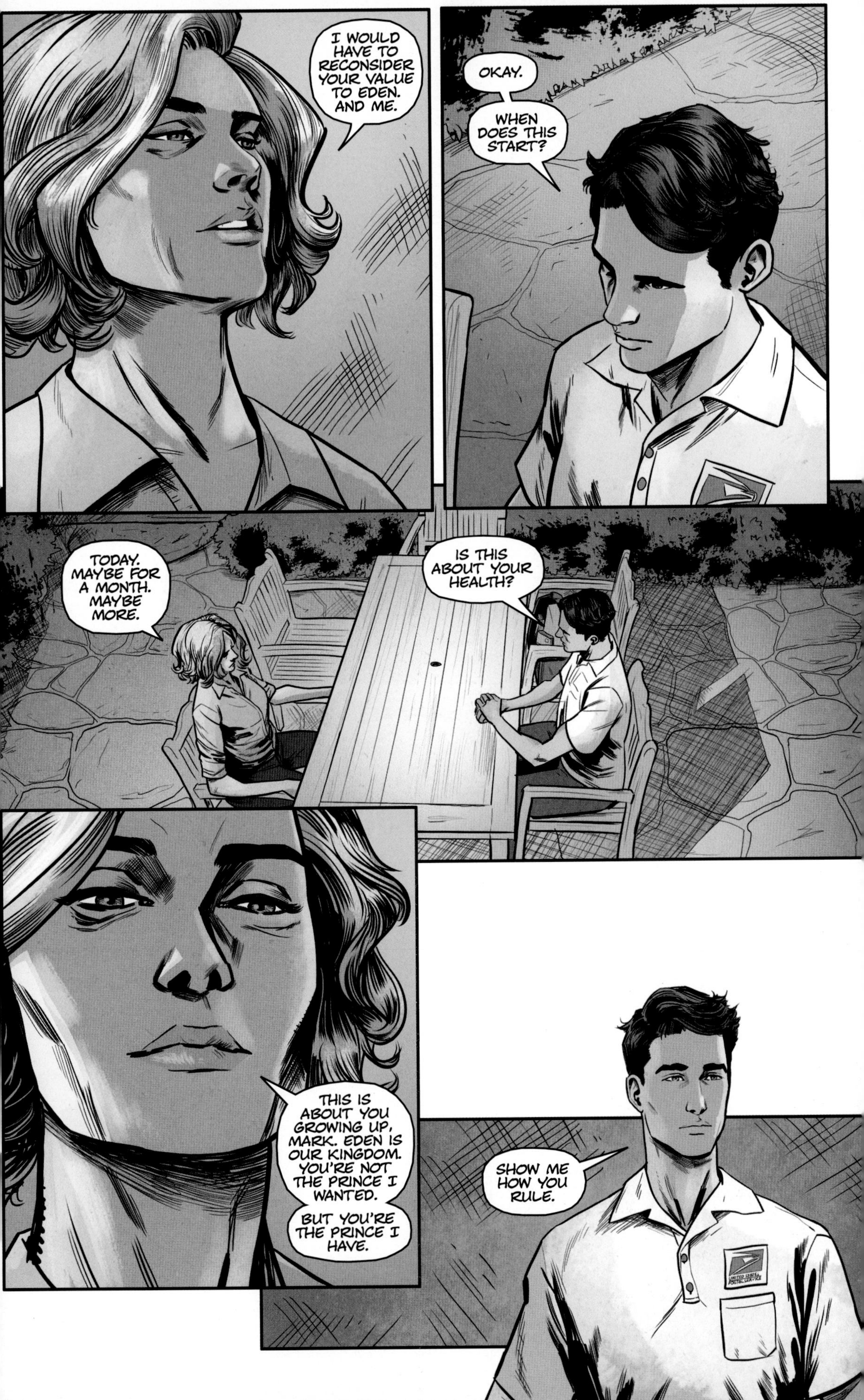
I WOULD HAVE TO RECONSIDER YOUR VALUE TO EDEN. AND ME.
OKAY.
WHEN DOES THIS START?
TODAY. MAYBE FOR A MONTH. MAYBE MORE.
IS THIS ABOUT YOUR HEALTH?
THIS IS ABOUT YOU GROWING UP, MARK. EDEN IS OUR KINGDOM. YOU'RE NOT THE PRINCE I WANTED.
BUT YOU'RE THE PRINCE I HAVE.
SHOW ME HOW YOU RULE.

"WHERE AM I?

"I KNOW YOU'RE THERE. I CAN HEAR YOU.

"MY CHEST HURTS LIKE A BITCH. I NEED TO CLEAN THESE WOUNDS.

"FUCKING SALT? YOU SHOULD HAVE USED LEAD.

"WHEN I GET OUT OF HERE, I'M GOING TO USE LEAD."

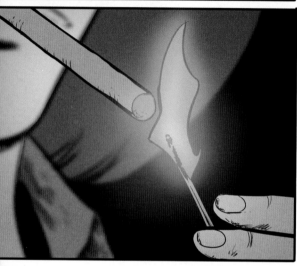

WE TENDED YOUR WOUNDS, AGENT BREMBLE. WE'VE TAKEN GOOD CARE OF YOU. WE'LL CONTINUE TO TAKE GOOD CARE OF YOU.

BECAUSE THAT IS OUR WAY.

NICE WIG. BUT I KNOW WHO YOU ARE.

YOU'RE THE BITCH WHO SHOT ME. SO WHAT HAPPENS NEXT?

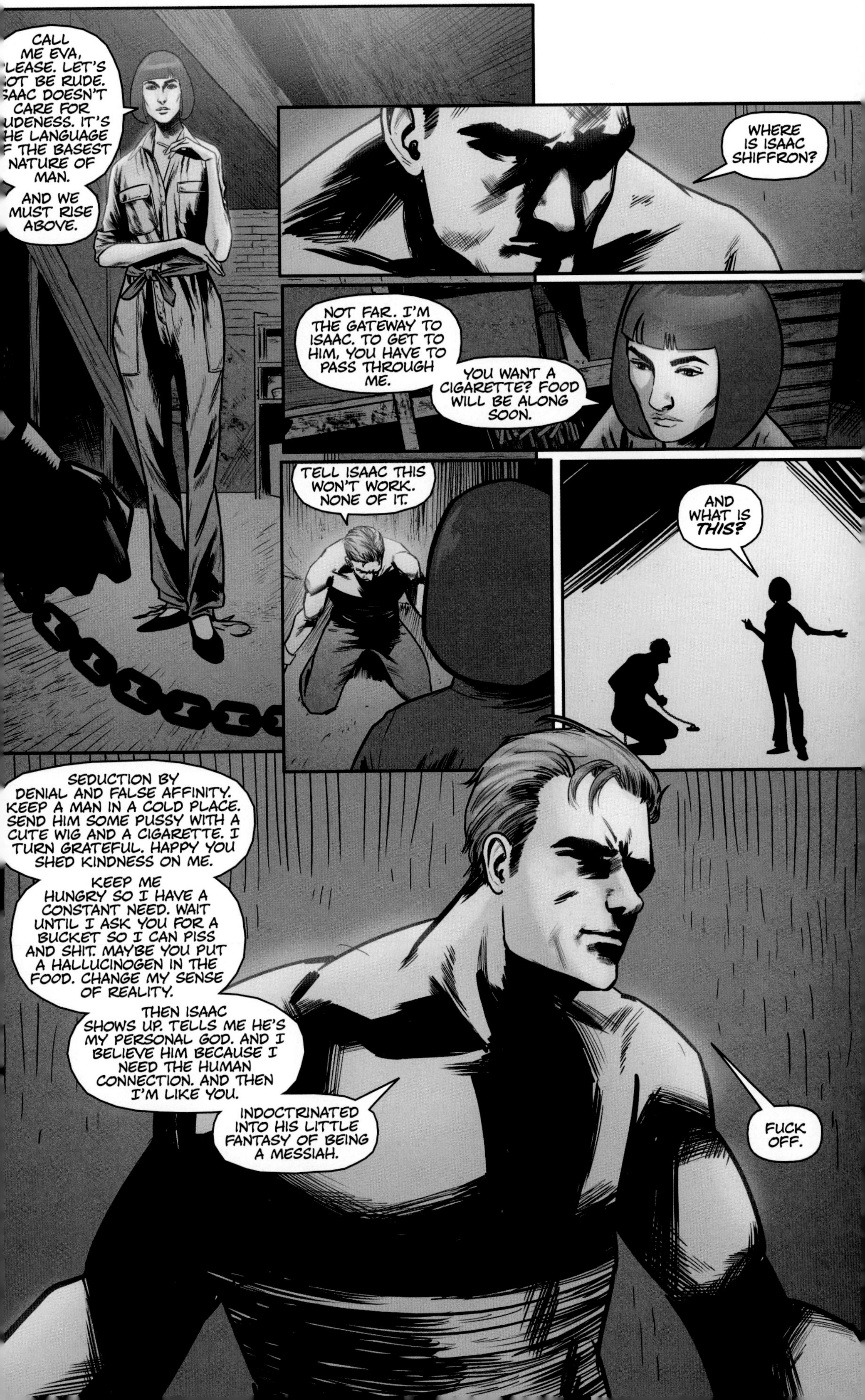
CALL ME EVA, LEASE. LET'S OT BE RUDE. SAAC DOESN'T CARE FOR UDENESS. IT'S HE LANGUAGE F THE BASEST NATURE OF MAN.
AND WE MUST RISE ABOVE.
WHERE IS ISAAC SHIFFRON?
NOT FAR. I'M THE GATEWAY TO ISAAC. TO GET TO HIM, YOU HAVE TO PASS THROUGH ME.
YOU WANT A CIGARETTE? FOOD WILL BE ALONG SOON.
TELL ISAAC THIS WON'T WORK. NONE OF IT.
AND WHAT IS *THIS?*
SEDUCTION BY DENIAL AND FALSE AFFINITY. KEEP A MAN IN A COLD PLACE. SEND HIM SOME PUSSY WITH A CUTE WIG AND A CIGARETTE. I TURN GRATEFUL. HAPPY YOU SHED KINDNESS ON ME.
KEEP ME HUNGRY SO I HAVE A CONSTANT NEED. WAIT UNTIL I ASK YOU FOR A BUCKET SO I CAN PISS AND SHIT. MAYBE YOU PUT A HALLUCINOGEN IN THE FOOD. CHANGE MY SENSE OF REALITY.
THEN ISAAC SHOWS UP. TELLS ME HE'S MY PERSONAL GOD. AND I BELIEVE HIM BECAUSE I NEED THE HUMAN CONNECTION. AND THEN I'M LIKE YOU.
INDOCTRINATED INTO HIS LITTLE FANTASY OF BEING A MESSIAH.
FUCK OFF.

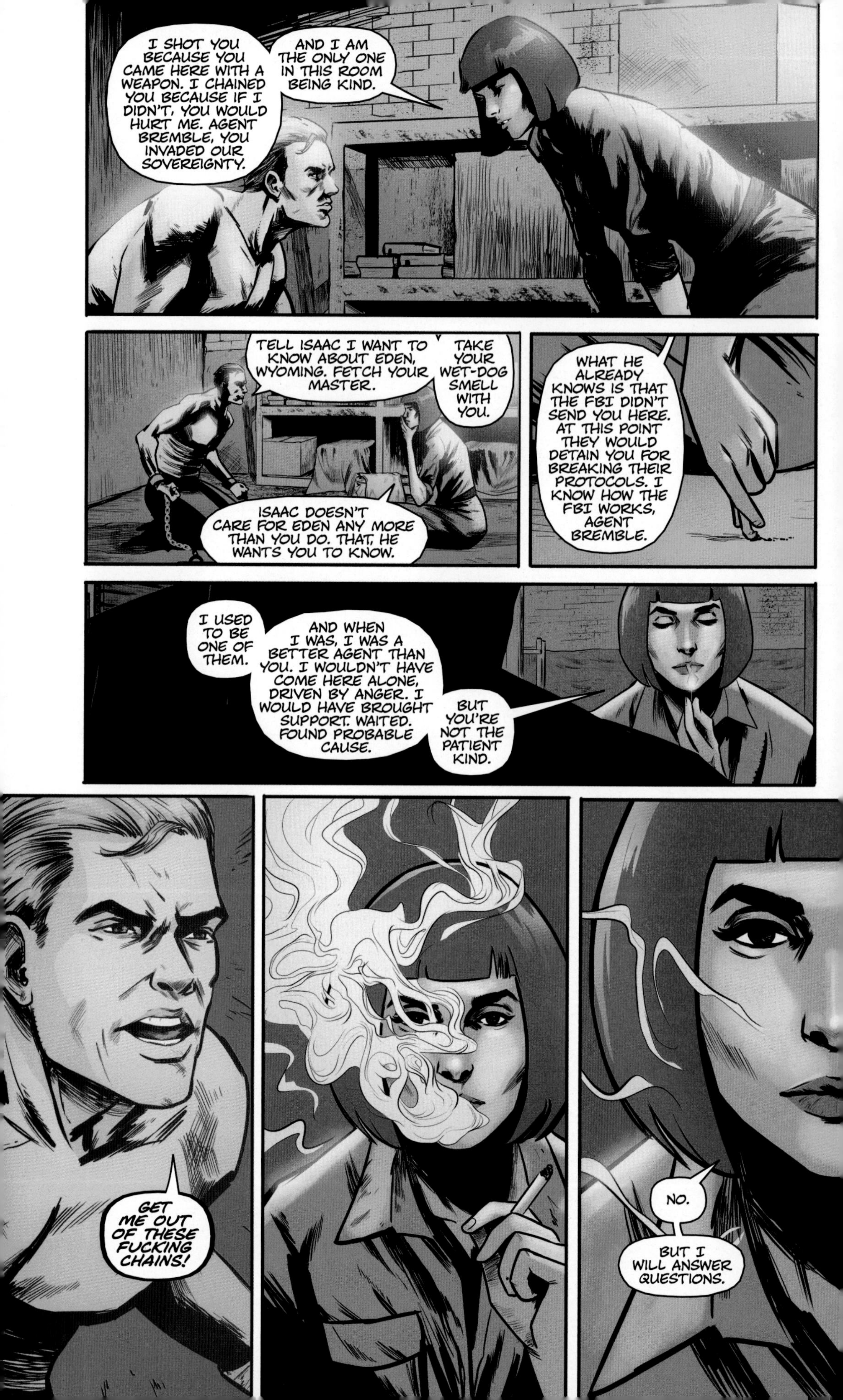
I SHOT YOU BECAUSE YOU CAME HERE WITH A WEAPON. I CHAINED YOU BECAUSE IF I DIDN'T, YOU WOULD HURT ME. AGENT BREMBLE, YOU INVADED OUR SOVEREIGNTY.
AND I AM THE ONLY ONE IN THIS ROOM BEING KIND.
TELL ISAAC I WANT TO KNOW ABOUT EDEN, WYOMING. FETCH YOUR MASTER.
TAKE YOUR WET-DOG SMELL WITH YOU.
ISAAC DOESN'T CARE FOR EDEN ANY MORE THAN YOU DO. THAT, HE WANTS YOU TO KNOW.
WHAT HE ALREADY KNOWS IS THAT THE FBI DIDN'T SEND YOU HERE. AT THIS POINT THEY WOULD DETAIN YOU FOR BREAKING THEIR PROTOCOLS. I KNOW HOW THE FBI WORKS, AGENT BREMBLE.
I USED TO BE ONE OF THEM.
AND WHEN I WAS, I WAS A BETTER AGENT THAN YOU. I WOULDN'T HAVE COME HERE ALONE, DRIVEN BY ANGER. I WOULD HAVE BROUGHT SUPPORT. WAITED. FOUND PROBABLE CAUSE.
BUT YOU'RE NOT THE PATIENT KIND.
GET ME OUT OF THESE FUCKING CHAINS!
NO.
BUT I WILL ANSWER QUESTIONS.

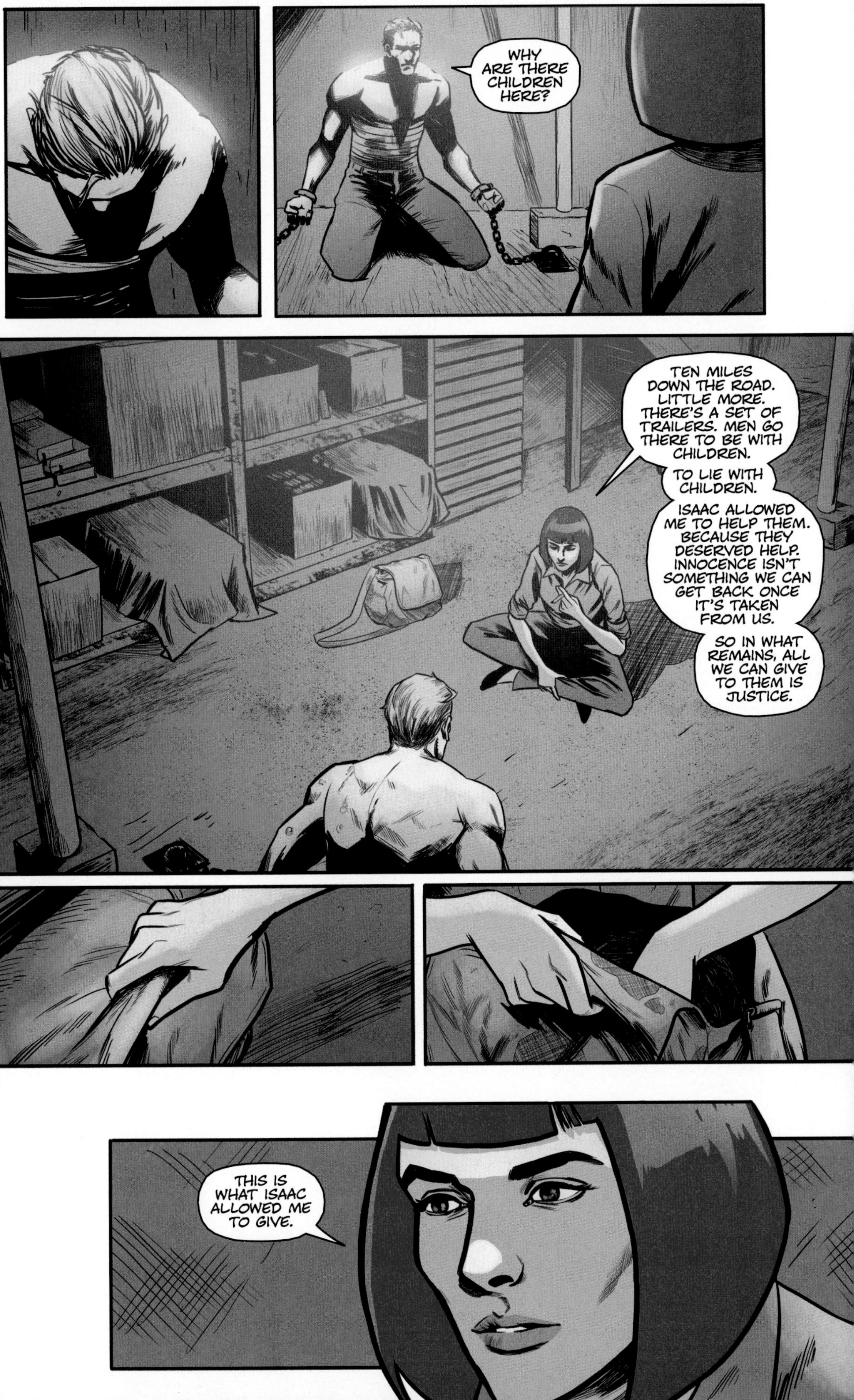
WHY ARE THERE CHILDREN HERE?
TEN MILES DOWN THE ROAD. LITTLE MORE. THERE'S A SET OF TRAILERS. MEN GO THERE TO BE WITH CHILDREN.
TO LIE WITH CHILDREN.
ISAAC ALLOWED ME TO HELP THEM. BECAUSE THEY DESERVED HELP. INNOCENCE ISN'T SOMETHING WE CAN GET BACK ONCE IT'S TAKEN FROM US.
SO IN WHAT REMAINS, ALL WE CAN GIVE TO THEM IS JUSTICE.
THIS IS WHAT ISAAC ALLOWED ME TO GIVE.

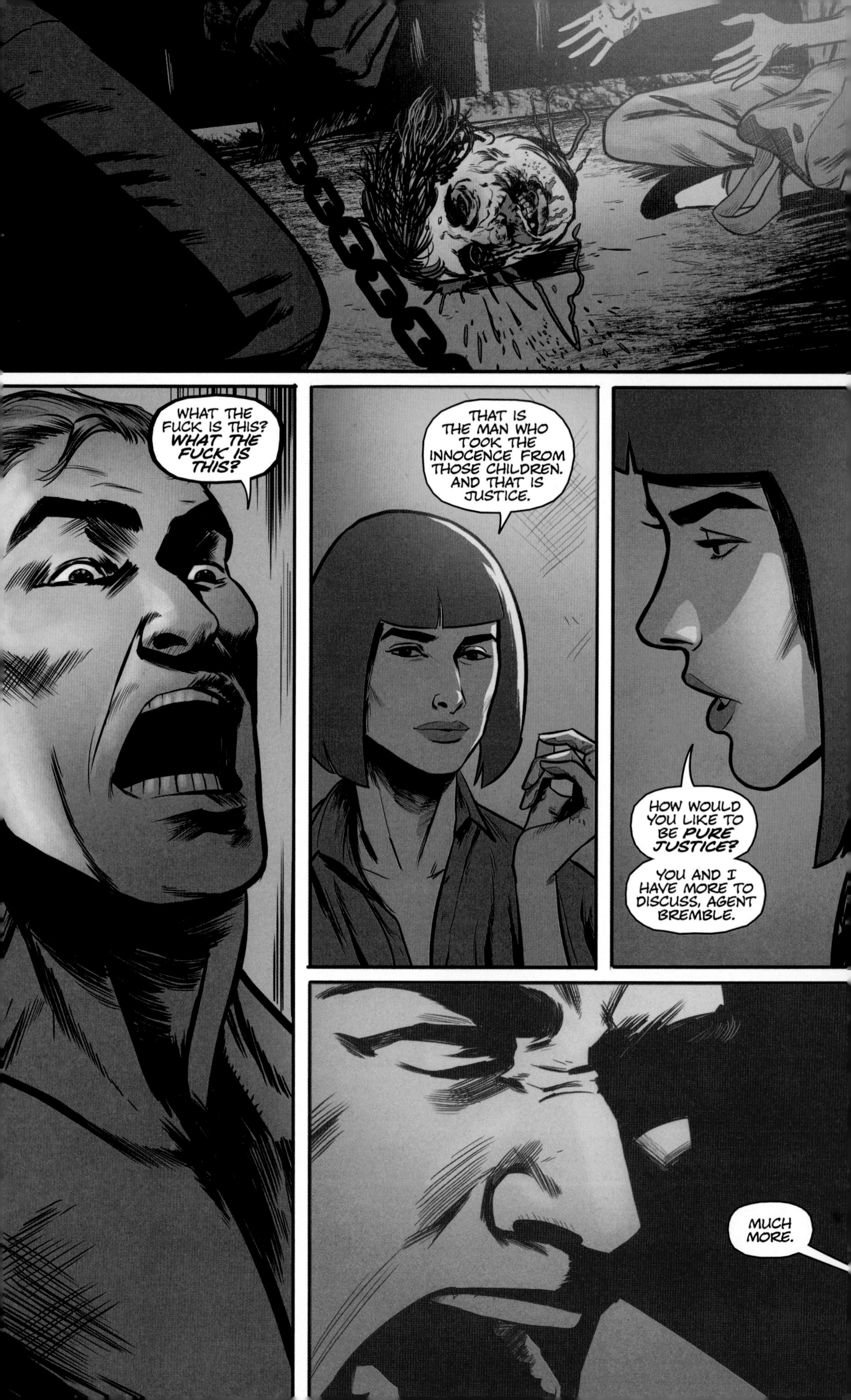
WHAT THE FUCK IS THIS? ***WHAT THE FUCK IS THIS?***
THAT IS THE MAN WHO TOOK THE INNOCENCE FROM THOSE CHILDREN. AND THAT IS JUSTICE.
HOW WOULD YOU LIKE TO BE ***PURE JUSTICE?***
YOU AND I HAVE MORE TO DISCUSS, AGENT BREMBLE.
MUCH MORE.

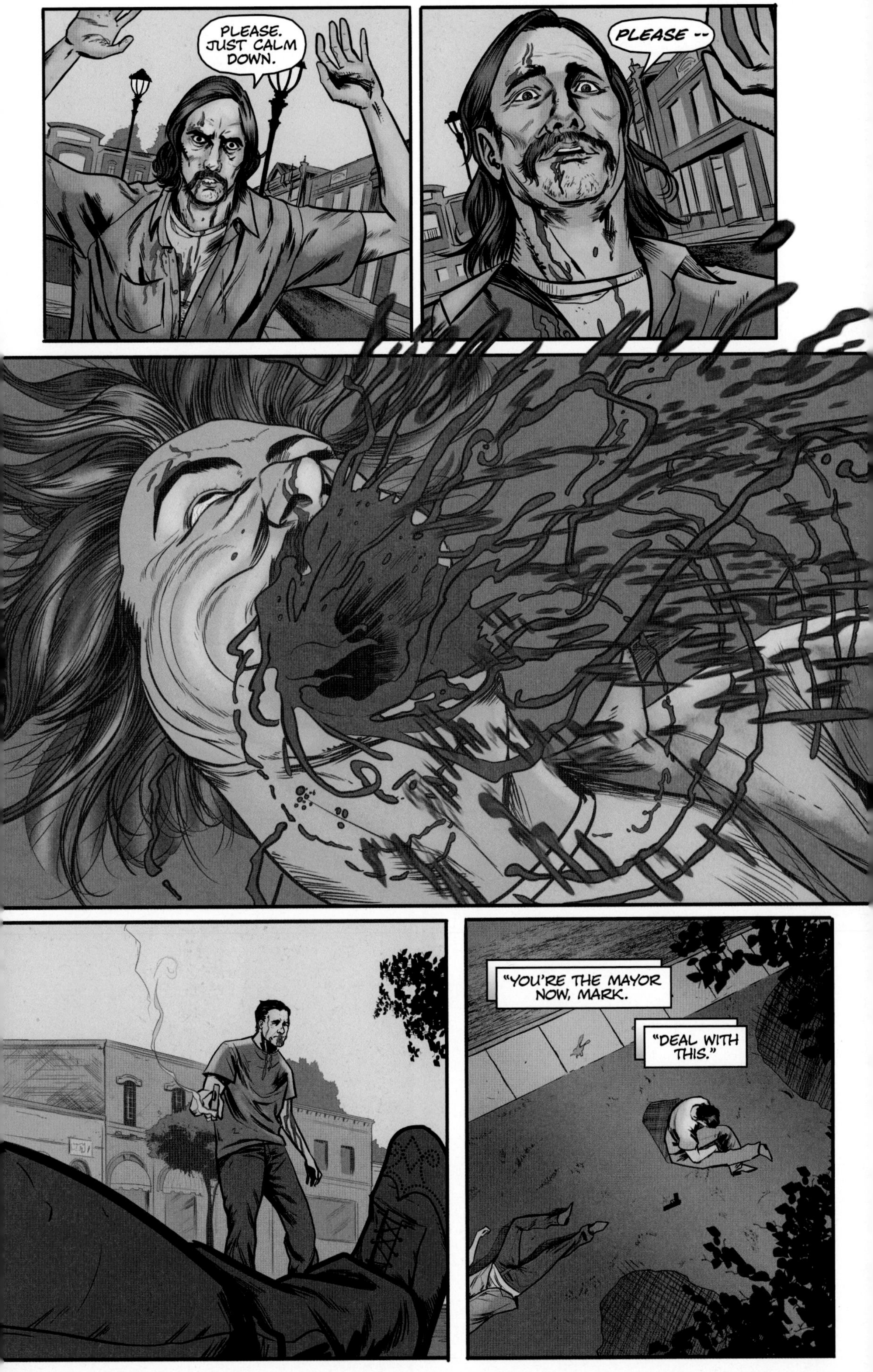
PLEASE. JUST CALM DOWN.
PLEASE --
"YOU'RE THE MAYOR NOW, MARK.
"DEAL WITH THIS."

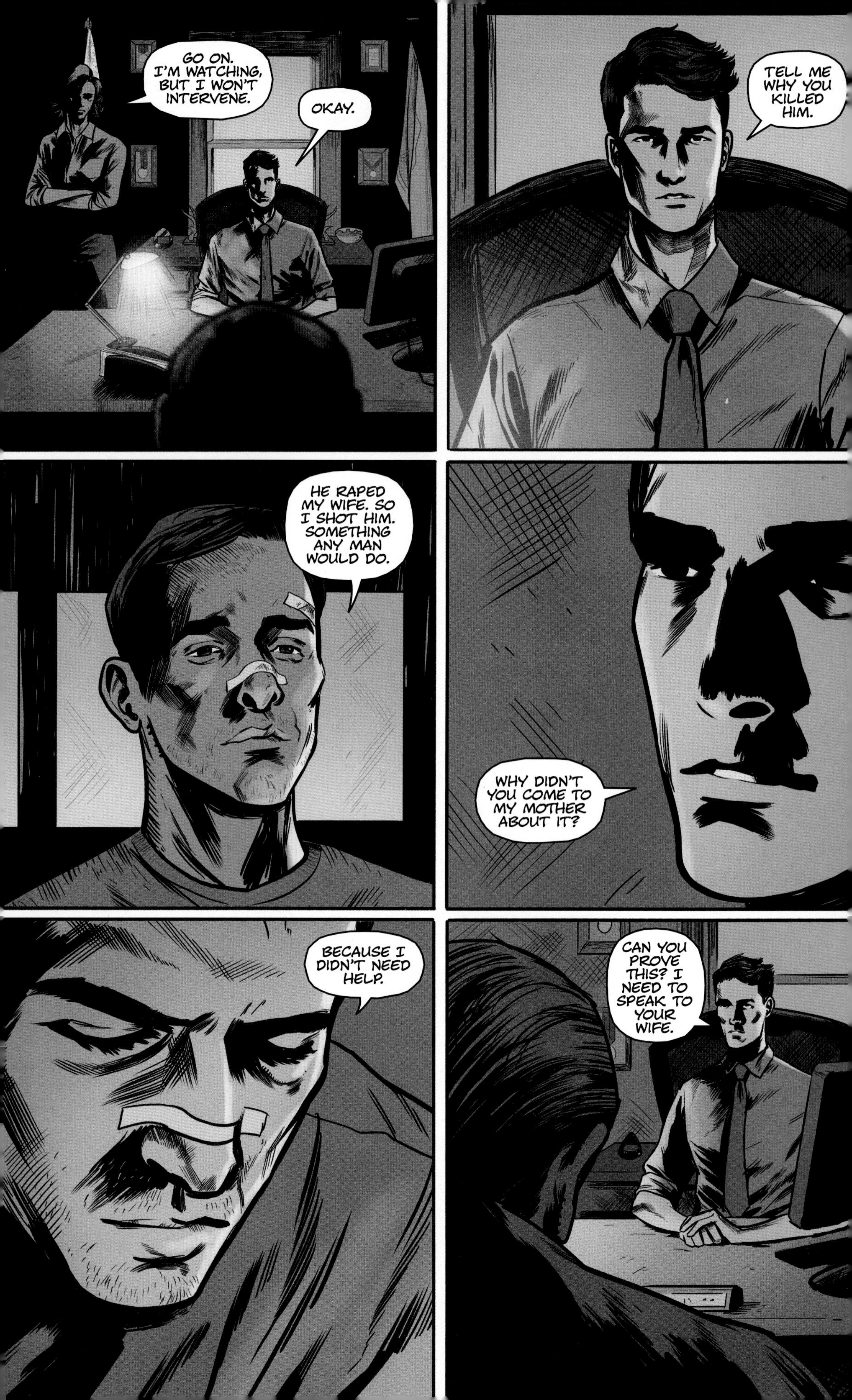
GO ON. I'M WATCHING, BUT I WON'T INTERVENE.
OKAY.
TELL ME WHY YOU KILLED HIM.
HE RAPED MY WIFE. SO I SHOT HIM. SOMETHING ANY MAN WOULD DO.
WHY DIDN'T YOU COME TO MY MOTHER ABOUT IT?
BECAUSE I DIDN'T NEED HELP.
CAN YOU PROVE THIS? I NEED TO SPEAK TO YOUR WIFE.

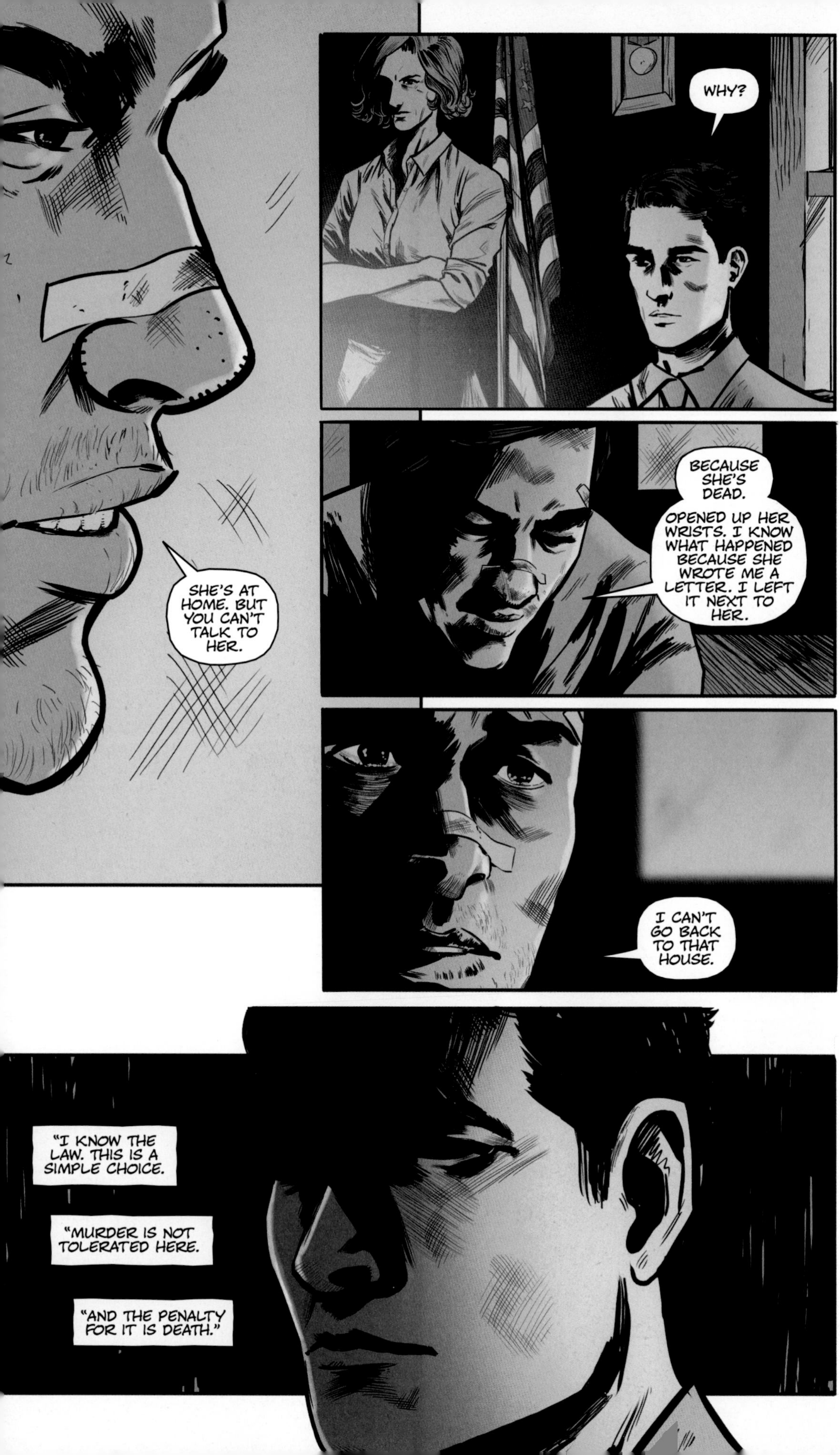
WHY?
SHE'S AT HOME. BUT YOU CAN'T TALK TO HER.
BECAUSE SHE'S DEAD.
OPENED UP HER WRISTS. I KNOW WHAT HAPPENED BECAUSE SHE WROTE ME A LETTER. I LEFT IT NEXT TO HER.
I CAN'T GO BACK TO THAT HOUSE.
"I KNOW THE LAW. THIS IS A SIMPLE CHOICE.
"MURDER IS NOT TOLERATED HERE.
"AND THE PENALTY FOR IT IS DEATH."

GO TO SHERIFF MAGNUM. TELL HIM WHAT YOU'VE TOLD ME. HE WILL GO BACK WITH YOU TO YOUR HOUSE AND HELP TEND TO THE REMAINS OF YOUR WIFE.

YOU DON'T HAVE TO LIVE IN THAT HOUSE, BUT WE DON'T HAVE ANOTHER HOUSE TO GIVE YOU, MR. VASQUEZ.

THINK OF YOUR HOUSE LIKE A PRISON. IT WILL OPERATE IN THE SAME WAY. NOW GO.

MARK --

GO, MR. VASQUEZ.

EDEN TOWN HALL

"YOU CAN'T ALLOW HIM TO --"

"I'M NOT.

"TONIGHT, MR. VASQUEZ WILL SLEEP. AT SOME POINT. THREE A.M. WILL BE A SAFE TIME."

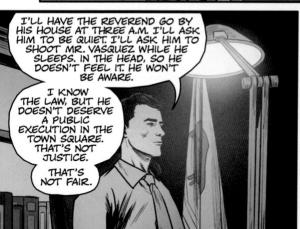

I'LL HAVE THE REVEREND GO BY HIS HOUSE AT THREE A.M. I'LL ASK HIM TO BE QUIET. I'LL ASK HIM TO SHOOT MR. VASQUEZ WHILE HE SLEEPS. IN THE HEAD, SO HE DOESN'T FEEL IT. HE WON'T BE AWARE.

I KNOW THE LAW, BUT HE DOESN'T DESERVE A PUBLIC EXECUTION IN THE TOWN SQUARE. THAT'S NOT JUSTICE.

THAT'S NOT FAIR.

TOMORROW MORNING I'M GOING TO MEET WITH A FEW PEOPLE HERE.

FOR WHAT?

TO CHANGE THINGS. FOR THE BETTER.

MARK. WHAT ARE YOU GOING TO DO?

SHE'S AFRAID OF ME.

AND SOMETHING INSIDE ME IS SATISFIED.

WHAT YOU ASKED ME TO DO. YOU ELECTED ME TO BE TEMPORARY MAYOR IN A DEMOCRACY WHERE YOU HAVE THE ONLY VOTE.

MOM --

ELECTIONS HAVE CONSEQUENCES.

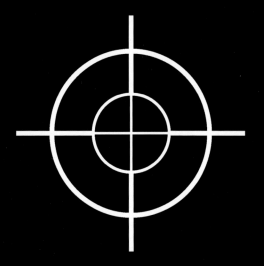

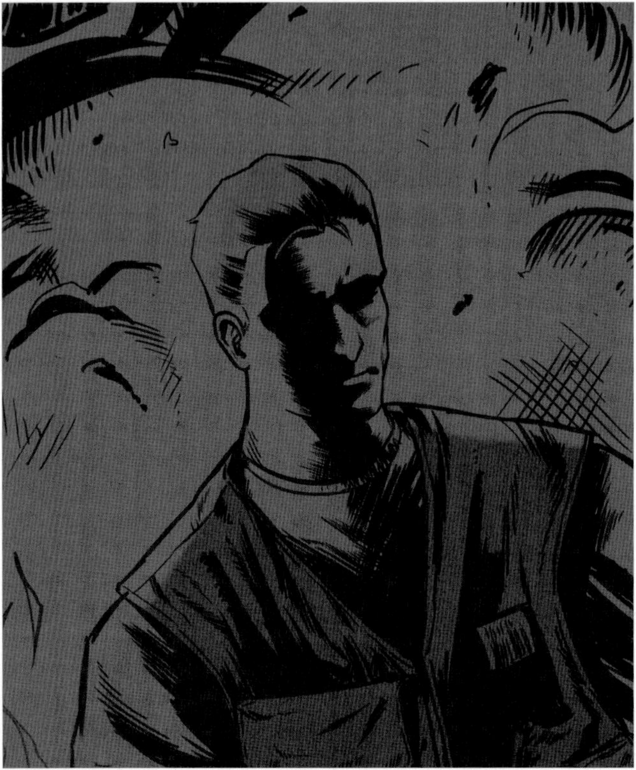

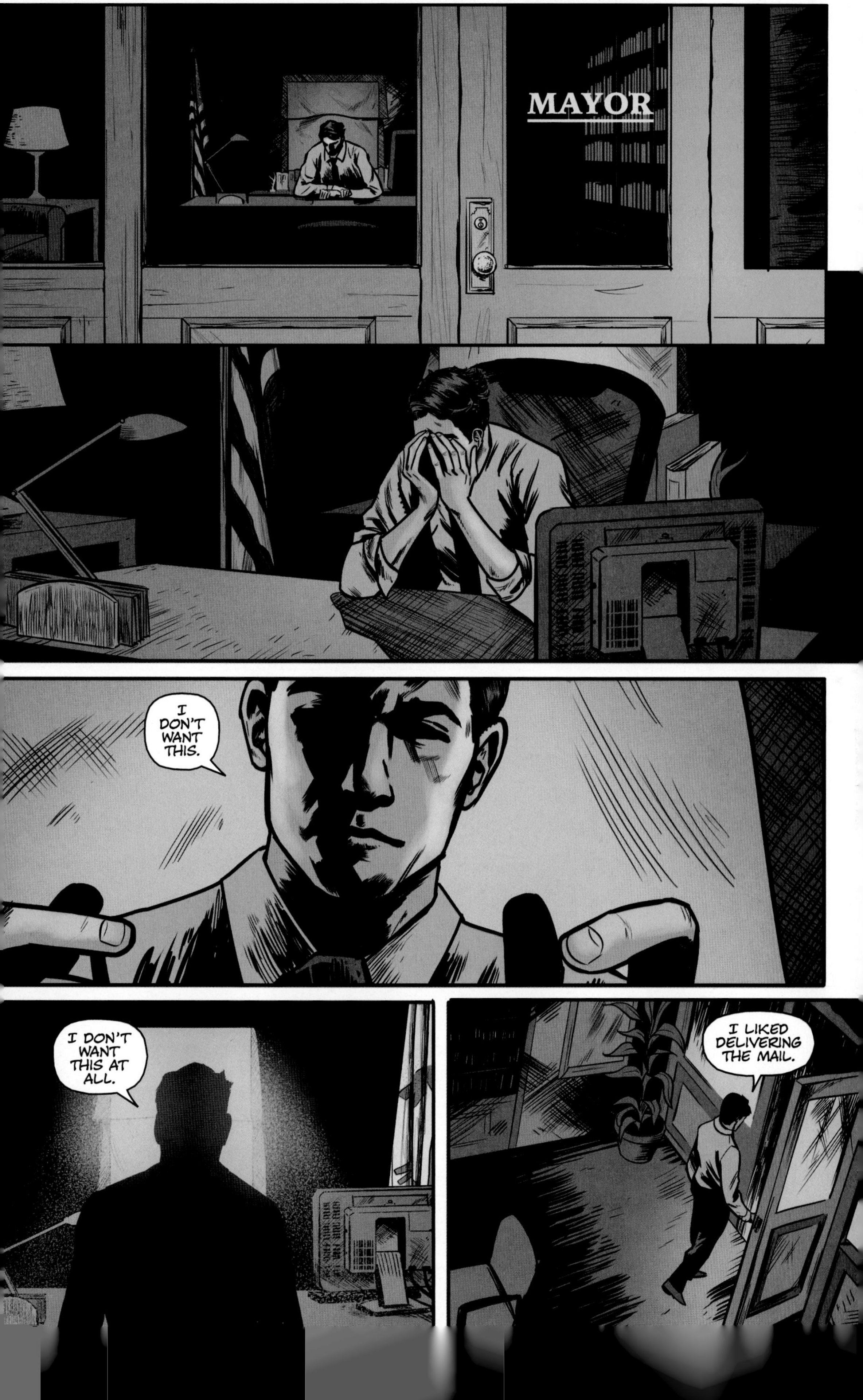
MAYOR
I DON'T WANT THIS.
I DON'T WANT THIS AT ALL.
I LIKED DELIVERING THE MAIL.

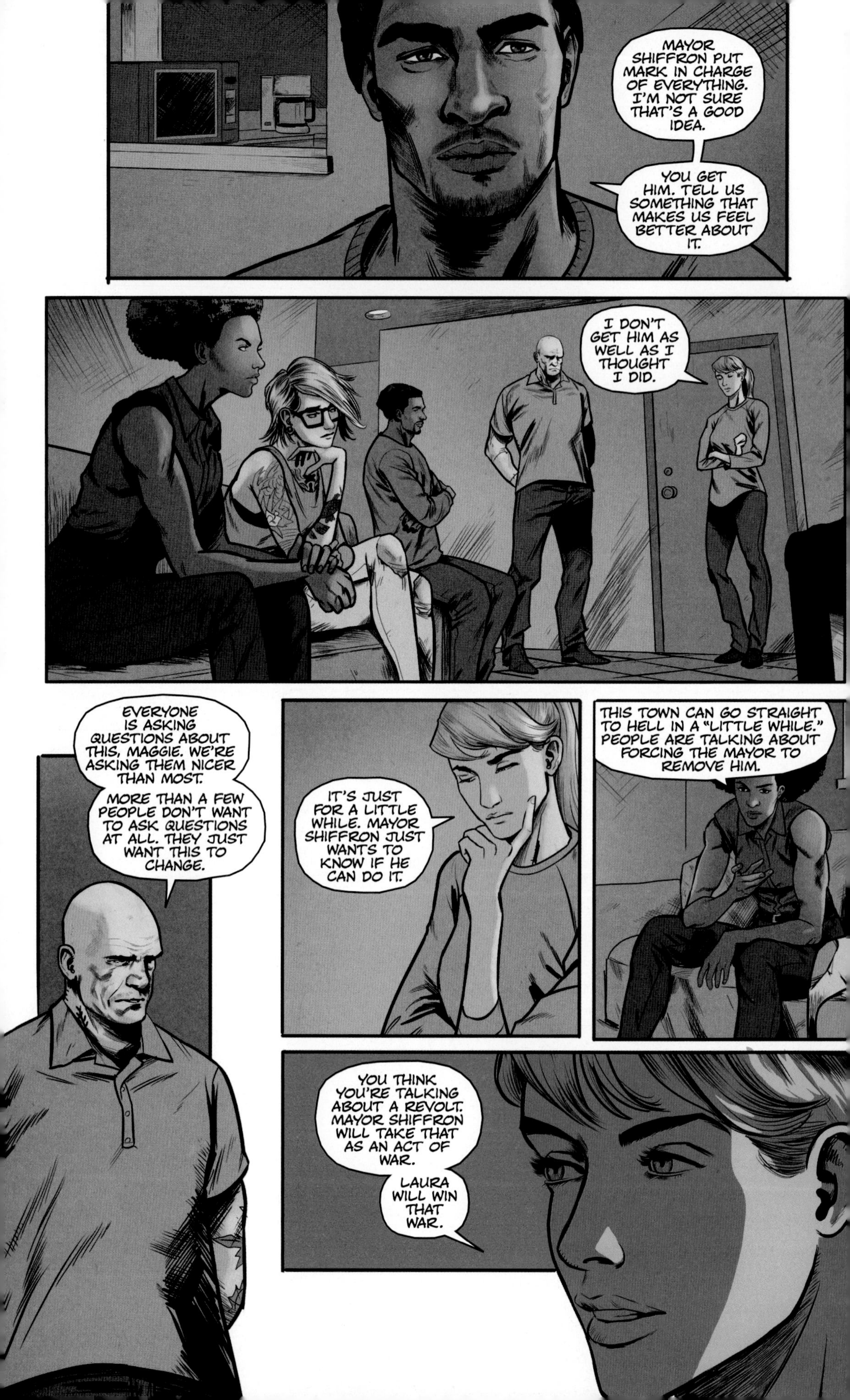
MAYOR SHIFFRON PUT MARK IN CHARGE OF EVERYTHING. I'M NOT SURE THAT'S A GOOD IDEA.
YOU GET HIM. TELL US SOMETHING THAT MAKES US FEEL BETTER ABOUT IT.
I DON'T GET HIM AS WELL AS I THOUGHT I DID.
EVERYONE IS ASKING QUESTIONS ABOUT THIS, MAGGIE. WE'RE ASKING THEM NICER THAN MOST.
MORE THAN A FEW PEOPLE DON'T WANT TO ASK QUESTIONS AT ALL. THEY JUST WANT THIS TO CHANGE.
IT'S JUST FOR A LITTLE WHILE. MAYOR SHIFFRON JUST WANTS TO KNOW IF HE CAN DO IT.
THIS TOWN CAN GO STRAIGHT TO HELL IN A "LITTLE WHILE." PEOPLE ARE TALKING ABOUT FORCING THE MAYOR TO REMOVE HIM.
YOU THINK YOU'RE TALKING ABOUT A REVOLT. MAYOR SHIFFRON WILL TAKE THAT AS AN ACT OF WAR.
LAURA WILL WIN THAT WAR.

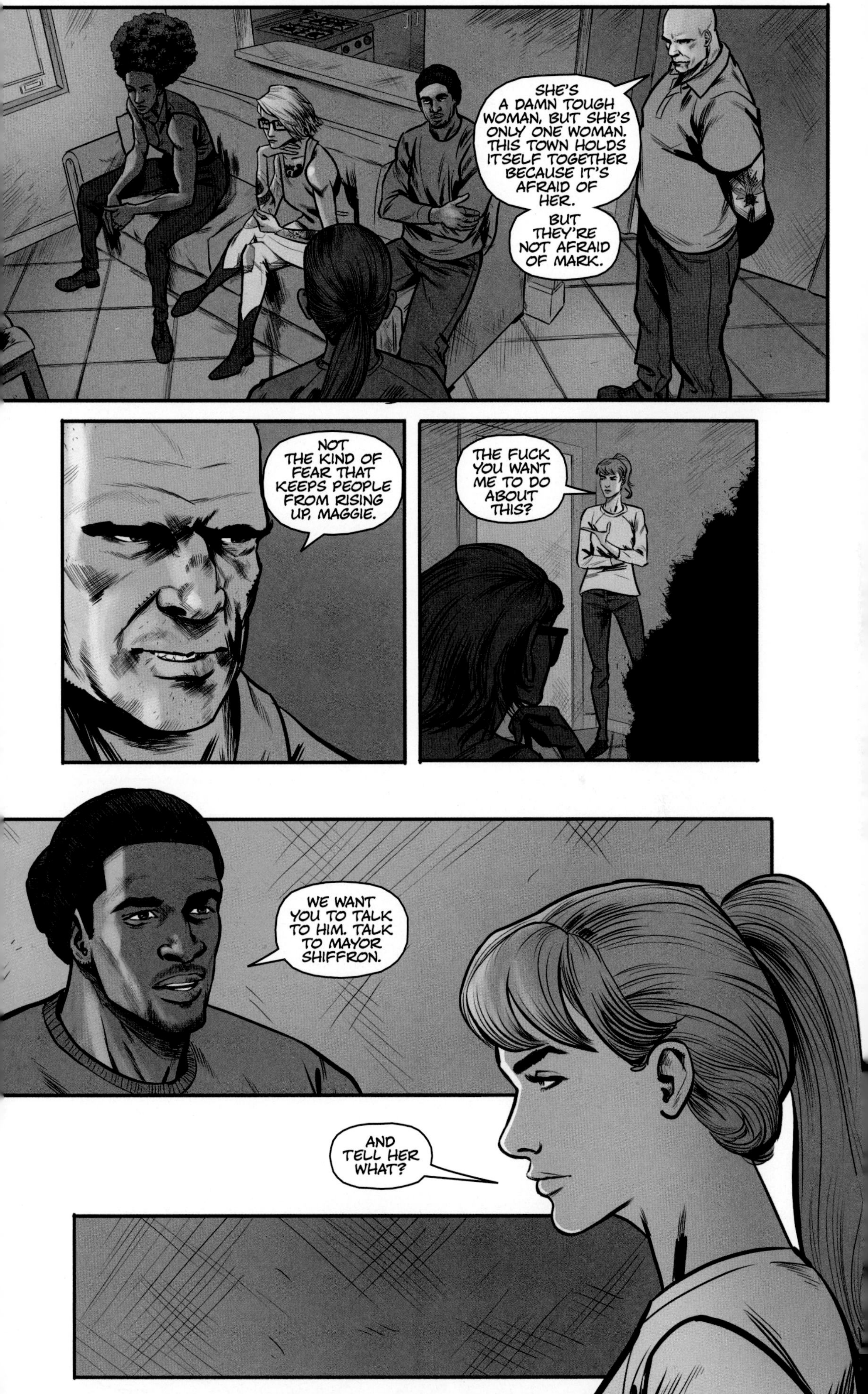
SHE'S A DAMN TOUGH WOMAN, BUT SHE'S ONLY ONE WOMAN. THIS TOWN HOLDS ITSELF TOGETHER BECAUSE IT'S AFRAID OF HER.
BUT THEY'RE NOT AFRAID OF MARK.
NOT THE KIND OF FEAR THAT KEEPS PEOPLE FROM RISING UP, MAGGIE.
THE FUCK YOU WANT ME TO DO ABOUT THIS?
WE WANT YOU TO TALK TO HIM. TALK TO MAYOR SHIFFRON.
AND TELL HER WHAT?

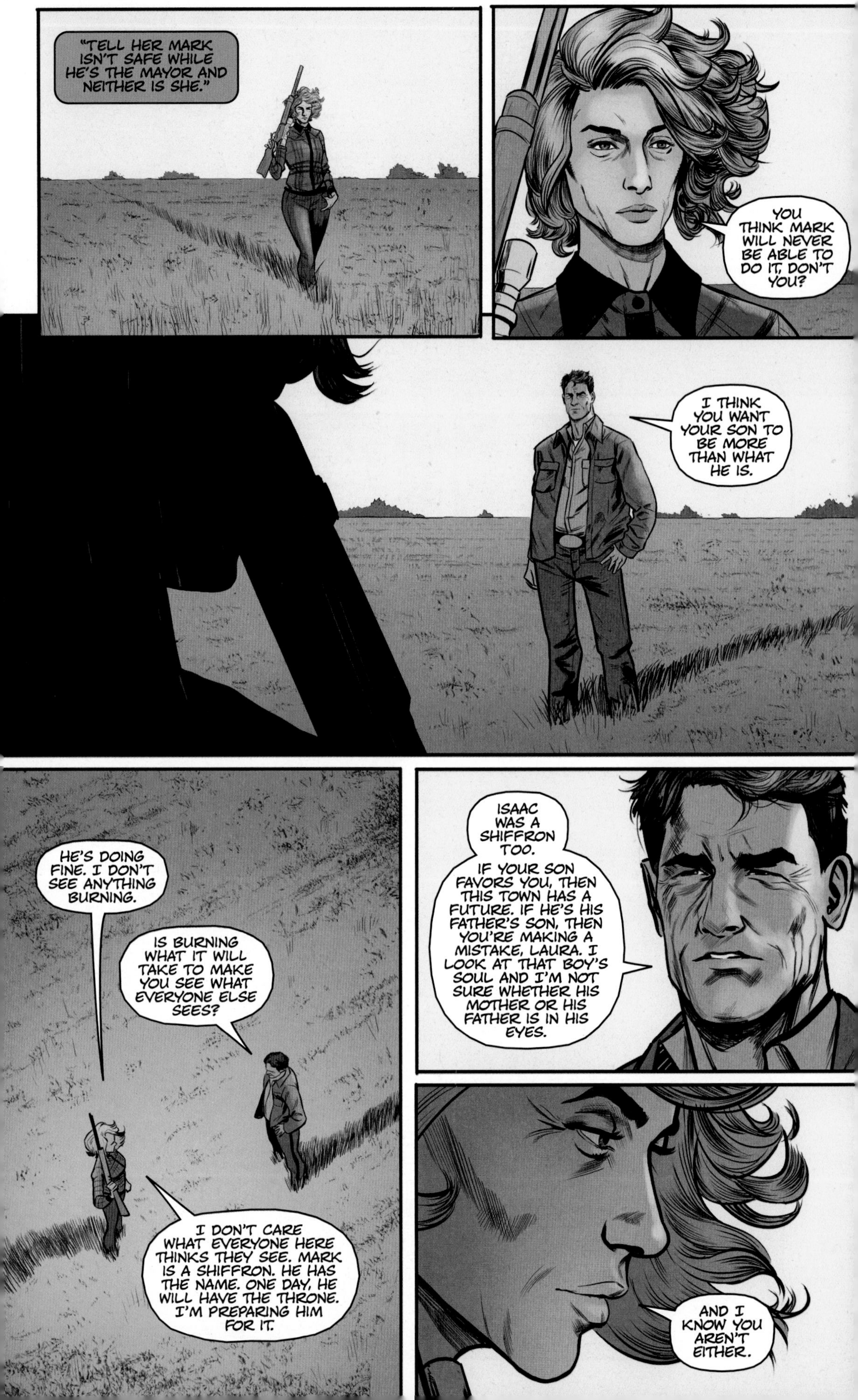
"TELL HER MARK ISN'T SAFE WHILE HE'S THE MAYOR AND NEITHER IS SHE."
YOU THINK MARK WILL NEVER BE ABLE TO DO IT, DON'T YOU?
I THINK YOU WANT YOUR SON TO BE MORE THAN WHAT HE IS.
HE'S DOING FINE. I DON'T SEE ANYTHING BURNING.
IS BURNING WHAT IT WILL TAKE TO MAKE YOU SEE WHAT EVERYONE ELSE SEES?
I DON'T CARE WHAT EVERYONE HERE THINKS THEY SEE. MARK IS A SHIFFRON. HE HAS THE NAME. ONE DAY, HE WILL HAVE THE THRONE. I'M PREPARING HIM FOR IT.
ISAAC WAS A SHIFFRON TOO.
IF YOUR SON FAVORS YOU, THEN THIS TOWN HAS A FUTURE. IF HE'S HIS FATHER'S SON, THEN YOU'RE MAKING A MISTAKE, LAURA. I LOOK AT THAT BOY'S SOUL AND I'M NOT SURE WHETHER HIS MOTHER OR HIS FATHER IS IN HIS EYES.
AND I KNOW YOU AREN'T EITHER.

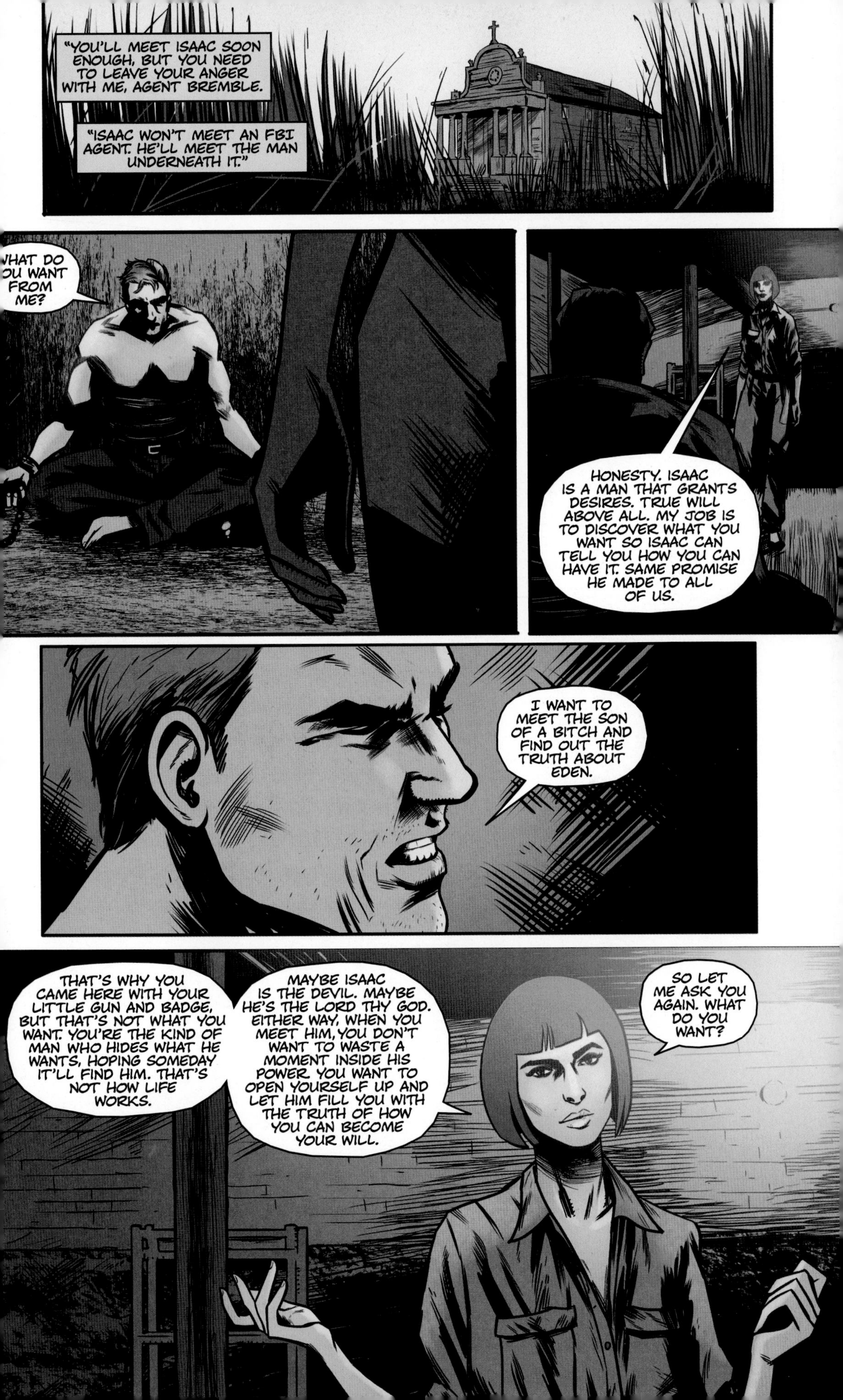
"YOU'LL MEET ISAAC SOON ENOUGH, BUT YOU NEED TO LEAVE YOUR ANGER WITH ME, AGENT BREMBLE.
"ISAAC WON'T MEET AN FBI AGENT. HE'LL MEET THE MAN UNDERNEATH IT."
WHAT DO YOU WANT FROM ME?
HONESTY. ISAAC IS A MAN THAT GRANTS DESIRES. TRUE WILL ABOVE ALL. MY JOB IS TO DISCOVER WHAT YOU WANT SO ISAAC CAN TELL YOU HOW YOU CAN HAVE IT. SAME PROMISE HE MADE TO ALL OF US.
I WANT TO MEET THE SON OF A BITCH AND FIND OUT THE TRUTH ABOUT EDEN.
THAT'S WHY YOU CAME HERE WITH YOUR LITTLE GUN AND BADGE, BUT THAT'S NOT WHAT YOU WANT. YOU'RE THE KIND OF MAN WHO HIDES WHAT HE WANTS, HOPING SOMEDAY IT'LL FIND HIM. THAT'S NOT HOW LIFE WORKS.
MAYBE ISAAC IS THE DEVIL. MAYBE HE'S THE LORD THY GOD. EITHER WAY, WHEN YOU MEET HIM, YOU DON'T WANT TO WASTE A MOMENT INSIDE HIS POWER. YOU WANT TO OPEN YOURSELF UP AND LET HIM FILL YOU WITH THE TRUTH OF HOW YOU CAN BECOME YOUR WILL.
SO LET ME ASK YOU AGAIN. WHAT DO YOU WANT?

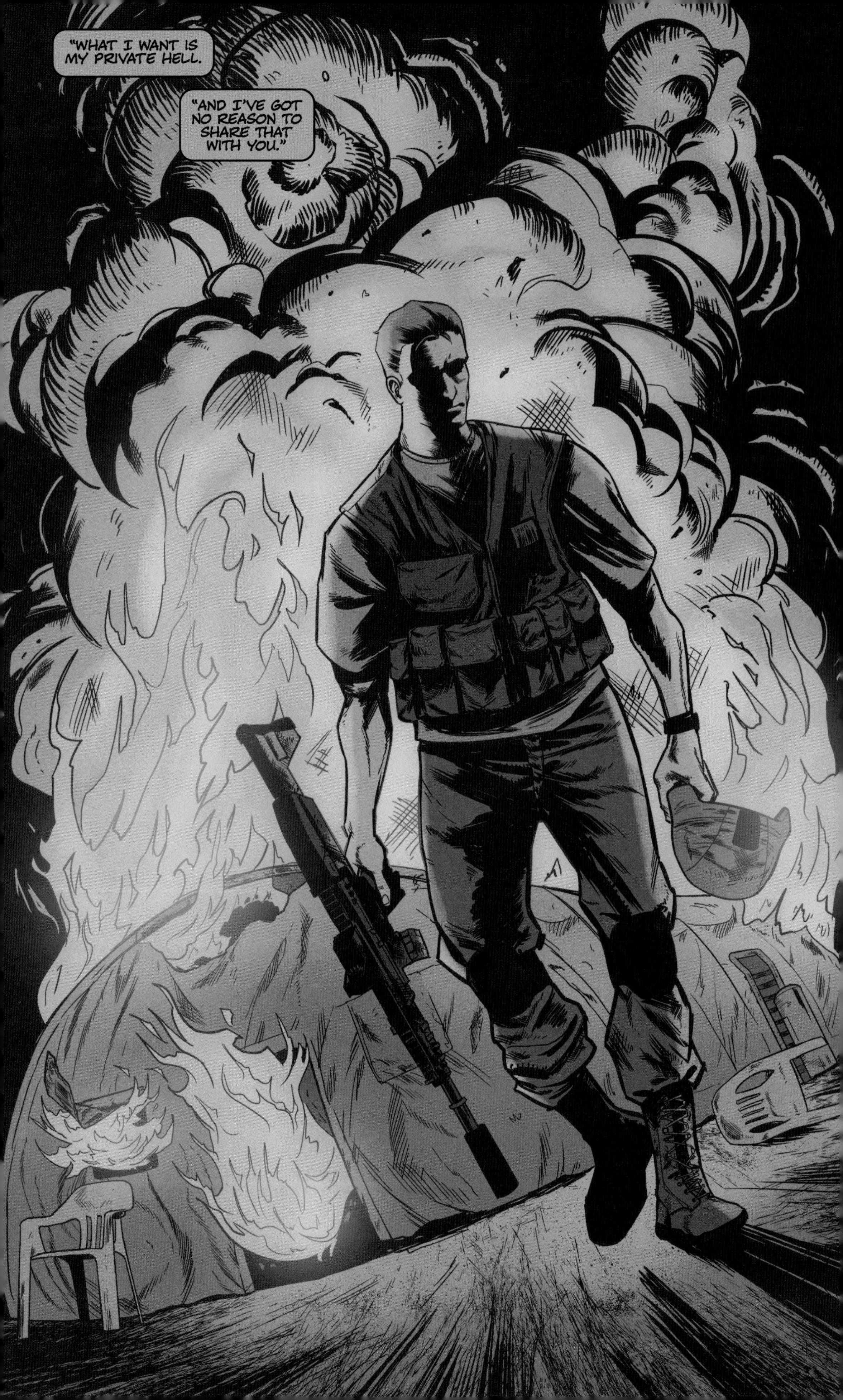
"WHAT I WANT IS MY PRIVATE HELL.
"AND I'VE GOT NO REASON TO SHARE THAT WITH YOU."

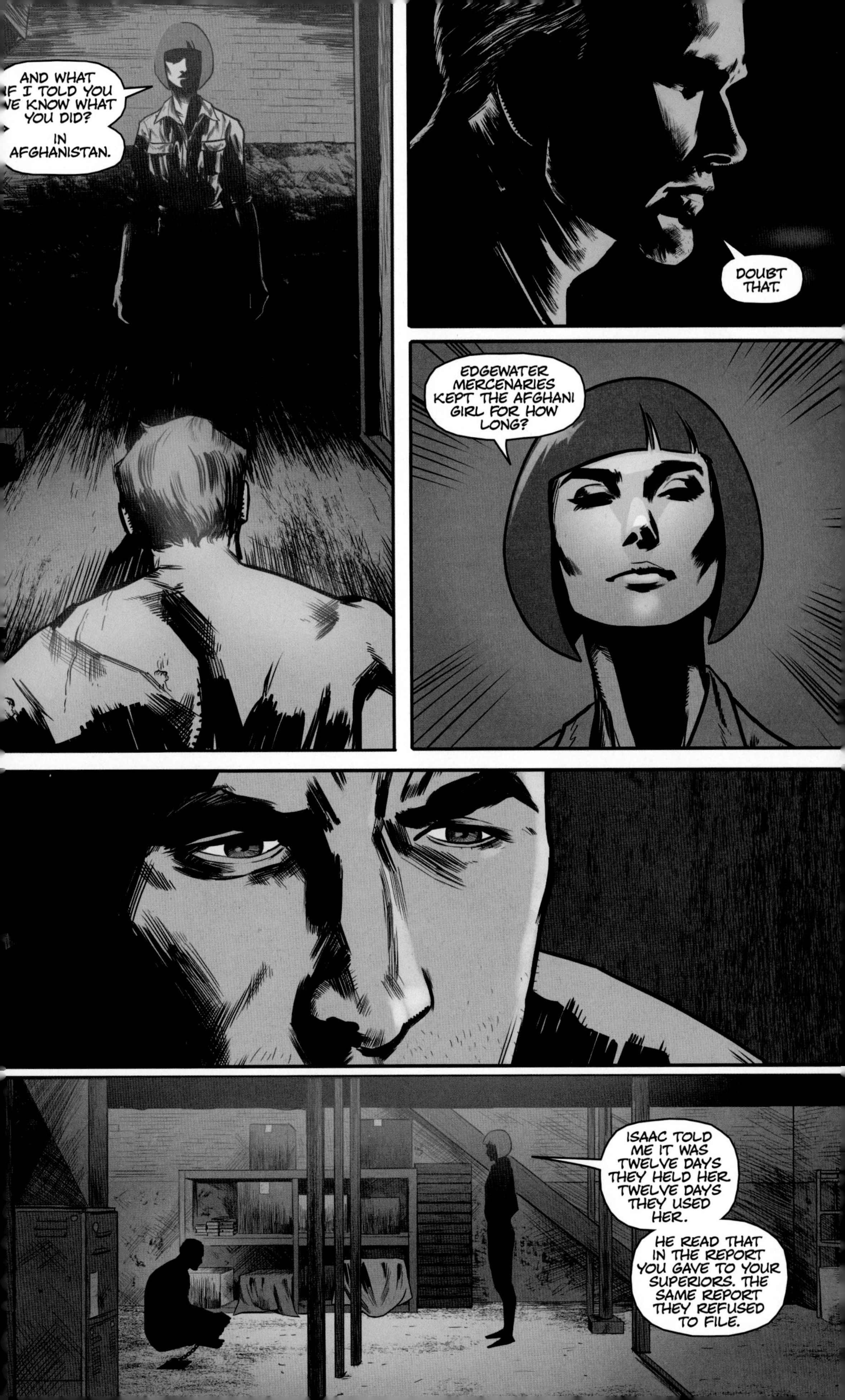
AND WHAT IF I TOLD YOU WE KNOW WHAT YOU DID?
IN AFGHANISTAN.
DOUBT THAT.
EDGEWATER MERCENARIES KEPT THE AFGHANI GIRL FOR HOW LONG?
ISAAC TOLD ME IT WAS TWELVE DAYS THEY HELD HER. TWELVE DAYS THEY USED HER.
HE READ THAT IN THE REPORT YOU GAVE TO YOUR SUPERIORS. THE SAME REPORT THEY REFUSED TO FILE.

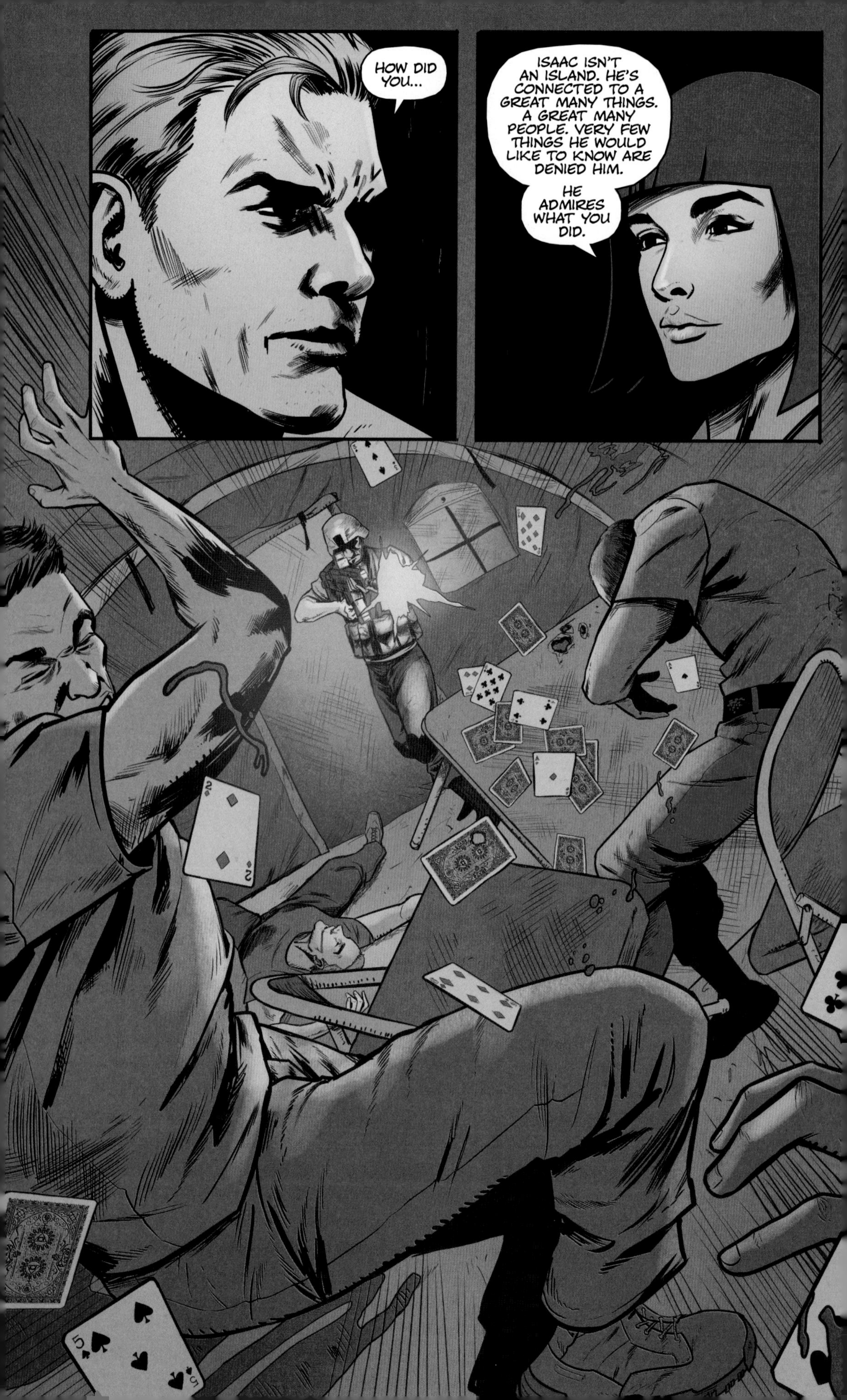
HOW DID YOU...
ISAAC ISN'T AN ISLAND. HE'S CONNECTED TO A GREAT MANY THINGS. A GREAT MANY PEOPLE. VERY FEW THINGS HE WOULD LIKE TO KNOW ARE DENIED HIM.
HE ADMIRES WHAT YOU DID.

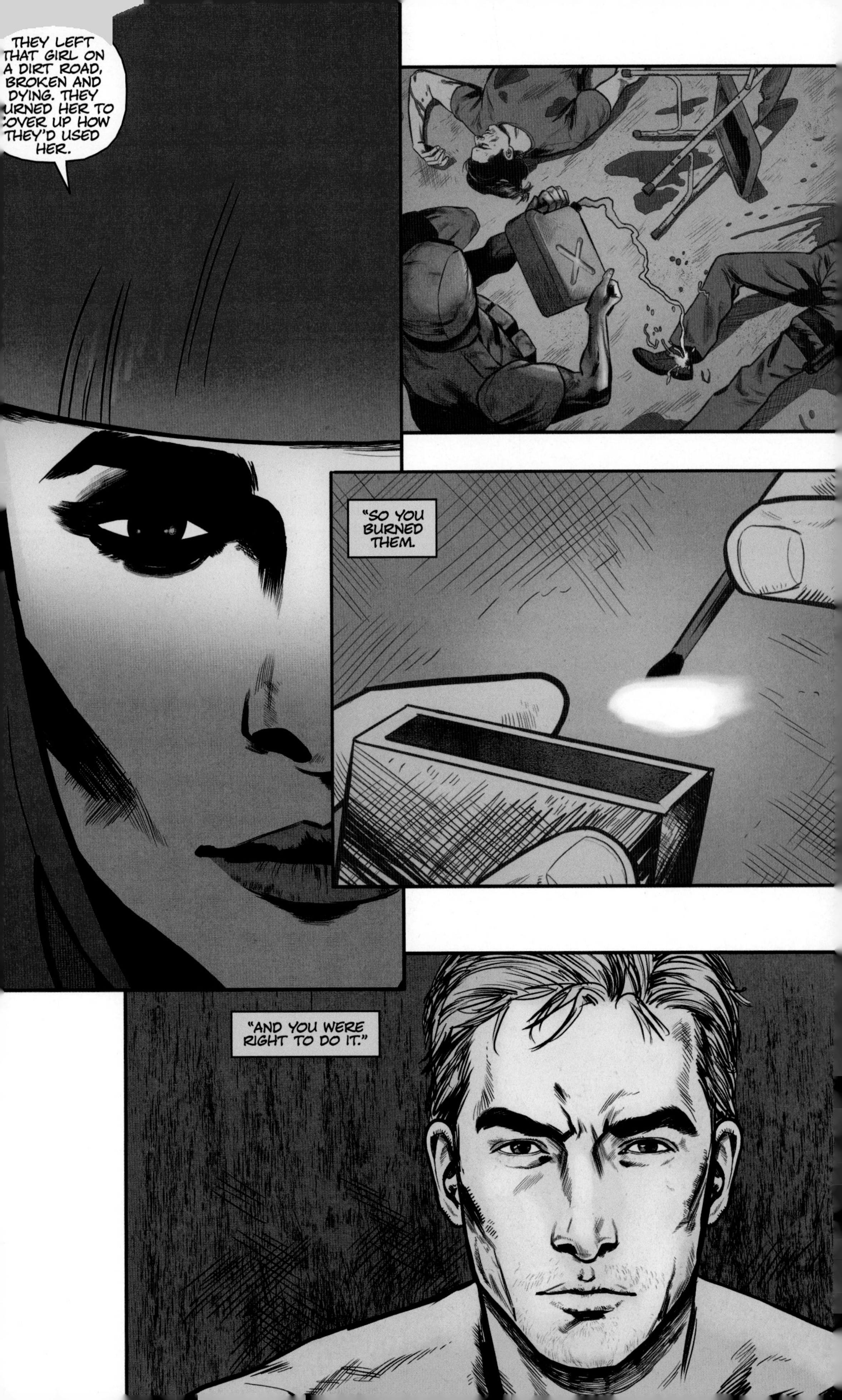
THEY LEFT THAT GIRL ON A DIRT ROAD, BROKEN AND DYING. THEY BURNED HER TO COVER UP HOW THEY'D USED HER.
"SO YOU BURNED THEM.
"AND YOU WERE RIGHT TO DO IT."

YOU'RE A MAN WHO BELIEVES IN JUSTICE. BUT YOU HAVEN'T BEEN ABLE TO FIND IT. NOT IN THE DESERT AND NOT IN THE FBI.

YOU THINK ISAAC SHIFFRON IS YOUR ENEMY, BUT HE BELIEVES THE SAME THINGS YOU DO. HE BELIEVES EDEN IS A FALSE KINGDOM PROTECTED BY THE SAME MEN THAT GIVE YOUR ORDERS.

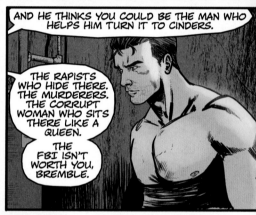

AND HE THINKS YOU COULD BE THE MAN WHO HELPS HIM TURN IT TO CINDERS.

THE RAPISTS WHO HIDE THERE. THE MURDERERS. THE CORRUPT WOMAN WHO SITS THERE LIKE A QUEEN.

THE FBI ISN'T WORTH YOU, BREMBLE.

AND YOU'RE NOT WORTH ISAAC'S COMPASSION. BUT IF YOU OPEN YOUR MIND, YOU MIGHT BE. YOU DON'T WANT LAW. YOU WANT JUSTICE.

JUSTICE REQUIRES WAR.

AND ISAAC WANTS TO SHOW YOU WHERE THAT WAR SHOULD BE WAGED.

HE'S BEEN WAITING FOR YOU TO FIND HIM.

YOU WERE MADE TO CALL HIS VISION YOUR HOME.

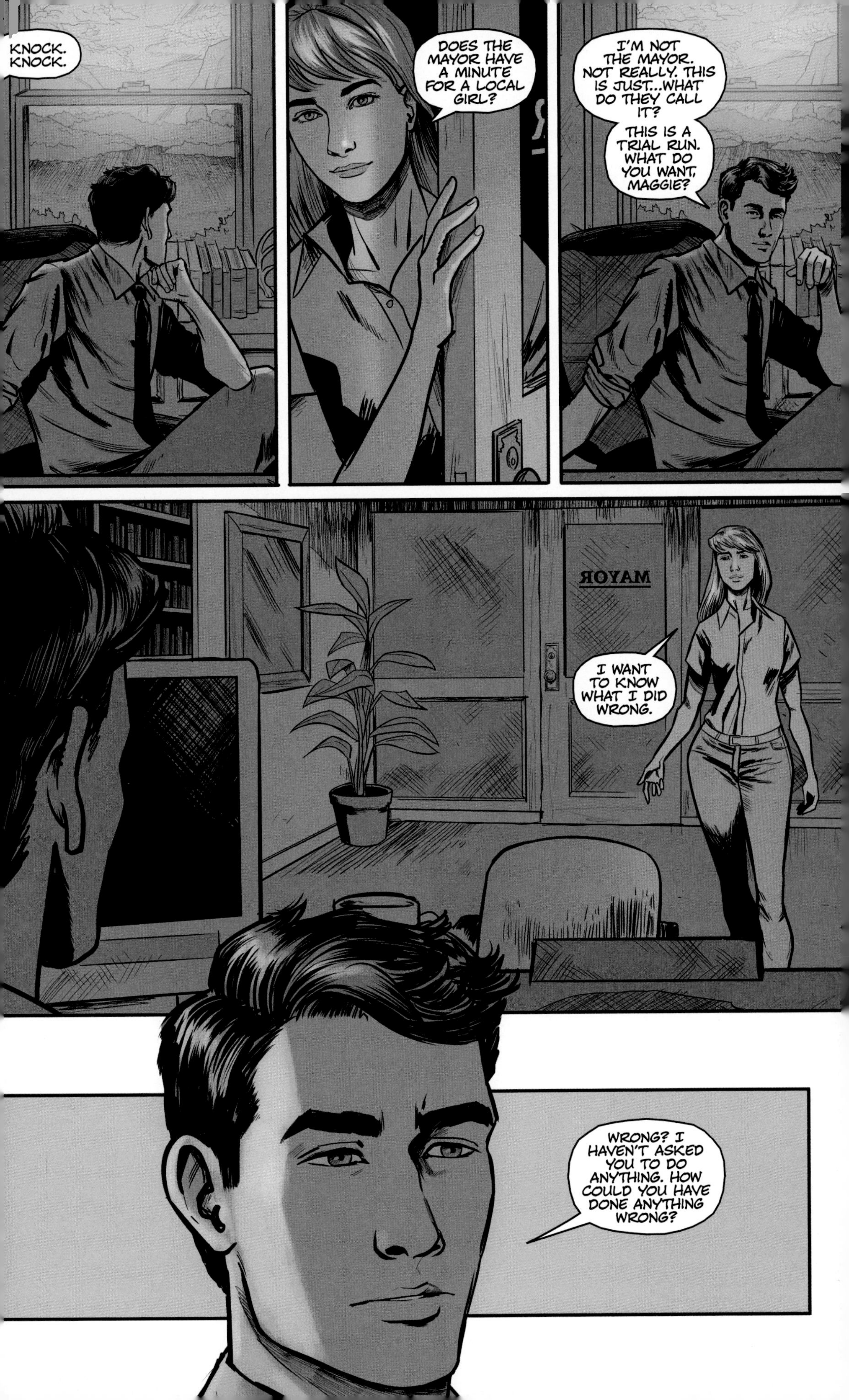
KNOCK.
KNOCK.
DOES THE MAYOR HAVE A MINUTE FOR A LOCAL GIRL?
I'M NOT THE MAYOR. NOT REALLY. THIS IS JUST...WHAT DO THEY CALL IT?
THIS IS A TRIAL RUN. WHAT DO YOU WANT, MAGGIE?
MAYOR
I WANT TO KNOW WHAT I DID WRONG.
WRONG? I HAVEN'T ASKED YOU TO DO ANYTHING. HOW COULD YOU HAVE DONE ANYTHING WRONG?

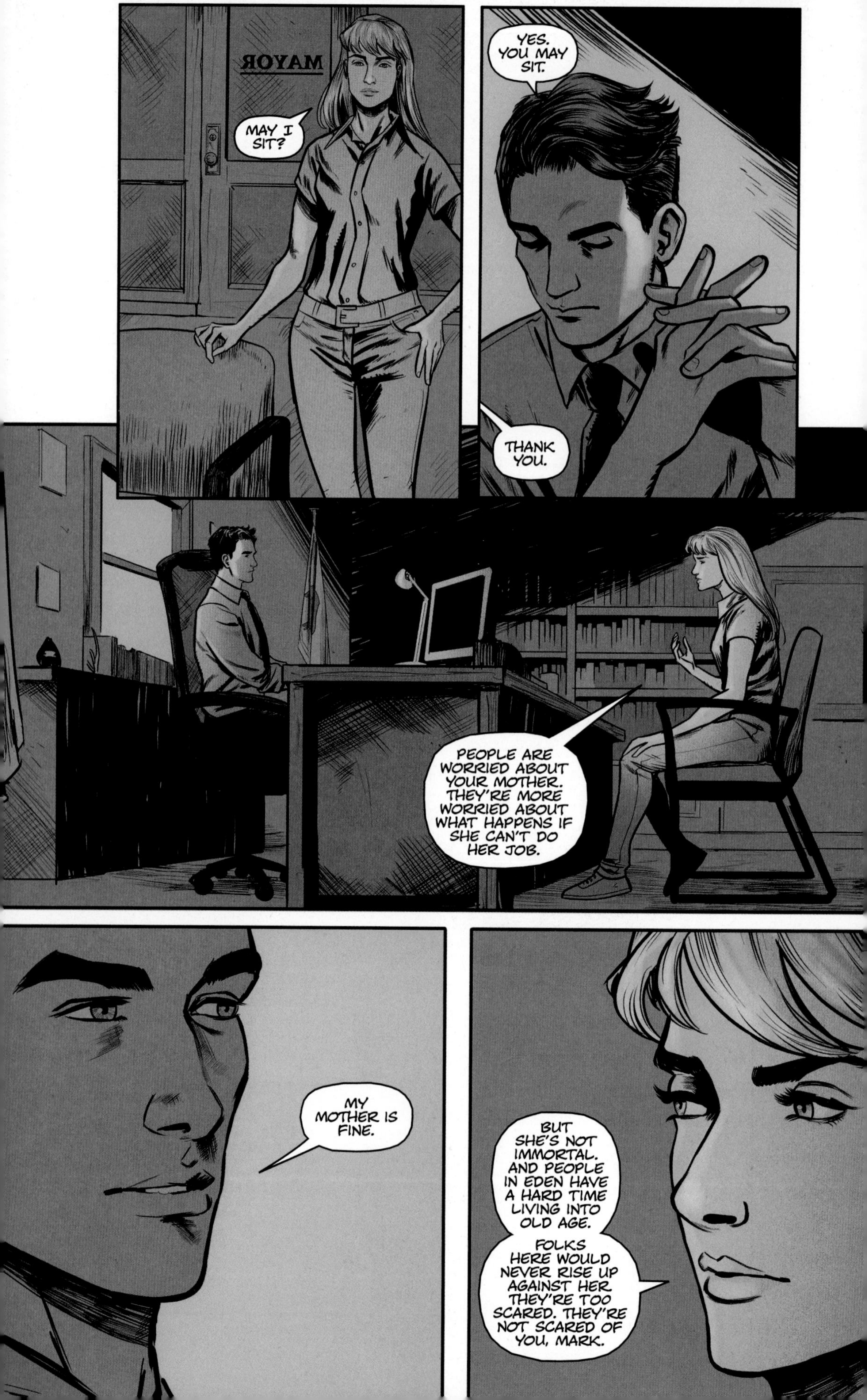
ROYAM
MAY I SIT?
YES. YOU MAY SIT.
THANK YOU.
PEOPLE ARE WORRIED ABOUT YOUR MOTHER. THEY'RE MORE WORRIED ABOUT WHAT HAPPENS IF SHE CAN'T DO HER JOB.
MY MOTHER IS FINE.
BUT SHE'S NOT IMMORTAL. AND PEOPLE IN EDEN HAVE A HARD TIME LIVING INTO OLD AGE.
FOLKS HERE WOULD NEVER RISE UP AGAINST HER THEY'RE TOO SCARED. THEY'RE NOT SCARED OF YOU, MARK.

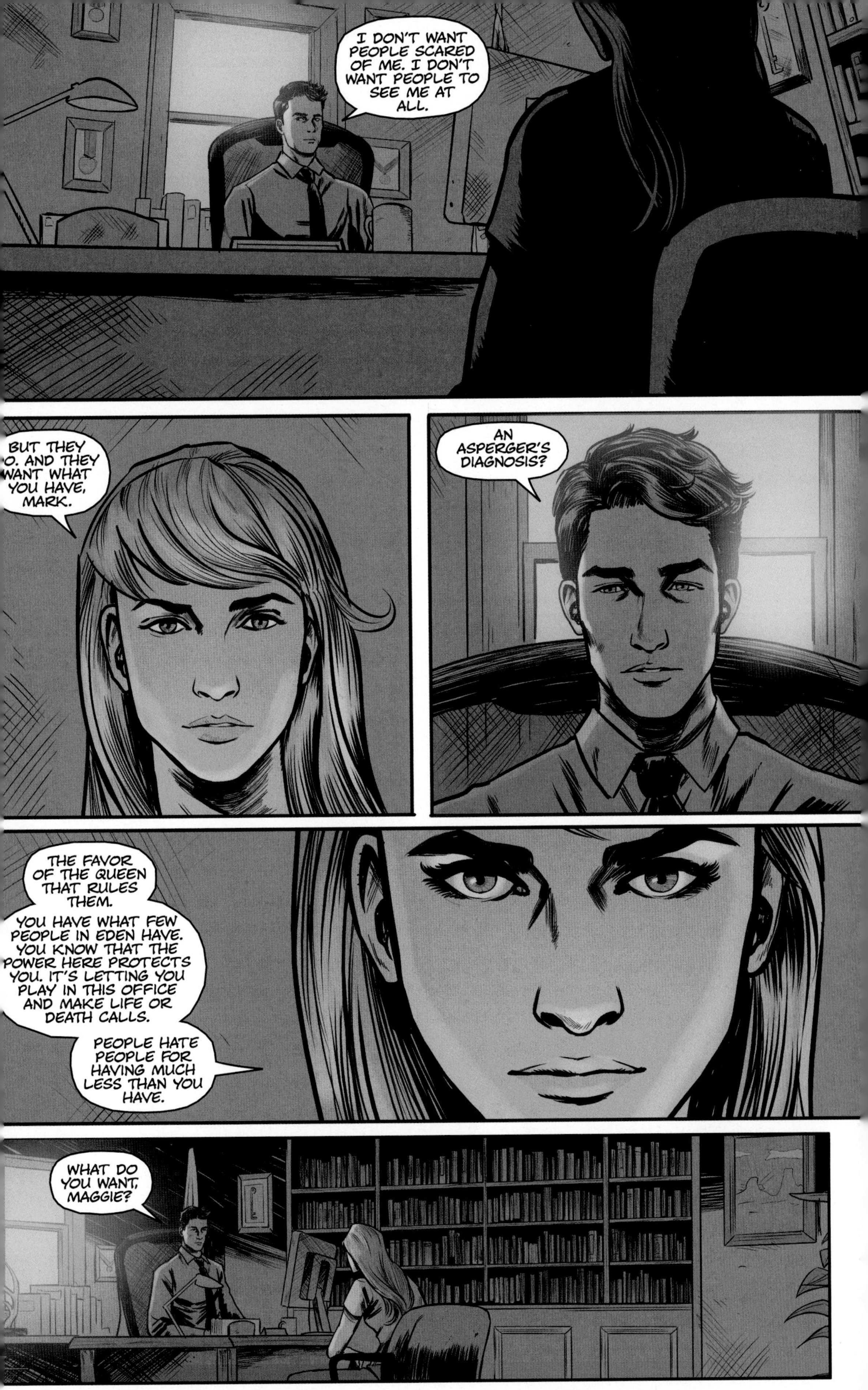
I DON'T WANT PEOPLE SCARED OF ME. I DON'T WANT PEOPLE TO SEE ME AT ALL.
BUT THEY O. AND THEY WANT WHAT YOU HAVE, MARK.
AN ASPERGER'S DIAGNOSIS?
THE FAVOR OF THE QUEEN THAT RULES THEM.
YOU HAVE WHAT FEW PEOPLE IN EDEN HAVE. YOU KNOW THAT THE POWER HERE PROTECTS YOU. IT'S LETTING YOU PLAY IN THIS OFFICE AND MAKE LIFE OR DEATH CALLS.
PEOPLE HATE PEOPLE FOR HAVING MUCH LESS THAN YOU HAVE.
WHAT DO YOU WANT, MAGGIE?

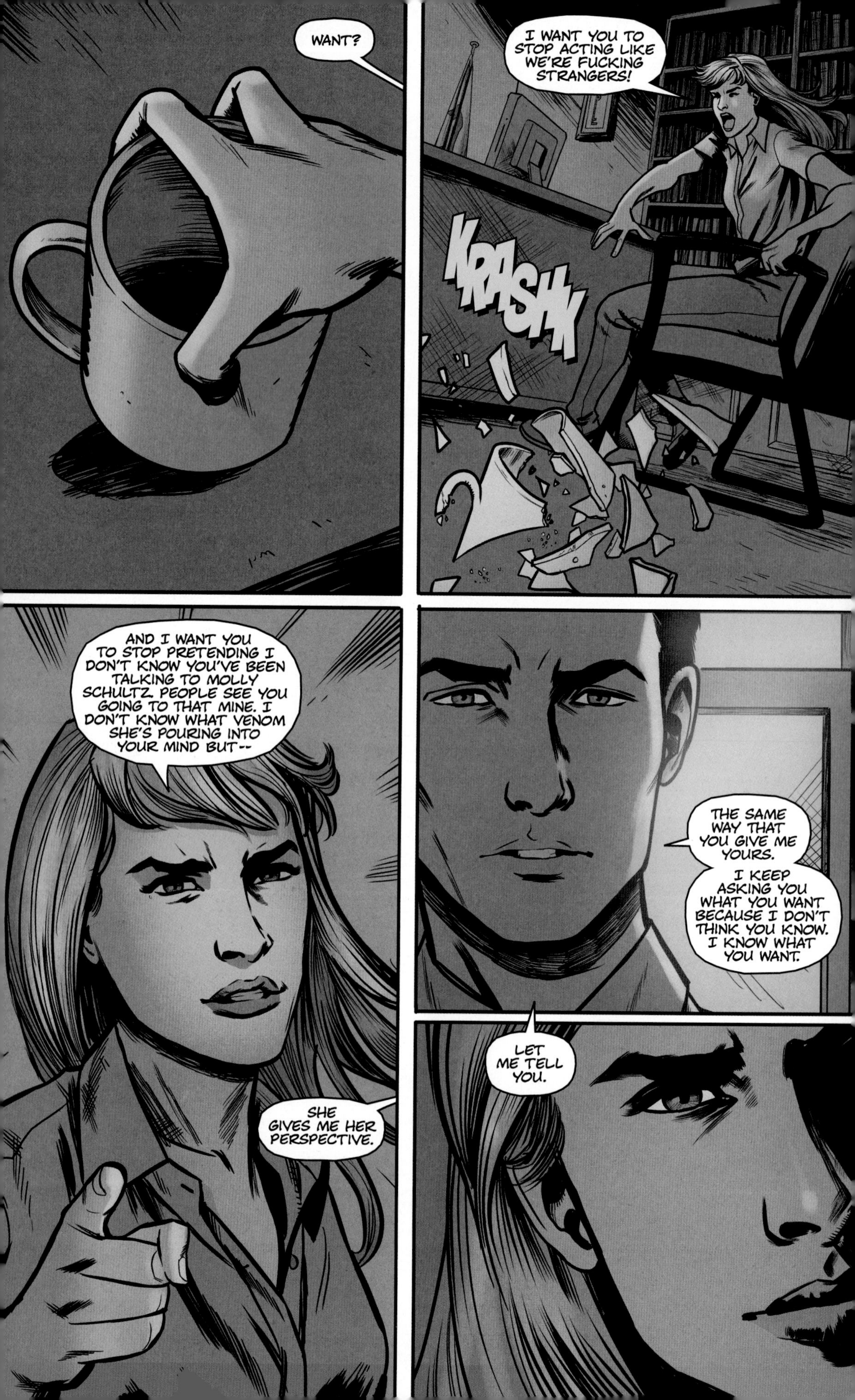
WANT?
I WANT YOU TO STOP ACTING LIKE WE'RE FUCKING STRANGERS!
KRASHK
AND I WANT YOU TO STOP PRETENDING I DON'T KNOW YOU'VE BEEN TALKING TO MOLLY SCHULTZ. PEOPLE SEE YOU GOING TO THAT MINE. I DON'T KNOW WHAT VENOM SHE'S POURING INTO YOUR MIND BUT--
SHE GIVES ME HER PERSPECTIVE.
THE SAME WAY THAT YOU GIVE ME YOURS.
I KEEP ASKING YOU WHAT YOU WANT BECAUSE I DON'T THINK YOU KNOW. I KNOW WHAT YOU WANT.
LET ME TELL YOU.

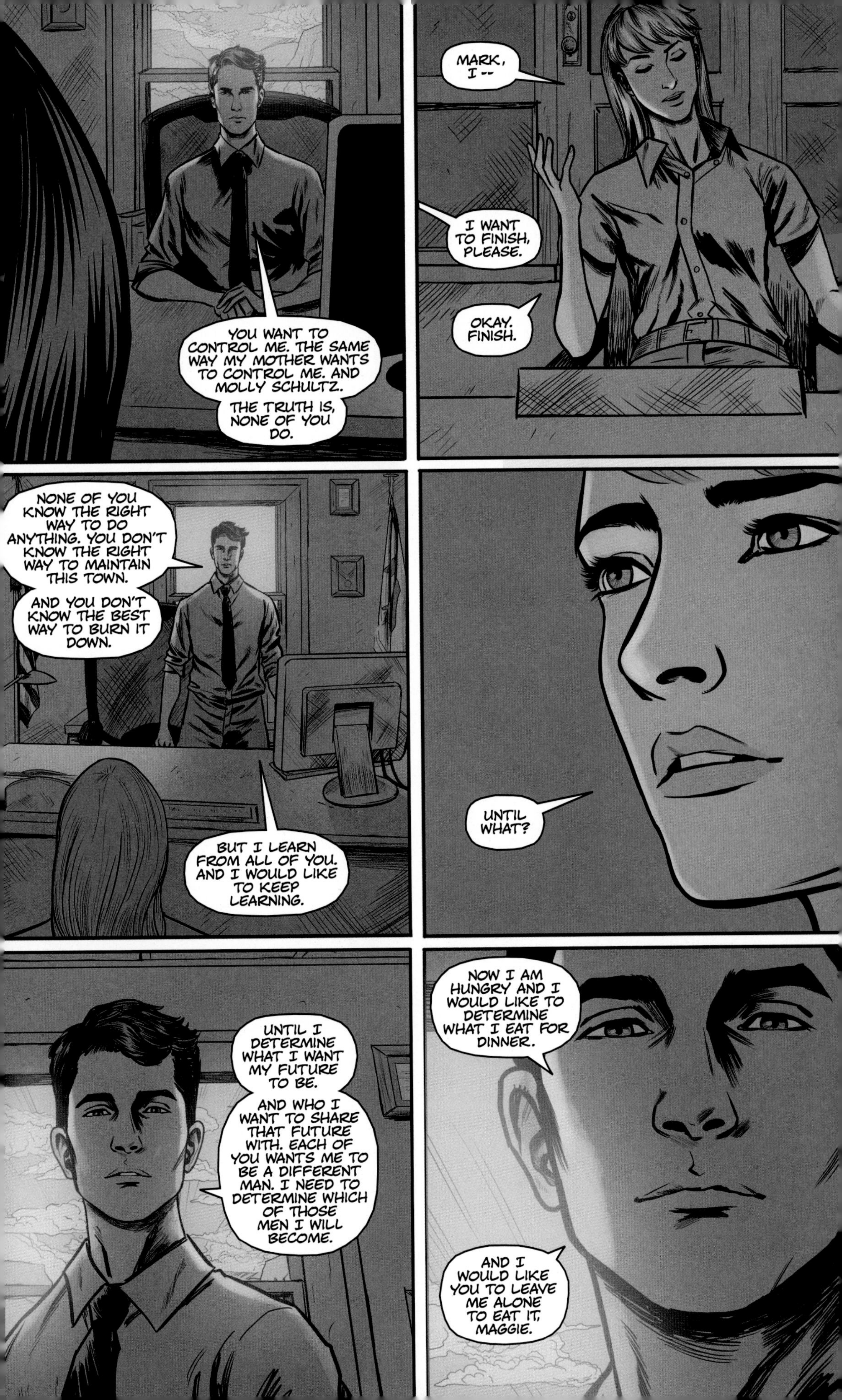
YOU WANT TO CONTROL ME. THE SAME WAY MY MOTHER WANTS TO CONTROL ME. AND MOLLY SCHULTZ.
THE TRUTH IS, NONE OF YOU DO.
MARK, I --
I WANT TO FINISH, PLEASE.
OKAY. FINISH.
NONE OF YOU KNOW THE RIGHT WAY TO DO ANYTHING. YOU DON'T KNOW THE RIGHT WAY TO MAINTAIN THIS TOWN.
AND YOU DON'T KNOW THE BEST WAY TO BURN IT DOWN.
BUT I LEARN FROM ALL OF YOU. AND I WOULD LIKE TO KEEP LEARNING.
UNTIL WHAT?
UNTIL I DETERMINE WHAT I WANT MY FUTURE TO BE.
AND WHO I WANT TO SHARE THAT FUTURE WITH. EACH OF YOU WANTS ME TO BE A DIFFERENT MAN. I NEED TO DETERMINE WHICH OF THOSE MEN I WILL BECOME.
NOW I AM HUNGRY AND I WOULD LIKE TO DETERMINE WHAT I EAT FOR DINNER.
AND I WOULD LIKE YOU TO LEAVE ME ALONE TO EAT IT, MAGGIE.

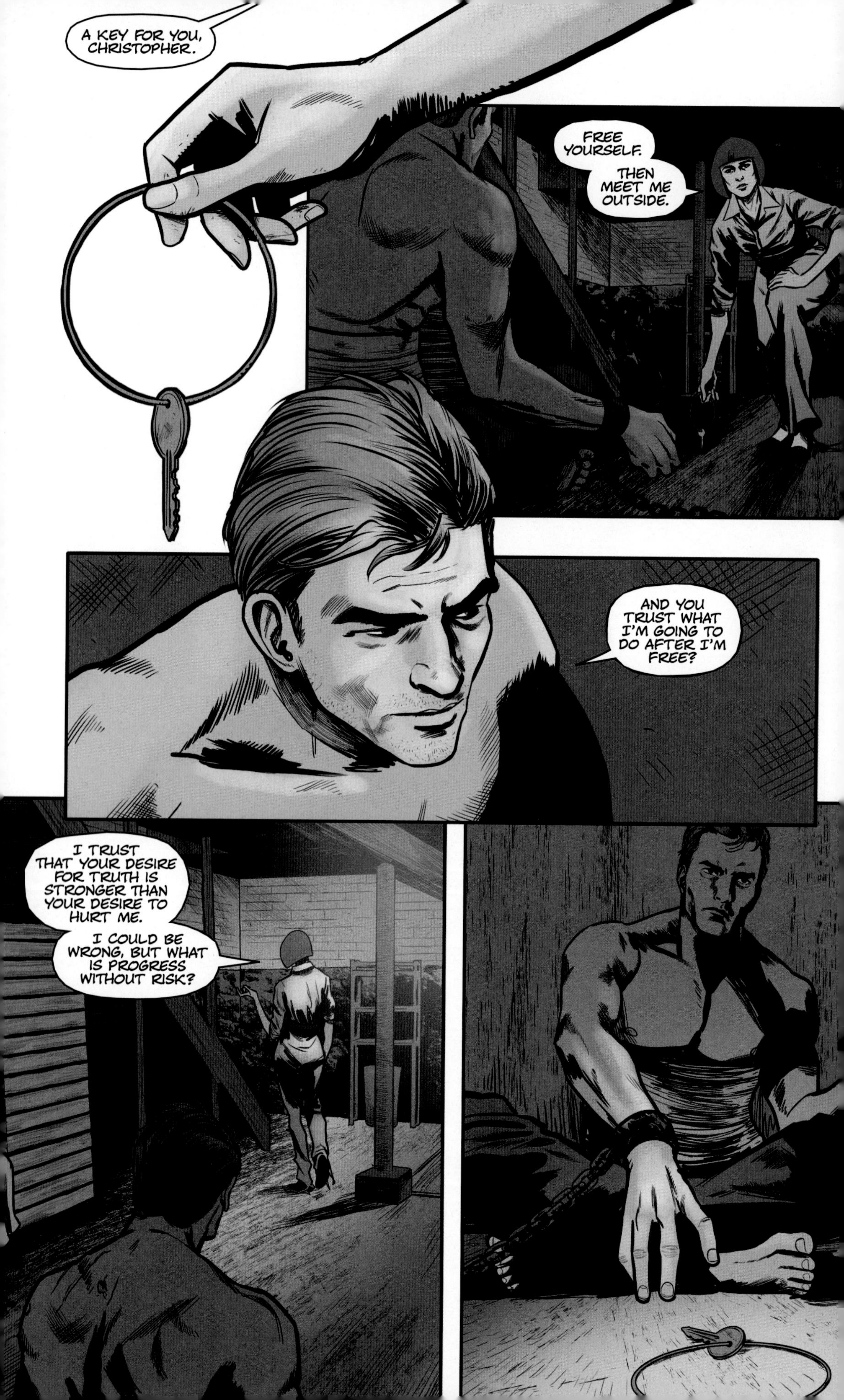
A KEY FOR YOU, CHRISTOPHER.
FREE YOURSELF.
THEN MEET ME OUTSIDE.
AND YOU TRUST WHAT I'M GOING TO DO AFTER I'M FREE?
I TRUST THAT YOUR DESIRE FOR TRUTH IS STRONGER THAN YOUR DESIRE TO HURT ME.
I COULD BE WRONG, BUT WHAT IS PROGRESS WITHOUT RISK?

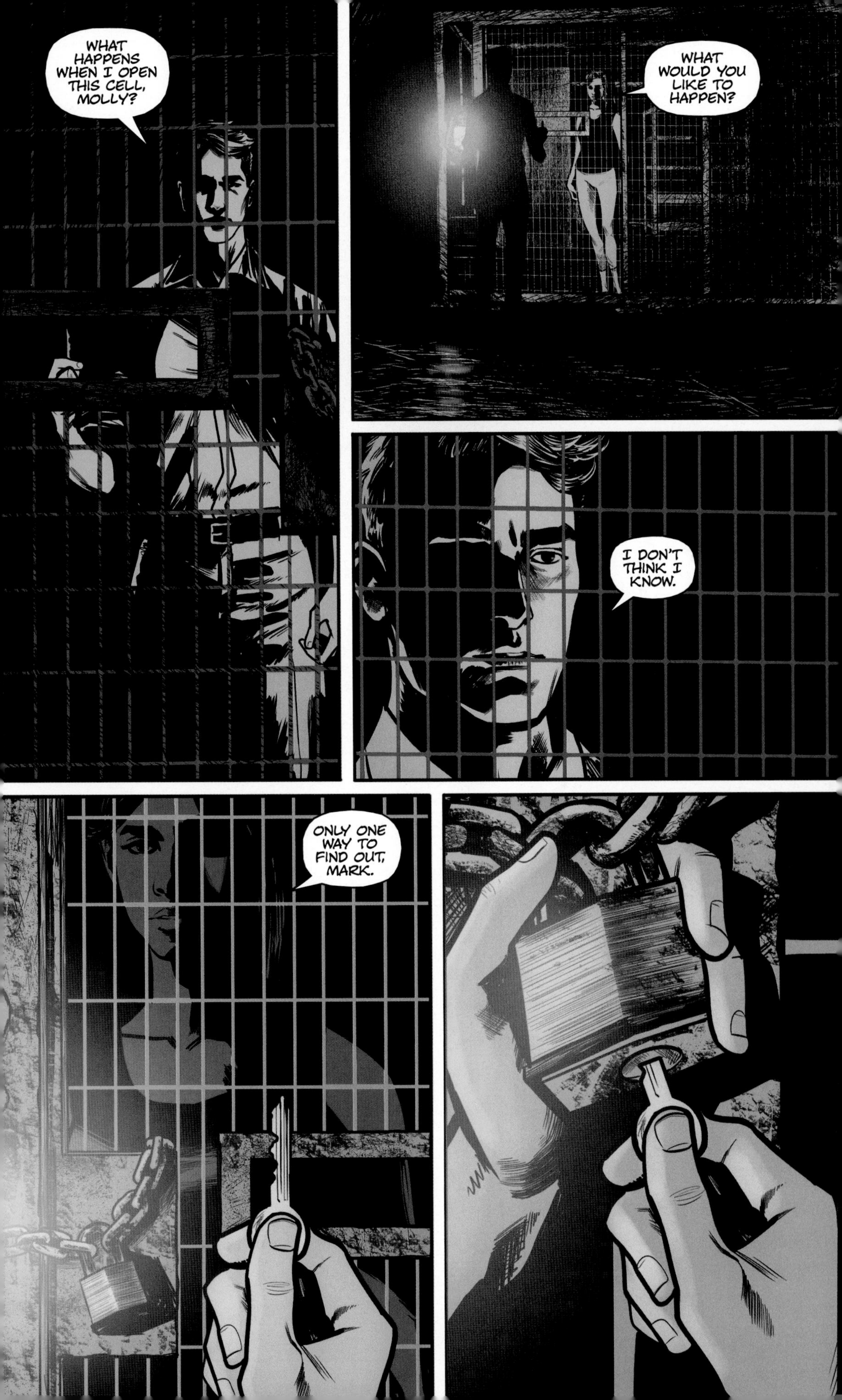
WHAT HAPPENS WHEN I OPEN THIS CELL, MOLLY?
WHAT WOULD YOU LIKE TO HAPPEN?
I DON'T THINK I KNOW.
ONLY ONE WAY TO FIND OUT, MARK.

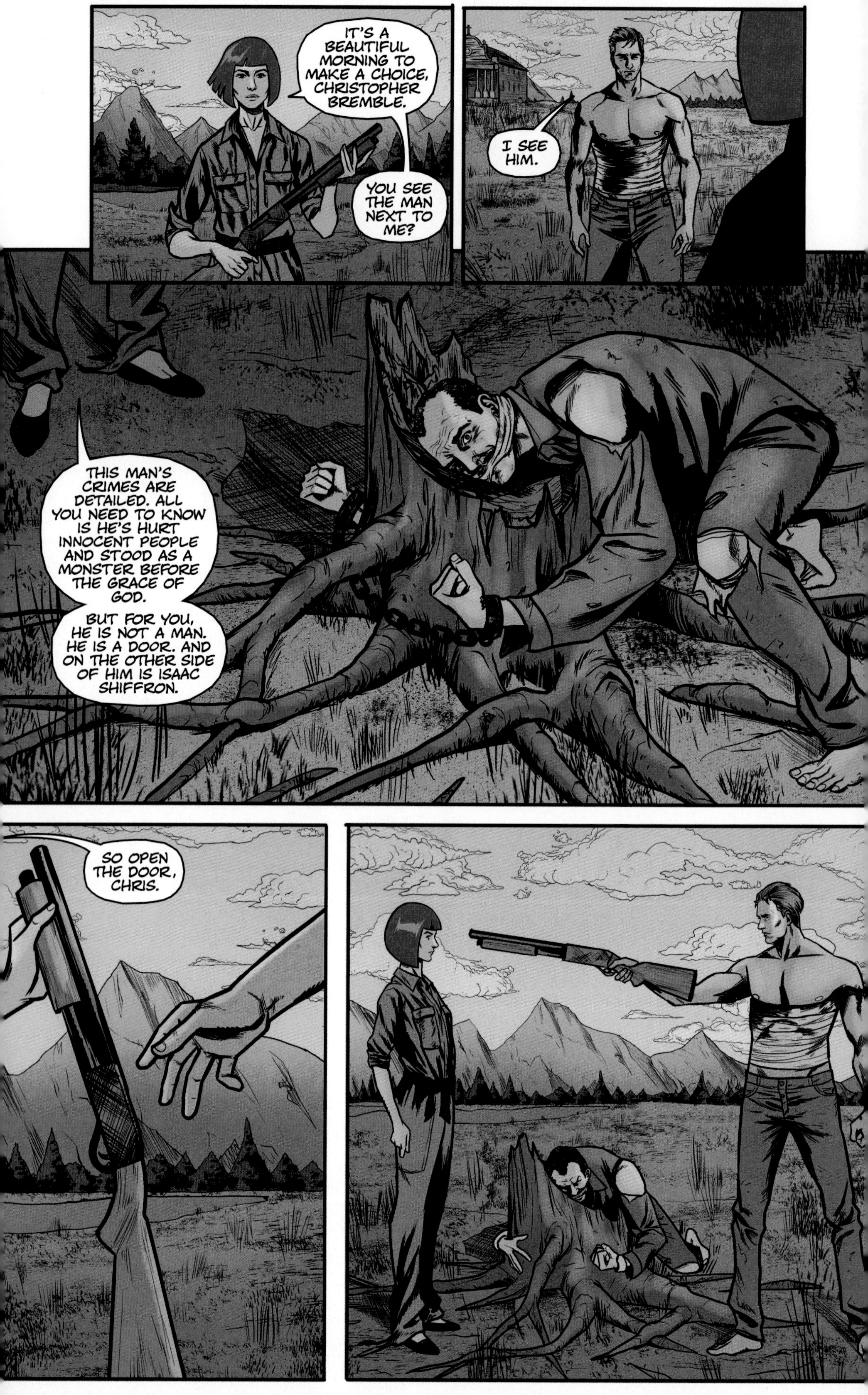

IT'S A BEAUTIFUL MORNING TO MAKE A CHOICE, CHRISTOPHER BREMBLE.
YOU SEE THE MAN NEXT TO ME?
I SEE HIM.
THIS MAN'S CRIMES ARE DETAILED. ALL YOU NEED TO KNOW IS HE'S HURT INNOCENT PEOPLE AND STOOD AS A MONSTER BEFORE THE GRACE OF GOD.
BUT FOR YOU, HE IS NOT A MAN. HE IS A DOOR. AND ON THE OTHER SIDE OF HIM IS ISAAC SHIFFRON.
SO OPEN THE DOOR, CHRIS.

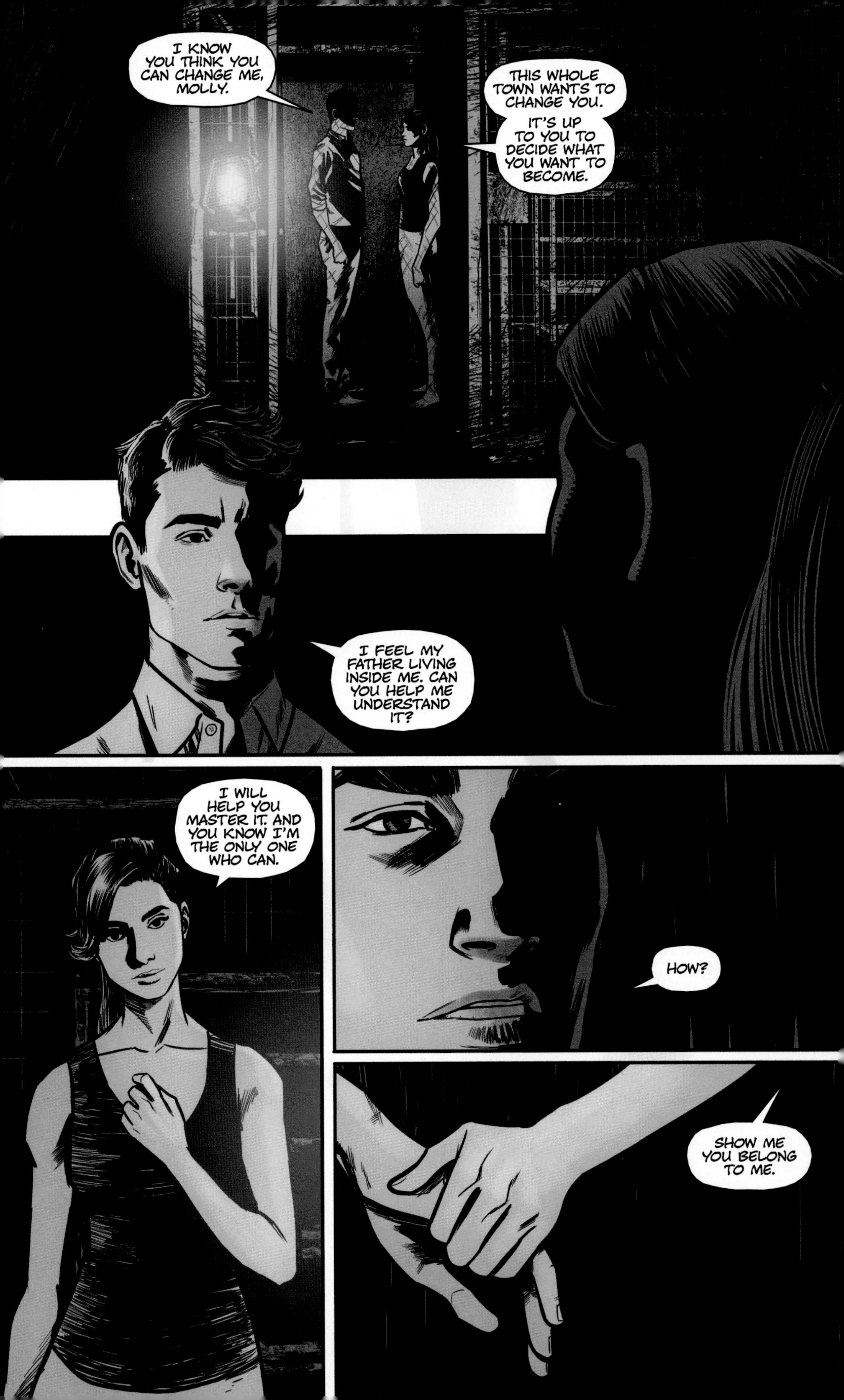
I KNOW YOU THINK YOU CAN CHANGE ME, MOLLY.
THIS WHOLE TOWN WANTS TO CHANGE YOU.
IT'S UP TO YOU TO DECIDE WHAT YOU WANT TO BECOME.
I FEEL MY FATHER LIVING INSIDE ME. CAN YOU HELP ME UNDERSTAND IT?
I WILL HELP YOU MASTER IT. AND YOU KNOW I'M THE ONLY ONE WHO CAN.
HOW?
SHOW ME YOU BELONG TO ME.

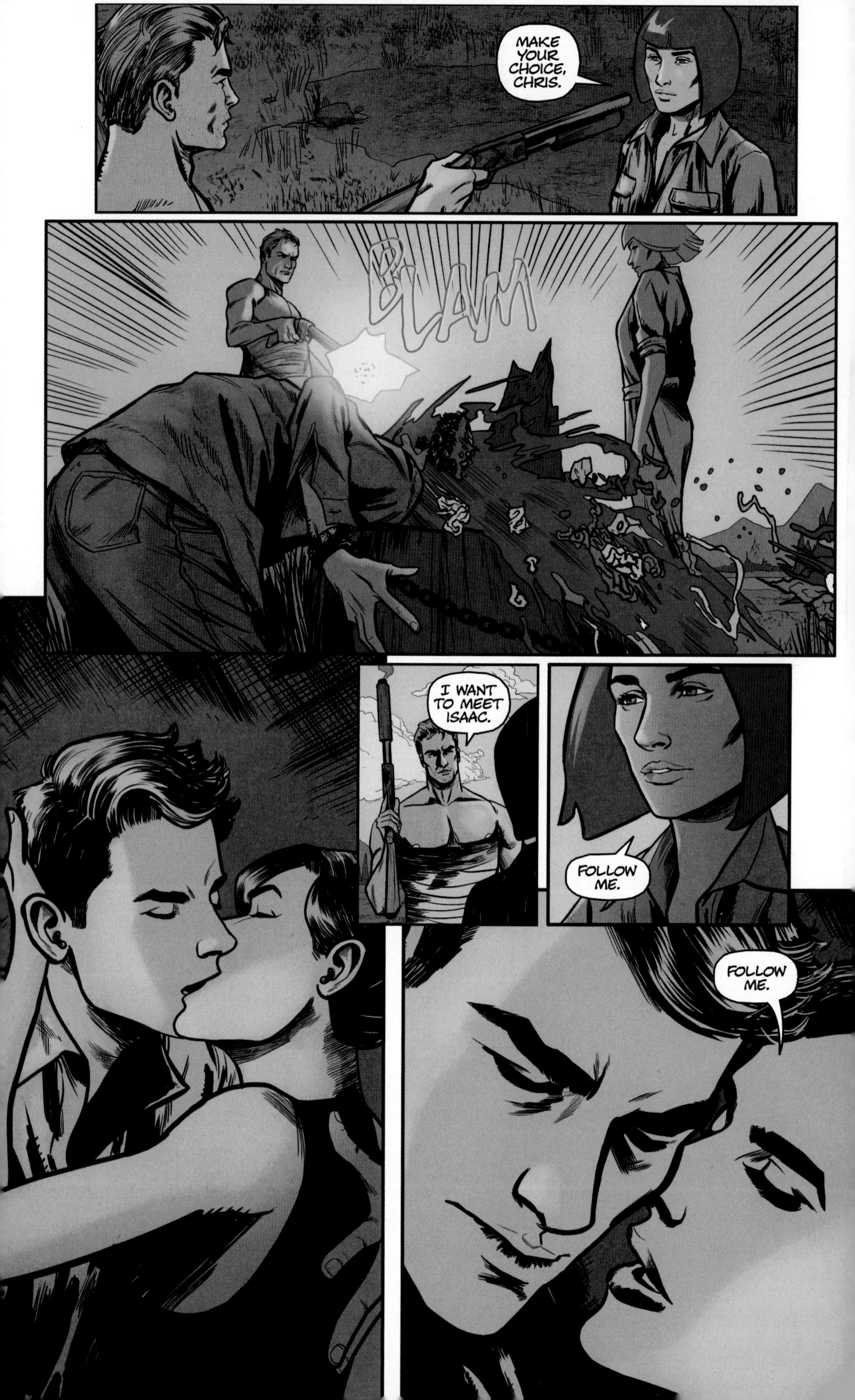
MAKE YOUR CHOICE, CHRIS.
BLAM
I WANT TO MEET ISAAC.
FOLLOW ME.
FOLLOW ME.

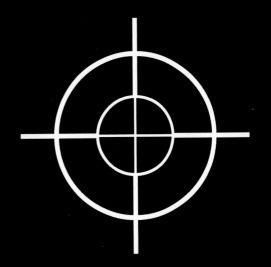

CHAPTER 19

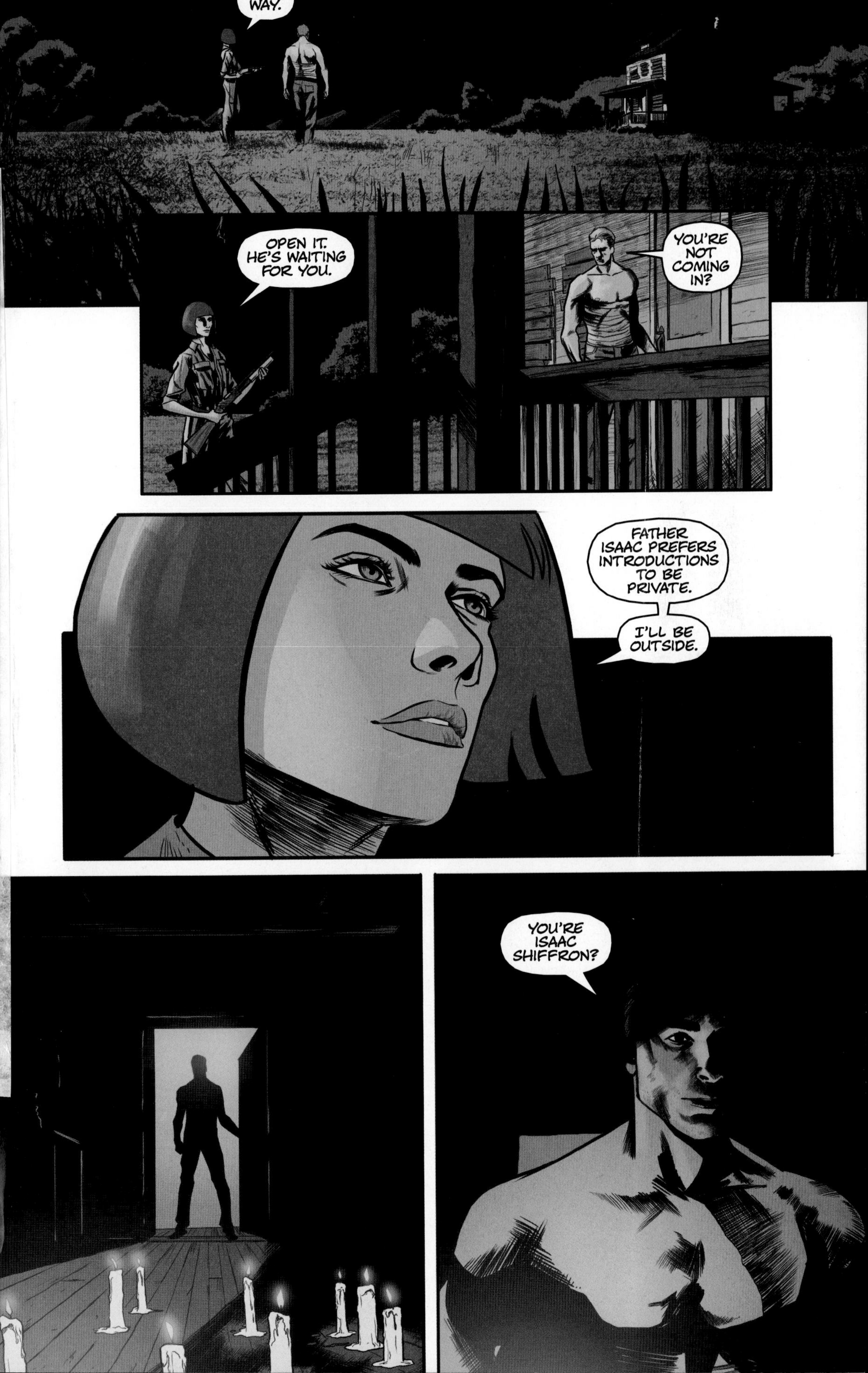
THIS WAY.
OPEN IT. HE'S WAITING FOR YOU.
YOU'RE NOT COMING IN?
FATHER ISAAC PREFERS INTRODUCTIONS TO BE PRIVATE.
I'LL BE OUTSIDE.
YOU'RE ISAAC SHIFFRON?

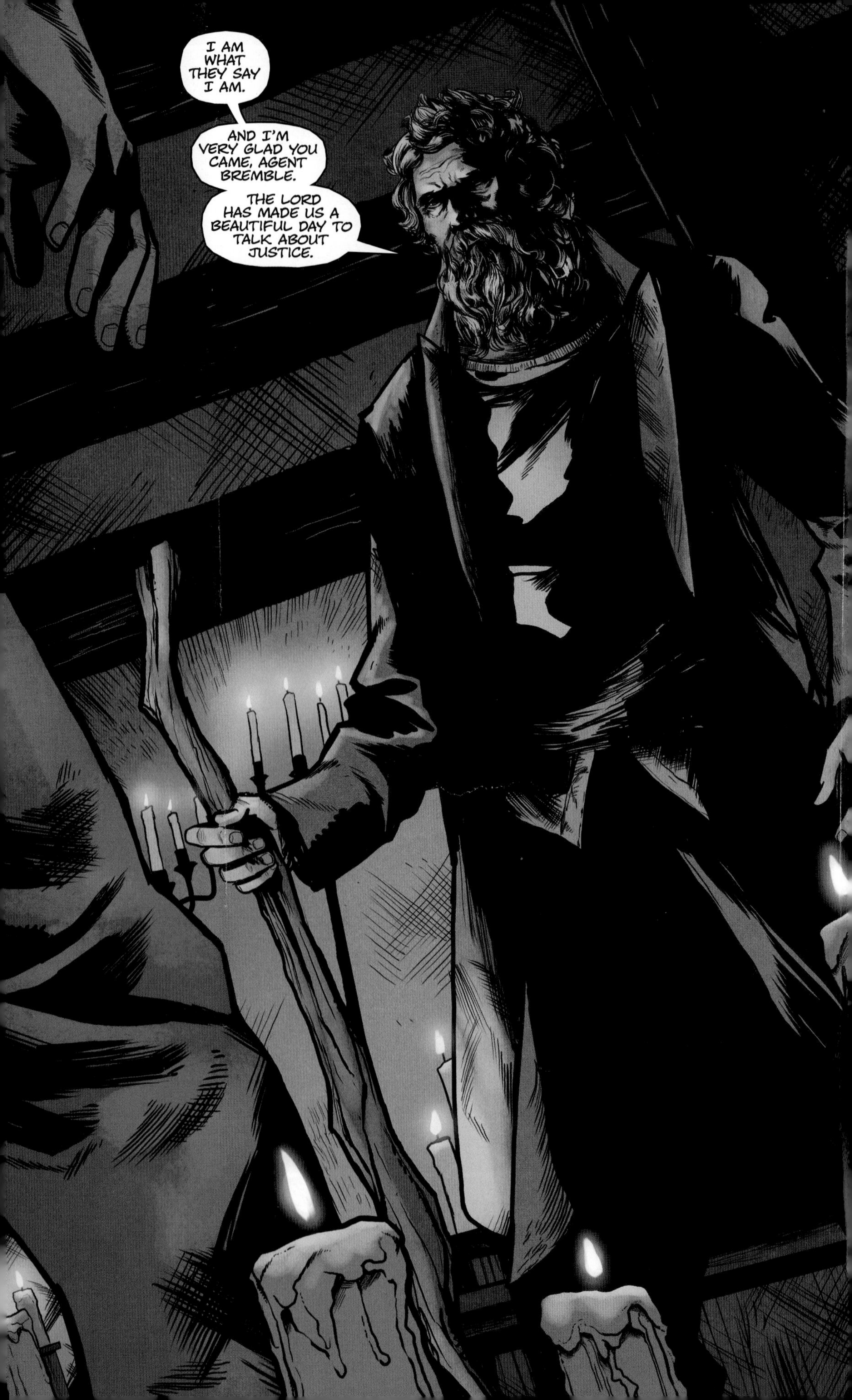
I AM WHAT THEY SAY I AM.
AND I'M VERY GLAD YOU CAME, AGENT BREMBLE.
THE LORD HAS MADE US A BEAUTIFUL DAY TO TALK ABOUT JUSTICE.

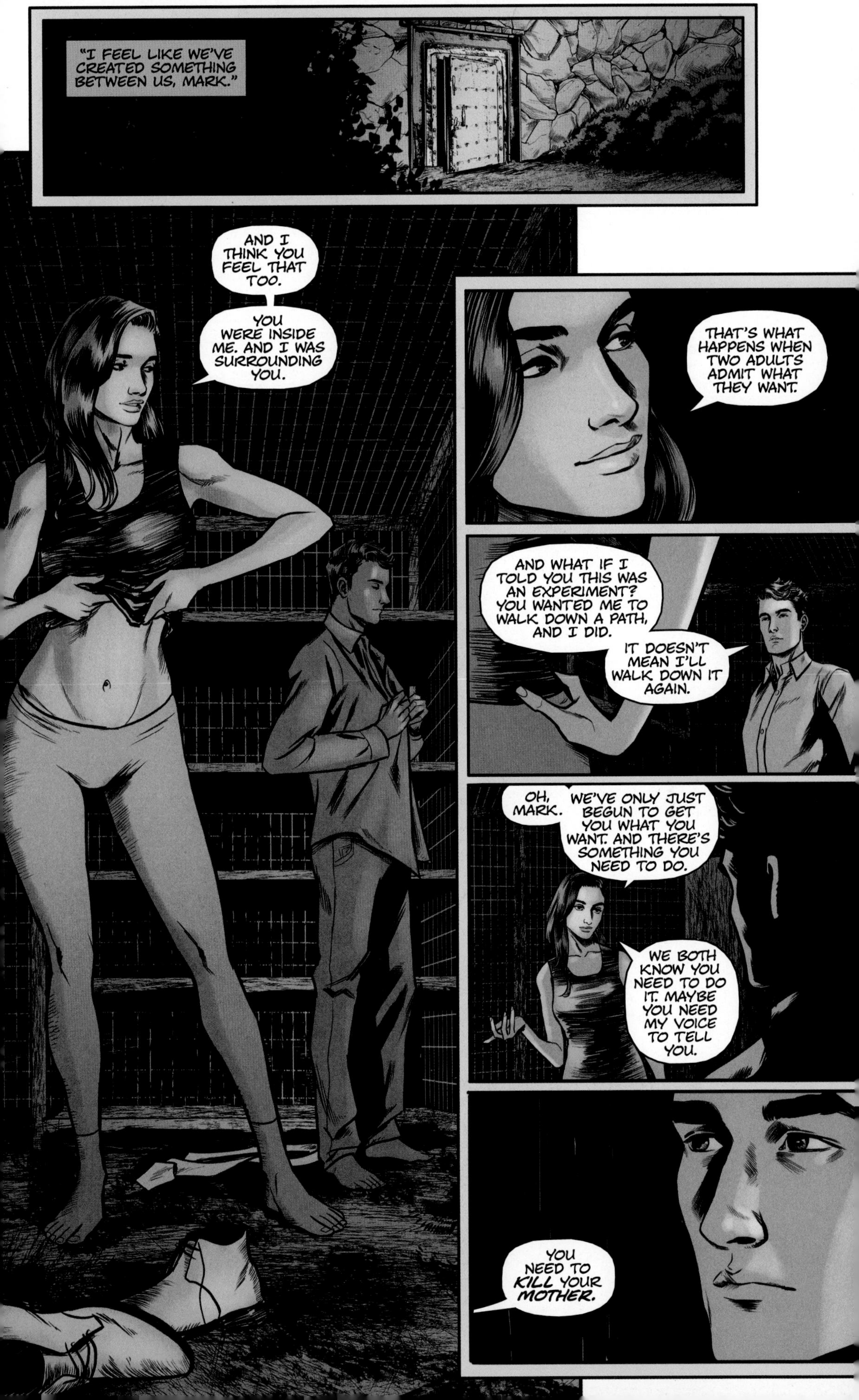

"I FEEL LIKE WE'VE CREATED SOMETHING BETWEEN US, MARK."
AND I THINK YOU FEEL THAT TOO.
YOU WERE INSIDE ME. AND I WAS SURROUNDING YOU.
THAT'S WHAT HAPPENS WHEN TWO ADULTS ADMIT WHAT THEY WANT.
AND WHAT IF I TOLD YOU THIS WAS AN EXPERIMENT? YOU WANTED ME TO WALK DOWN A PATH, AND I DID.
IT DOESN'T MEAN I'LL WALK DOWN IT AGAIN.
OH, MARK.
WE'VE ONLY JUST BEGUN TO GET YOU WHAT YOU WANT. AND THERE'S SOMETHING YOU NEED TO DO.
WE BOTH KNOW YOU NEED TO DO IT. MAYBE YOU NEED MY VOICE TO TELL YOU.
YOU NEED TO *KILL* YOUR *MOTHER*.

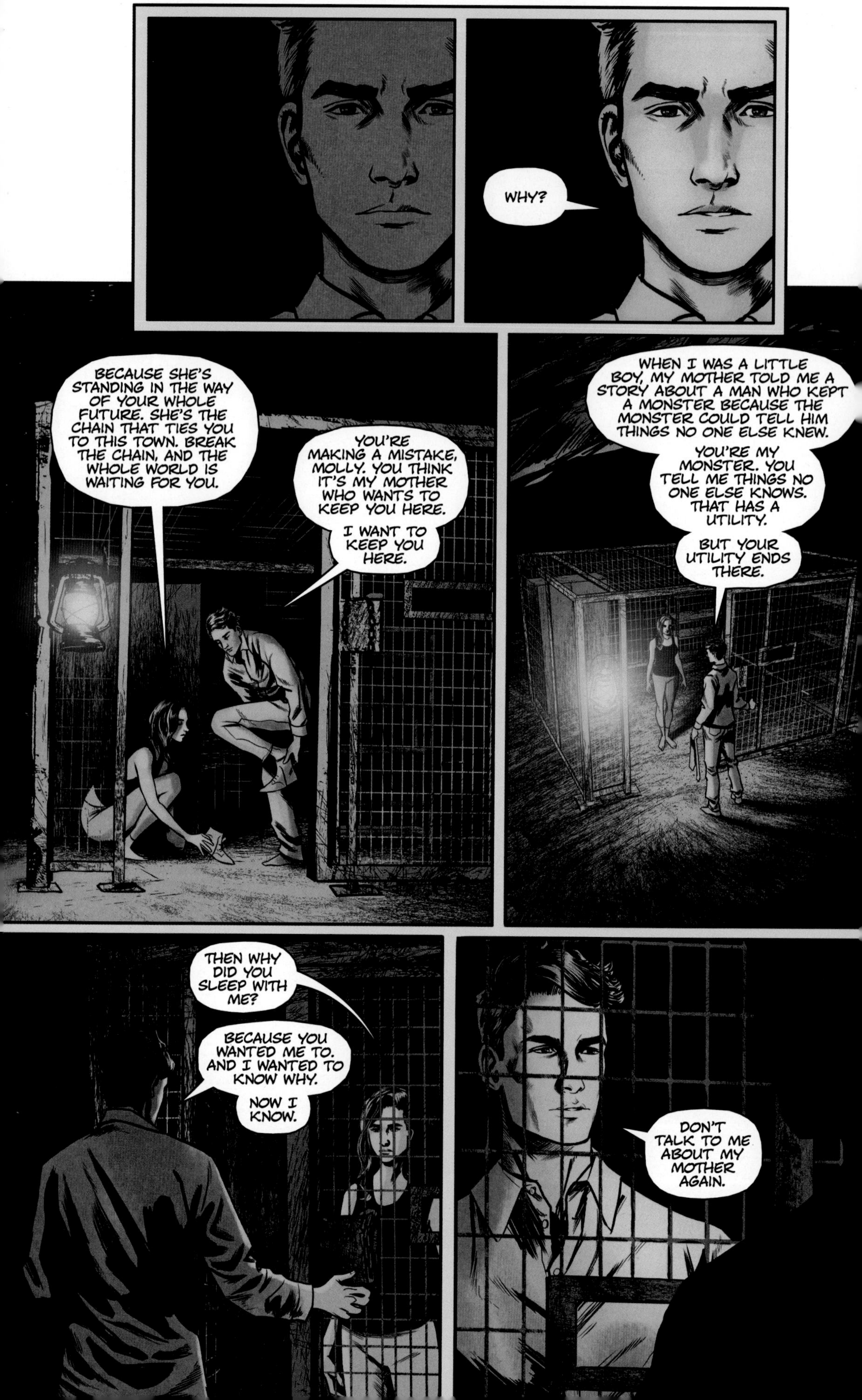
WHY?
BECAUSE SHE'S STANDING IN THE WAY OF YOUR WHOLE FUTURE. SHE'S THE CHAIN THAT TIES YOU TO THIS TOWN. BREAK THE CHAIN, AND THE WHOLE WORLD IS WAITING FOR YOU.
YOU'RE MAKING A MISTAKE, MOLLY. YOU THINK IT'S MY MOTHER WHO WANTS TO KEEP YOU HERE.
I WANT TO KEEP YOU HERE.
WHEN I WAS A LITTLE BOY, MY MOTHER TOLD ME A STORY ABOUT A MAN WHO KEPT A MONSTER BECAUSE THE MONSTER COULD TELL HIM THINGS NO ONE ELSE KNEW.
YOU'RE MY MONSTER. YOU TELL ME THINGS NO ONE ELSE KNOWS. THAT HAS A UTILITY.
BUT YOUR UTILITY ENDS THERE.
THEN WHY DID YOU SLEEP WITH ME?
BECAUSE YOU WANTED ME TO. AND I WANTED TO KNOW WHY.
NOW I KNOW.
DON'T TALK TO ME ABOUT MY MOTHER AGAIN.

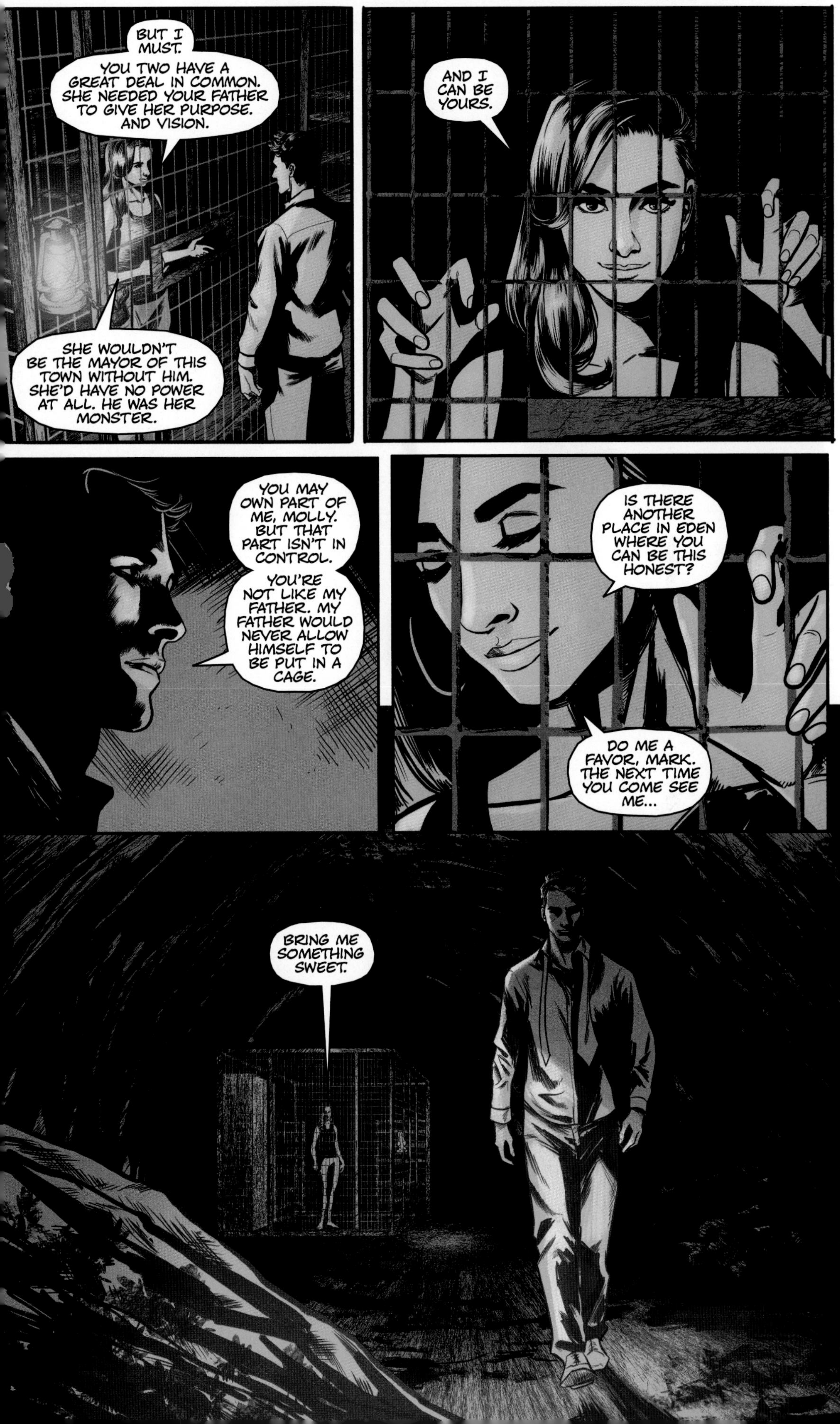
BUT I MUST.
YOU TWO HAVE A GREAT DEAL IN COMMON. SHE NEEDED YOUR FATHER TO GIVE HER PURPOSE. AND VISION.
SHE WOULDN'T BE THE MAYOR OF THIS TOWN WITHOUT HIM. SHE'D HAVE NO POWER AT ALL. HE WAS HER MONSTER.
AND I CAN BE YOURS.
YOU MAY OWN PART OF ME, MOLLY. BUT THAT PART ISN'T IN CONTROL.
YOU'RE NOT LIKE MY FATHER. MY FATHER WOULD NEVER ALLOW HIMSELF TO BE PUT IN A CAGE.
IS THERE ANOTHER PLACE IN EDEN WHERE YOU CAN BE THIS HONEST?
DO ME A FAVOR, MARK. THE NEXT TIME YOU COME SEE ME...
BRING ME SOMETHING SWEET.

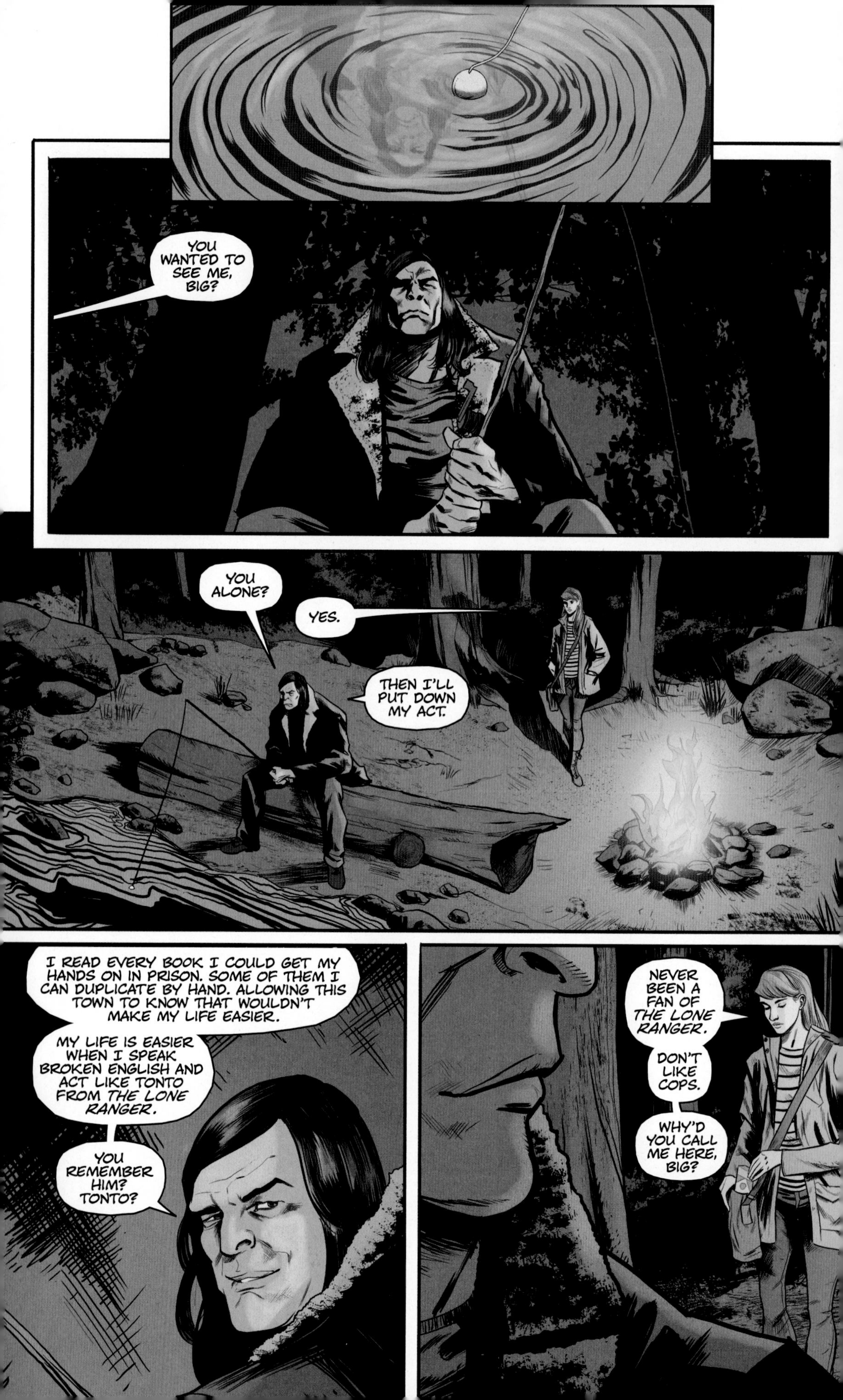
YOU WANTED TO SEE ME, BIG?
YOU ALONE?
YES.
THEN I'LL PUT DOWN MY ACT.
I READ EVERY BOOK I COULD GET MY HANDS ON IN PRISON. SOME OF THEM I CAN DUPLICATE BY HAND. ALLOWING THIS TOWN TO KNOW THAT WOULDN'T MAKE MY LIFE EASIER.
MY LIFE IS EASIER WHEN I SPEAK BROKEN ENGLISH AND ACT LIKE TONTO FROM *THE LONE RANGER*.
YOU REMEMBER HIM? TONTO?
NEVER BEEN A FAN OF *THE LONE RANGER*.
DON'T LIKE COPS.
WHY'D YOU CALL ME HERE, BIG?

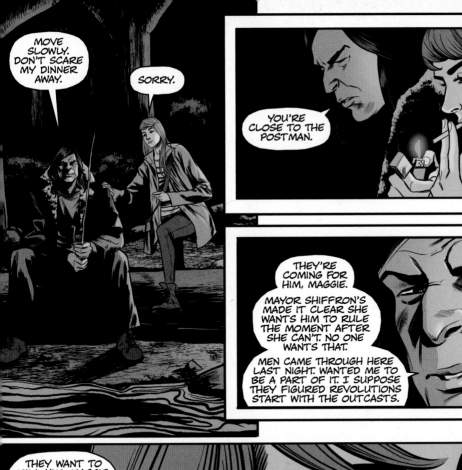

MOVE SLOWLY. DON'T SCARE MY DINNER AWAY.

SORRY.

YOU'RE CLOSE TO THE POSTMAN.

I WAS.

THEY'RE COMING FOR HIM, MAGGIE.

MAYOR SHIFFRON'S MADE IT CLEAR SHE WANTS HIM TO RULE THE MOMENT AFTER SHE CAN'T. NO ONE WANTS THAT.

MEN CAME THROUGH HERE LAST NIGHT. WANTED ME TO BE A PART OF IT. I SUPPOSE THEY FIGURED REVOLUTIONS START WITH THE OUTCASTS.

THEY WANT TO KILL HIM, MAGGIE. THEY'LL GO THROUGH MAYOR SHIFFRON TO DO IT.

WHICH MEN?

DOESN'T MATTER. THEY ASKED ME TO SWEAR I WOULD KEEP THEIR NAMES HIDDEN. AND I WILL.

BUT I DECLINED THEIR INTENTIONS. I LIKE THAT BOY. HE'S HONEST.

I LIKE HIM TOO, BIG.

WHY YOU TELLING ME THIS?

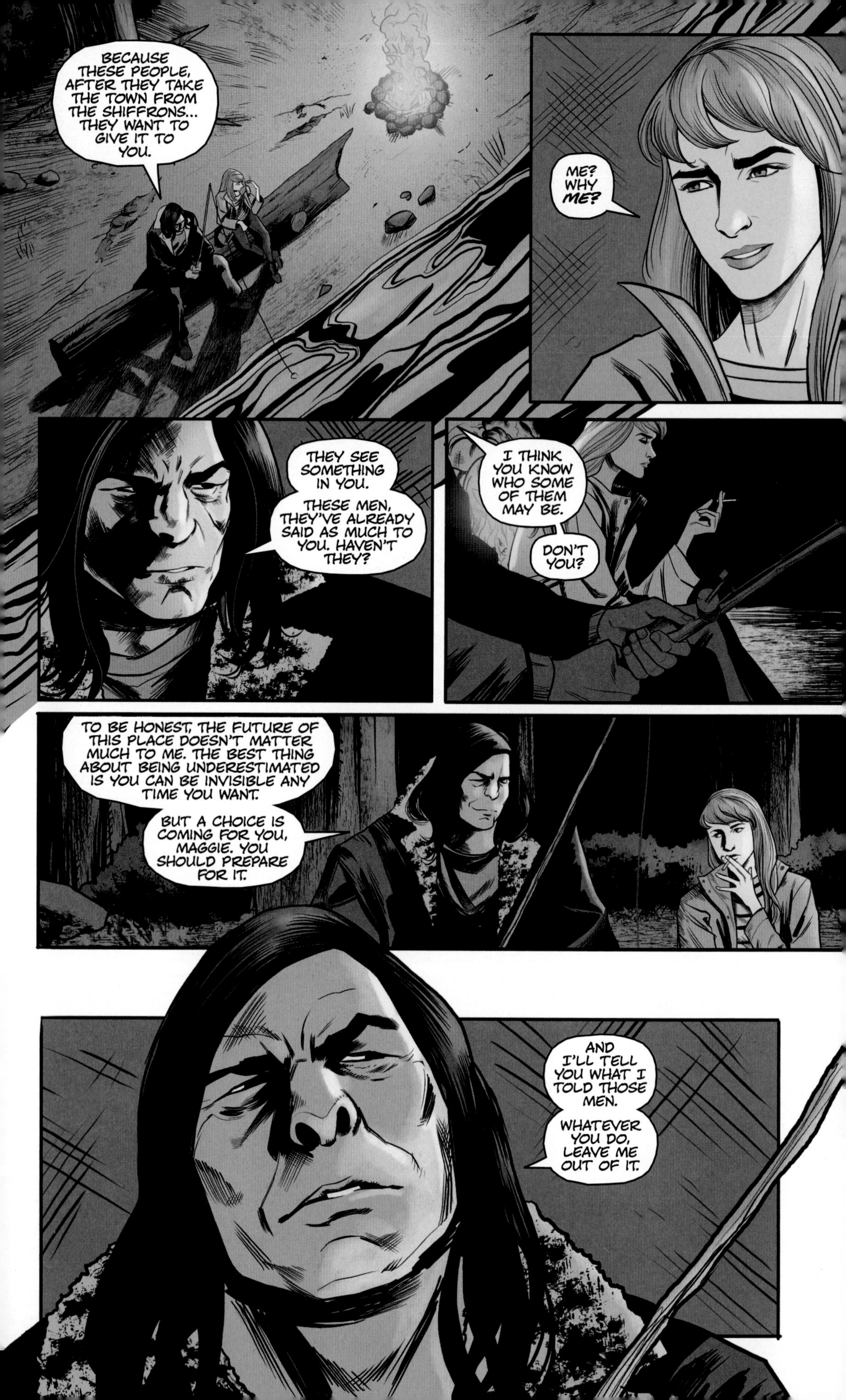
BECAUSE THESE PEOPLE, AFTER THEY TAKE THE TOWN FROM THE SHIFFRONS... THEY WANT TO GIVE IT TO YOU.
ME? WHY *ME?*
THEY SEE SOMETHING IN YOU.
THESE MEN, THEY'VE ALREADY SAID AS MUCH TO YOU. HAVEN'T THEY?
I THINK YOU KNOW WHO SOME OF THEM MAY BE.
DON'T YOU?
TO BE HONEST, THE FUTURE OF THIS PLACE DOESN'T MATTER MUCH TO ME. THE BEST THING ABOUT BEING UNDERESTIMATED IS YOU CAN BE INVISIBLE ANY TIME YOU WANT.
BUT A CHOICE IS COMING FOR YOU, MAGGIE. YOU SHOULD PREPARE FOR IT.
AND I'LL TELL YOU WHAT I TOLD THOSE MEN.
WHATEVER YOU DO, LEAVE ME OUT OF IT.

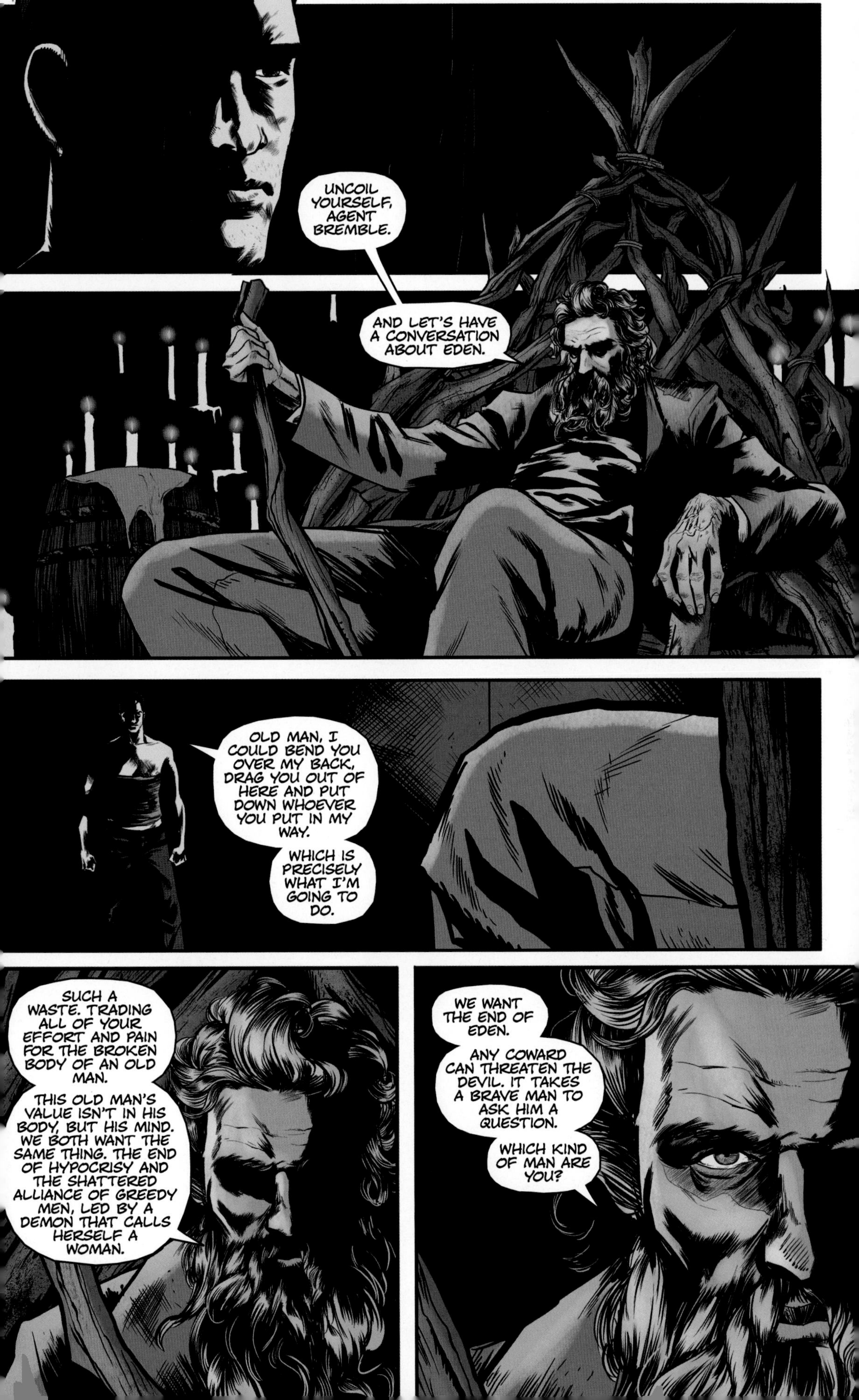
UNCOIL YOURSELF, AGENT BREMBLE.
AND LET'S HAVE A CONVERSATION ABOUT EDEN.
OLD MAN, I COULD BEND YOU OVER MY BACK, DRAG YOU OUT OF HERE AND PUT DOWN WHOEVER YOU PUT IN MY WAY.
WHICH IS PRECISELY WHAT I'M GOING TO DO.
SUCH A WASTE. TRADING ALL OF YOUR EFFORT AND PAIN FOR THE BROKEN BODY OF AN OLD MAN.
THIS OLD MAN'S VALUE ISN'T IN HIS BODY, BUT HIS MIND. WE BOTH WANT THE SAME THING. THE END OF HYPOCRISY AND THE SHATTERED ALLIANCE OF GREEDY MEN, LED BY A DEMON THAT CALLS HERSELF A WOMAN.
WE WANT THE END OF EDEN.
ANY COWARD CAN THREATEN THE DEVIL. IT TAKES A BRAVE MAN TO ASK HIM A QUESTION.
WHICH KIND OF MAN ARE YOU?

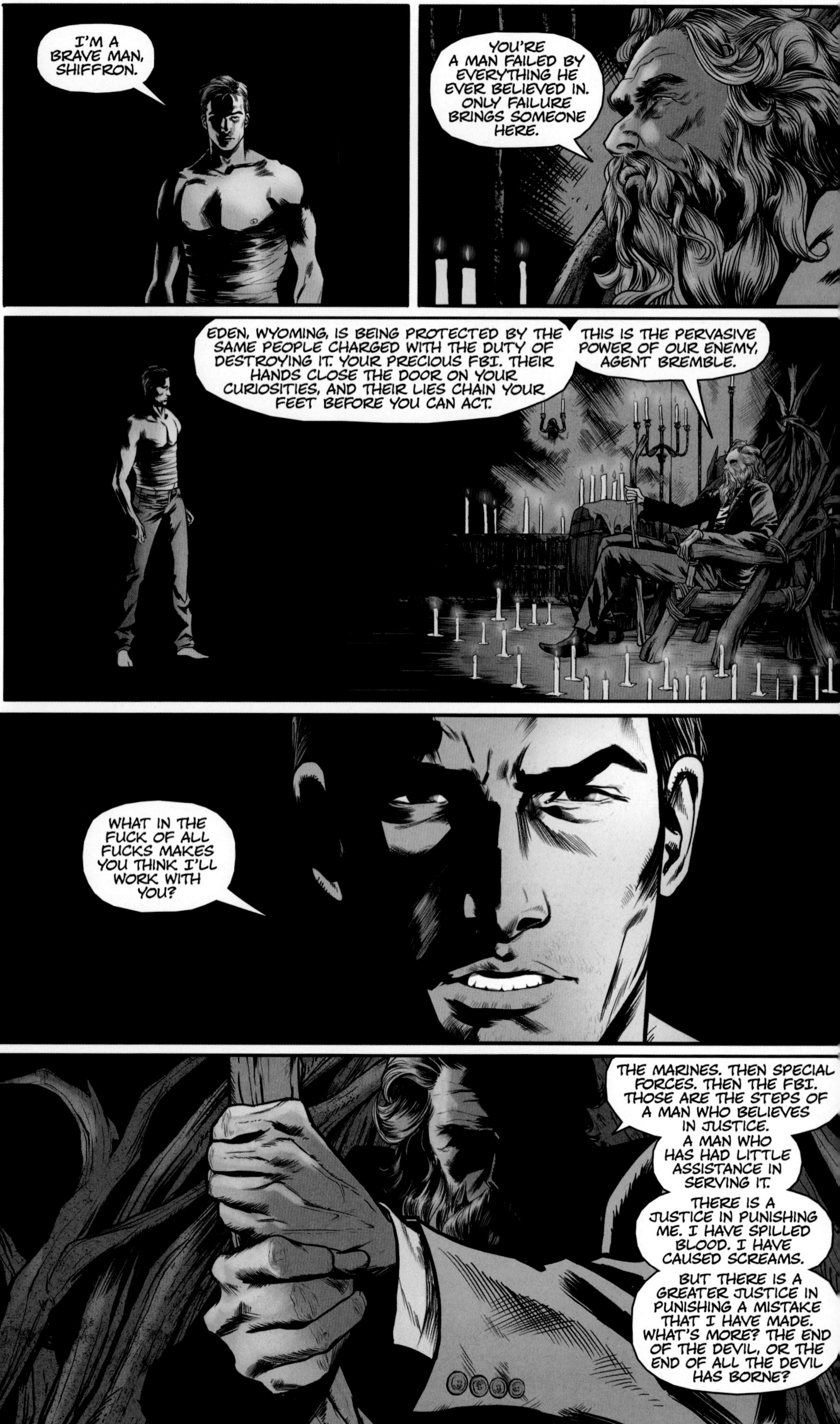
I'M A BRAVE MAN, SHIFFRON.
YOU'RE A MAN FAILED BY EVERYTHING HE EVER BELIEVED IN. ONLY FAILURE BRINGS SOMEONE HERE.
EDEN, WYOMING, IS BEING PROTECTED BY THE SAME PEOPLE CHARGED WITH THE DUTY OF DESTROYING IT. YOUR PRECIOUS FBI. THEIR HANDS CLOSE THE DOOR ON YOUR CURIOSITIES, AND THEIR LIES CHAIN YOUR FEET BEFORE YOU CAN ACT.
THIS IS THE PERVASIVE POWER OF OUR ENEMY, AGENT BREMBLE.
WHAT IN THE FUCK OF ALL FUCKS MAKES YOU THINK I'LL WORK WITH YOU?
THE MARINES. THEN SPECIAL FORCES. THEN THE FBI. THOSE ARE THE STEPS OF A MAN WHO BELIEVES IN JUSTICE.
A MAN WHO HAS HAD LITTLE ASSISTANCE IN SERVING IT.
THERE IS A JUSTICE IN PUNISHING ME. I HAVE SPILLED BLOOD. I HAVE CAUSED SCREAMS.
BUT THERE IS A GREATER JUSTICE IN PUNISHING A MISTAKE THAT I HAVE MADE. WHAT'S MORE? THE END OF THE DEVIL, OR THE END OF ALL THE DEVIL HAS BORNE?

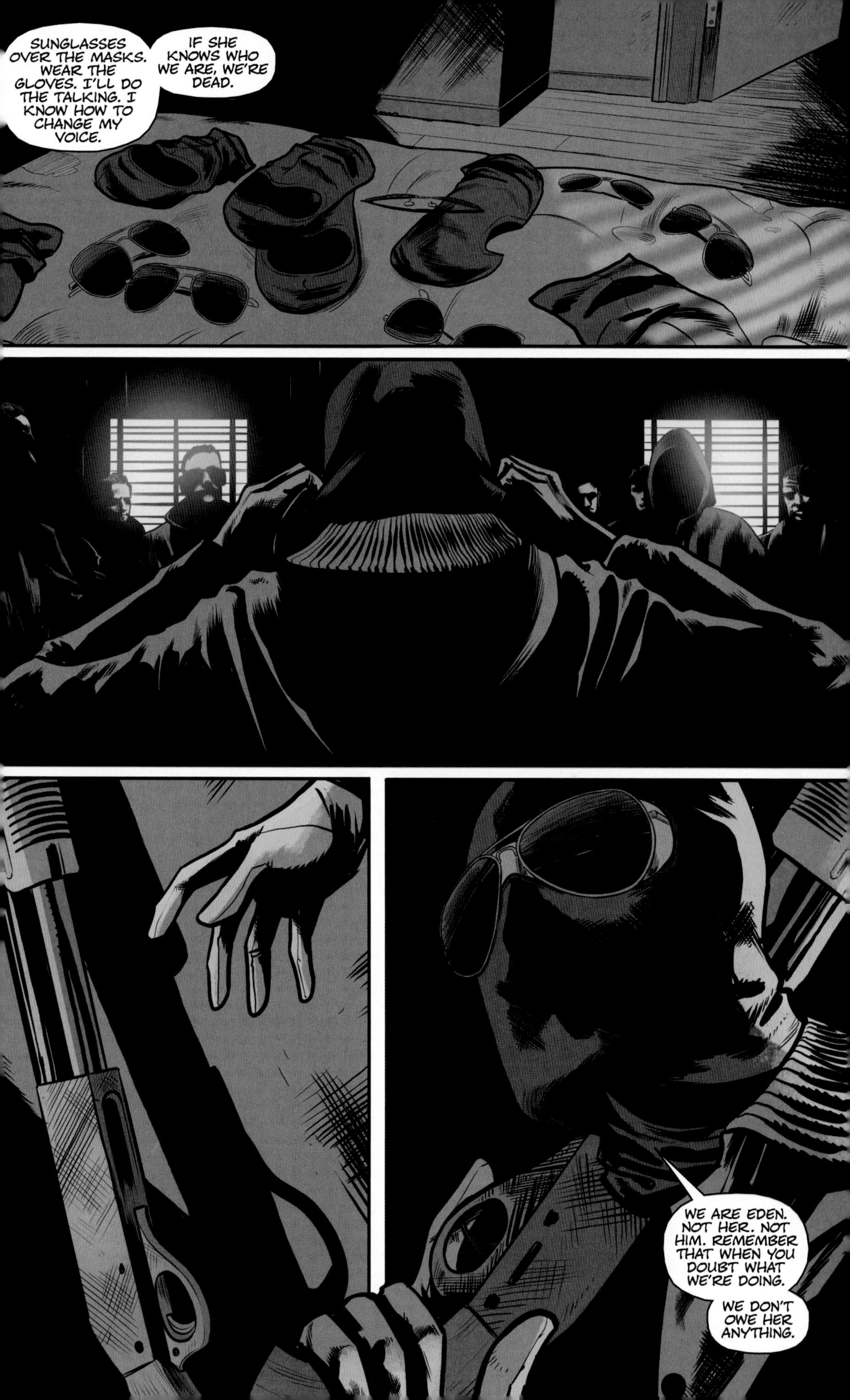
SUNGLASSES OVER THE MASKS. WEAR THE GLOVES. I'LL DO THE TALKING. I KNOW HOW TO CHANGE MY VOICE.
IF SHE KNOWS WHO WE ARE, WE'RE DEAD.
WE ARE EDEN. NOT HER. NOT HIM. REMEMBER THAT WHEN YOU DOUBT WHAT WE'RE DOING.
WE DON'T OWE HER ANYTHING.

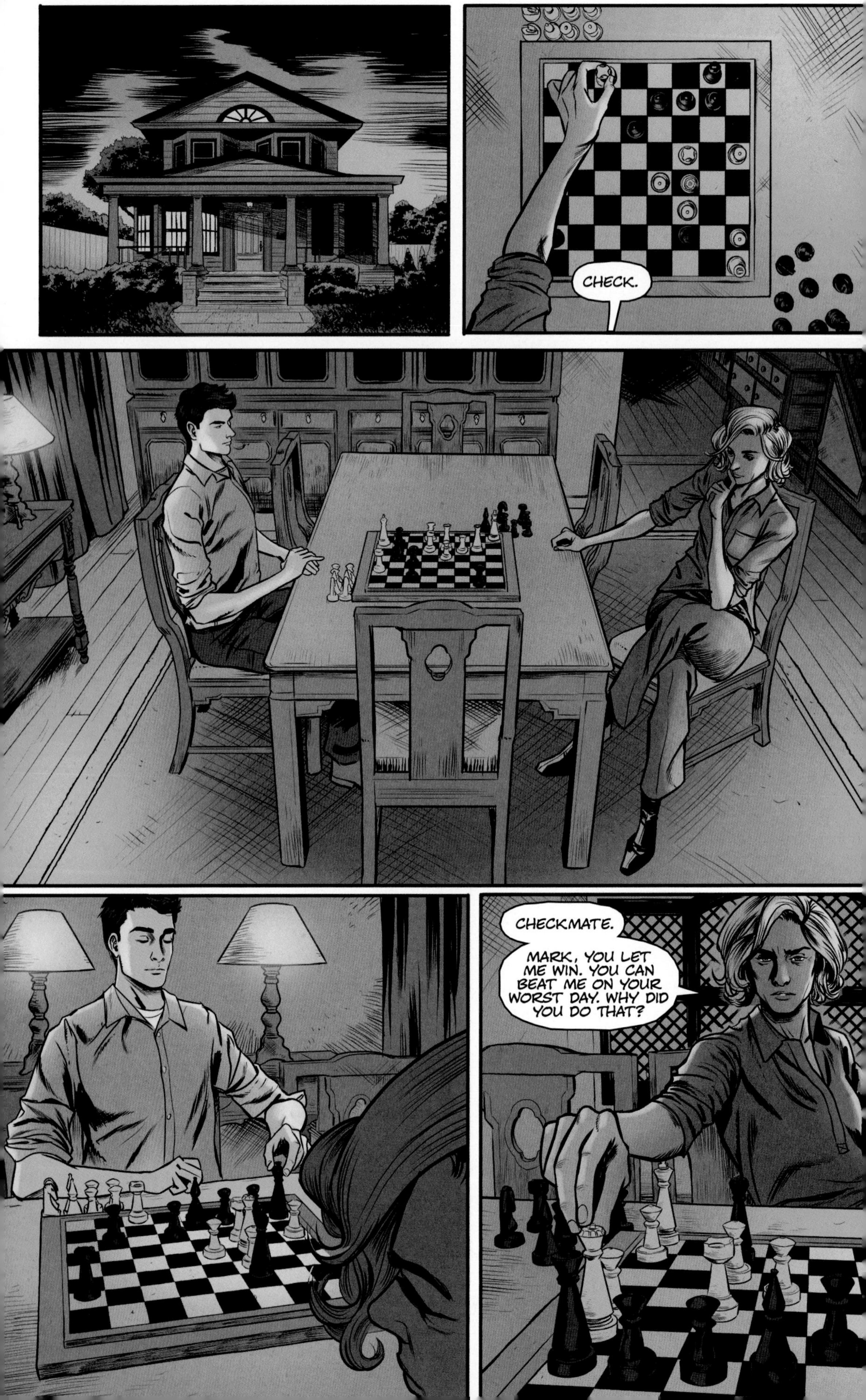
CHECK.
CHECKMATE.
MARK, YOU LET ME WIN. YOU CAN BEAT ME ON YOUR WORST DAY. WHY DID YOU DO THAT?

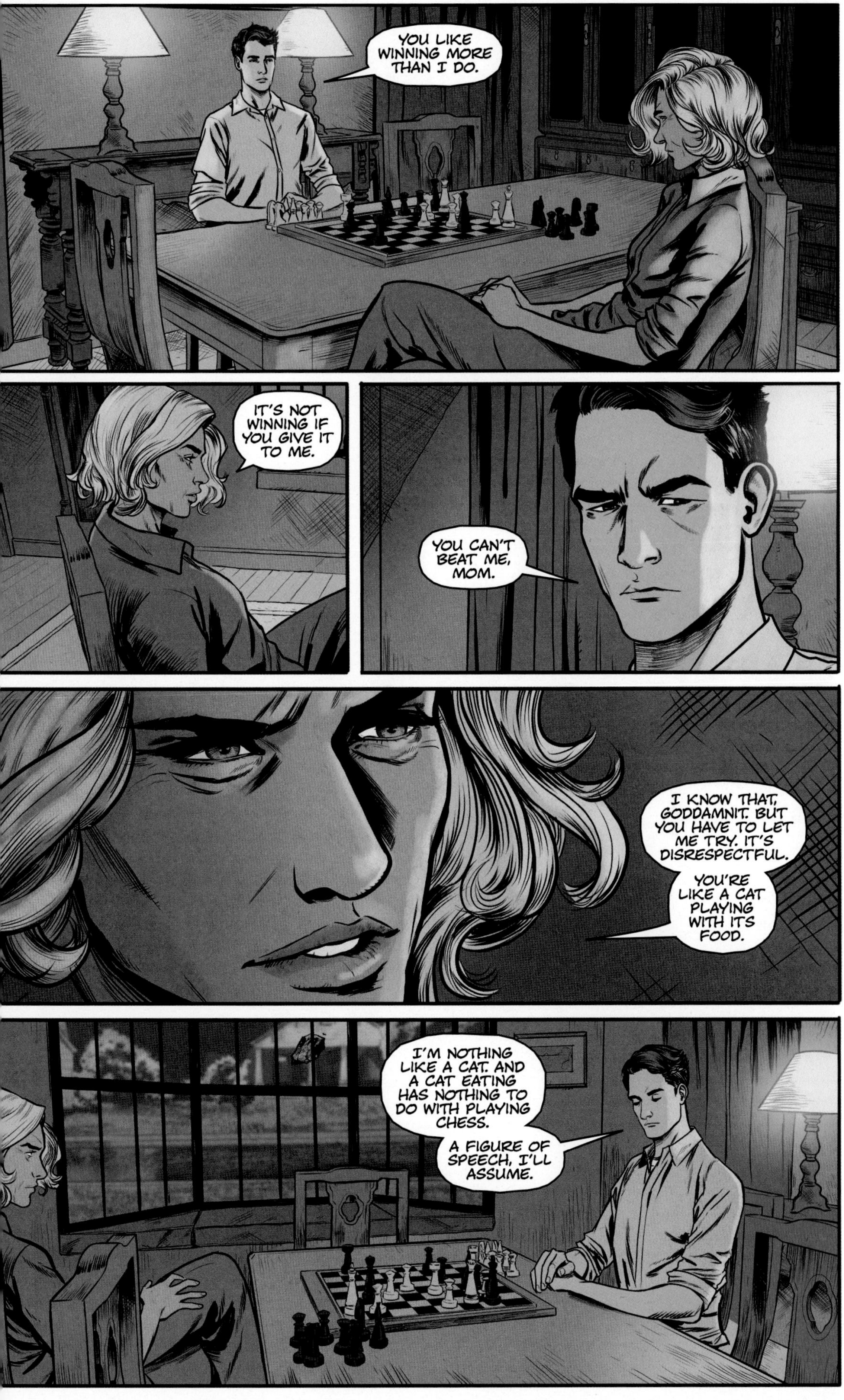
YOU LIKE WINNING MORE THAN I DO.
IT'S NOT WINNING IF YOU GIVE IT TO ME.
YOU CAN'T BEAT ME, MOM.
I KNOW THAT, GODDAMNIT. BUT YOU HAVE TO LET ME TRY. IT'S DISRESPECTFUL.
YOU'RE LIKE A CAT PLAYING WITH ITS FOOD.
I'M NOTHING LIKE A CAT. AND A CAT EATING HAS NOTHING TO DO WITH PLAYING CHESS.
A FIGURE OF SPEECH, I'LL ASSUME.

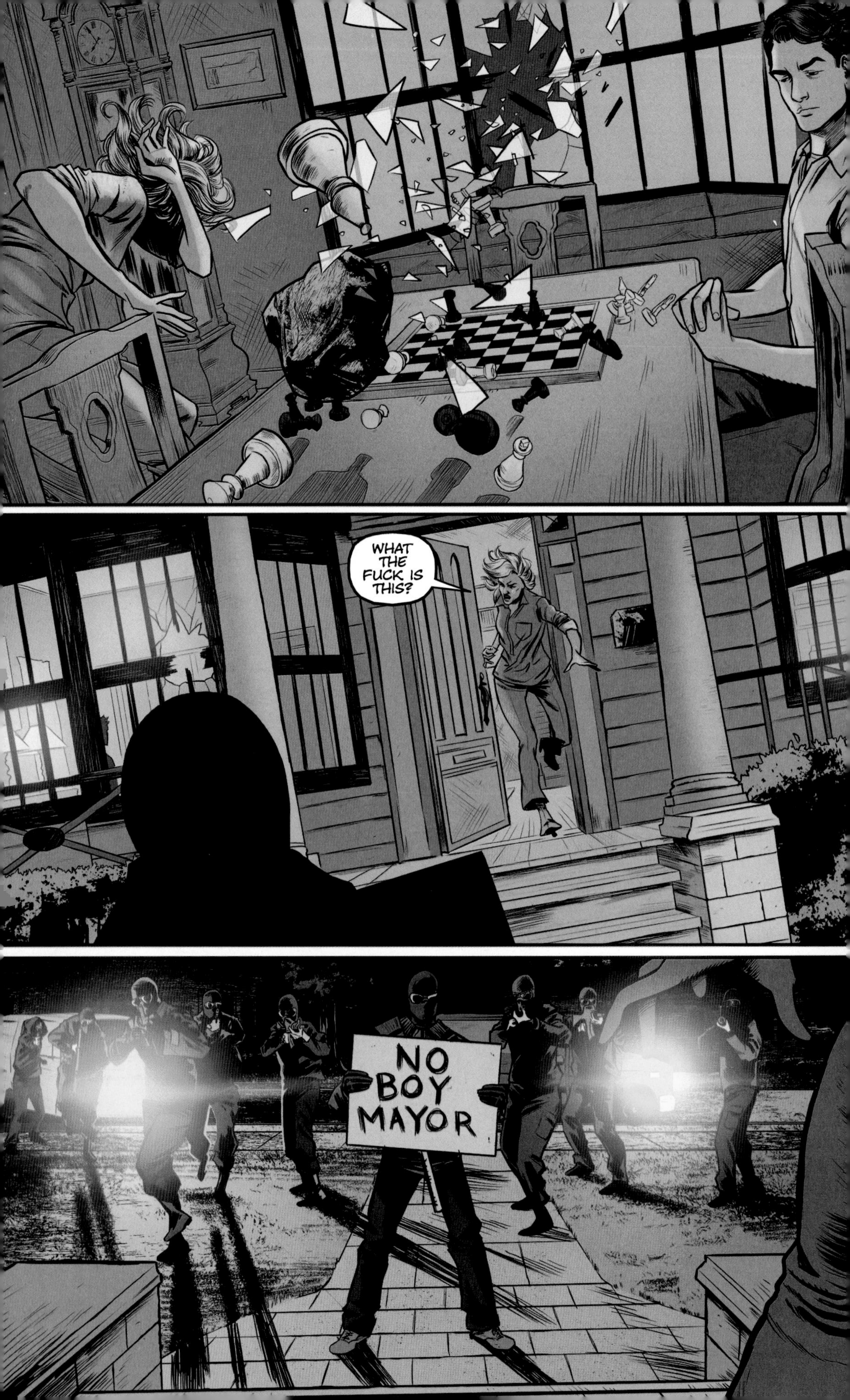
WHAT THE FUCK IS THIS?
NO BOY MAYOR

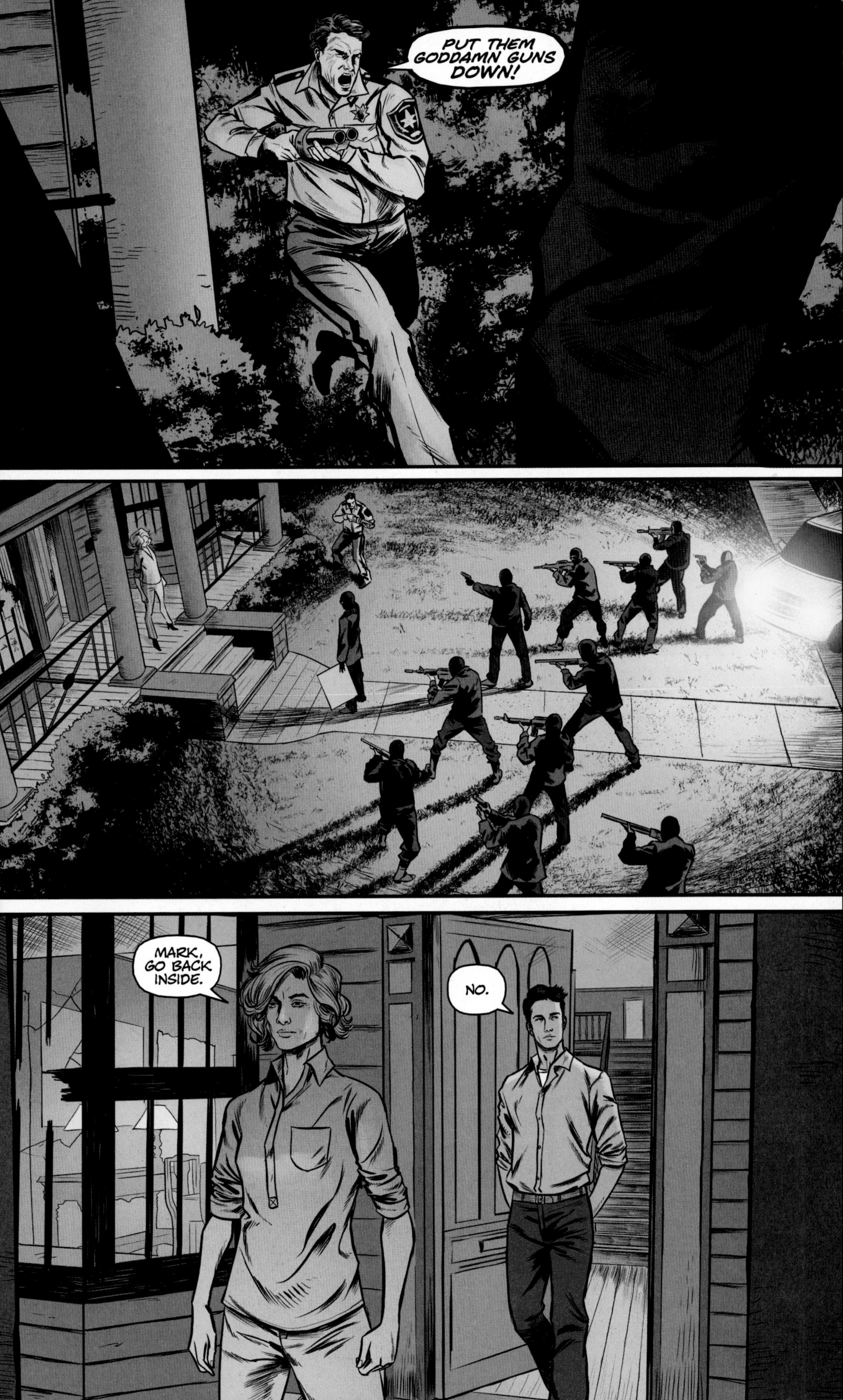
PUT THEM GODDAMN GUNS DOWN!
MARK, GO BACK INSIDE.
NO.

MASKS, GLOVES AND GLASSES TO MAKE IT HARD TO IDENTIFY YOU. ALL OF YOU WEARING ALL BLACK.

USING A SIGN SO WE CAN'T HEAR YOUR VOICES.

IT'S SMART. A GOOD, SMART PLAN.

MARK, YOU CAN DETERMINE WHO THESE FOLKS ARE. GIMME NAMES.

AND I'LL PUT THEM DOWN.

YOU SONS OF BITCHES HEAR ME!

I WILL FIND OUT WHO YOU ARE AND I'LL TIE YOU ALL TO A FUCKING POST AND WATCH YOU DIE FROM MY WINDOW!

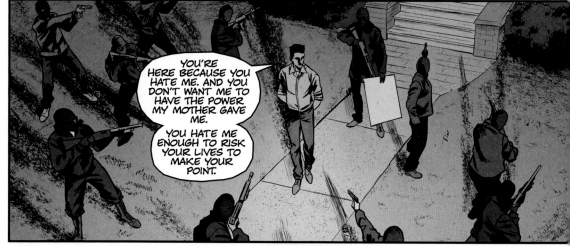

YOU'RE HERE BECAUSE YOU HATE ME. AND YOU DON'T WANT ME TO HAVE THE POWER MY MOTHER GAVE ME.

YOU HATE ME ENOUGH TO RISK YOUR LIVES TO MAKE YOUR POINT.

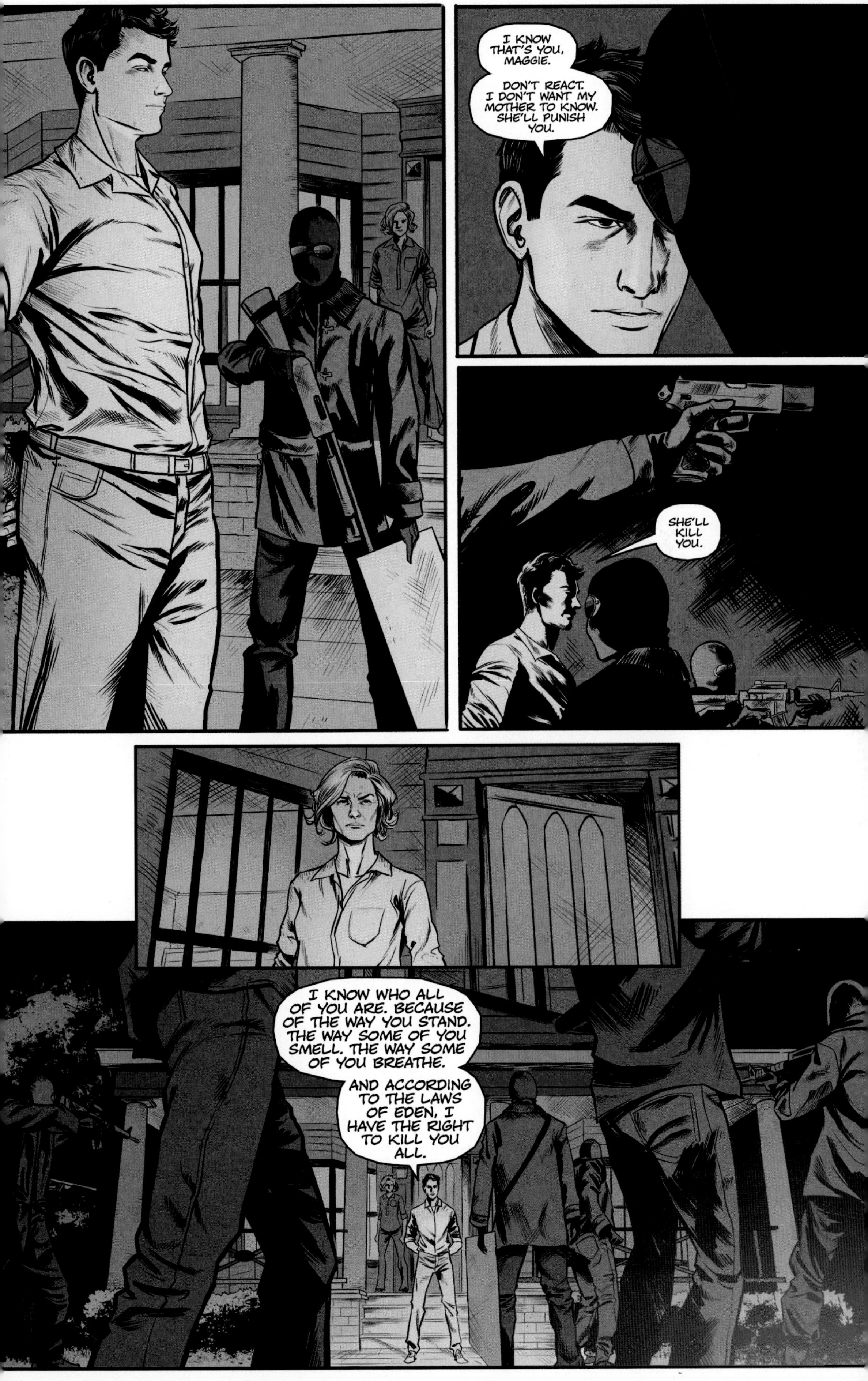
I KNOW THAT'S YOU, MAGGIE.
DON'T REACT. I DON'T WANT MY MOTHER TO KNOW. SHE'LL PUNISH YOU.
SHE'LL KILL YOU.
I KNOW WHO ALL OF YOU ARE. BECAUSE OF THE WAY YOU STAND. THE WAY SOME OF YOU SMELL. THE WAY SOME OF YOU BREATHE.
AND ACCORDING TO THE LAWS OF EDEN, I HAVE THE RIGHT TO KILL YOU ALL.

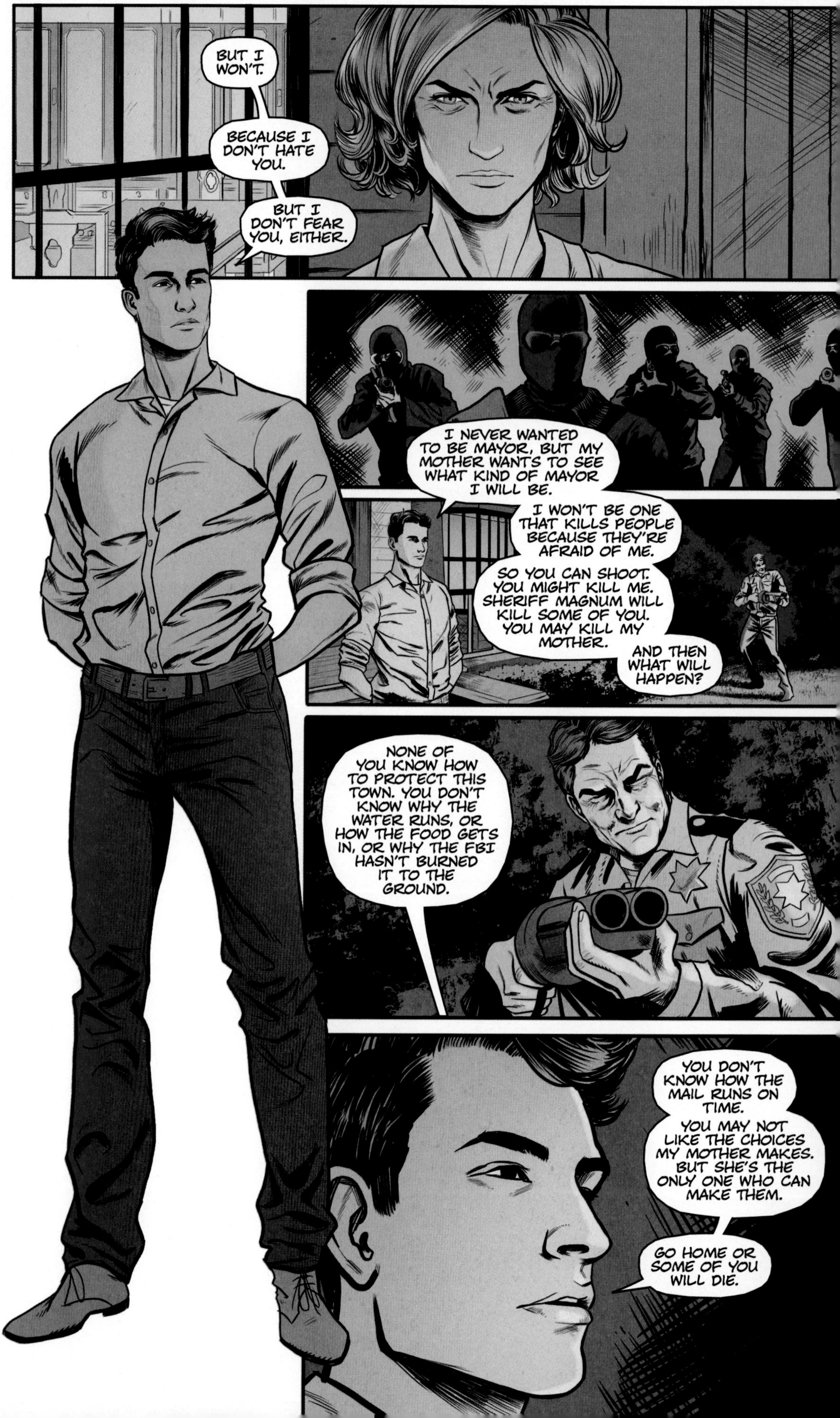
BUT I WON'T.
BECAUSE I DON'T HATE YOU.
BUT I DON'T FEAR YOU, EITHER.
I NEVER WANTED TO BE MAYOR, BUT MY MOTHER WANTS TO SEE WHAT KIND OF MAYOR I WILL BE.
I WON'T BE ONE THAT KILLS PEOPLE BECAUSE THEY'RE AFRAID OF ME.
SO YOU CAN SHOOT. YOU MIGHT KILL ME. SHERIFF MAGNUM WILL KILL SOME OF YOU. YOU MAY KILL MY MOTHER.
AND THEN WHAT WILL HAPPEN?
NONE OF YOU KNOW HOW TO PROTECT THIS TOWN. YOU DON'T KNOW WHY THE WATER RUNS, OR HOW THE FOOD GETS IN, OR WHY THE FBI HASN'T BURNED IT TO THE GROUND.
YOU DON'T KNOW HOW THE MAIL RUNS ON TIME.
YOU MAY NOT LIKE THE CHOICES MY MOTHER MAKES. BUT SHE'S THE ONLY ONE WHO CAN MAKE THEM.
GO HOME OR SOME OF YOU WILL DIE.

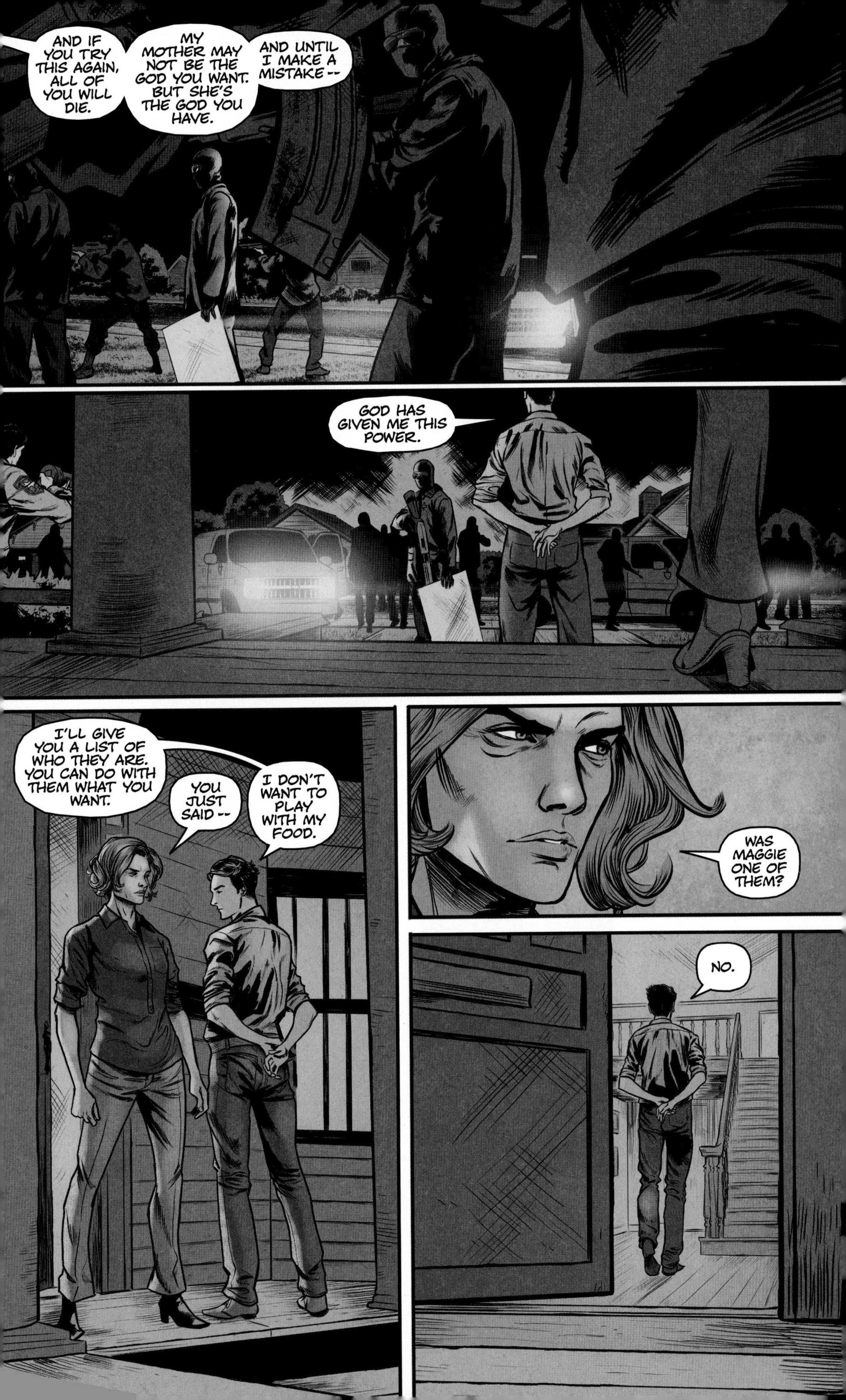
AND IF YOU TRY THIS AGAIN, ALL OF YOU WILL DIE.
MY MOTHER MAY NOT BE THE GOD YOU WANT. BUT SHE'S THE GOD YOU HAVE.
AND UNTIL I MAKE A MISTAKE --
GOD HAS GIVEN ME THIS POWER.
I'LL GIVE YOU A LIST OF WHO THEY ARE. YOU CAN DO WITH THEM WHAT YOU WANT.
YOU JUST SAID --
I DON'T WANT TO PLAY WITH MY FOOD.
WAS MAGGIE ONE OF THEM?
NO.

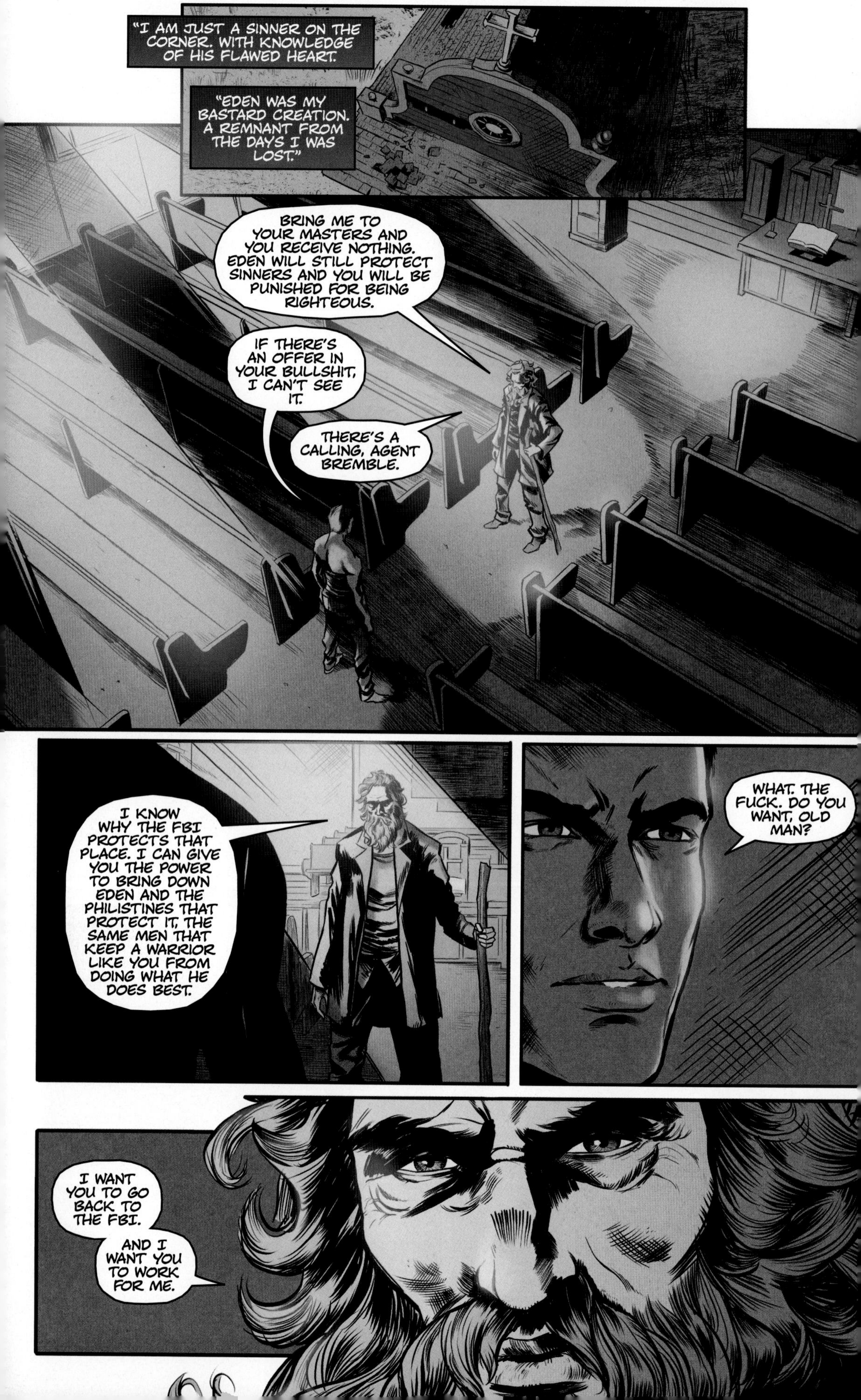
"I AM JUST A SINNER ON THE CORNER. WITH KNOWLEDGE OF HIS FLAWED HEART.
"EDEN WAS MY BASTARD CREATION. A REMNANT FROM THE DAYS I WAS LOST."
BRING ME TO YOUR MASTERS AND YOU RECEIVE NOTHING. EDEN WILL STILL PROTECT SINNERS AND YOU WILL BE PUNISHED FOR BEING RIGHTEOUS.
IF THERE'S AN OFFER IN YOUR BULLSHIT, I CAN'T SEE IT.
THERE'S A CALLING, AGENT BREMBLE.
I KNOW WHY THE FBI PROTECTS THAT PLACE. I CAN GIVE YOU THE POWER TO BRING DOWN EDEN AND THE PHILISTINES THAT PROTECT IT, THE SAME MEN THAT KEEP A WARRIOR LIKE YOU FROM DOING WHAT HE DOES BEST.
WHAT. THE FUCK. DO YOU WANT, OLD MAN?
I WANT YOU TO GO BACK TO THE FBI.
AND I WANT YOU TO WORK FOR ME.

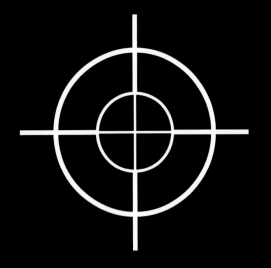

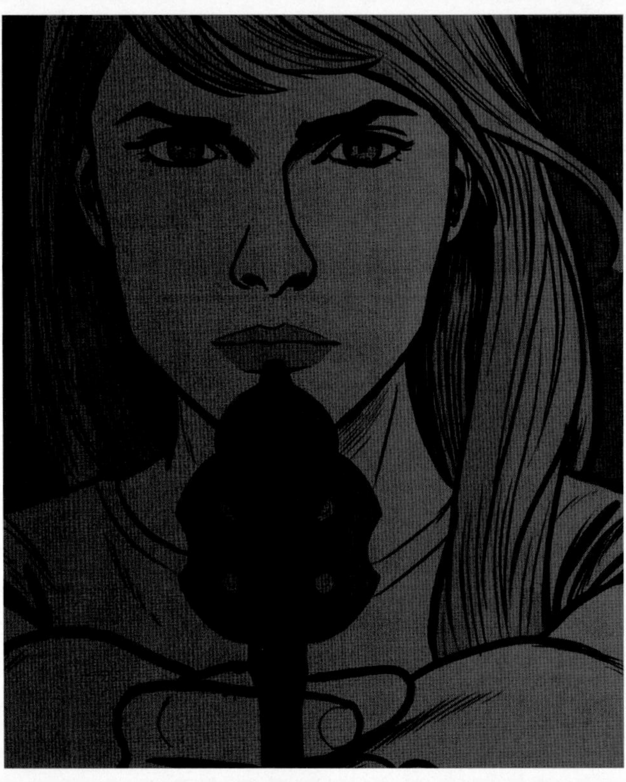

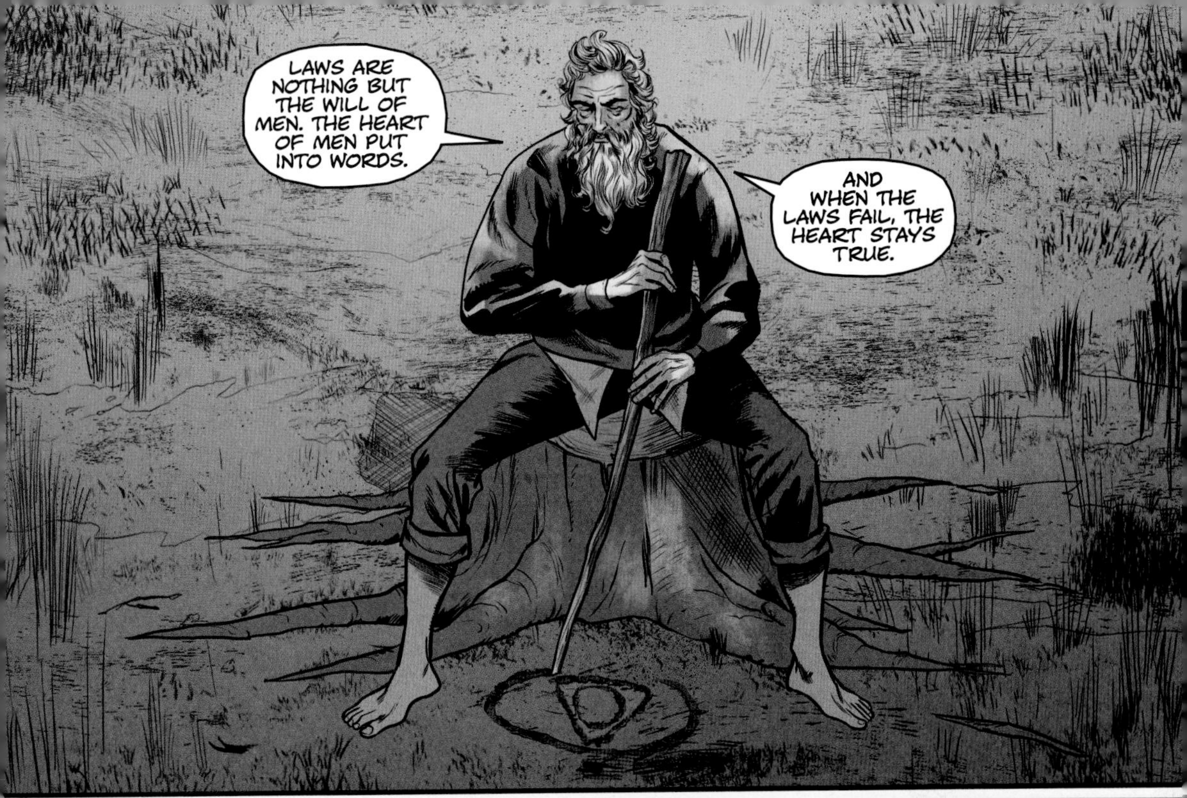
LAWS ARE NOTHING BUT THE WILL OF MEN. THE HEART OF MEN PUT INTO WORDS.
AND WHEN THE LAWS FAIL, THE HEART STAYS TRUE.

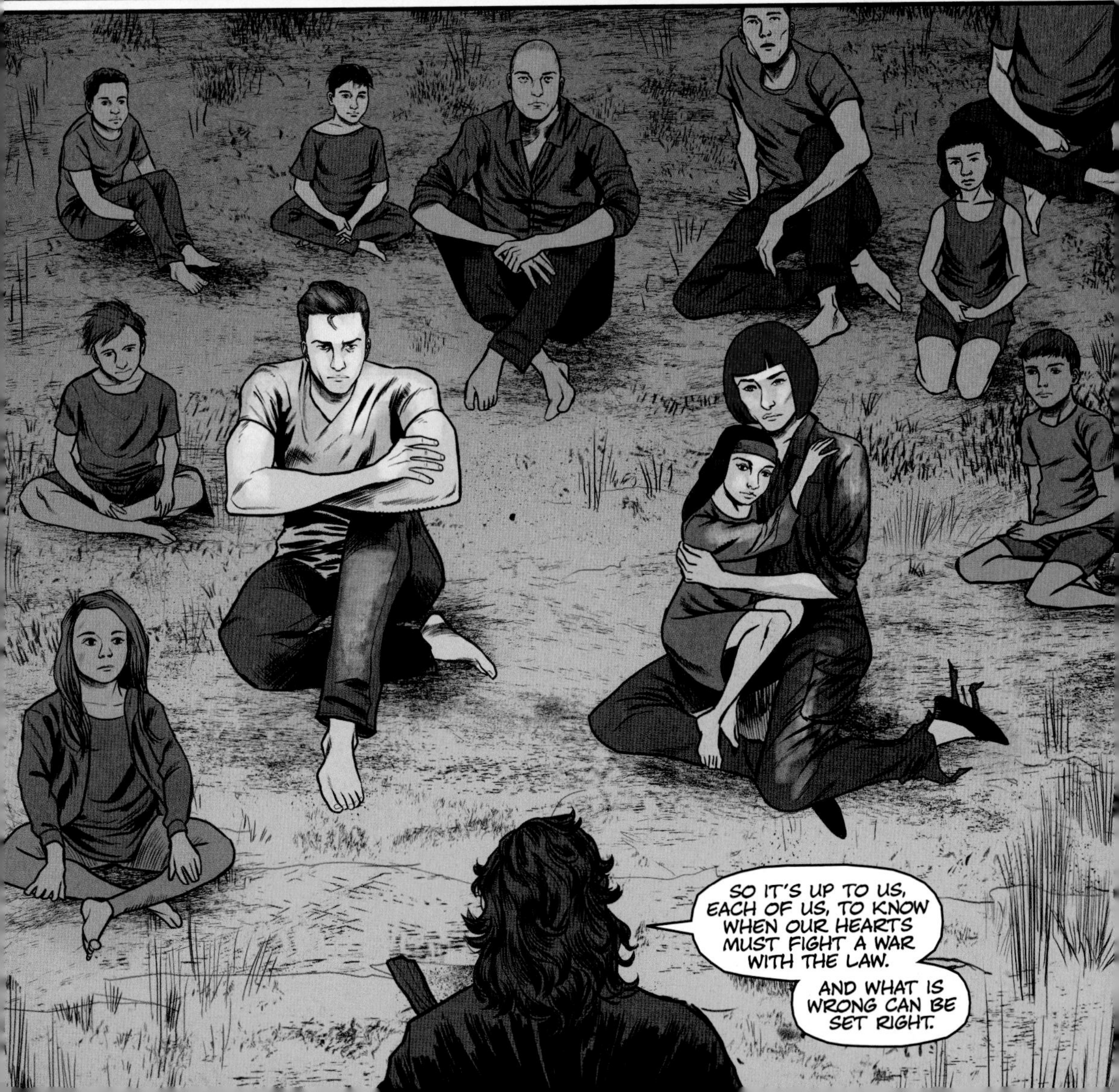
SO IT'S UP TO US, EACH OF US, TO KNOW WHEN OUR HEARTS MUST FIGHT A WAR WITH THE LAW.
AND WHAT IS WRONG CAN BE SET RIGHT.

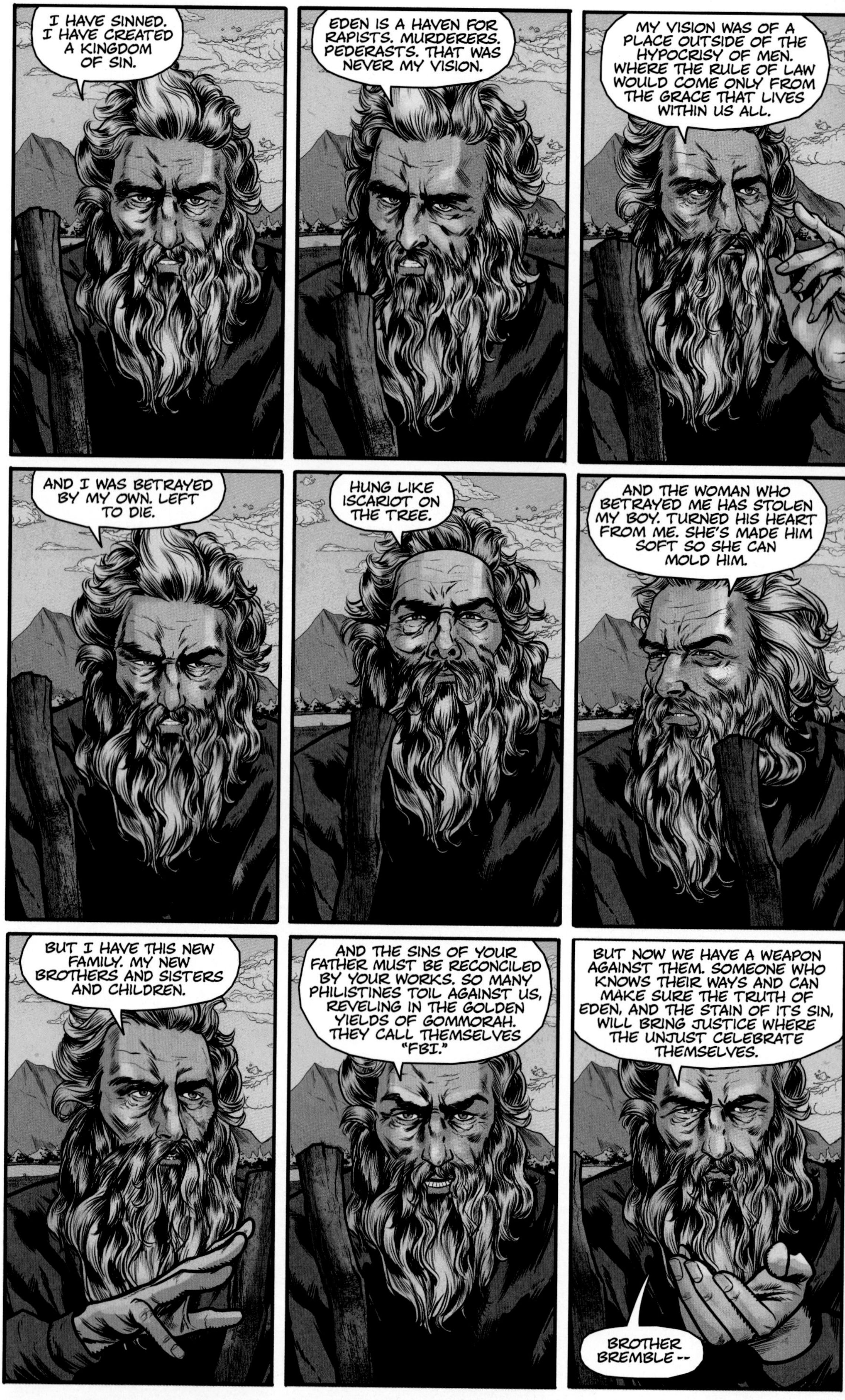
I HAVE SINNED. I HAVE CREATED A KINGDOM OF SIN.
EDEN IS A HAVEN FOR RAPISTS. MURDERERS. PEDERASTS. THAT WAS NEVER MY VISION.
MY VISION WAS OF A PLACE OUTSIDE OF THE HYPOCRISY OF MEN. WHERE THE RULE OF LAW WOULD COME ONLY FROM THE GRACE THAT LIVES WITHIN US ALL.
AND I WAS BETRAYED BY MY OWN. LEFT TO DIE.
HUNG LIKE ISCARIOT ON THE TREE.
AND THE WOMAN WHO BETRAYED ME HAS STOLEN MY BOY. TURNED HIS HEART FROM ME. SHE'S MADE HIM SOFT SO SHE CAN MOLD HIM.
BUT I HAVE THIS NEW FAMILY. MY NEW BROTHERS AND SISTERS AND CHILDREN.
AND THE SINS OF YOUR FATHER MUST BE RECONCILED BY YOUR WORKS. SO MANY PHILISTINES TOIL AGAINST US, REVELING IN THE GOLDEN YIELDS OF GOMMORAH. THEY CALL THEMSELVES "FBI."
BUT NOW WE HAVE A WEAPON AGAINST THEM. SOMEONE WHO KNOWS THEIR WAYS AND CAN MAKE SURE THE TRUTH OF EDEN, AND THE STAIN OF ITS SIN, WILL BRING JUSTICE WHERE THE UNJUST CELEBRATE THEMSELVES.
BROTHER BREMBLE --

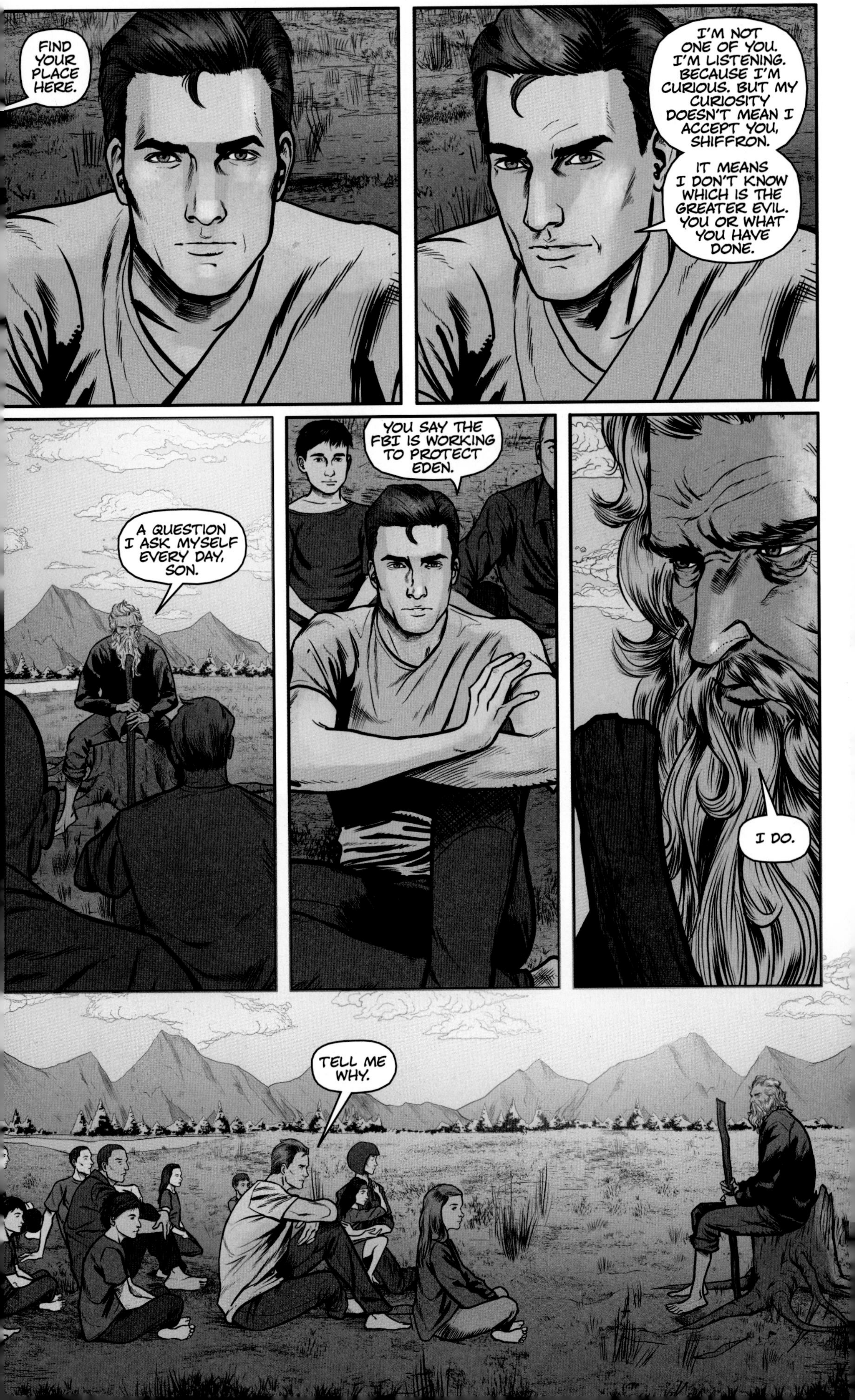
FIND YOUR PLACE HERE.
I'M NOT ONE OF YOU. I'M LISTENING. BECAUSE I'M CURIOUS. BUT MY CURIOSITY DOESN'T MEAN I ACCEPT YOU, SHIFFRON.
IT MEANS I DON'T KNOW WHICH IS THE GREATER EVIL. YOU OR WHAT YOU HAVE DONE.
A QUESTION I ASK MYSELF EVERY DAY, SON.
YOU SAY THE FBI IS WORKING TO PROTECT EDEN.
I DO.
TELL ME WHY.

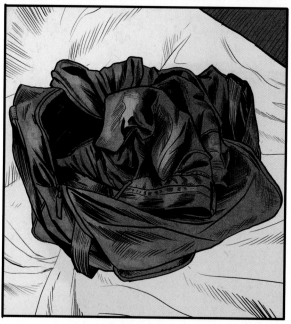

WHY DO YOU HAVE A GUN?

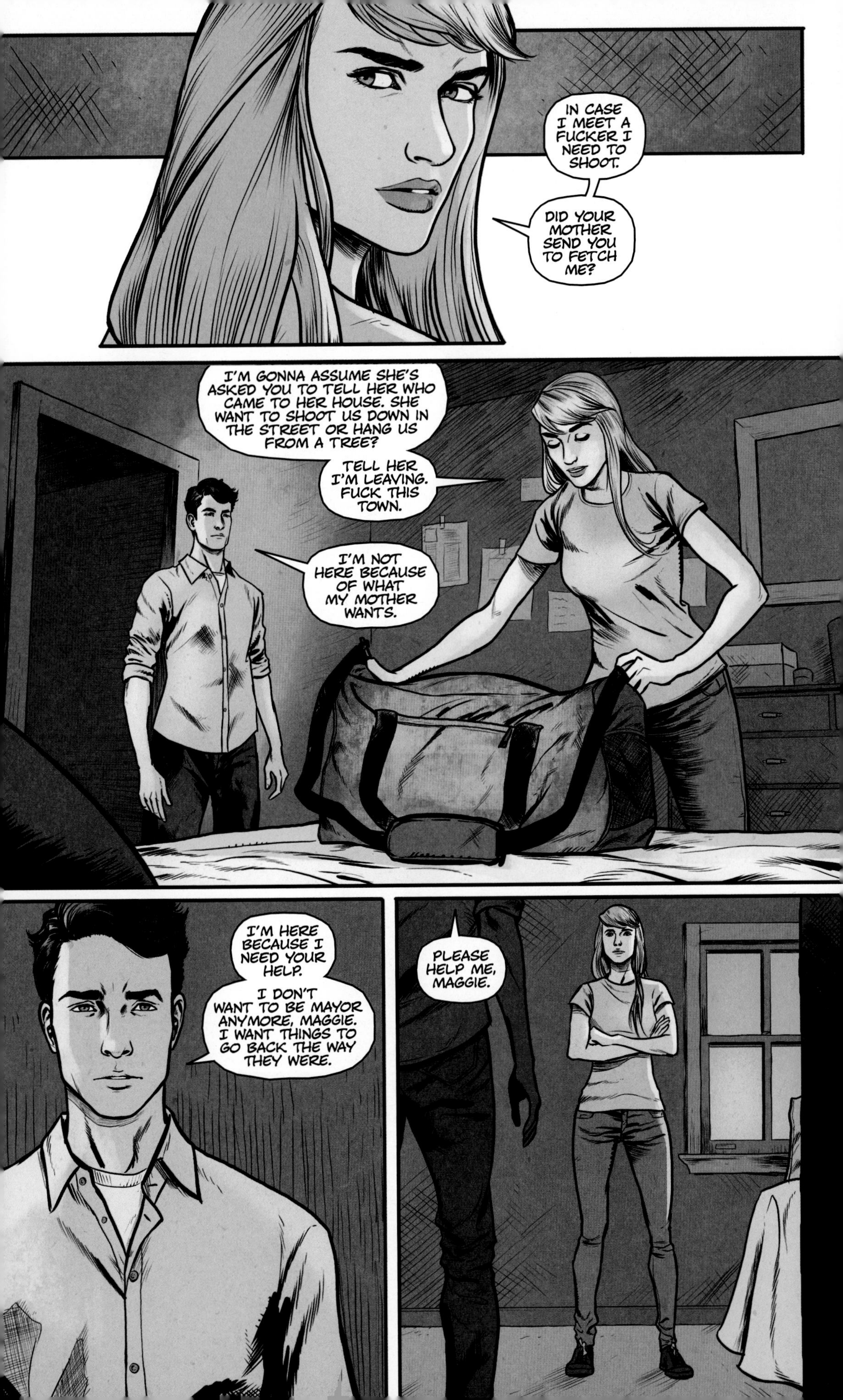
IN CASE I MEET A FUCKER I NEED TO SHOOT.
DID YOUR MOTHER SEND YOU TO FETCH ME?
I'M GONNA ASSUME SHE'S ASKED YOU TO TELL HER WHO CAME TO HER HOUSE. SHE WANT TO SHOOT US DOWN IN THE STREET OR HANG US FROM A TREE?
TELL HER I'M LEAVING. FUCK THIS TOWN.
I'M NOT HERE BECAUSE OF WHAT MY MOTHER WANTS.
I'M HERE BECAUSE I NEED YOUR HELP.
I DON'T WANT TO BE MAYOR ANYMORE, MAGGIE. I WANT THINGS TO GO BACK THE WAY THEY WERE.
PLEASE HELP ME, MAGGIE.

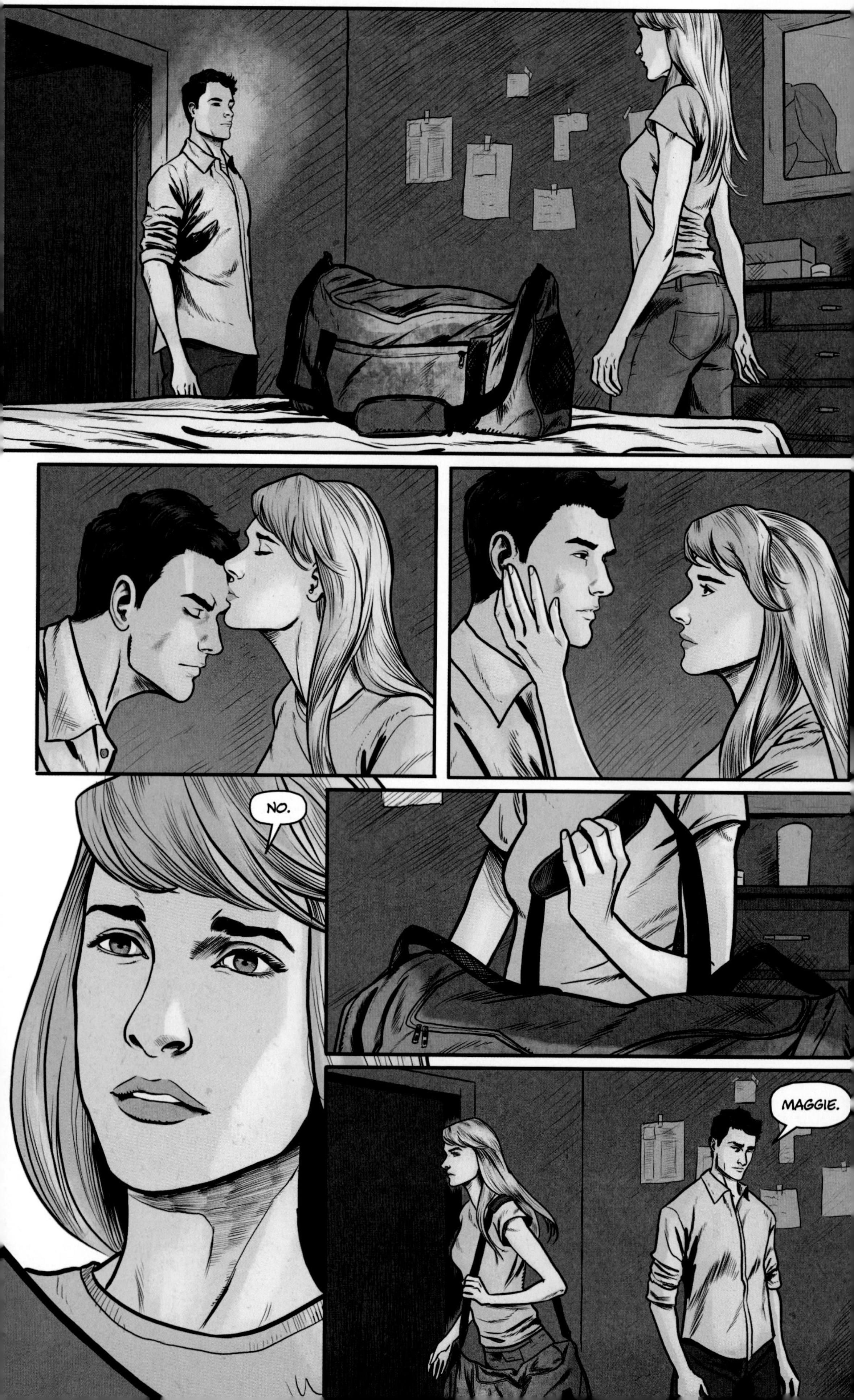
NO.
MAGGIE.

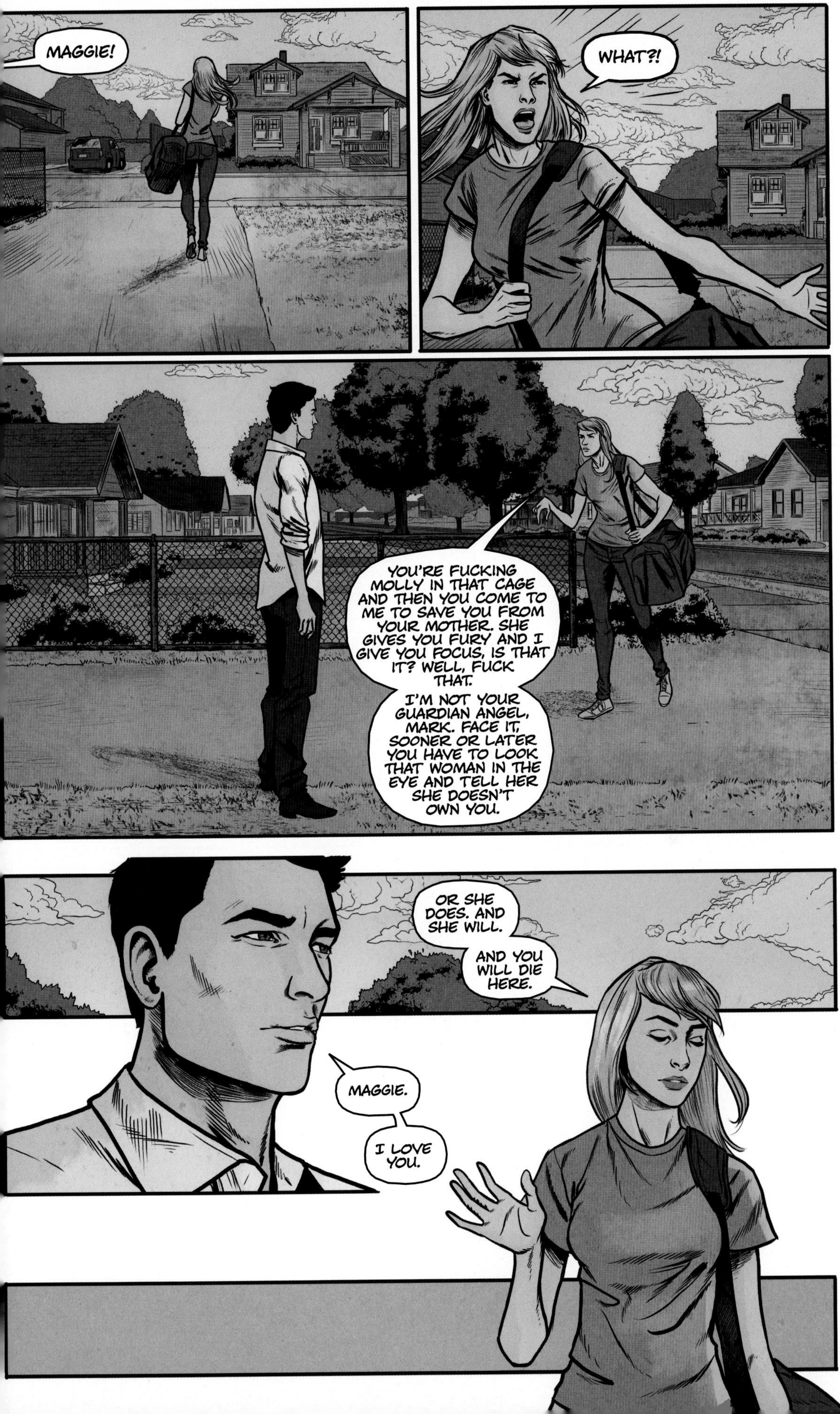
MAGGIE!
WHAT?!
YOU'RE FUCKING MOLLY IN THAT CAGE AND THEN YOU COME TO ME TO SAVE YOU FROM YOUR MOTHER. SHE GIVES YOU FURY AND I GIVE YOU FOCUS, IS THAT IT? WELL, FUCK THAT.
I'M NOT YOUR GUARDIAN ANGEL, MARK. FACE IT, SOONER OR LATER YOU HAVE TO LOOK THAT WOMAN IN THE EYE AND TELL HER SHE DOESN'T OWN YOU.
OR SHE DOES. AND SHE WILL.
AND YOU WILL DIE HERE.
MAGGIE.
I LOVE YOU.

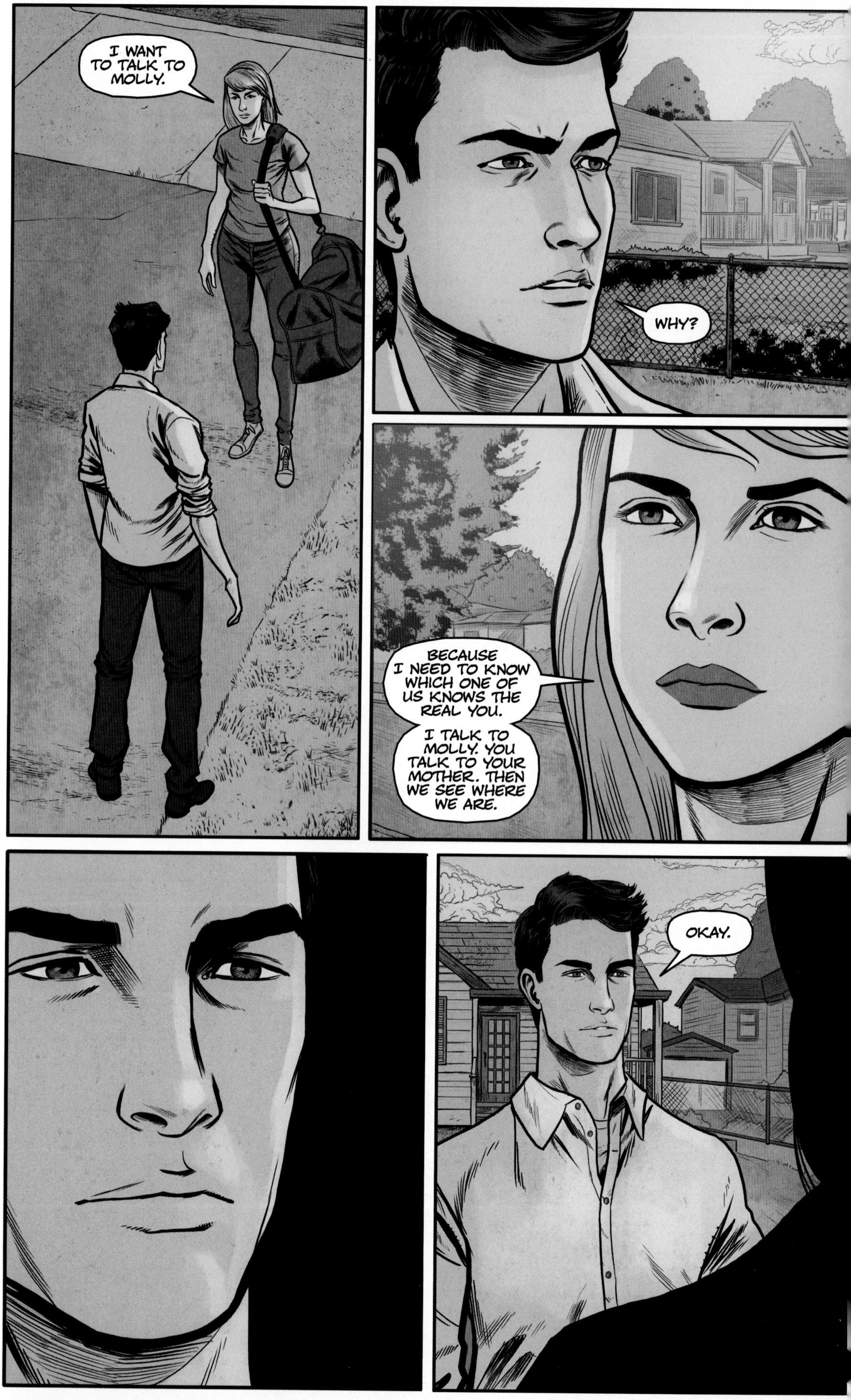
I WANT TO TALK TO MOLLY.
WHY?
BECAUSE I NEED TO KNOW WHICH ONE OF US KNOWS THE REAL YOU.
I TALK TO MOLLY. YOU TALK TO YOUR MOTHER. THEN WE SEE WHERE WE ARE.
OKAY.

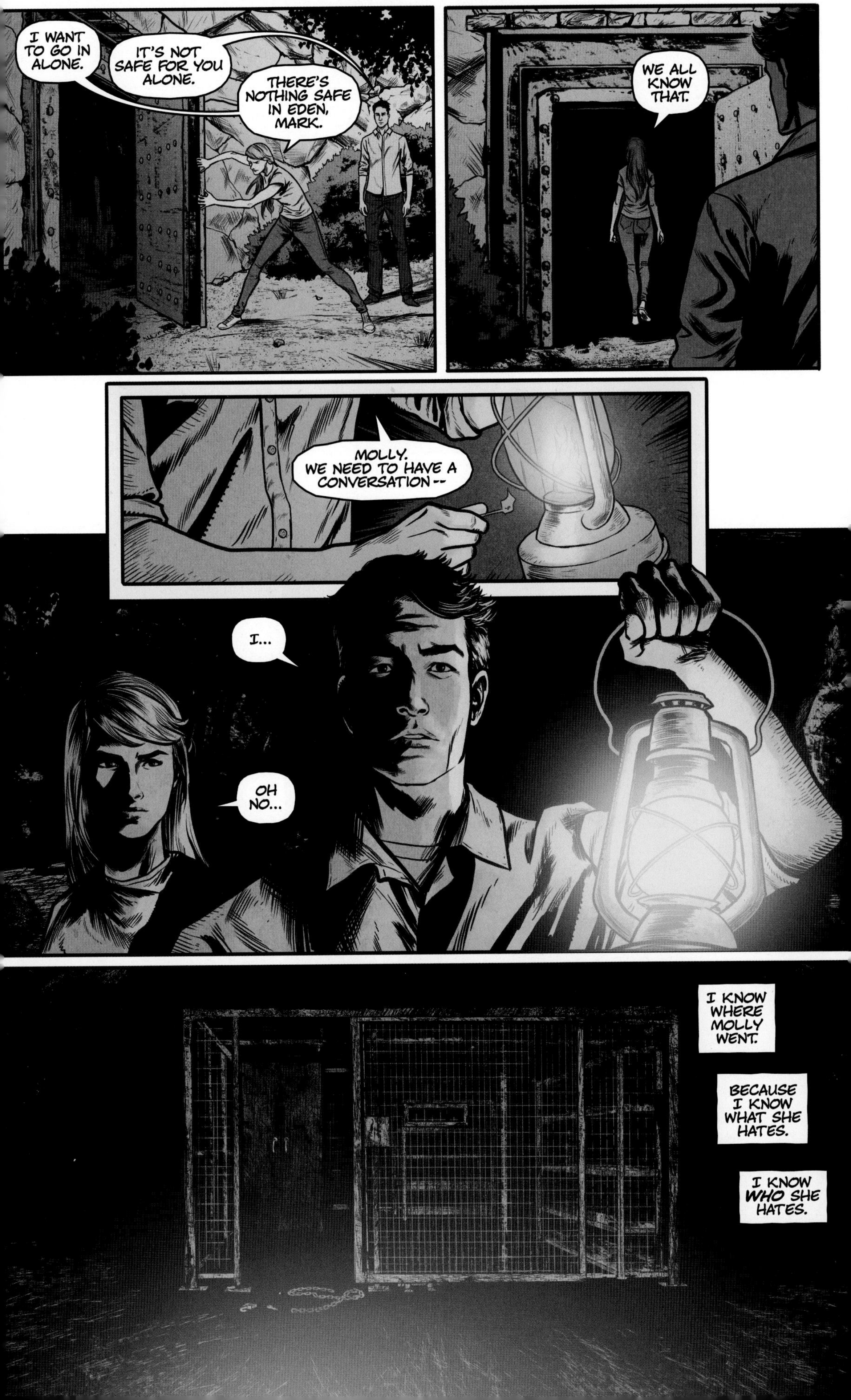

I WANT TO GO IN ALONE.
IT'S NOT SAFE FOR YOU ALONE.
THERE'S NOTHING SAFE IN EDEN, MARK.
WE ALL KNOW THAT.
MOLLY. WE NEED TO HAVE A CONVERSATION --
I...
OH NO...
I KNOW WHERE MOLLY WENT.
BECAUSE I KNOW WHAT SHE HATES.
I KNOW *WHO* SHE HATES.

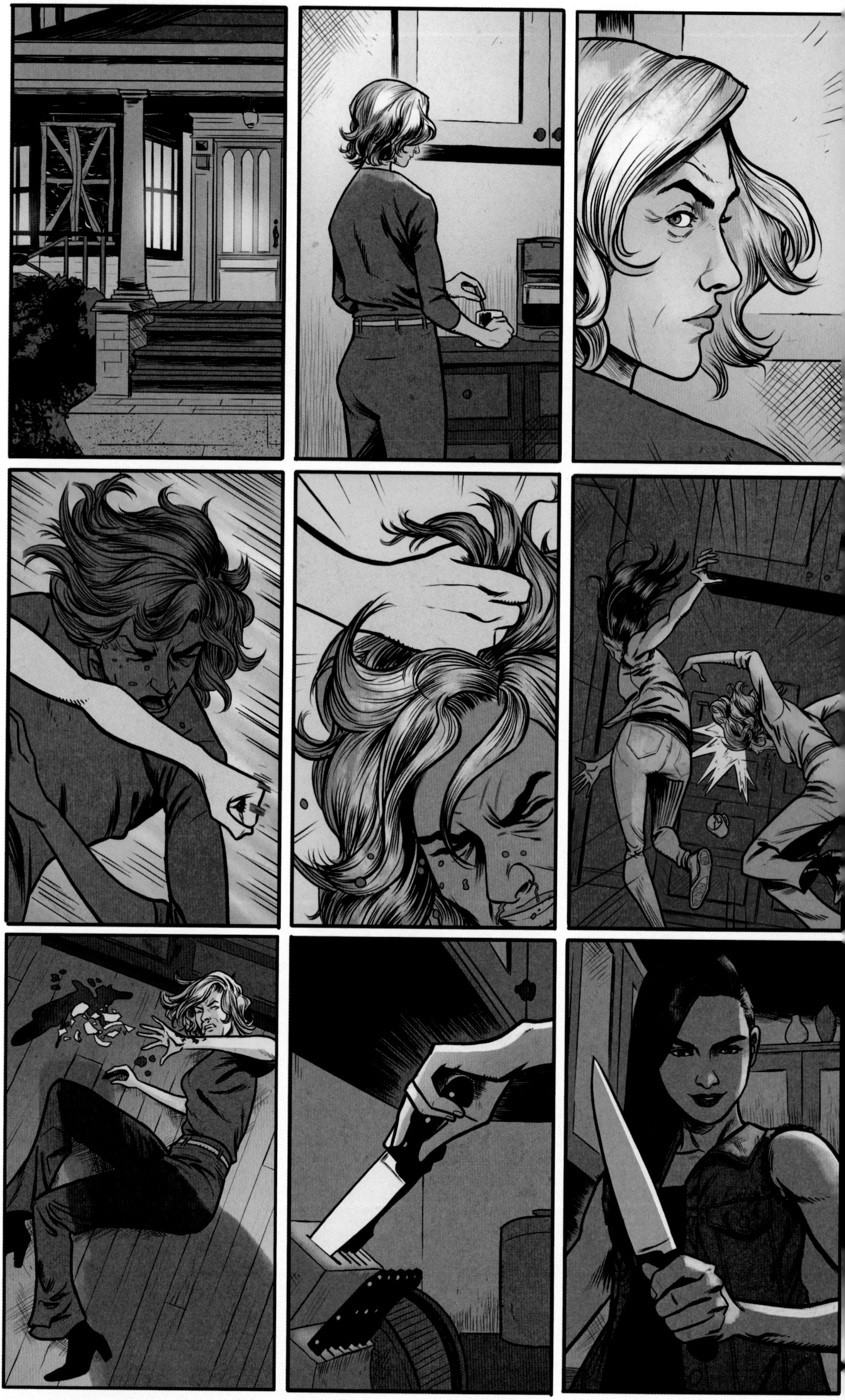

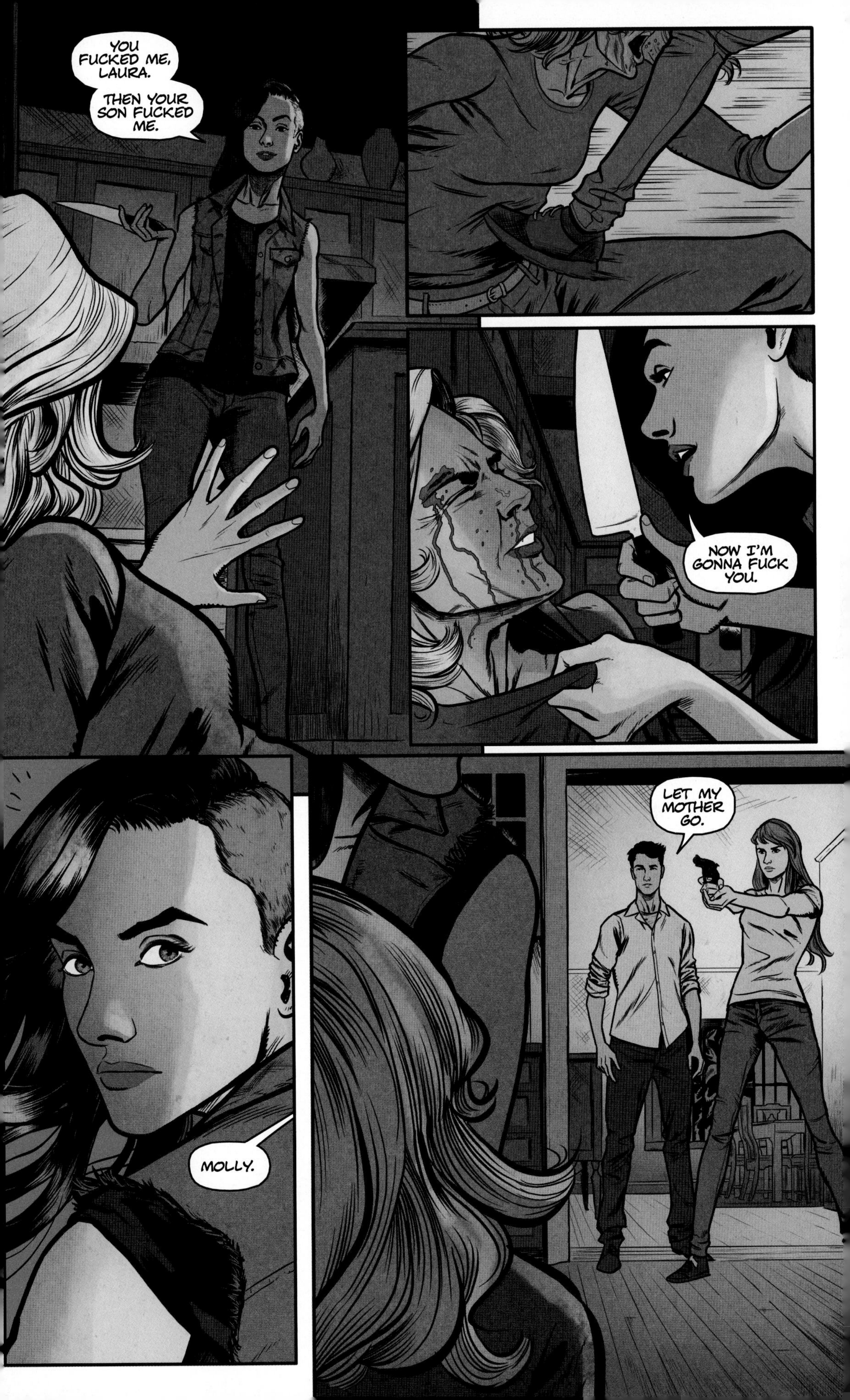
YOU FUCKED ME, LAURA.
THEN YOUR SON FUCKED ME.
NOW I'M GONNA FUCK YOU.
MOLLY.
LET MY MOTHER GO.

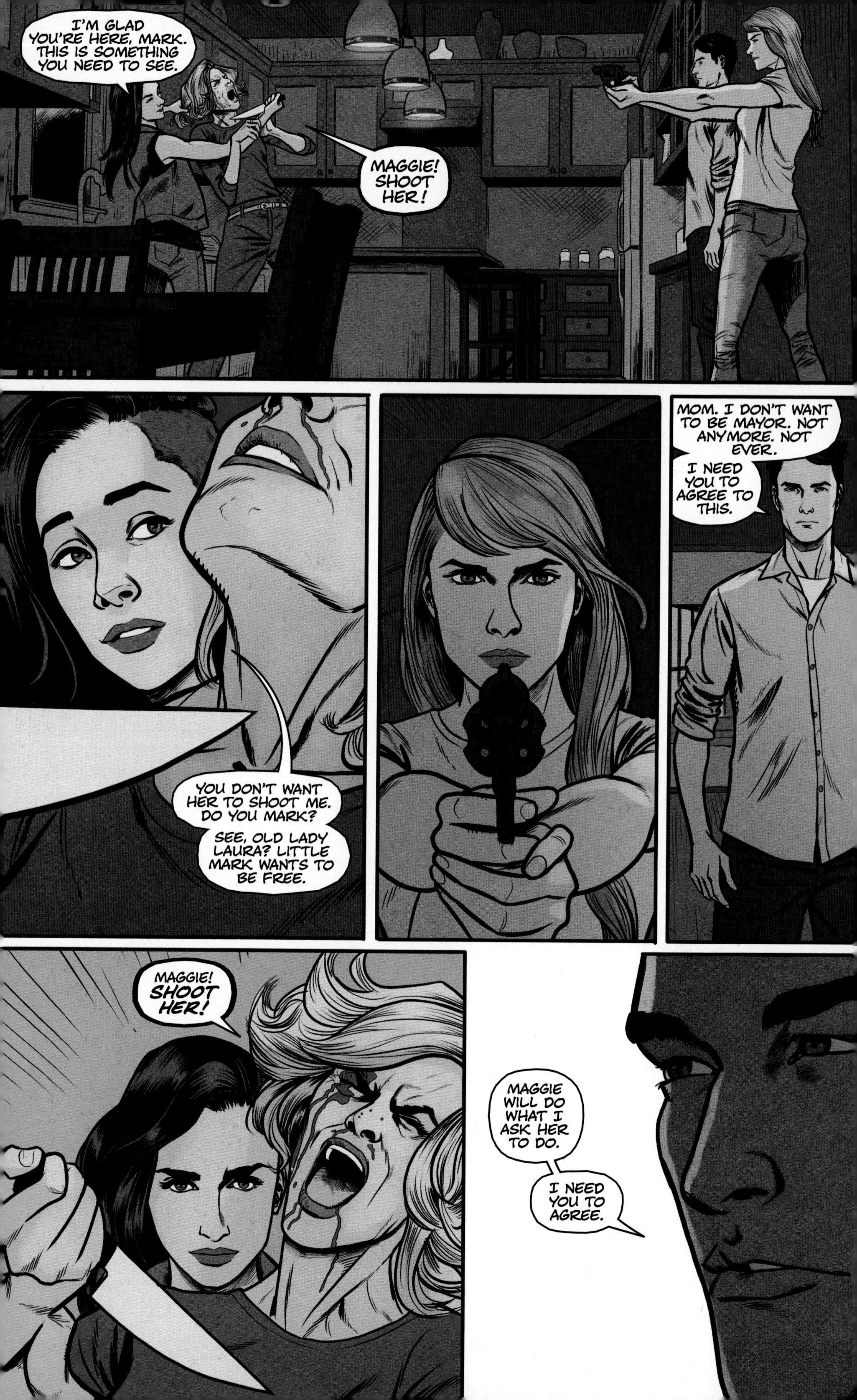
I'M GLAD YOU'RE HERE, MARK. THIS IS SOMETHING YOU NEED TO SEE.
MAGGIE! SHOOT HER!
YOU DON'T WANT HER TO SHOOT ME. DO YOU MARK?
SEE, OLD LADY LAURA? LITTLE MARK WANTS TO BE FREE.
MOM. I DON'T WANT TO BE MAYOR. NOT ANYMORE. NOT EVER.
I NEED YOU TO AGREE TO THIS.
MAGGIE! SHOOT HER!
MAGGIE WILL DO WHAT I ASK HER TO DO.
I NEED YOU TO AGREE.

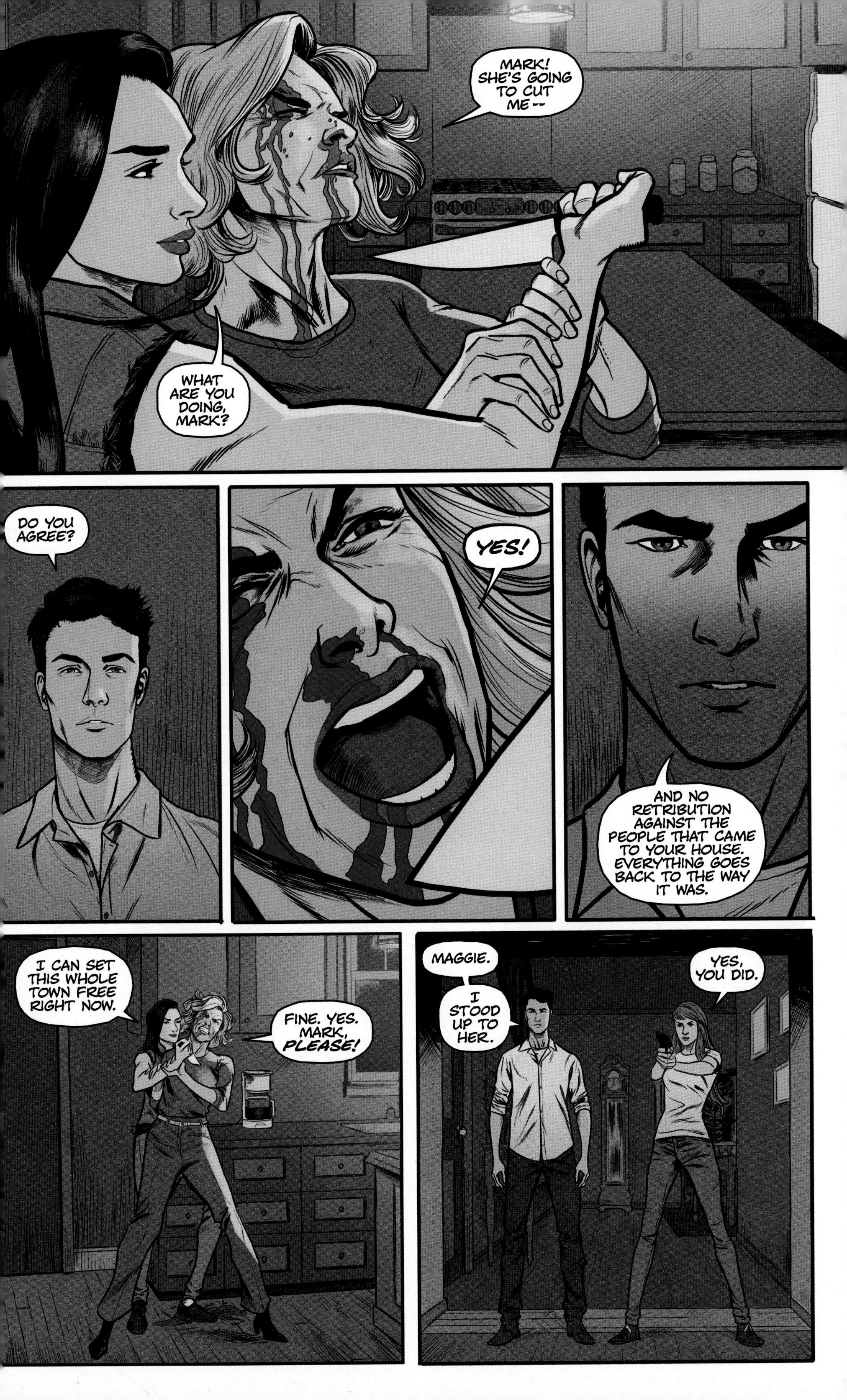
MARK! SHE'S GOING TO CUT ME --
WHAT ARE YOU DOING, MARK?
DO YOU AGREE?
YES!
AND NO RETRIBUTION AGAINST THE PEOPLE THAT CAME TO YOUR HOUSE. EVERYTHING GOES BACK TO THE WAY IT WAS.
I CAN SET THIS WHOLE TOWN FREE RIGHT NOW.
FINE. YES. MARK, PLEASE!
MAGGIE.
I STOOD UP TO HER.
YES, YOU DID.

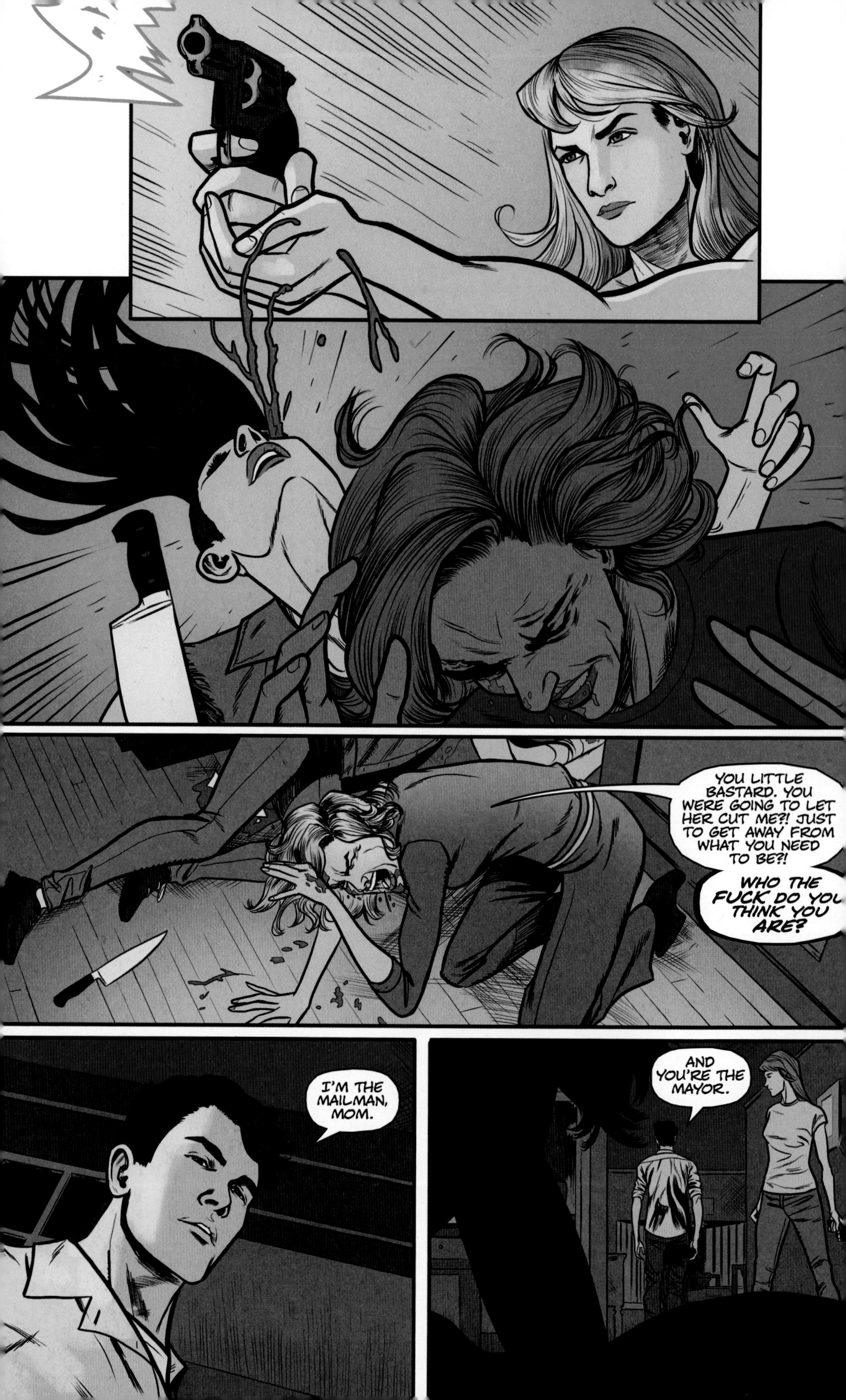
YOU LITTLE BASTARD. YOU WERE GOING TO LET HER CUT ME?! JUST TO GET AWAY FROM WHAT YOU NEED TO BE?!
WHO THE FUCK DO YOU THINK YOU ARE?
I'M THE MAILMAN, MOM.
AND YOU'RE THE MAYOR.

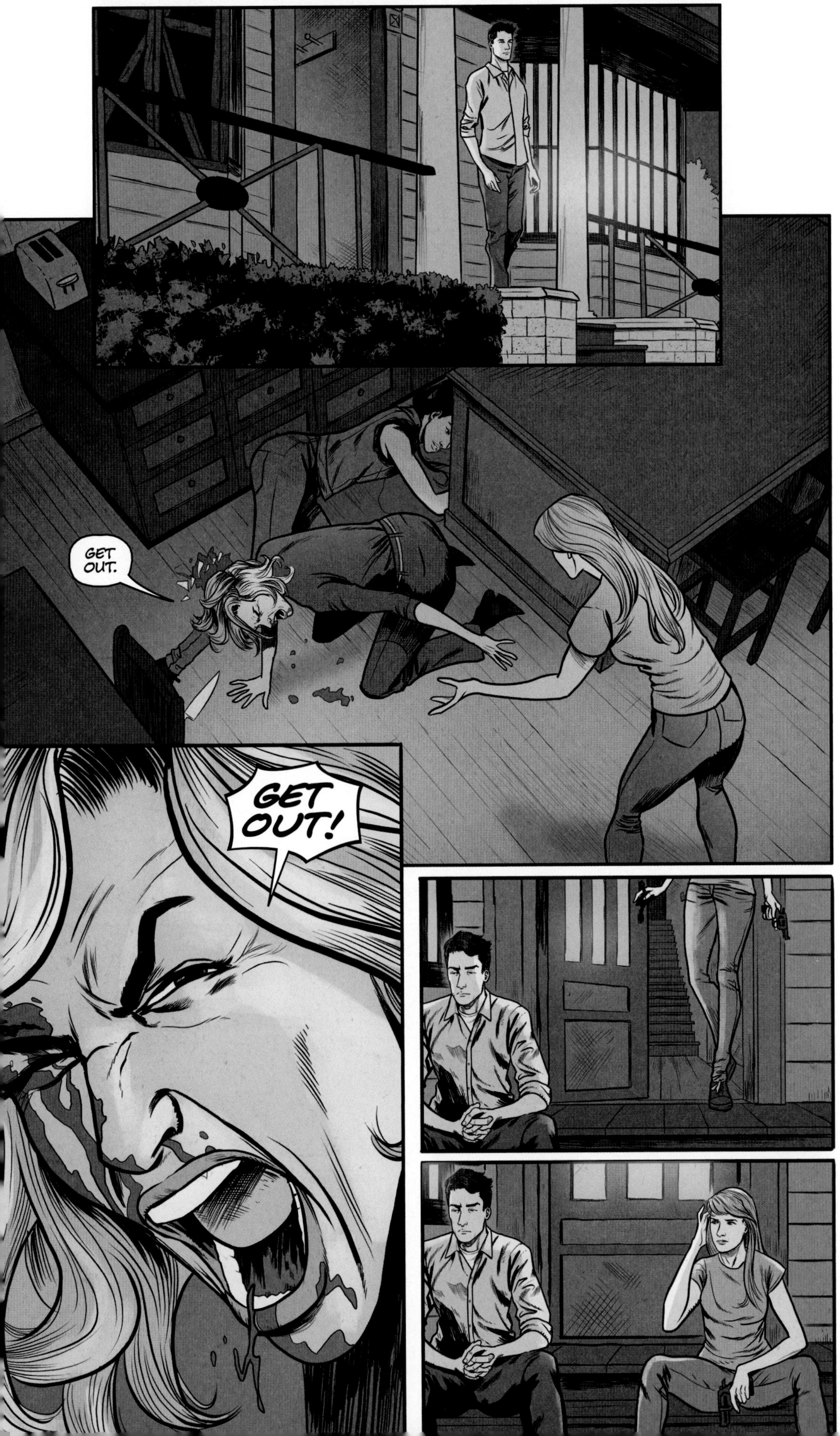
GET OUT.
GET OUT!

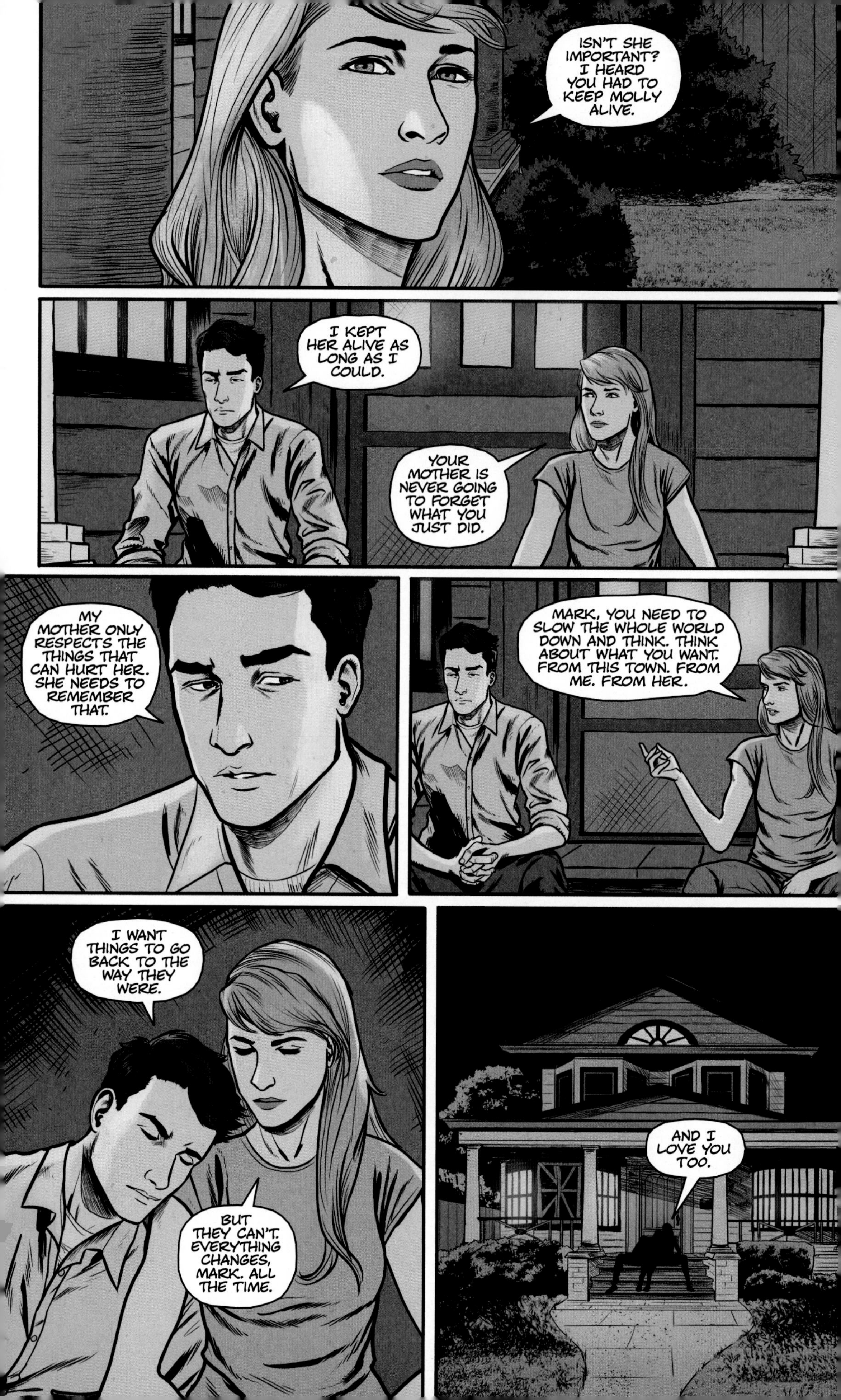
ISN'T SHE IMPORTANT? I HEARD YOU HAD TO KEEP MOLLY ALIVE.
I KEPT HER ALIVE AS LONG AS I COULD.
YOUR MOTHER IS NEVER GOING TO FORGET WHAT YOU JUST DID.
MY MOTHER ONLY RESPECTS THE THINGS THAT CAN HURT HER. SHE NEEDS TO REMEMBER THAT.
MARK, YOU NEED TO SLOW THE WHOLE WORLD DOWN AND THINK. THINK ABOUT WHAT YOU WANT. FROM THIS TOWN. FROM ME. FROM HER.
I WANT THINGS TO GO BACK TO THE WAY THEY WERE.
BUT THEY CAN'T. EVERYTHING CHANGES, MARK. ALL THE TIME.
AND I LOVE YOU TOO.

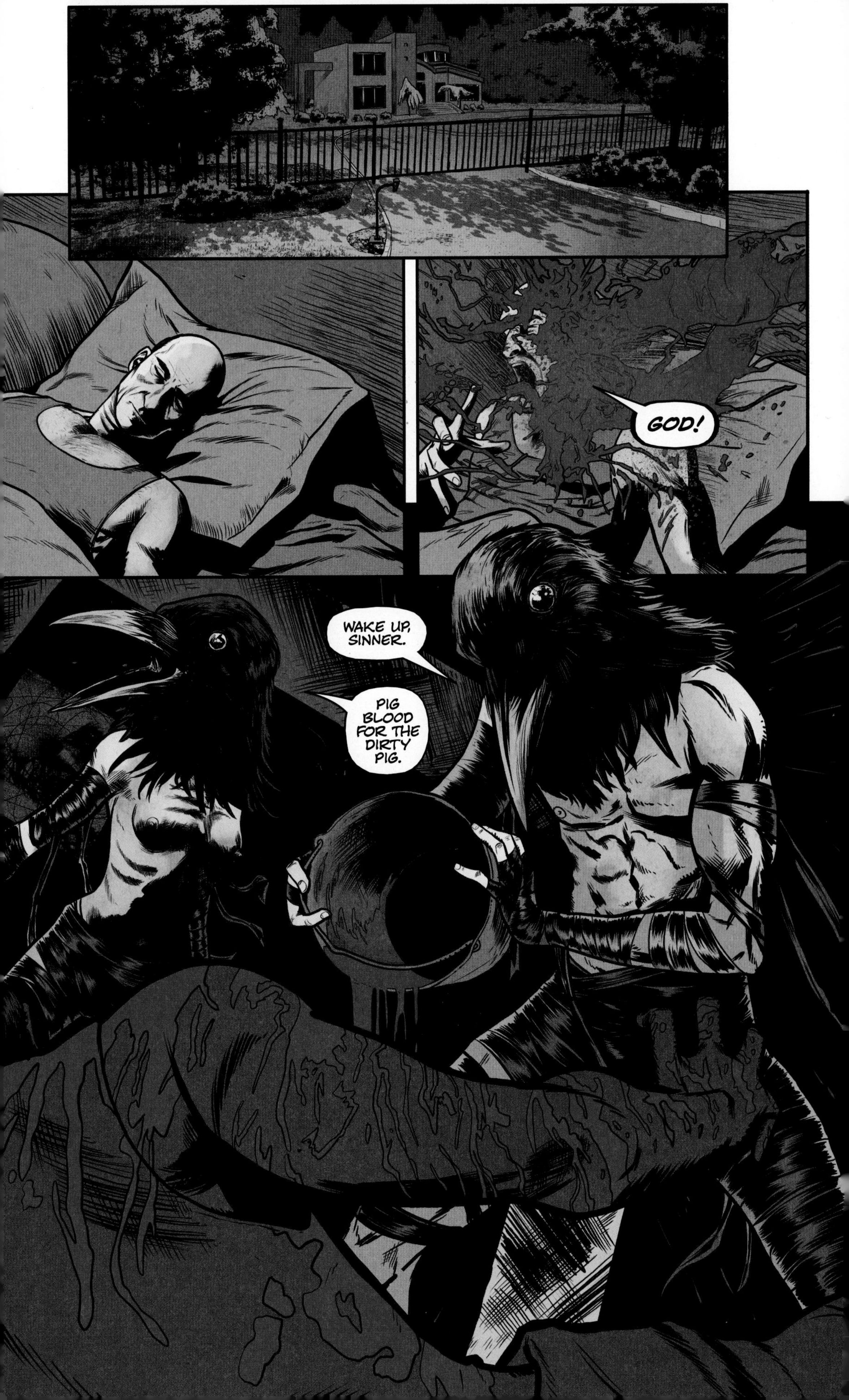
GOD!
WAKE UP, SINNER.
PIG BLOOD FOR THE DIRTY PIG.

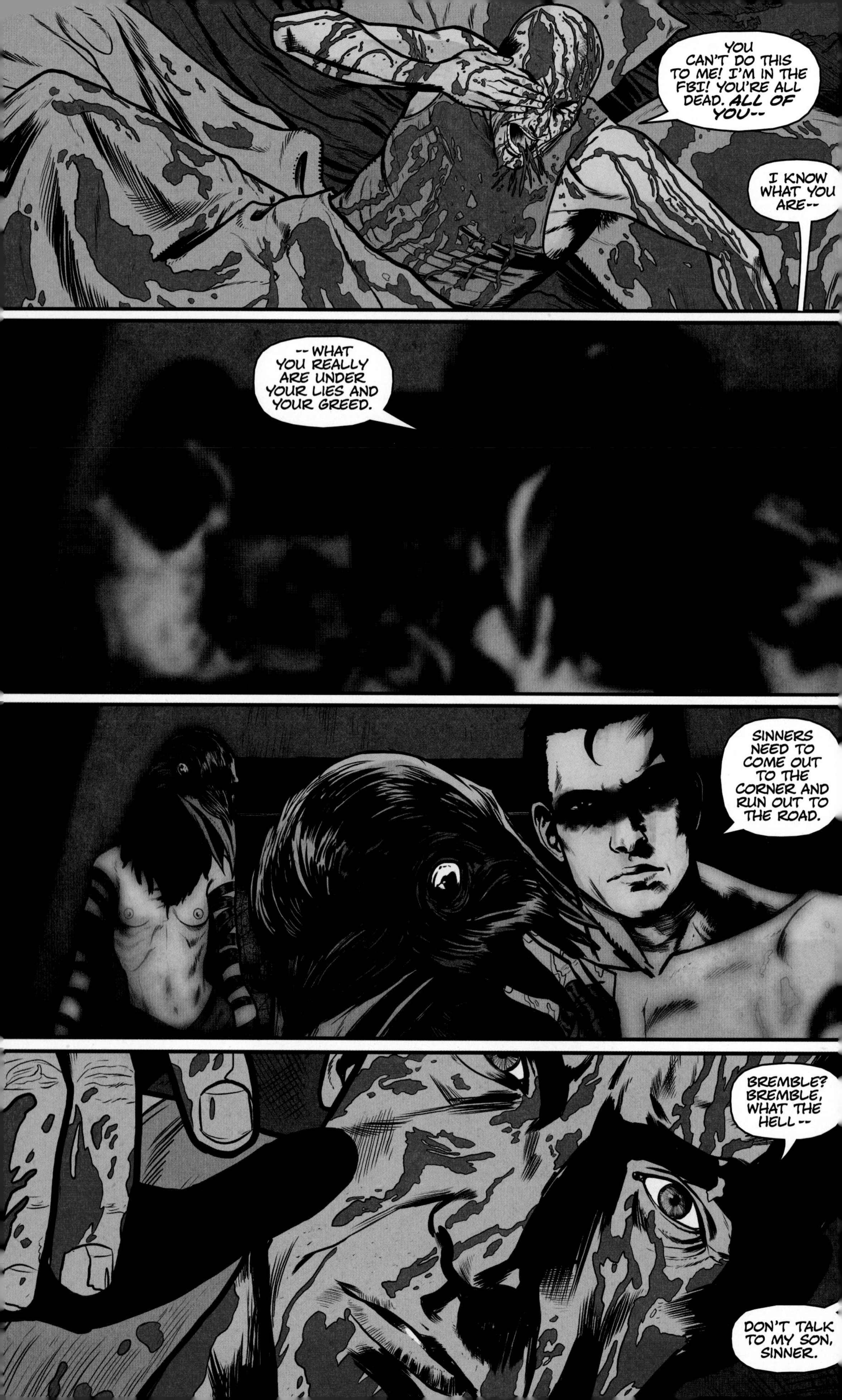
YOU CAN'T DO THIS TO ME! I'M IN THE FBI! YOU'RE ALL DEAD. ALL OF YOU--
I KNOW WHAT YOU ARE--
--WHAT YOU REALLY ARE UNDER YOUR LIES AND YOUR GREED.
SINNERS NEED TO COME OUT TO THE CORNER AND RUN OUT TO THE ROAD.
BREMBLE? BREMBLE, WHAT THE HELL--
DON'T TALK TO MY SON, SINNER.

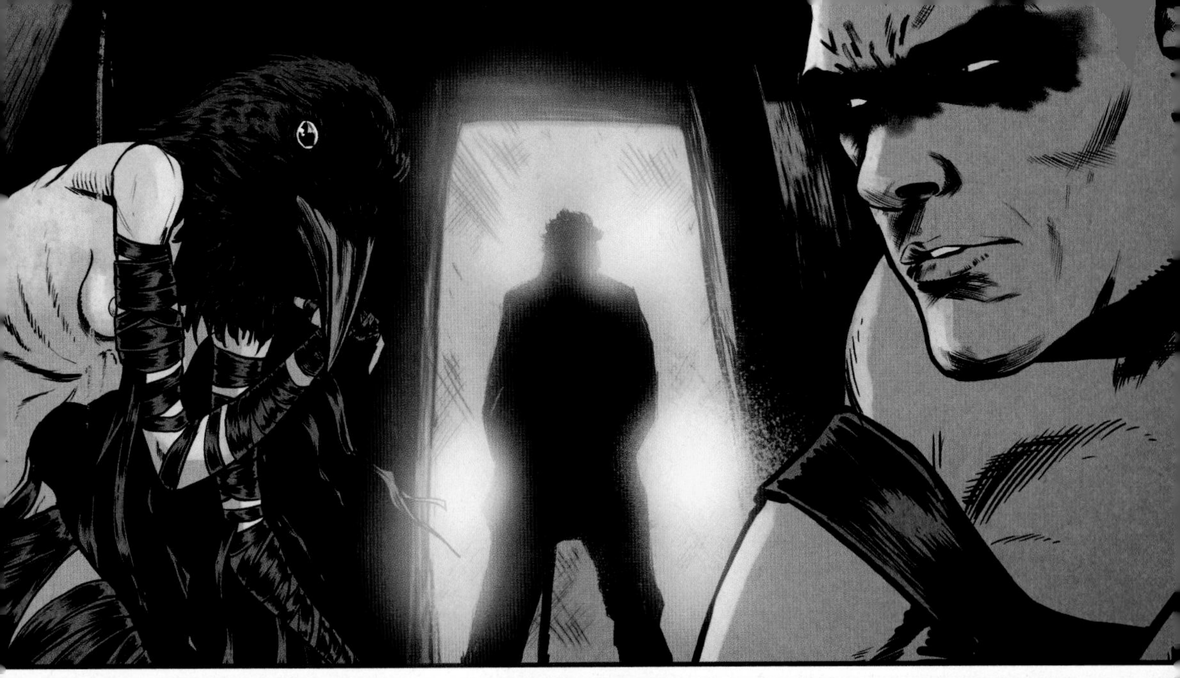

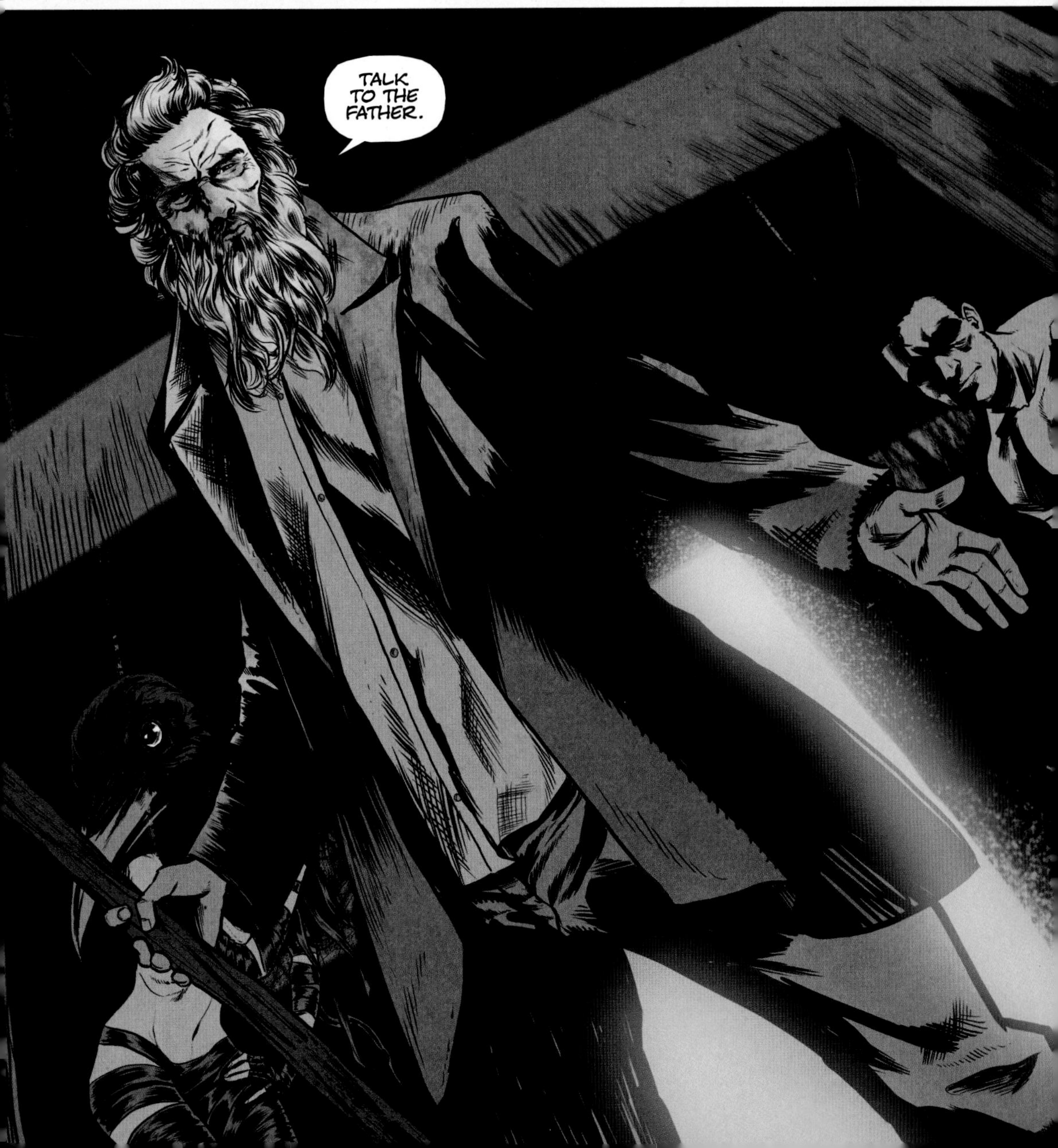
TALK TO THE FATHER.

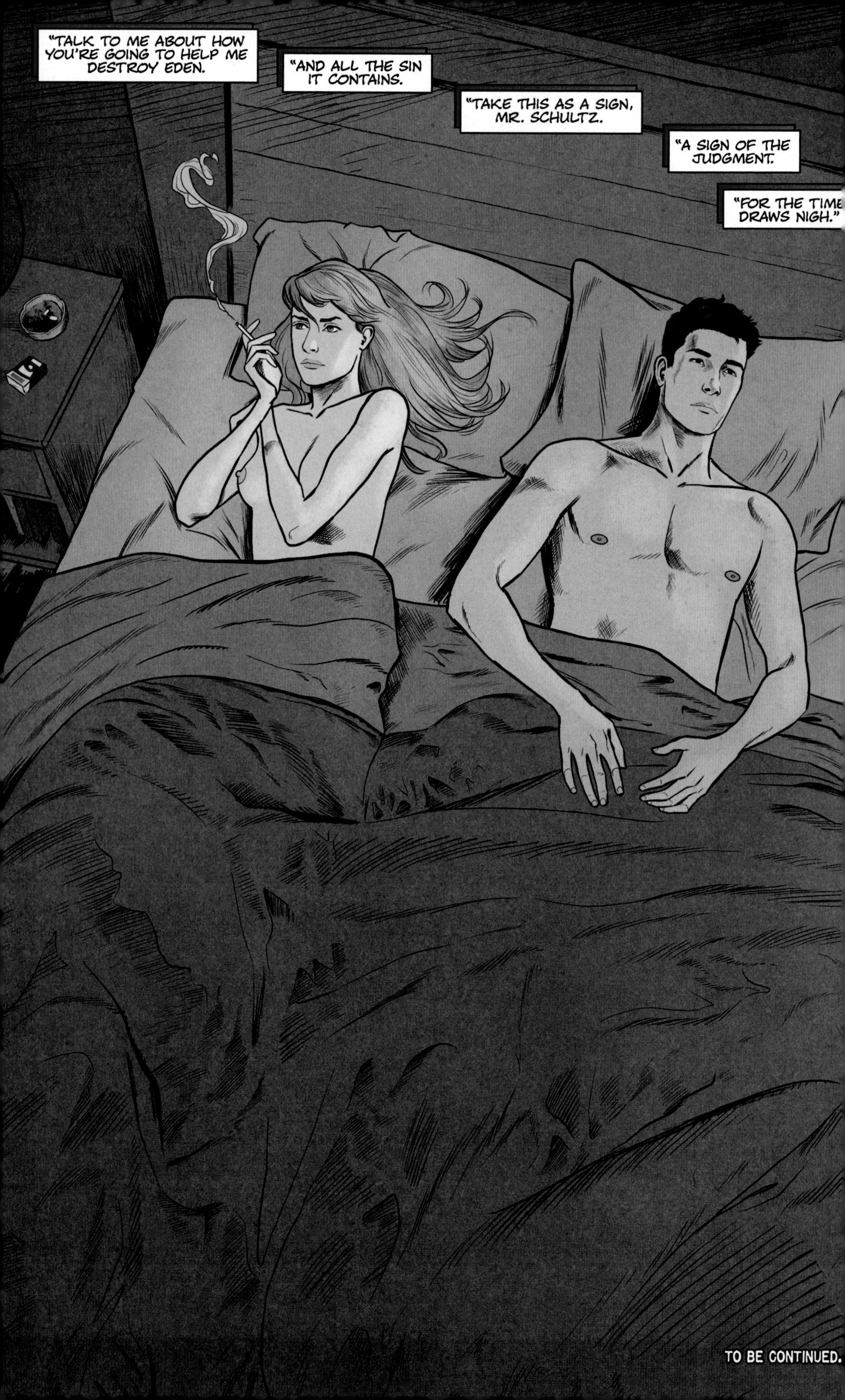
"TALK TO ME ABOUT HOW YOU'RE GOING TO HELP ME DESTROY EDEN.
"AND ALL THE SIN IT CONTAINS.
"TAKE THIS AS A SIGN, MR. SCHULTZ.
"A SIGN OF THE JUDGMENT.
"FOR THE TIME DRAWS NIGH."
TO BE CONTINUED.

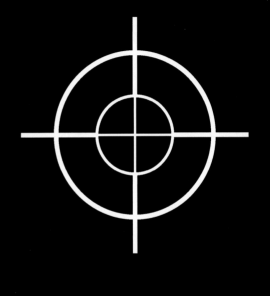

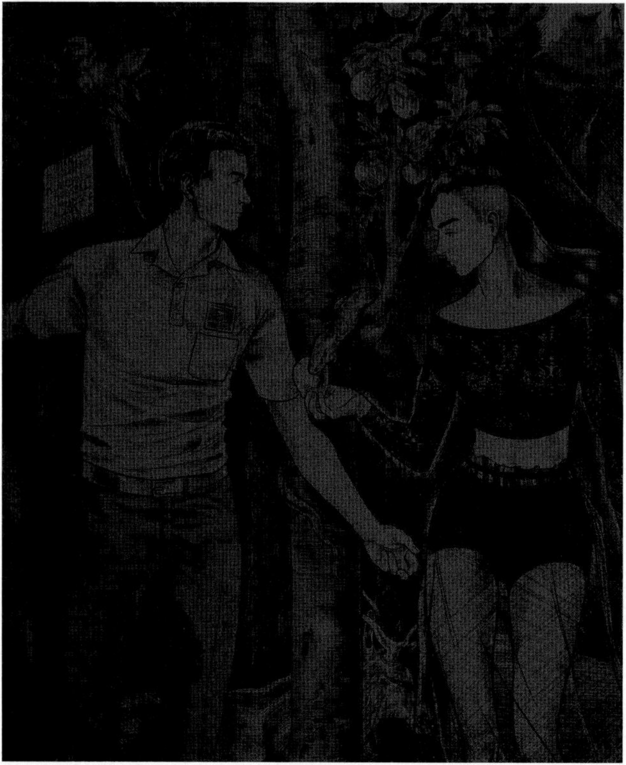

Postal #17
Linda Sejic

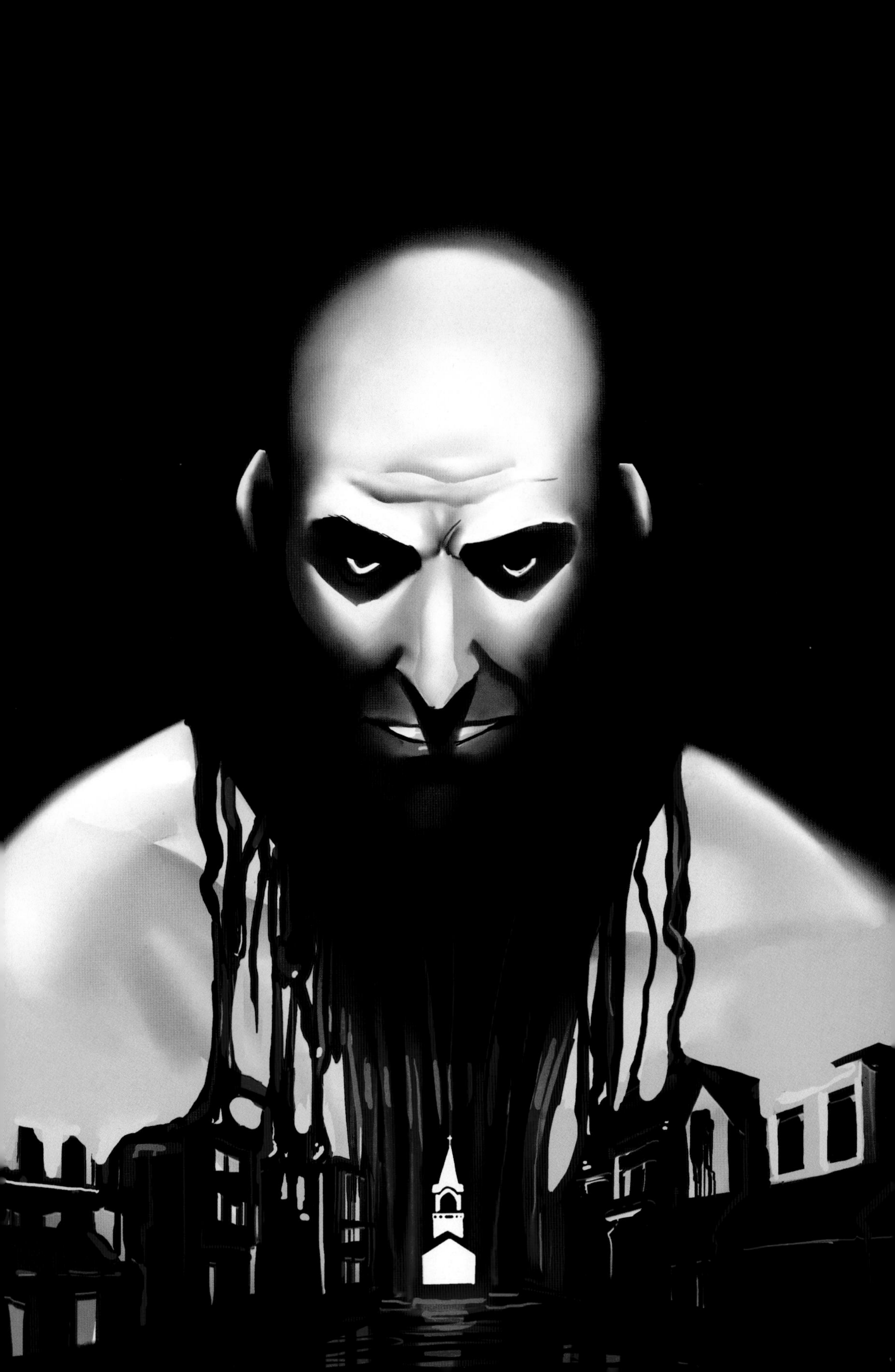

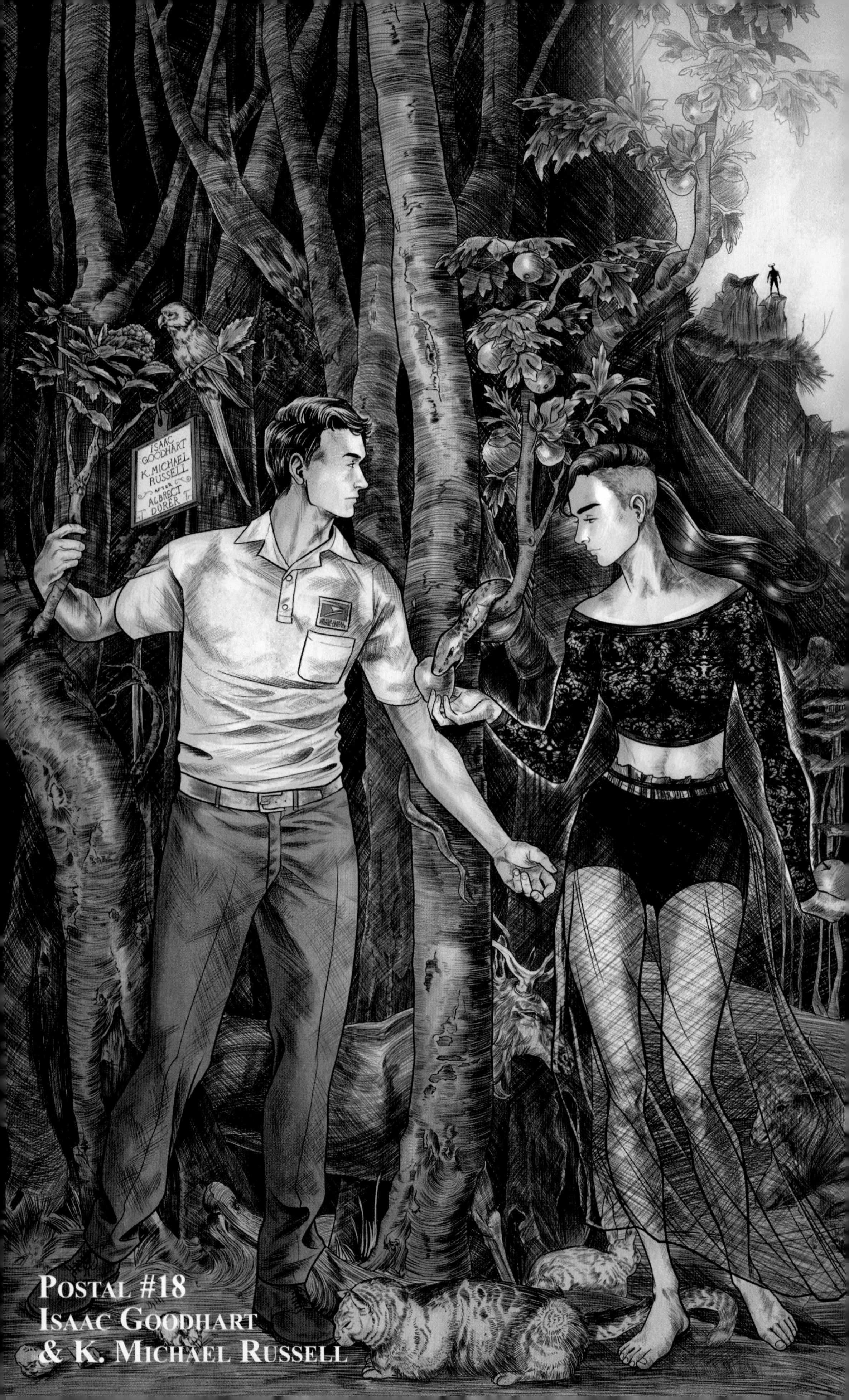
ISAAC
GOODHART
K. MICHAEL
RUSSELL
AFTER
ALBRECT
DURER

Postal #18
Isaac Goodhart
& K. Michael Russell

POSTAL #19
LINDA SEJIC

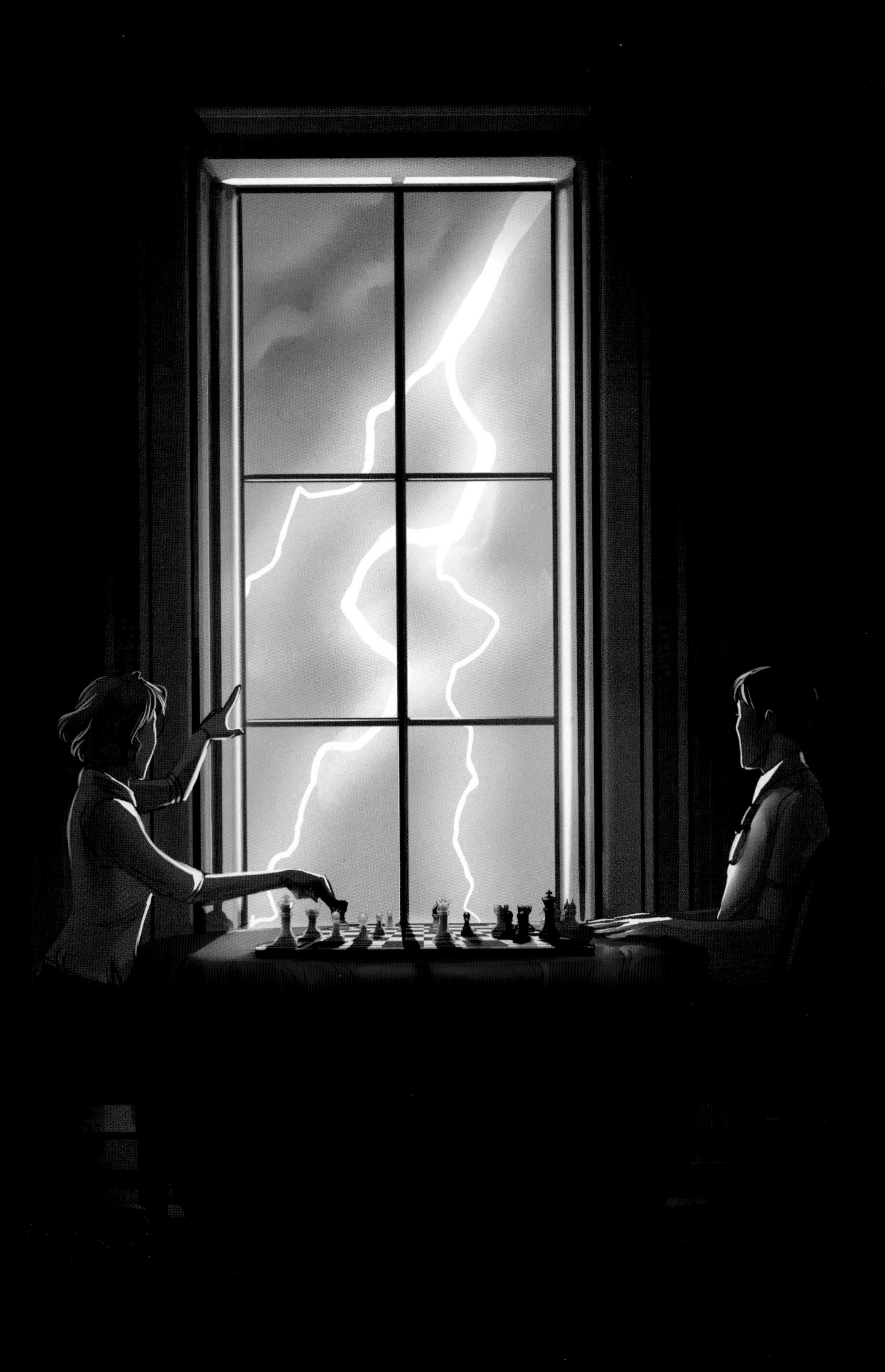

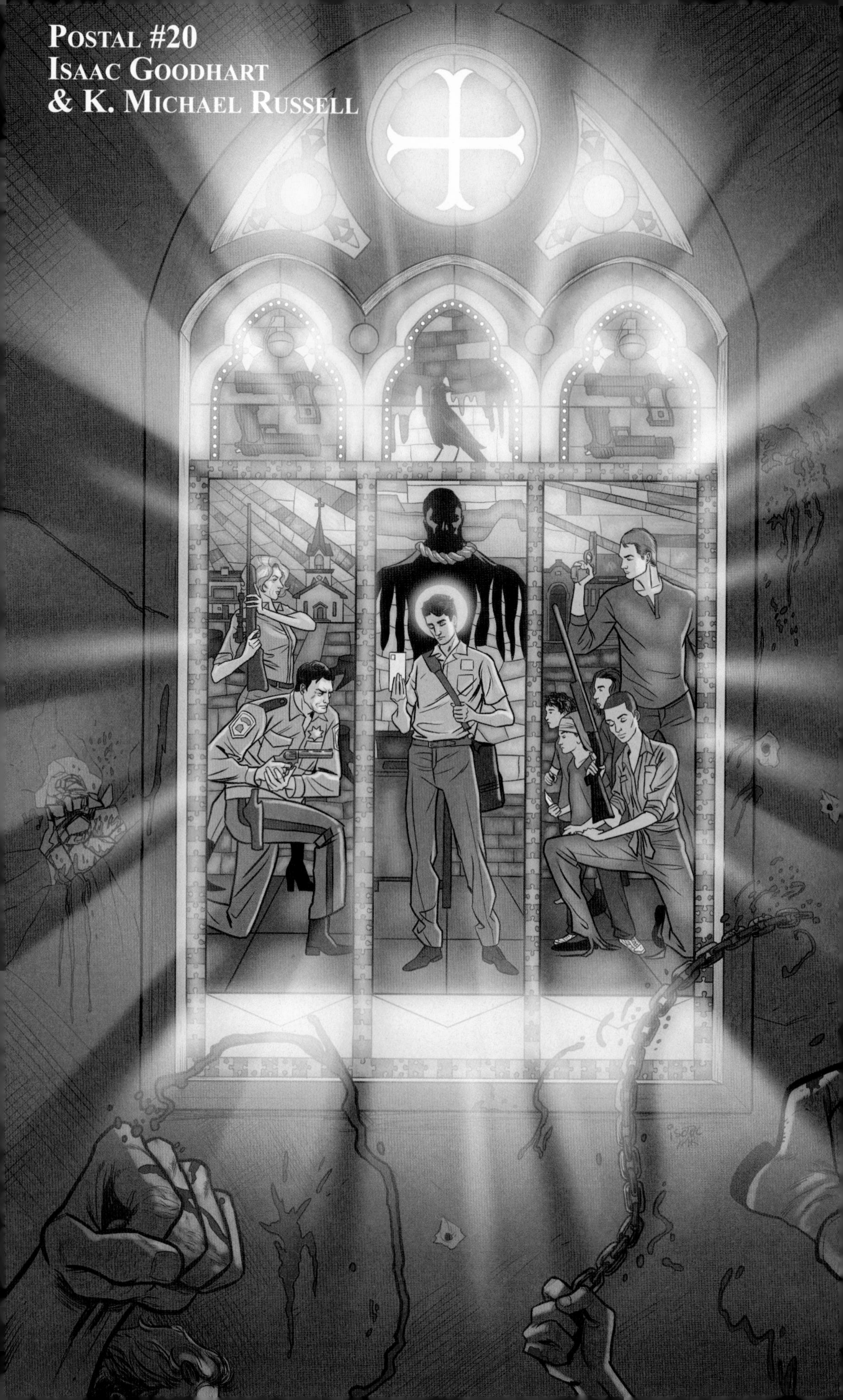

POSTAL #20
ISAAC GOODHART
& K. MICHAEL RUSSELL

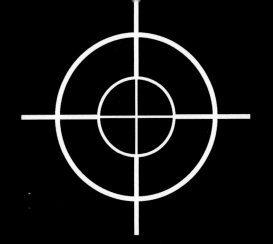

HAWKINS · HILL · SAEKI · VALENZA

GOLGOTHA

PREVIEW

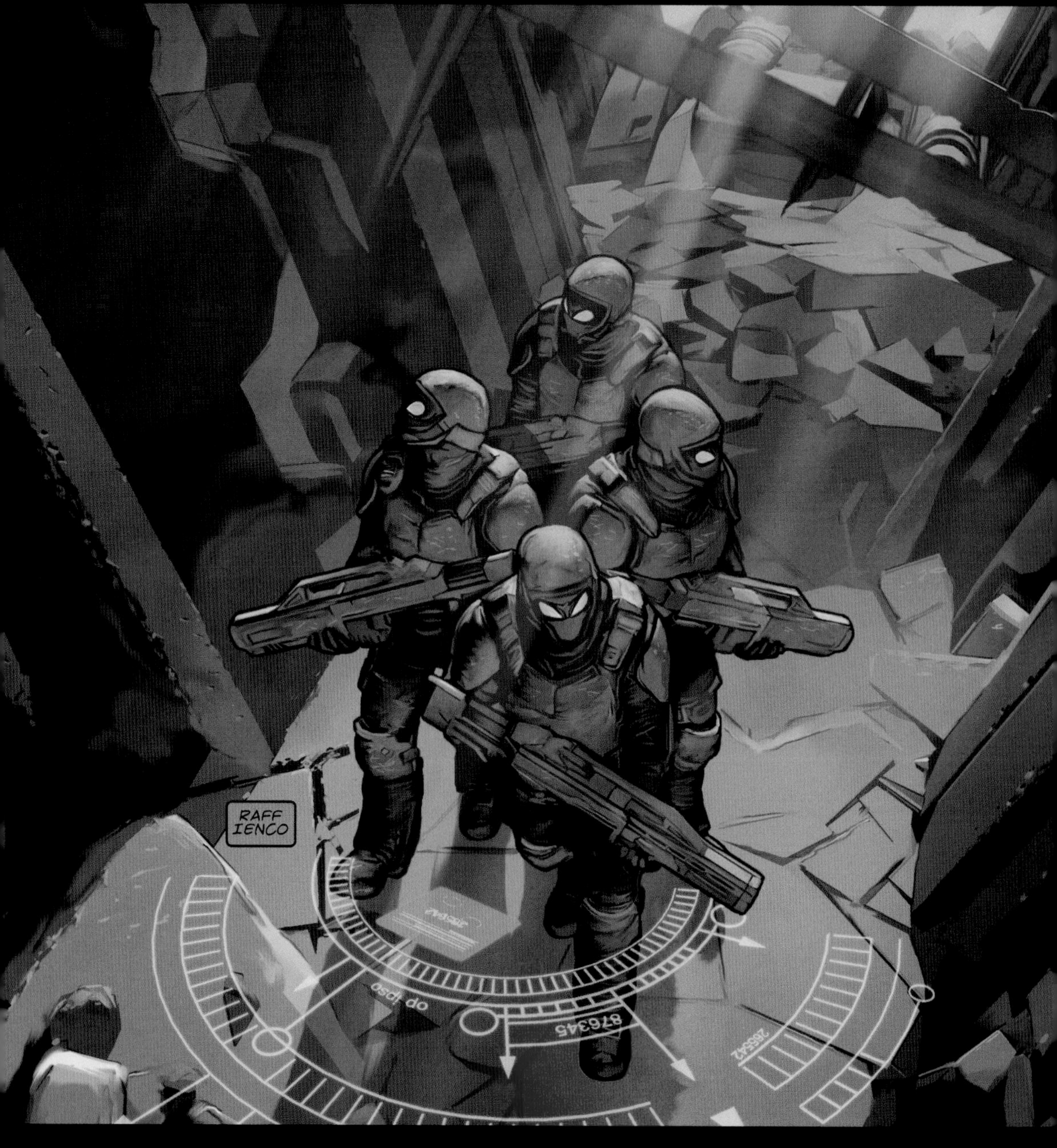
RAFF
IENCO

IN STORES
OCTOBER
2017

TOP COW 25 YEARS EST. 1992

THE FUTURE OF COMICS 25 image

MISSION STATEMENT

ISOCSS Golgotha.
Fleet number 18739840(09).
Modified Drawnheim MC-69B Taurus E-Class Vessel.

MISSION PARAMETERS:

Attempt to create the first human, mining colony beyond Earth.

DESTINATION: IAU-ACHILLES.

TIME TO DESTINATION: Est. 80 years.

ESSENTIAL CREW:

CARILLO, Anabelle.
(AEF. HUM-INT)

Born: **Chicago, Illinois.**

Decorated pilot in both sea and Earth Orbit operations.

Graduate of ISOC Naval Academy.

Unmarried. No children.

MEAD, Lancaster.
(Engineer)

Born: **San Diego, California.**

Graduate of MIT.

HIV Positive (Remission). Unmarried. No children.

ESSENTIAL CREW:

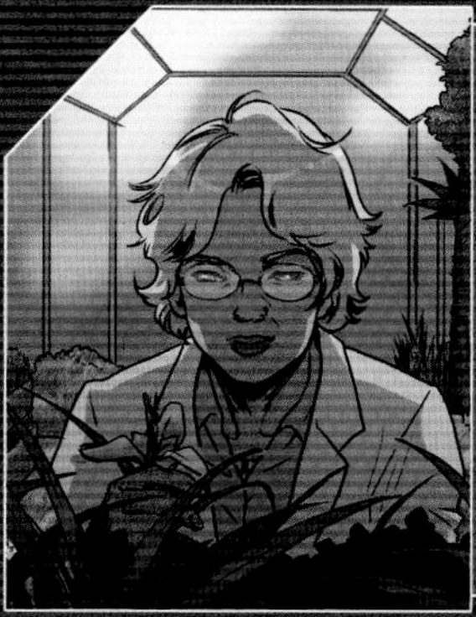

LIPPENCOTT, Charelene.
(PhD. Agrophysics)

Born: **Joplin, Missouri.**

Graduate Johns Hopkins (B.A. Applied Sciences), PhD Cornell University (Agrophysics).

Unmarried. No Children.

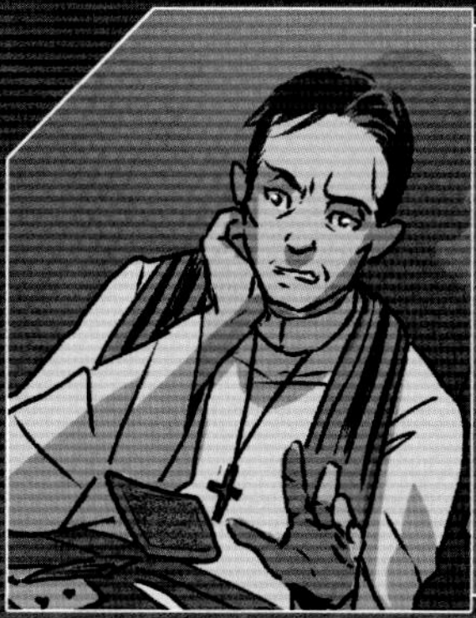

CHENG, David.
(Chaplain. AEF.)

Born: **New Orleans. Louisiana.** Base Chaplain, Flynn Air Force Base.

Graduate Saint Louis University (B.A. Religious Studies).

Widowed. Laura Cheng (Deceased). No Children.

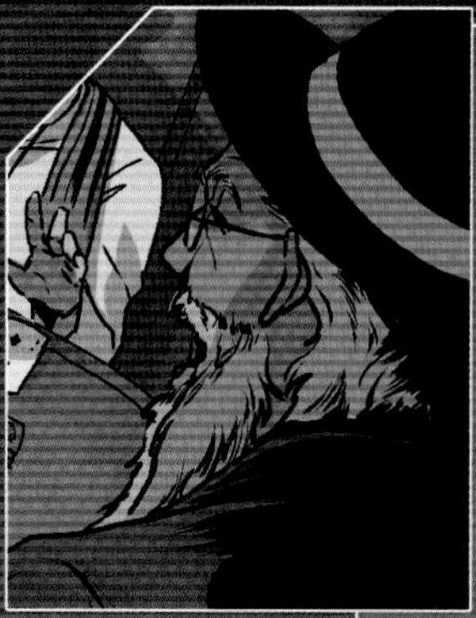

ROSENTHAL, Moshe.
(Rabbi. AEF.)

Born: **Haifa, Israel.** Dual Citizenship United States of America. Naturalized.

Graduate University of Haifa (B.A. Hebrew Literature and Language, Political Science).

Base Rabbi Rumsfeld Air Force Base.

Unmarried. No children.

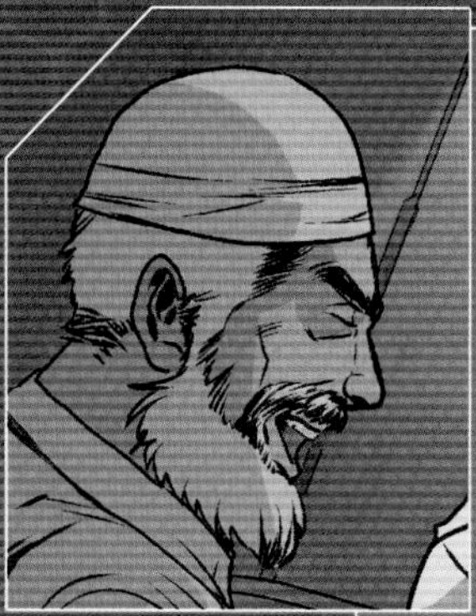

GAFANI, Abdul-Ghafaar.
(Imam. AEF.)

Born: **Istanbul, Turkey.** Dual-Citizenship-United States of America. Naturalized.

Graduate Harvard University (B.A. Philosophy). Founder North African Sunni Islam Mosque.

Served USMC, honorable discharge. Rank: Captain (declined).

Unmarried. No children.

ESSENTIAL CREW:

LAWTON, Michael.
(Cpt. 31st Special Forces Group. ISOC.)

Born: **Kansas City, Kansas.**

Graduated Wyandotte High School. No post graduate education.

Enlisted Marines. Served two tours Marine/Resource Coalition Conflict. Promoted to Special Forces.

Duty status: Active.

Married to Jennifer Lawton.
Expecting first child.

BARDOT, Cleménce.
(Applied Robotics. Kinematics. Control dynamics.)

Born: **Brooklyn, New York.**

Graduated Cornell University (B.A. Applied Robotics, M.S. Applied Robotics).

Winner Nobel Prize (Team Awarded).

Unmarried. No children.

CARPENTER, Jennifer.
(PhD. Xenobiologist.)

Born: **Los Angeles, California.**

Graduated UCLA (B.A. Biosafety) Graduated USC (PhD. Xenobiology).

Divorced. No children.

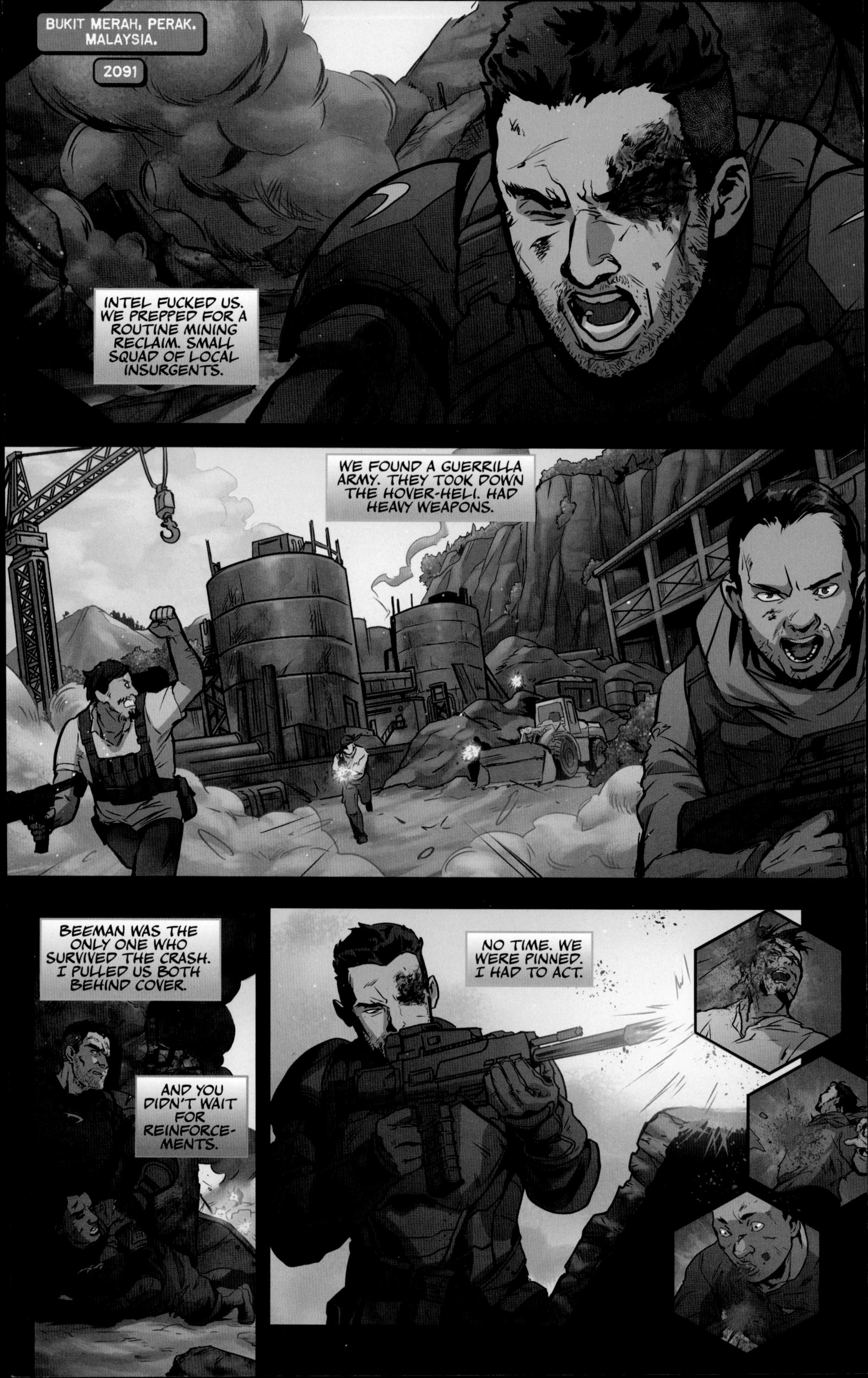
BUKIT MERAH, PERAK. MALAYSIA.
2091
INTEL FUCKED US. WE PREPPED FOR A ROUTINE MINING RECLAIM. SMALL SQUAD OF LOCAL INSURGENTS.
WE FOUND A GUERRILLA ARMY. THEY TOOK DOWN THE HOVER-HELI. HAD HEAVY WEAPONS.
BEEMAN WAS THE ONLY ONE WHO SURVIVED THE CRASH. I PULLED US BOTH BEHIND COVER.
AND YOU DIDN'T WAIT FOR REINFORCE-MENTS.
NO TIME. WE WERE PINNED. I HAD TO ACT.

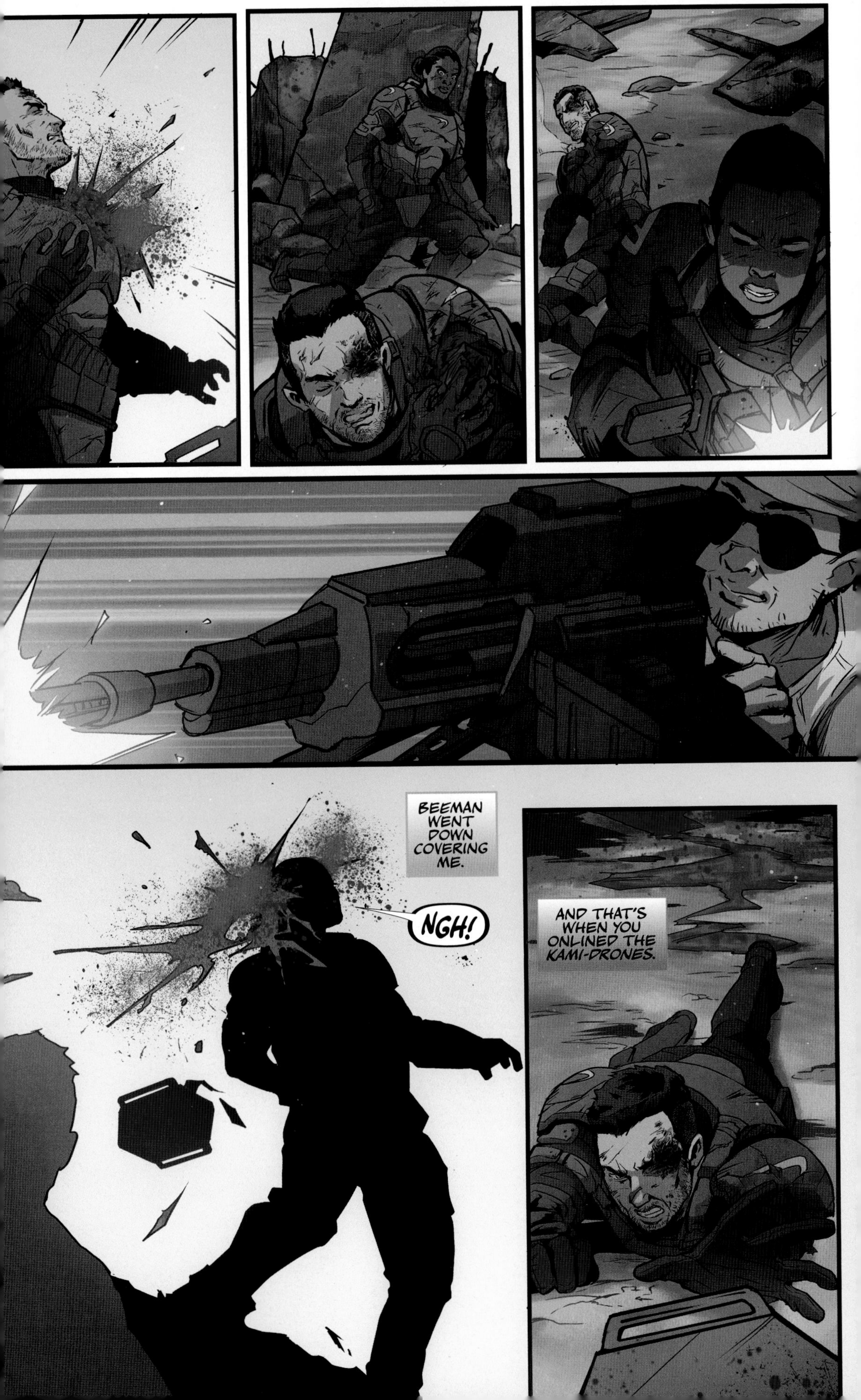
BEEMAN WENT DOWN COVERING ME.
NGH!
AND THAT'S WHEN YOU ONLINED THE KAMI-DRONES.

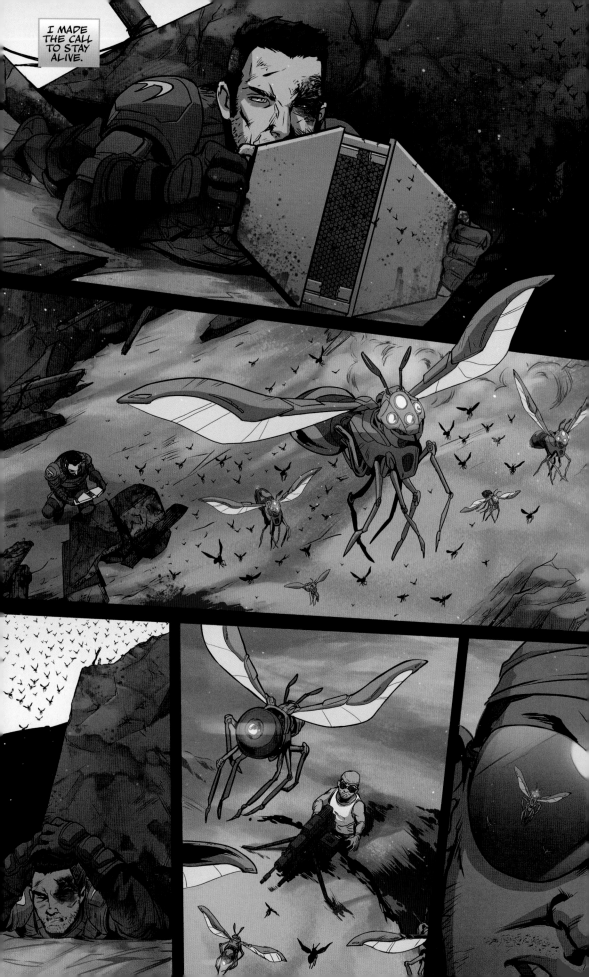

I MADE THE CALL TO STAY ALIVE.

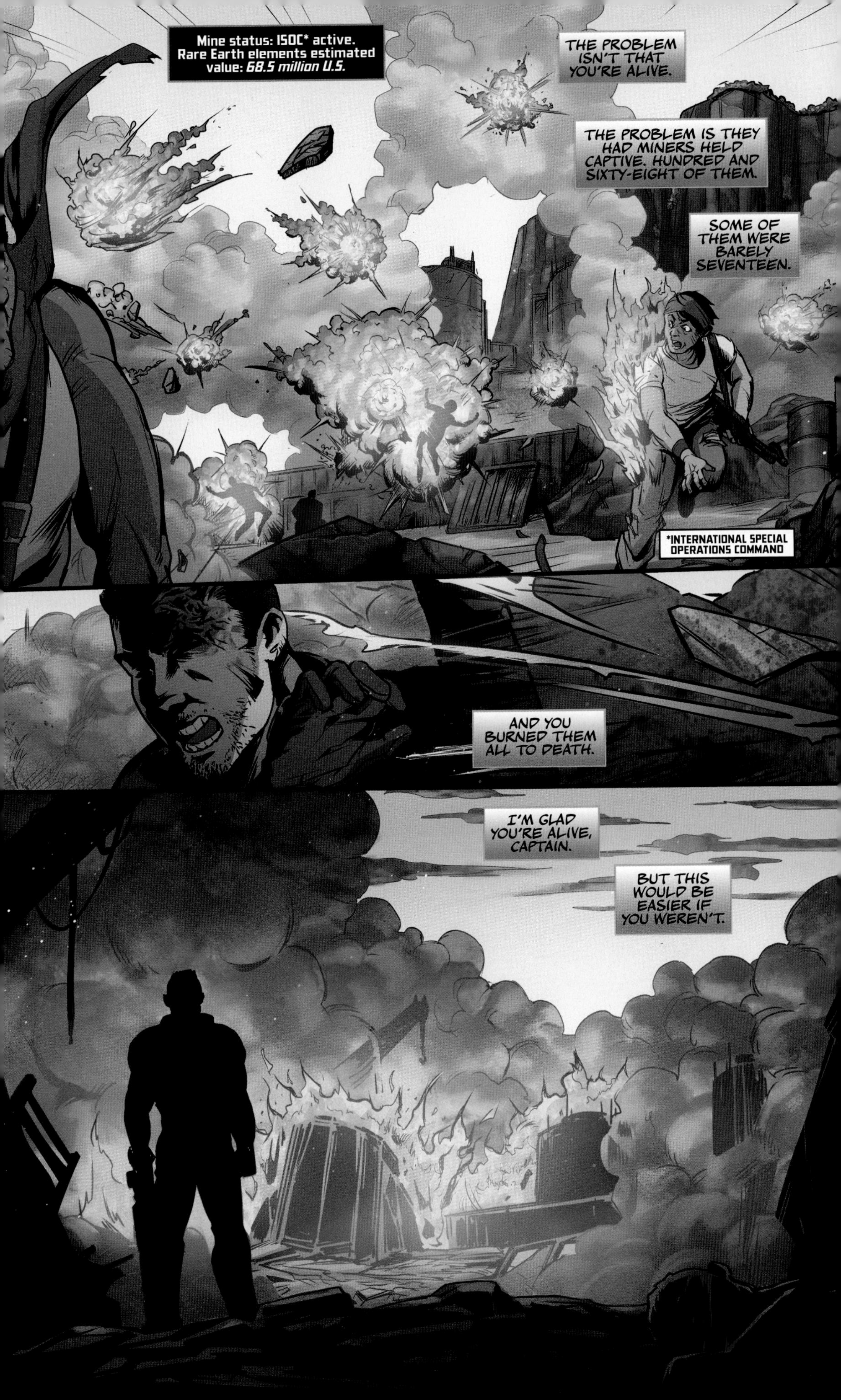
Mine status: ISOC* active.
Rare Earth elements estimated value: 68.5 million U.S.
THE PROBLEM ISN'T THAT YOU'RE ALIVE.
THE PROBLEM IS THEY HAD MINERS HELD CAPTIVE. HUNDRED AND SIXTY-EIGHT OF THEM.
SOME OF THEM WERE BARELY SEVENTEEN.
*INTERNATIONAL SPECIAL OPERATIONS COMMAND
AND YOU BURNED THEM ALL TO DEATH.
I'M GLAD YOU'RE ALIVE, CAPTAIN.
BUT THIS WOULD BE EASIER IF YOU WEREN'T.

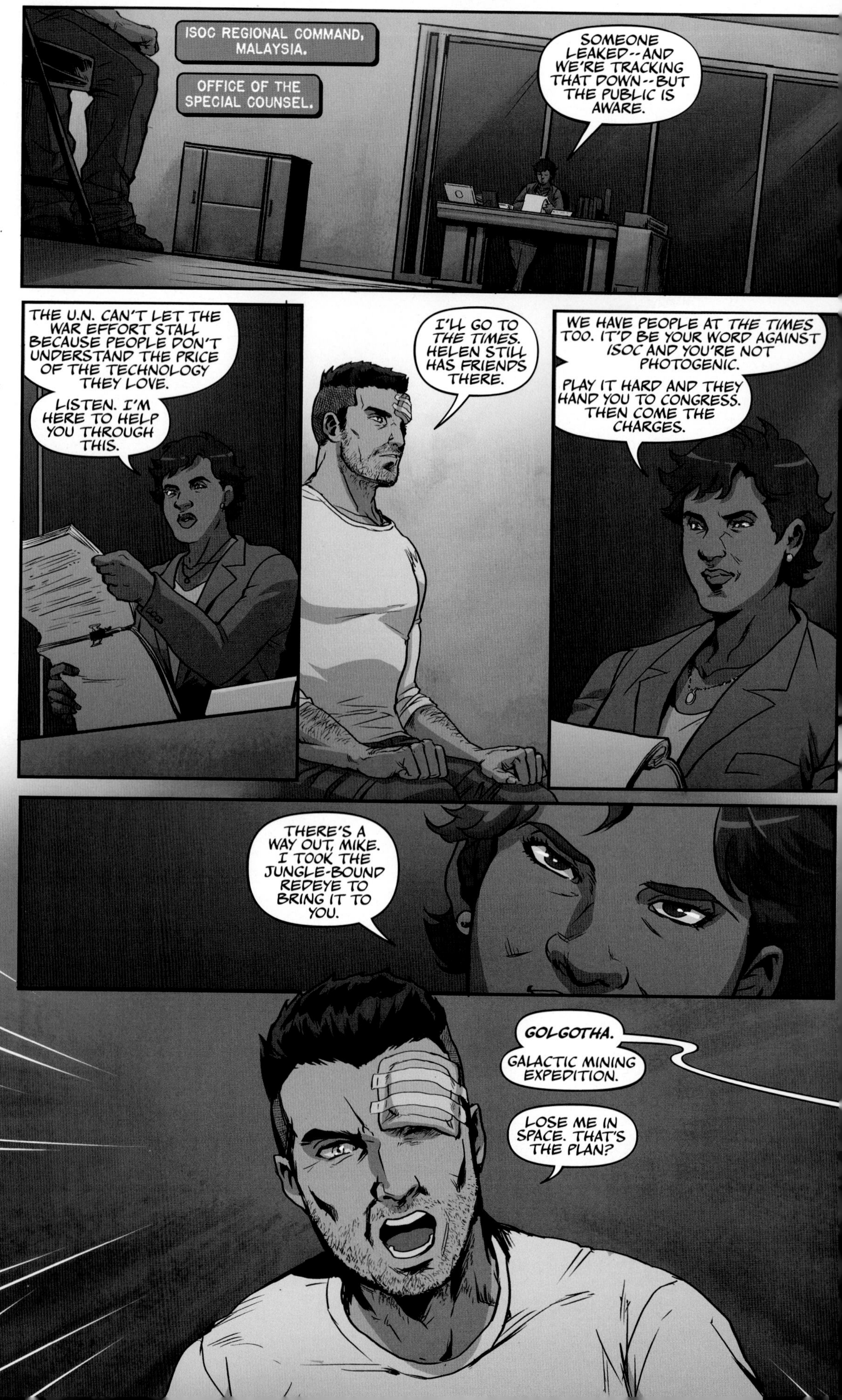
ISOC REGIONAL COMMAND, MALAYSIA.
OFFICE OF THE SPECIAL COUNSEL.
SOMEONE LEAKED--AND WE'RE TRACKING THAT DOWN--BUT THE PUBLIC IS AWARE.
THE U.N. CAN'T LET THE WAR EFFORT STALL BECAUSE PEOPLE DON'T UNDERSTAND THE PRICE OF THE TECHNOLOGY THEY LOVE.
LISTEN. I'M HERE TO HELP YOU THROUGH THIS.
I'LL GO TO THE TIMES. HELEN STILL HAS FRIENDS THERE.
WE HAVE PEOPLE AT THE TIMES TOO. IT'D BE YOUR WORD AGAINST ISOC AND YOU'RE NOT PHOTOGENIC.
PLAY IT HARD AND THEY HAND YOU TO CONGRESS. THEN COME THE CHARGES.
THERE'S A WAY OUT, MIKE. I TOOK THE JUNGLE-BOUND REDEYE TO BRING IT TO YOU.
GOLGOTHA.
GALACTIC MINING EXPEDITION.
LOSE ME IN SPACE. THAT'S THE PLAN?

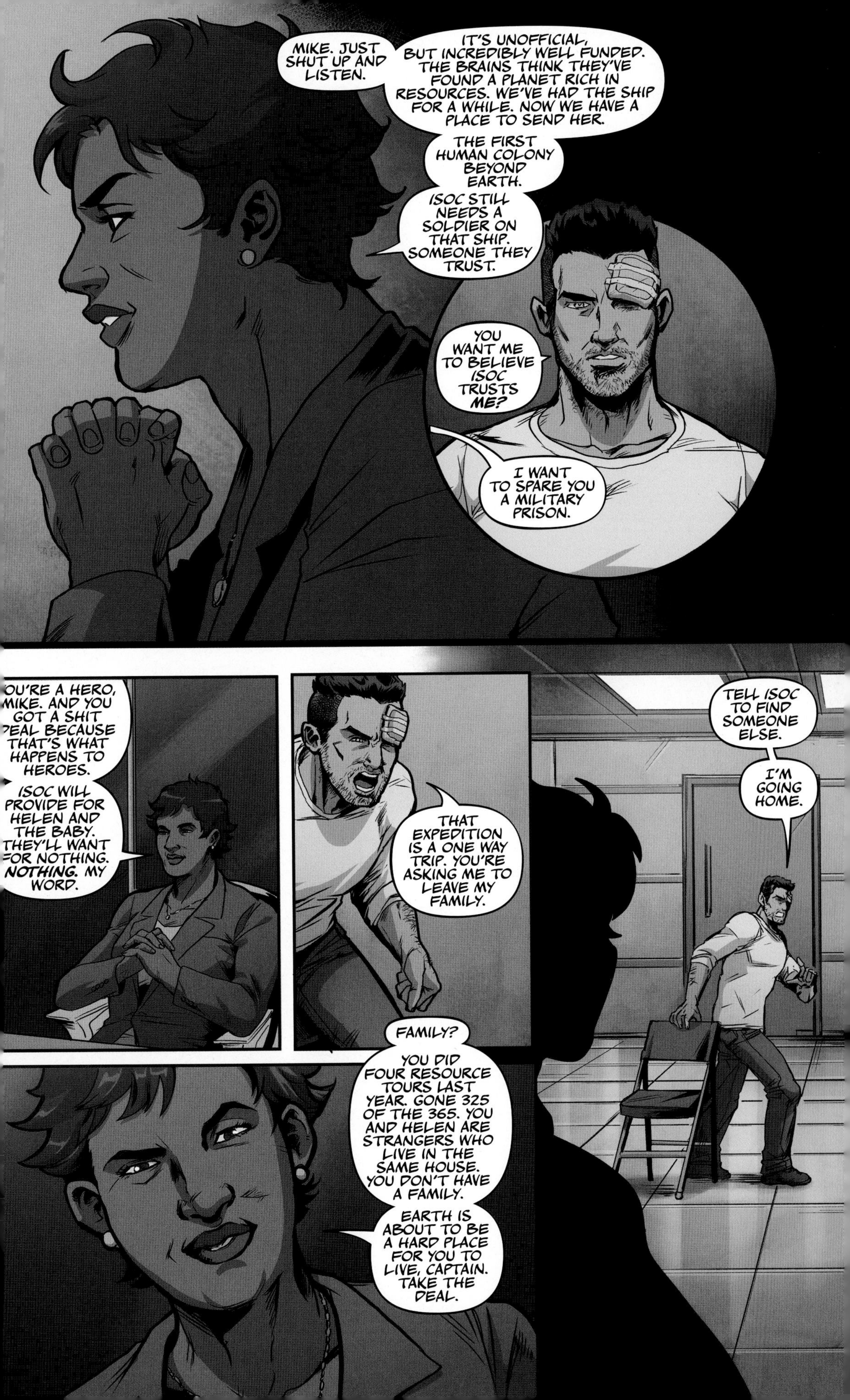
MIKE. JUST SHUT UP AND LISTEN.
IT'S UNOFFICIAL, BUT INCREDIBLY WELL FUNDED. THE BRAINS THINK THEY'VE FOUND A PLANET RICH IN RESOURCES. WE'VE HAD THE SHIP FOR A WHILE. NOW WE HAVE A PLACE TO SEND HER.
THE FIRST HUMAN COLONY BEYOND EARTH.
ISOC STILL NEEDS A SOLDIER ON THAT SHIP. SOMEONE THEY TRUST.
YOU WANT ME TO BELIEVE ISOC TRUSTS ME?
I WANT TO SPARE YOU A MILITARY PRISON.
OU'RE A HERO, MIKE. AND YOU GOT A SHIT DEAL BECAUSE THAT'S WHAT HAPPENS TO HEROES.
ISOC WILL PROVIDE FOR HELEN AND THE BABY. THEY'LL WANT FOR NOTHING. NOTHING. MY WORD.
THAT EXPEDITION IS A ONE WAY TRIP. YOU'RE ASKING ME TO LEAVE MY FAMILY.
TELL ISOC TO FIND SOMEONE ELSE.
I'M GOING HOME.
FAMILY?
YOU DID FOUR RESOURCE TOURS LAST YEAR. GONE 325 OF THE 365. YOU AND HELEN ARE STRANGERS WHO LIVE IN THE SAME HOUSE. YOU DON'T HAVE A FAMILY.
EARTH IS ABOUT TO BE A HARD PLACE FOR YOU TO LIVE, CAPTAIN. TAKE THE DEAL.

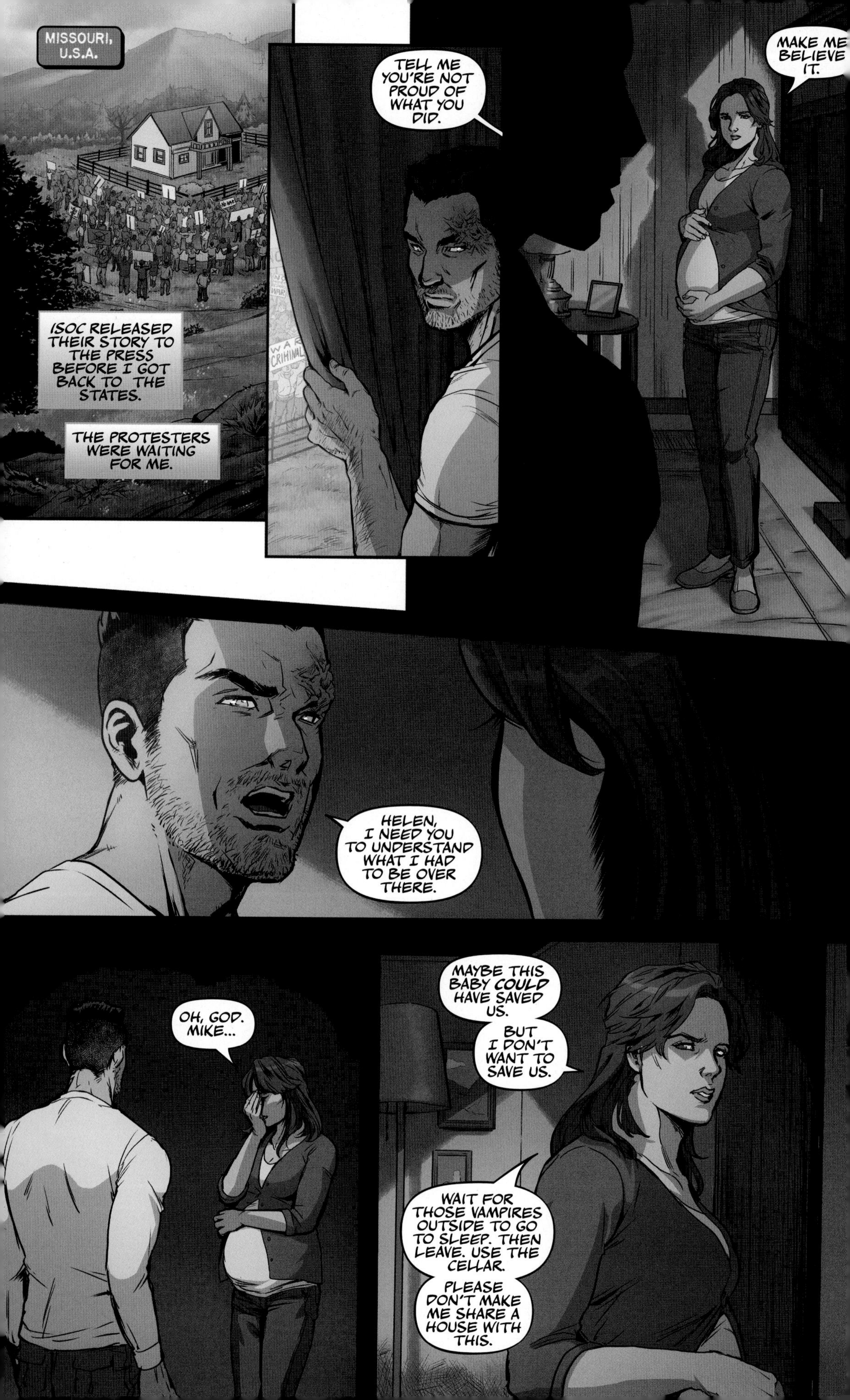
MISSOURI, U.S.A.
ISOC RELEASED THEIR STORY TO THE PRESS BEFORE I GOT BACK TO THE STATES.
THE PROTESTERS WERE WAITING FOR ME.
NO WAR
WAR CRIMINAL
TELL ME YOU'RE NOT PROUD OF WHAT YOU DID.
MAKE ME BELIEVE IT.
HELEN, I NEED YOU TO UNDERSTAND WHAT I HAD TO BE OVER THERE.
OH, GOD. MIKE...
MAYBE THIS BABY COULD HAVE SAVED US.
BUT I DON'T WANT TO SAVE US.
WAIT FOR THOSE VAMPIRES OUTSIDE TO GO TO SLEEP. THEN LEAVE. USE THE CELLAR.
PLEASE DON'T MAKE ME SHARE A HOUSE WITH THIS.

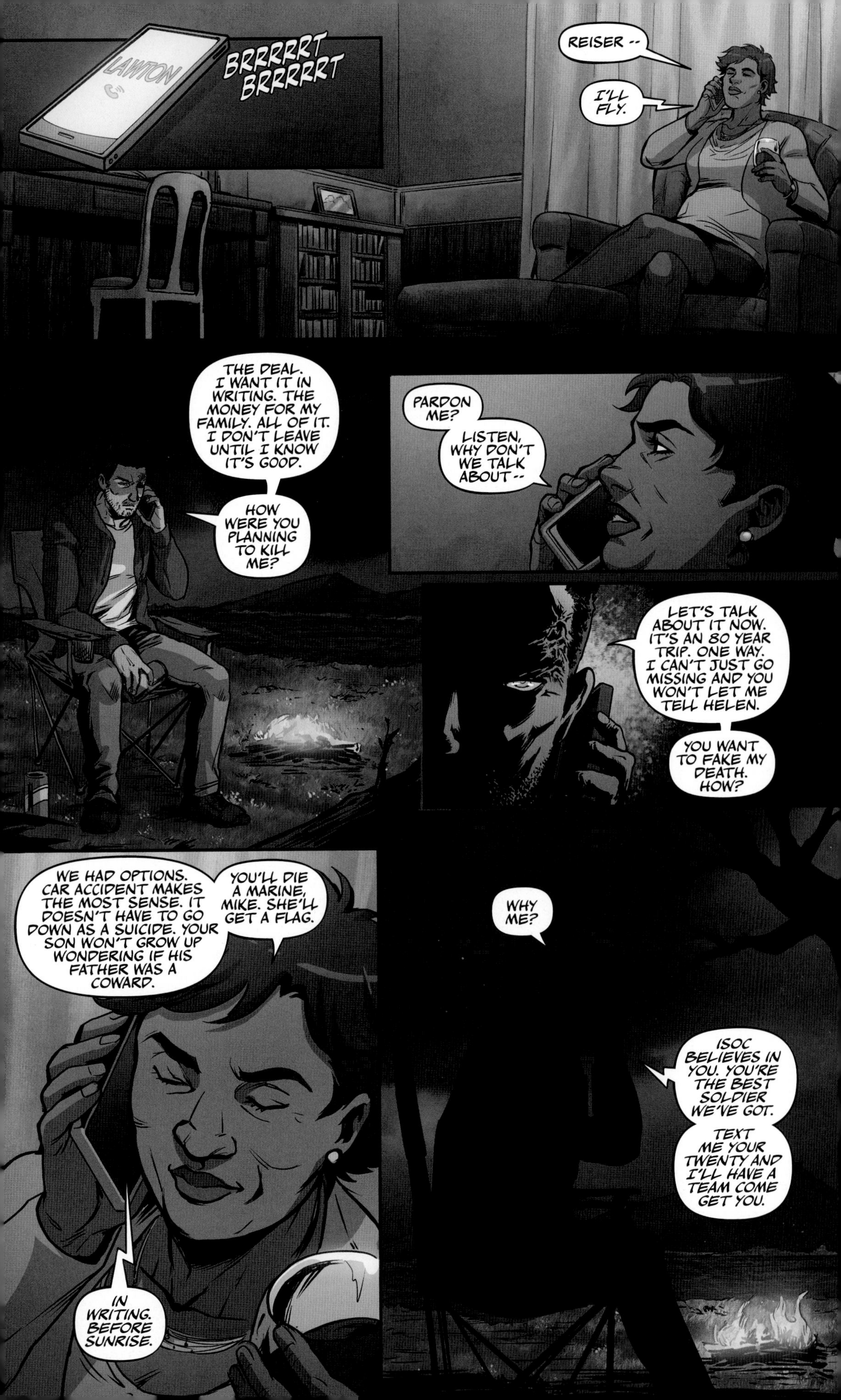
LAWTON
BRRRRRT BRRRRRT
REISER --
I'LL FLY.
THE DEAL. I WANT IT IN WRITING. THE MONEY FOR MY FAMILY. ALL OF IT. I DON'T LEAVE UNTIL I KNOW IT'S GOOD.
HOW WERE YOU PLANNING TO KILL ME?
PARDON ME?
LISTEN, WHY DON'T WE TALK ABOUT --
LET'S TALK ABOUT IT NOW. IT'S AN 80 YEAR TRIP. ONE WAY. I CAN'T JUST GO MISSING AND YOU WON'T LET ME TELL HELEN.
YOU WANT TO FAKE MY DEATH. HOW?
WE HAD OPTIONS. CAR ACCIDENT MAKES THE MOST SENSE. IT DOESN'T HAVE TO GO DOWN AS A SUICIDE. YOUR SON WON'T GROW UP WONDERING IF HIS FATHER WAS A COWARD.
YOU'LL DIE A MARINE, MIKE. SHE'LL GET A FLAG.
WHY ME?
ISOC BELIEVES IN YOU. YOU'RE THE BEST SOLDIER WE'VE GOT.
TEXT ME YOUR TWENTY AND I'LL HAVE A TEAM COME GET YOU.
IN WRITING. BEFORE SUNRISE.

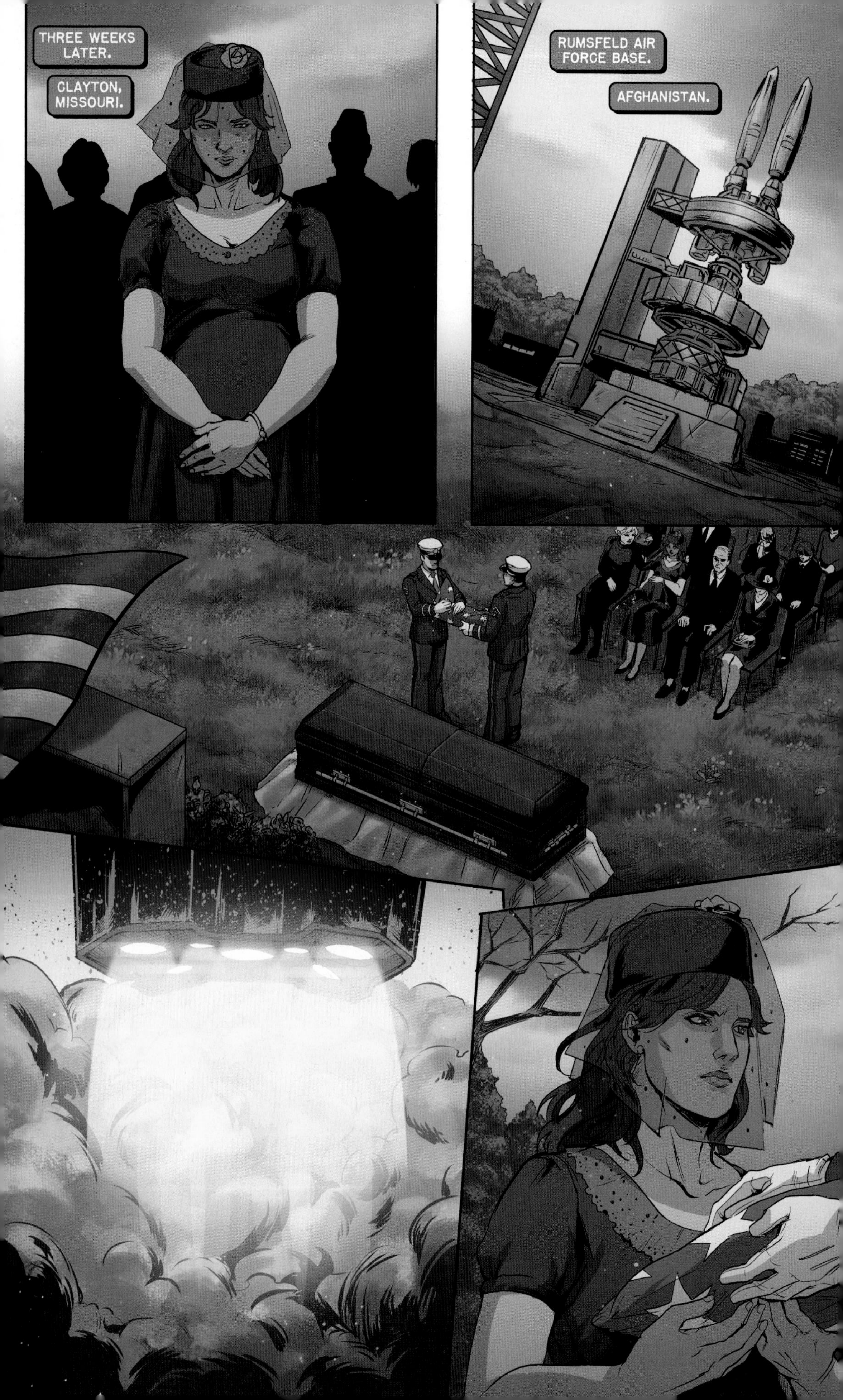
THREE WEEKS LATER.
CLAYTON, MISSOURI.
RUMSFELD AIR FORCE BASE.
AFGHANISTAN.

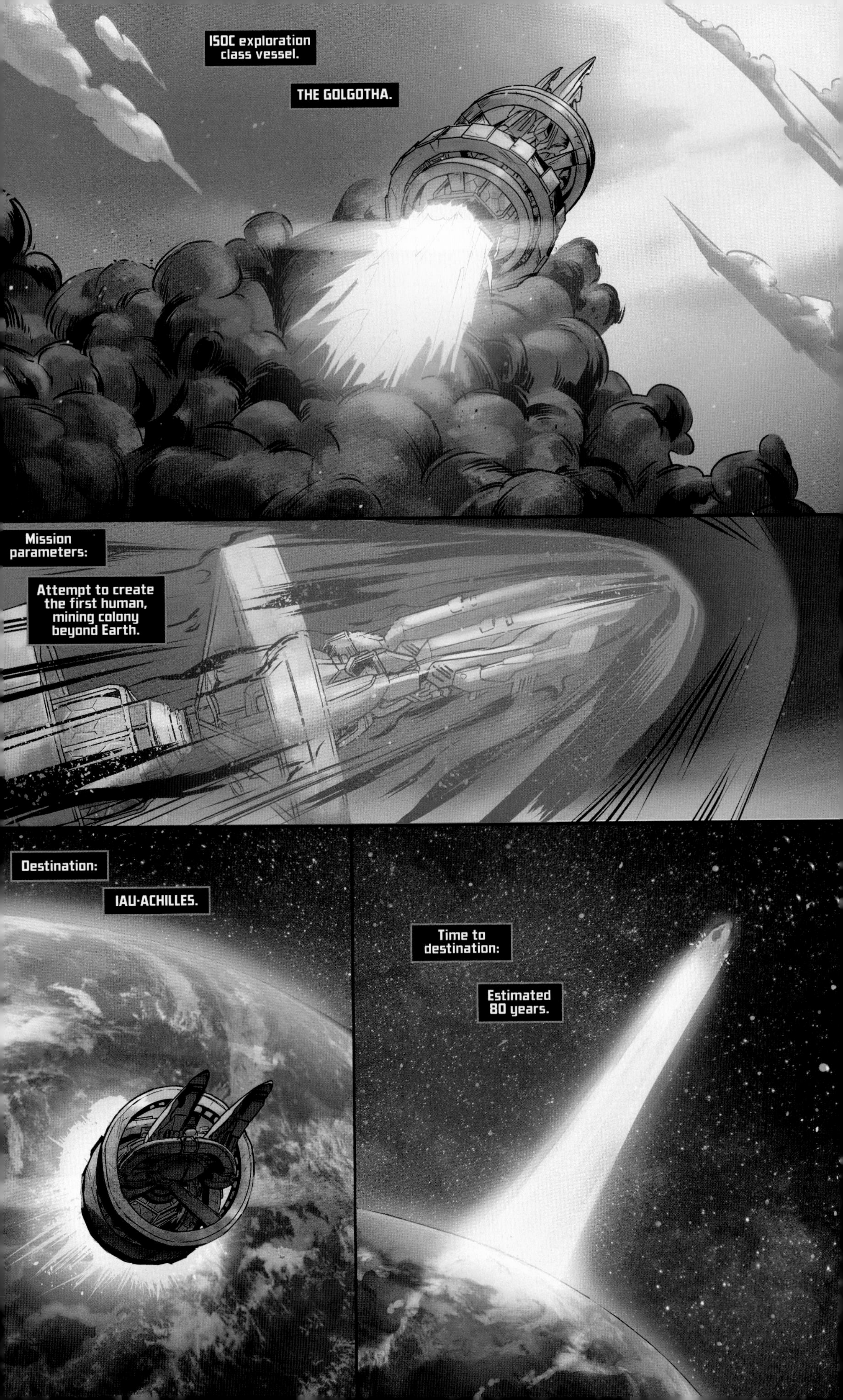
ISOC exploration class vessel.
THE GOLGOTHA.
Mission parameters:
Attempt to create the first human, mining colony beyond Earth.
Destination:
IAU-ACHILLES.
Time to destination:
Estimated 80 years.

Essential crew:

CARILLO, Anabelle. AEF. HUM-INT backup pilot to automated ship system.

MEAD, Lancaster. Engineer.

LIPPENCOTT, Charlene. PhD. Agrophysics.

GAFANI, Abdul-Ghafaar. Imam. AEF.

CHENG, David. Chaplain. AEF.

ROSENTHAL, Moshe. Rabbi. AEF.

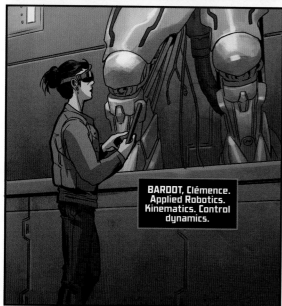

BARDOT, Clémence. Applied Robotics. Kinematics. Control dynamics.

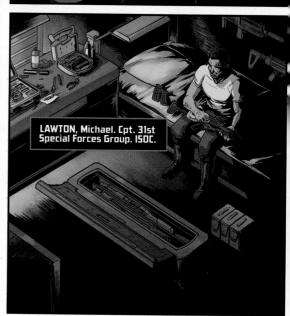

LAWTON, Michael. Cpt. 31st Special Forces Group. ISOC.

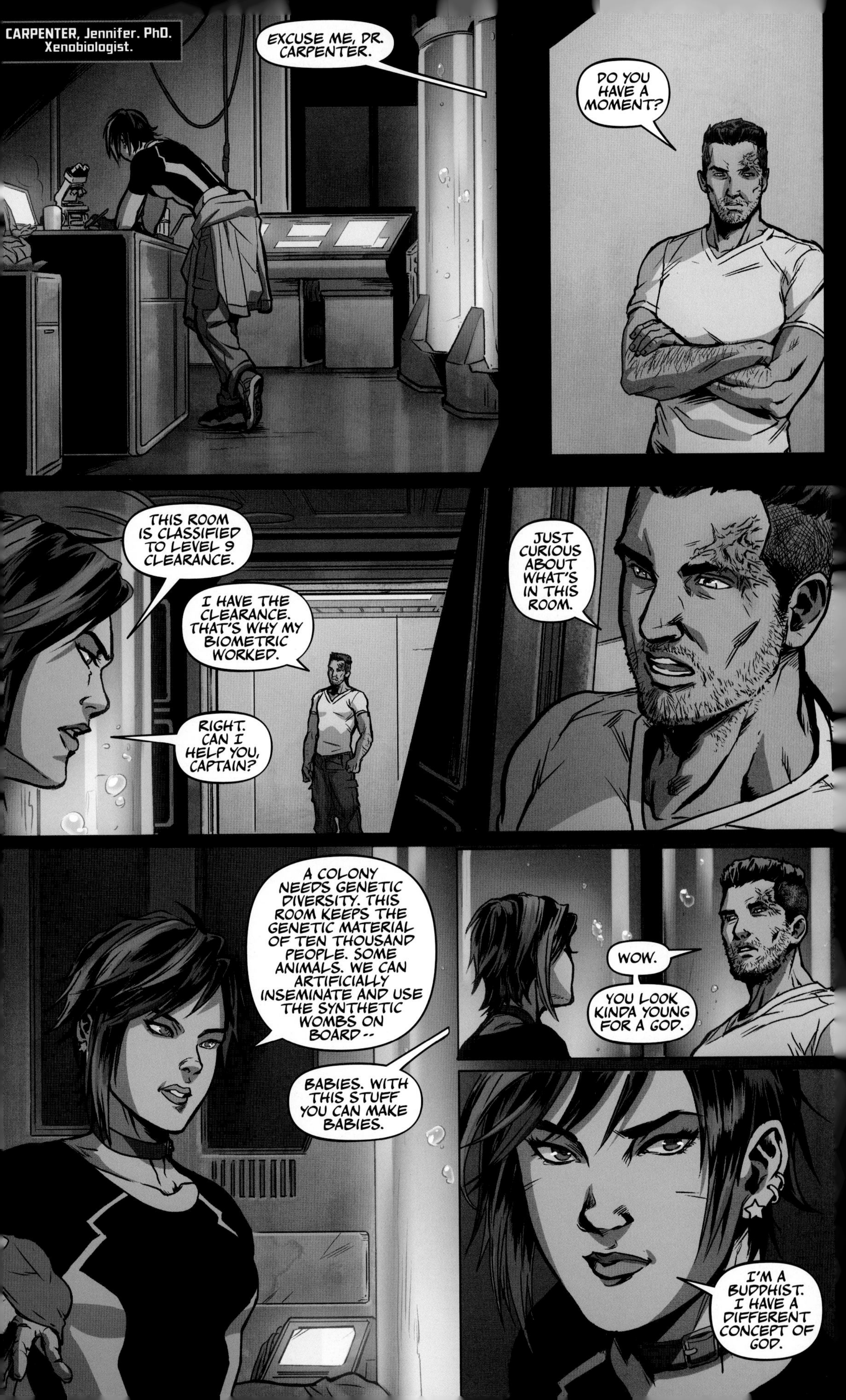
CARPENTER, Jennifer. PhD.
Xenobiologist.
EXCUSE ME, DR. CARPENTER.
DO YOU HAVE A MOMENT?
THIS ROOM IS CLASSIFIED TO LEVEL 9 CLEARANCE.
I HAVE THE CLEARANCE. THAT'S WHY MY BIOMETRIC WORKED.
RIGHT. CAN I HELP YOU, CAPTAIN?
JUST CURIOUS ABOUT WHAT'S IN THIS ROOM.
A COLONY NEEDS GENETIC DIVERSITY. THIS ROOM KEEPS THE GENETIC MATERIAL OF TEN THOUSAND PEOPLE. SOME ANIMALS. WE CAN ARTIFICIALLY INSEMINATE AND USE THE SYNTHETIC WOMBS ON BOARD--
BABIES. WITH THIS STUFF YOU CAN MAKE BABIES.
WOW.
YOU LOOK KINDA YOUNG FOR A GOD.
I'M A BUDDHIST. I HAVE A DIFFERENT CONCEPT OF GOD.

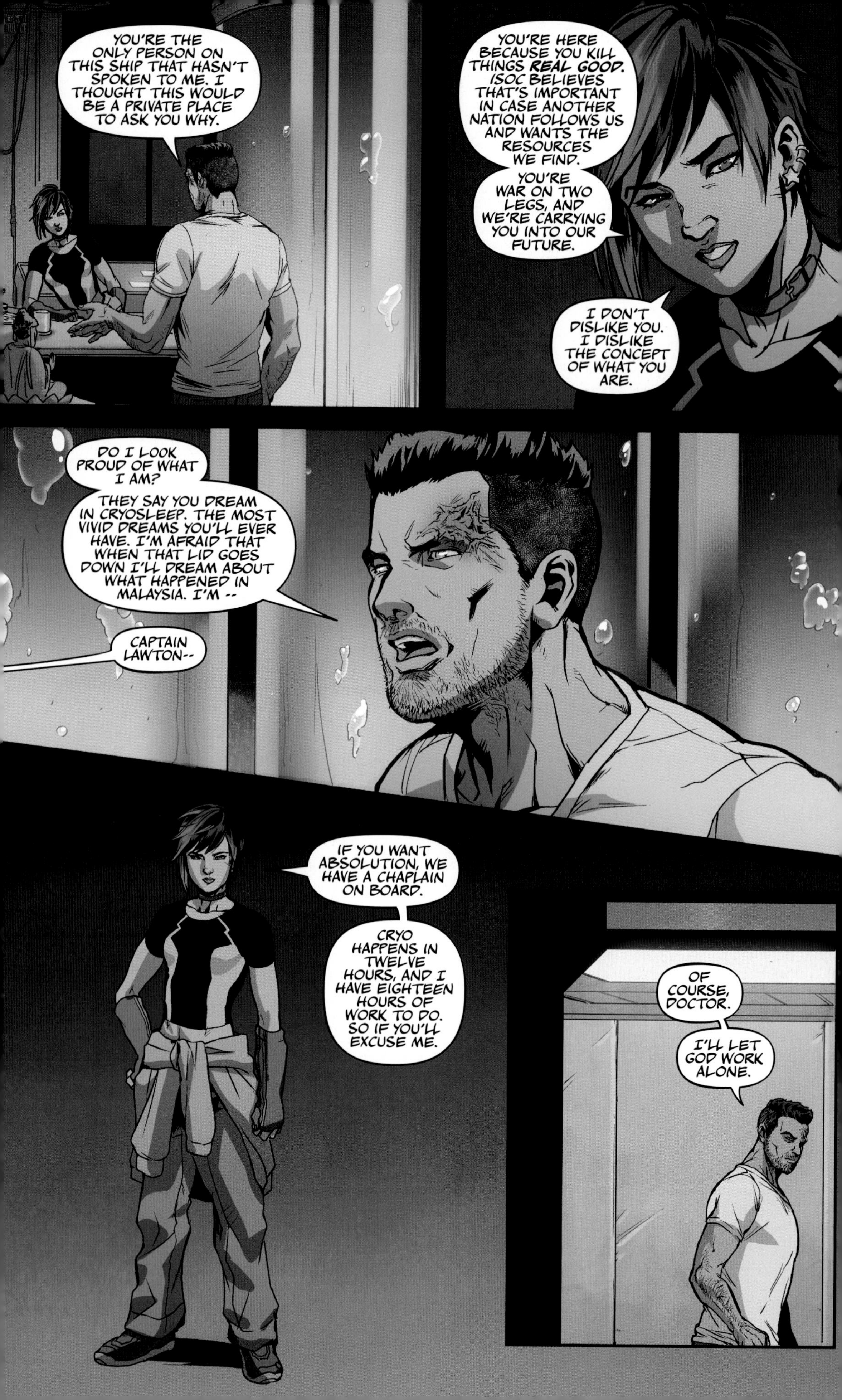
YOU'RE THE ONLY PERSON ON THIS SHIP THAT HASN'T SPOKEN TO ME. I THOUGHT THIS WOULD BE A PRIVATE PLACE TO ASK YOU WHY.
YOU'RE HERE BECAUSE YOU KILL THINGS REAL GOOD. ISOC BELIEVES THAT'S IMPORTANT IN CASE ANOTHER NATION FOLLOWS US AND WANTS THE RESOURCES WE FIND.
YOU'RE WAR ON TWO LEGS, AND WE'RE CARRYING YOU INTO OUR FUTURE.
I DON'T DISLIKE YOU. I DISLIKE THE CONCEPT OF WHAT YOU ARE.
DO I LOOK PROUD OF WHAT I AM?
THEY SAY YOU DREAM IN CRYOSLEEP. THE MOST VIVID DREAMS YOU'LL EVER HAVE. I'M AFRAID THAT WHEN THAT LID GOES DOWN I'LL DREAM ABOUT WHAT HAPPENED IN MALAYSIA. I'M --
CAPTAIN LAWTON--
IF YOU WANT ABSOLUTION, WE HAVE A CHAPLAIN ON BOARD.
CRYO HAPPENS IN TWELVE HOURS, AND I HAVE EIGHTEEN HOURS OF WORK TO DO. SO IF YOU'LL EXCUSE ME.
OF COURSE, DOCTOR.
I'LL LET GOD WORK ALONE.

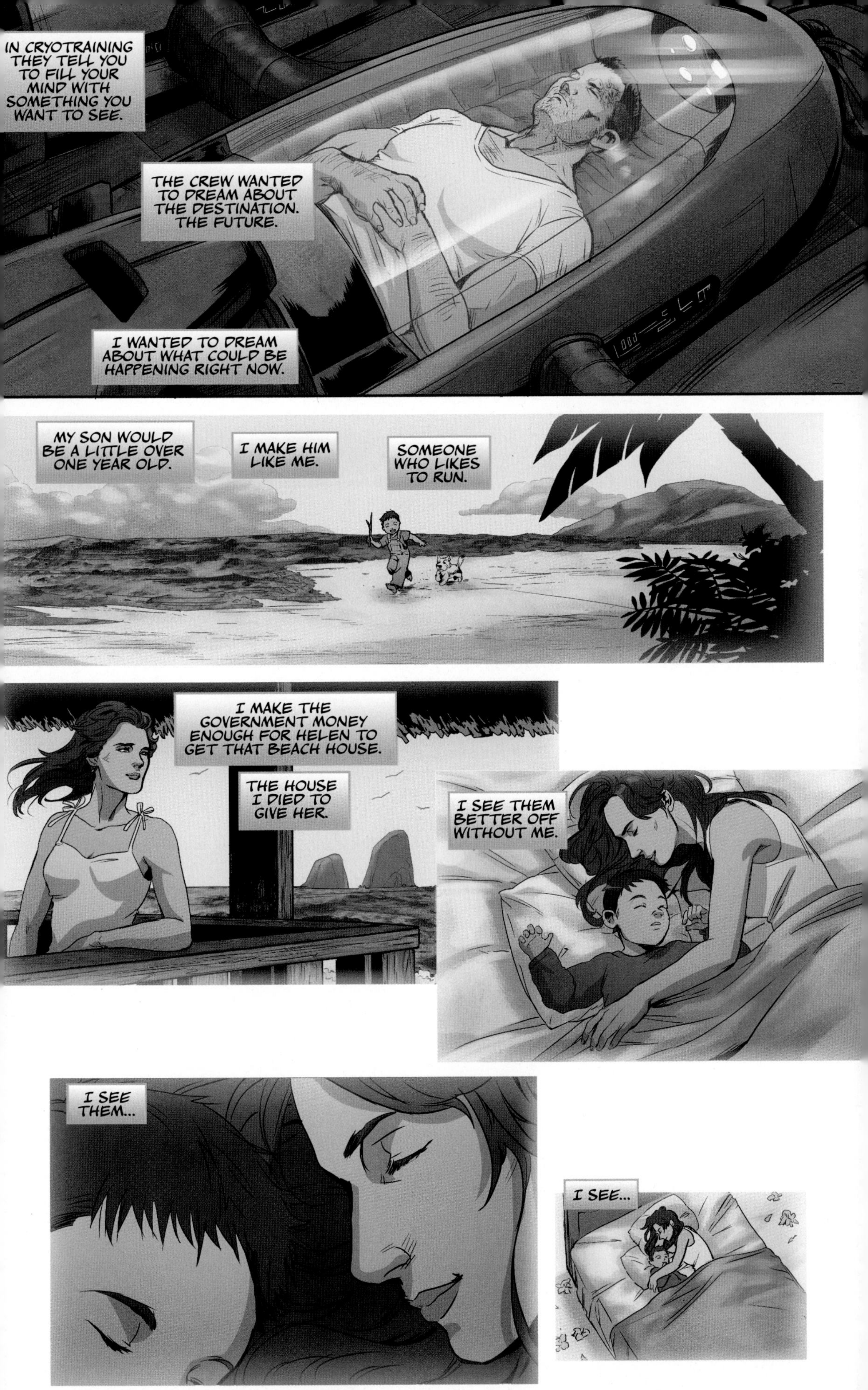
IN CRYOTRAINING THEY TELL YOU TO FILL YOUR MIND WITH SOMETHING YOU WANT TO SEE.
THE CREW WANTED TO DREAM ABOUT THE DESTINATION. THE FUTURE.
I WANTED TO DREAM ABOUT WHAT COULD BE HAPPENING RIGHT NOW.
MY SON WOULD BE A LITTLE OVER ONE YEAR OLD.
I MAKE HIM LIKE ME.
SOMEONE WHO LIKES TO RUN.
I MAKE THE GOVERNMENT MONEY ENOUGH FOR HELEN TO GET THAT BEACH HOUSE.
THE HOUSE I DIED TO GIVE HER.
I SEE THEM BETTER OFF WITHOUT ME.
I SEE THEM...
I SEE...

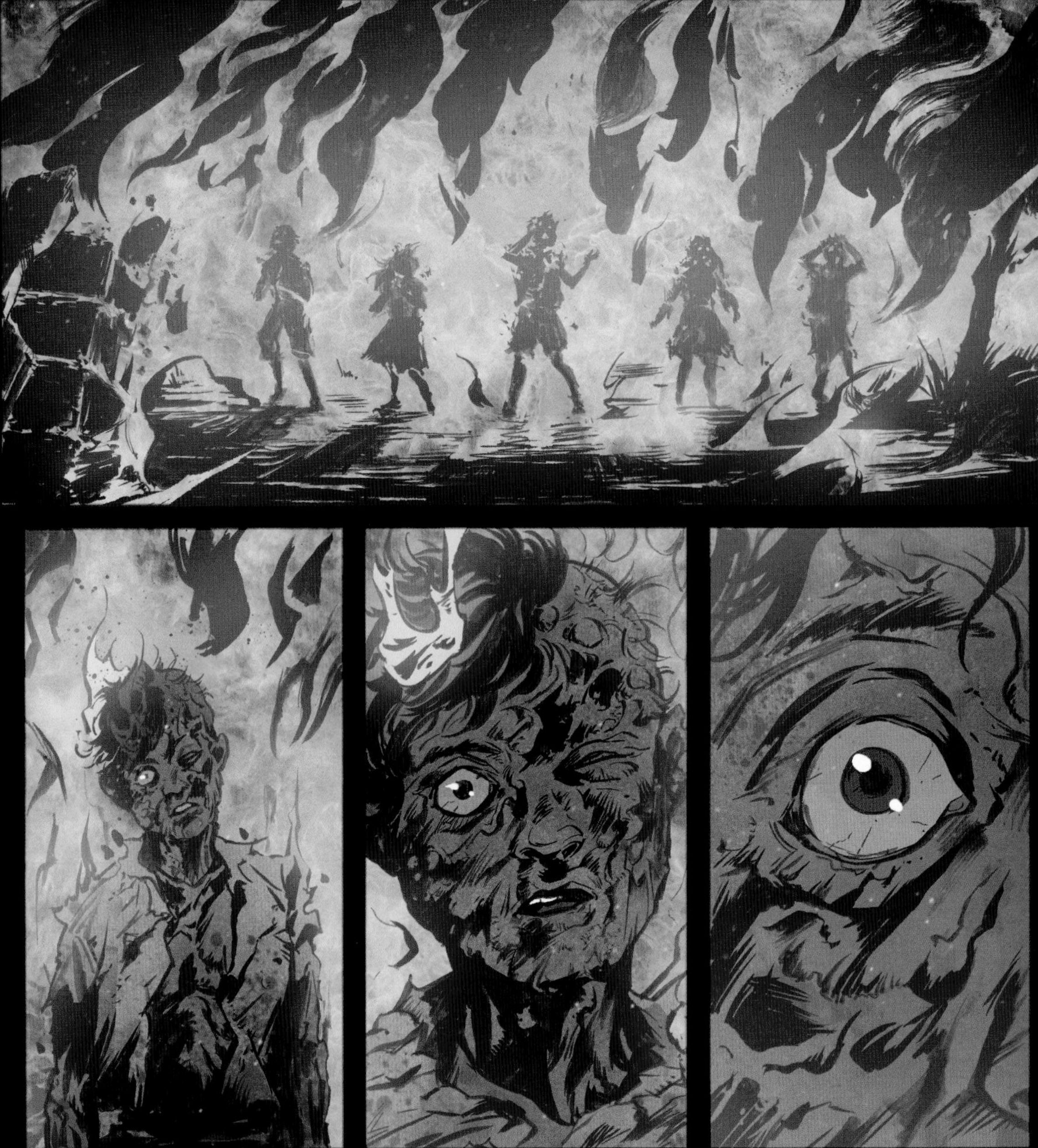

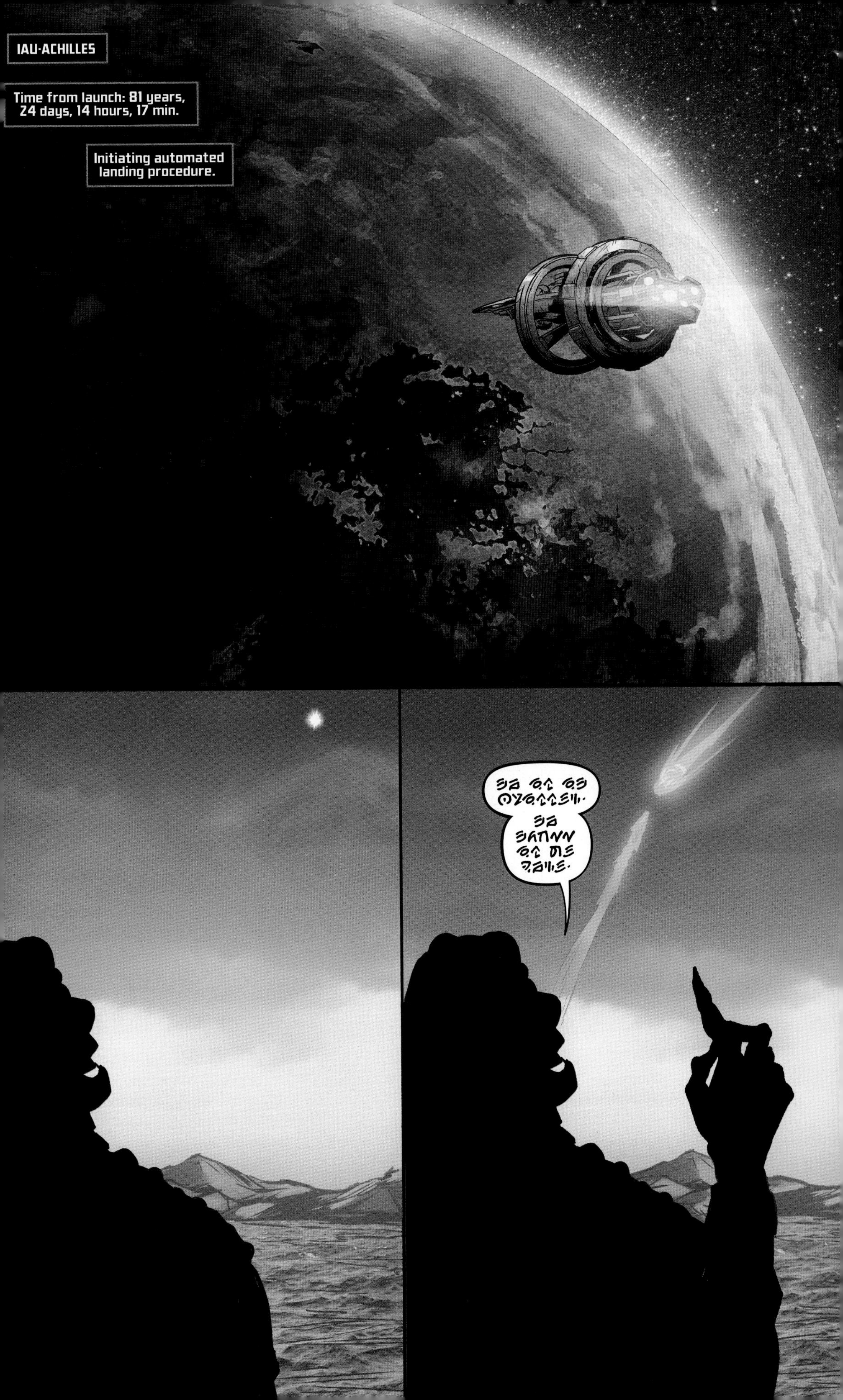
IAU-ACHILLES
Time from launch: 81 years, 24 days, 14 hours, 17 min.
Initiating automated landing procedure.

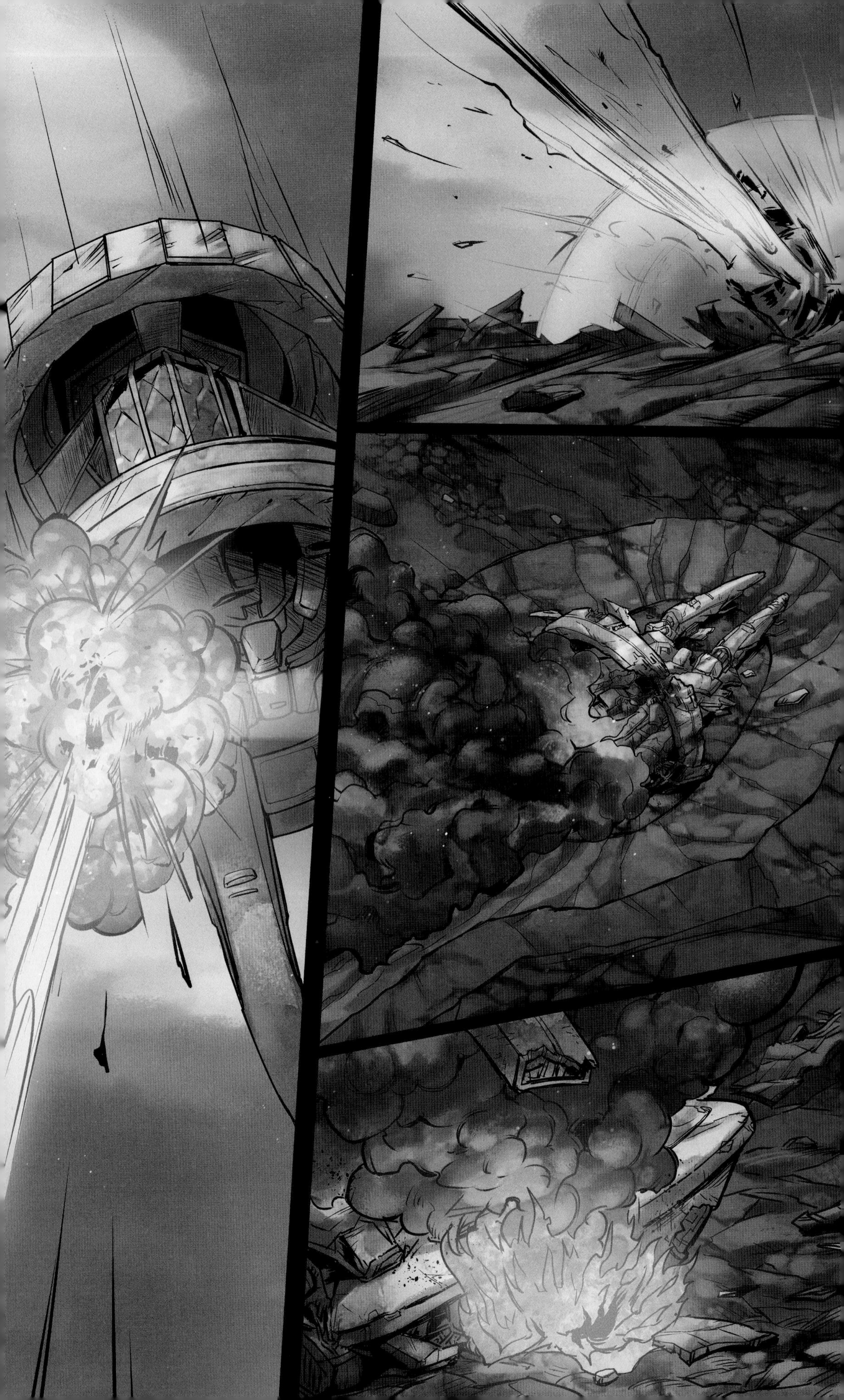

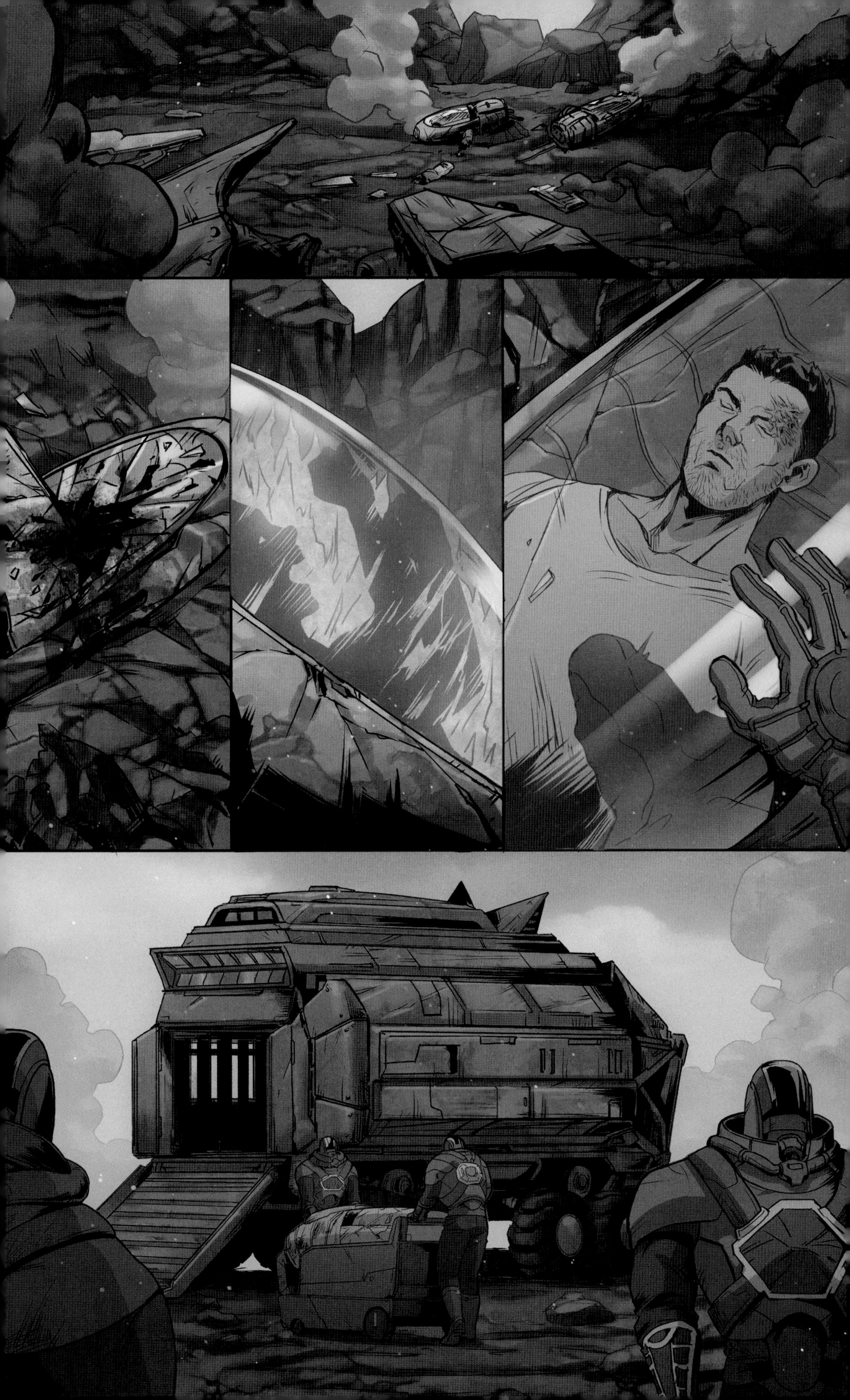

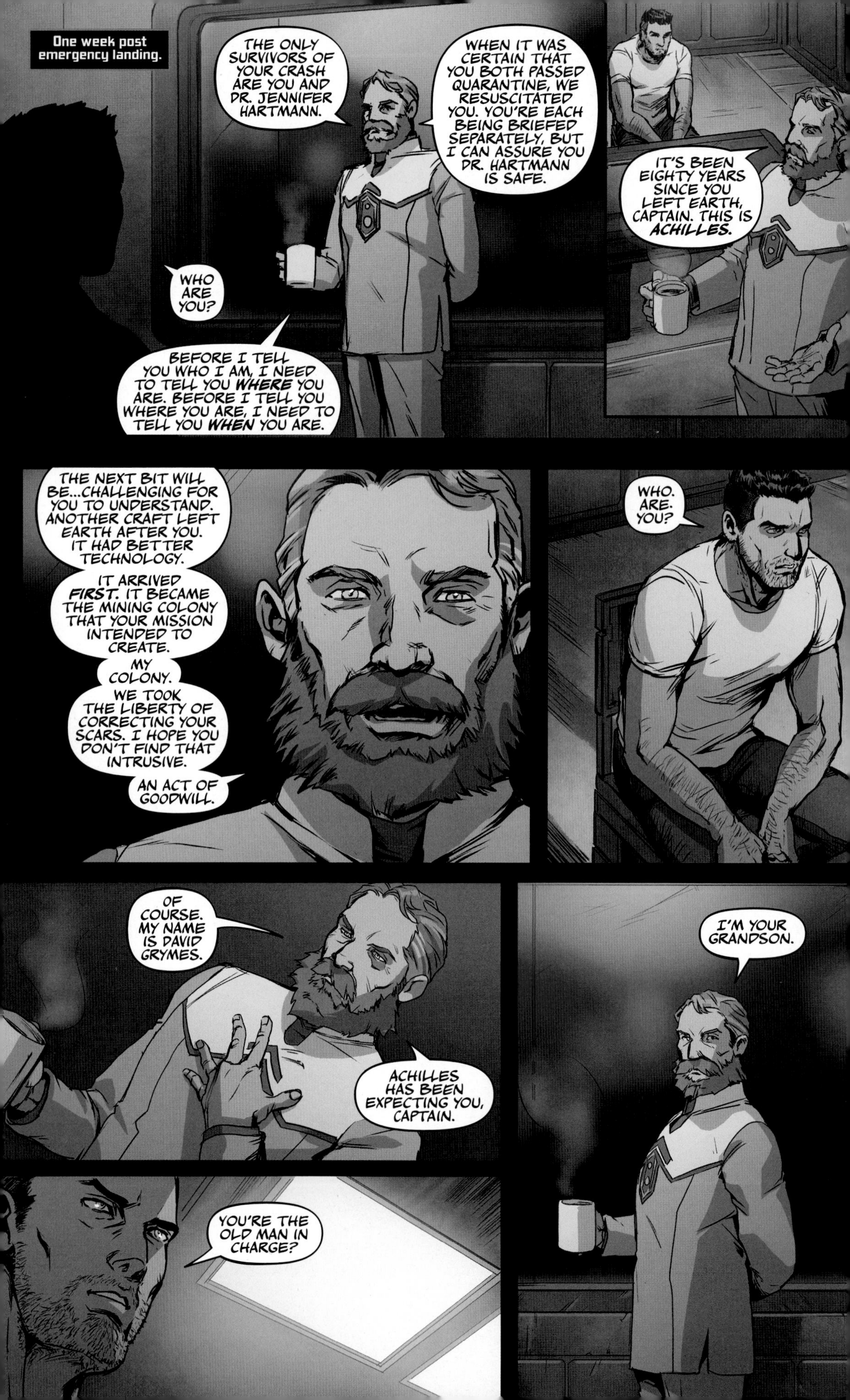
One week post emergency landing.
THE ONLY SURVIVORS OF YOUR CRASH ARE YOU AND DR. JENNIFER HARTMANN.
WHEN IT WAS CERTAIN THAT YOU BOTH PASSED QUARANTINE, WE RESUSCITATED YOU. YOU'RE EACH BEING BRIEFED SEPARATELY, BUT I CAN ASSURE YOU DR. HARTMANN IS SAFE.
WHO ARE YOU?
BEFORE I TELL YOU WHO I AM, I NEED TO TELL YOU WHERE YOU ARE. BEFORE I TELL YOU WHERE YOU ARE, I NEED TO TELL YOU WHEN YOU ARE.
IT'S BEEN EIGHTY YEARS SINCE YOU LEFT EARTH, CAPTAIN. THIS IS ACHILLES.
THE NEXT BIT WILL BE...CHALLENGING FOR YOU TO UNDERSTAND. ANOTHER CRAFT LEFT EARTH AFTER YOU. IT HAD BETTER TECHNOLOGY.
IT ARRIVED FIRST. IT BECAME THE MINING COLONY THAT YOUR MISSION INTENDED TO CREATE.
MY COLONY.
WE TOOK THE LIBERTY OF CORRECTING YOUR SCARS. I HOPE YOU DON'T FIND THAT INTRUSIVE.
AN ACT OF GOODWILL.
WHO. ARE. YOU?
OF COURSE. MY NAME IS DAVID GRYMES.
ACHILLES HAS BEEN EXPECTING YOU, CAPTAIN.
YOU'RE THE OLD MAN IN CHARGE?
I'M YOUR GRANDSON.

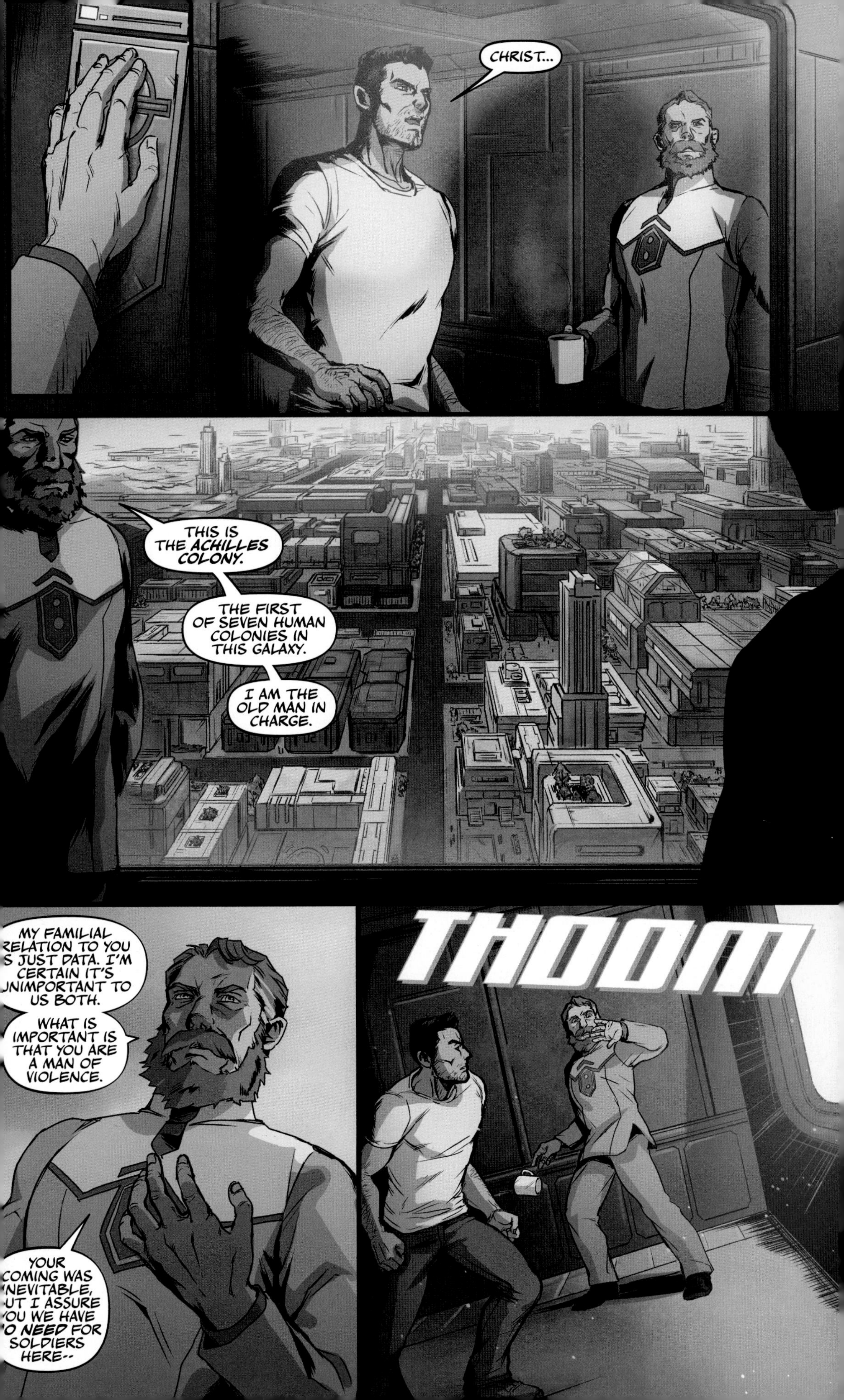
CHRIST...
THIS IS THE ACHILLES COLONY.
THE FIRST OF SEVEN HUMAN COLONIES IN THIS GALAXY.
I AM THE OLD MAN IN CHARGE.
MY FAMILIAL RELATION TO YOU IS JUST DATA. I'M CERTAIN IT'S UNIMPORTANT TO US BOTH.
WHAT IS IMPORTANT IS THAT YOU ARE A MAN OF VIOLENCE.
YOUR COMING WAS INEVITABLE, BUT I ASSURE YOU WE HAVE NO NEED FOR SOLDIERS HERE--
THOOM

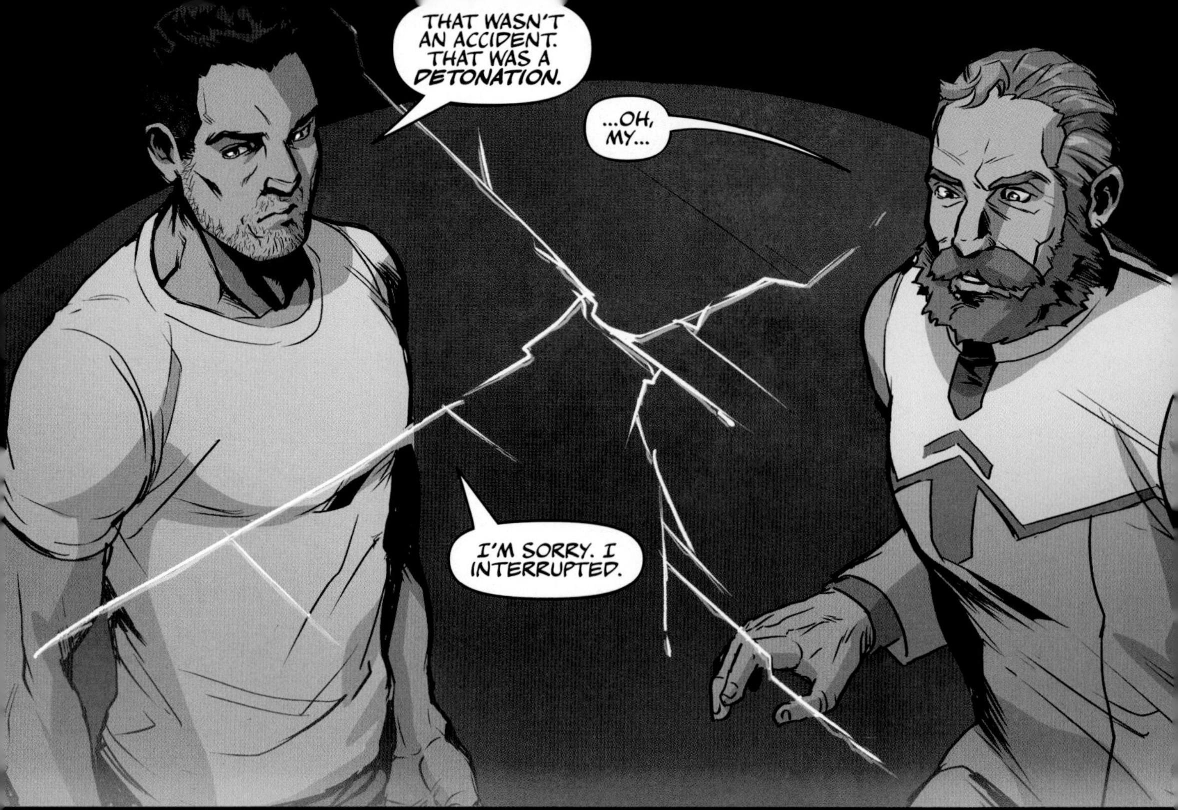
THAT WASN'T AN ACCIDENT. THAT WAS A DETONATION.
...OH, MY...
I'M SORRY. I INTERRUPTED.

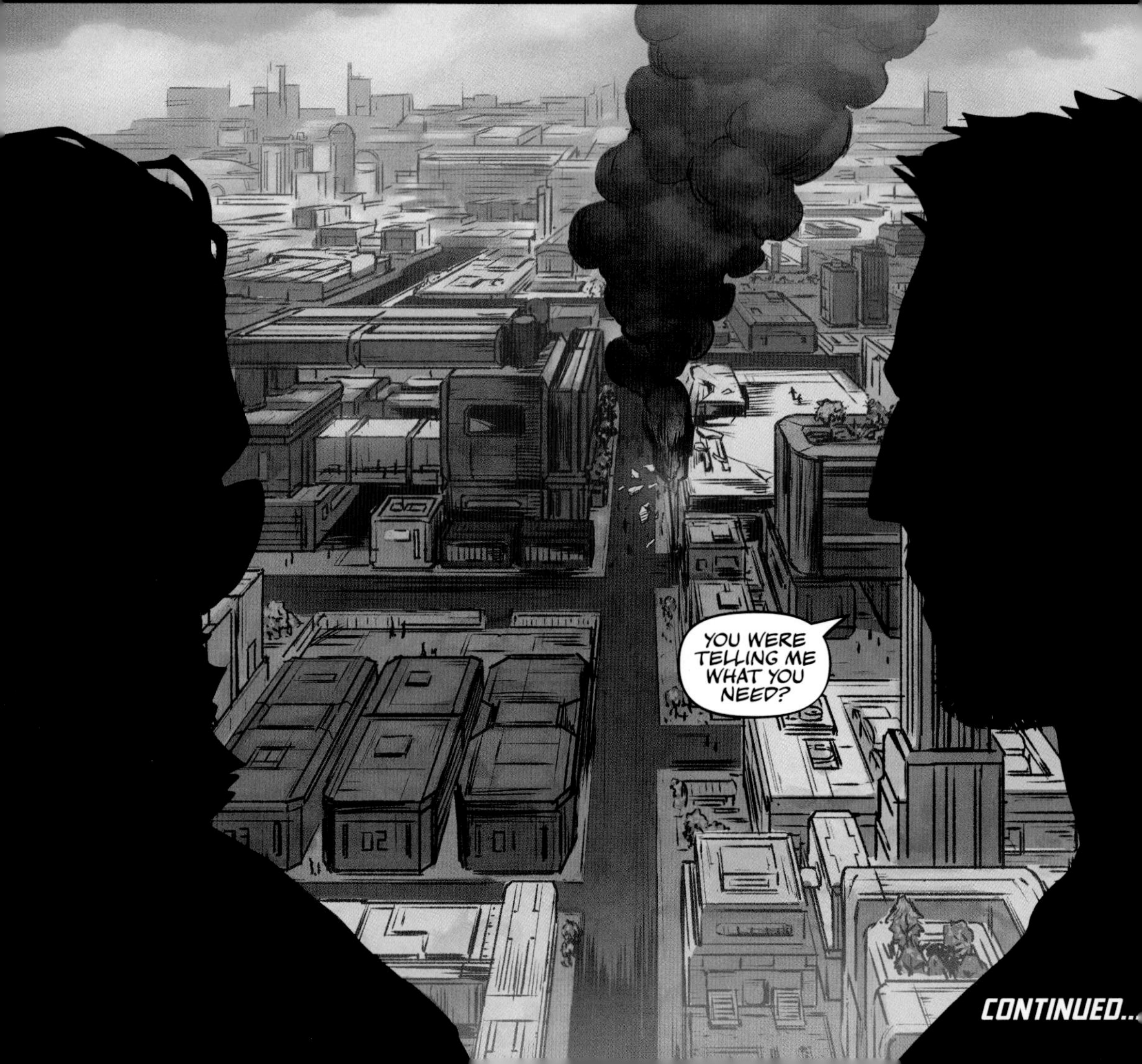
YOU WERE TELLING ME WHAT YOU NEED?
CONTINUED...

Meet the Creators of Postal

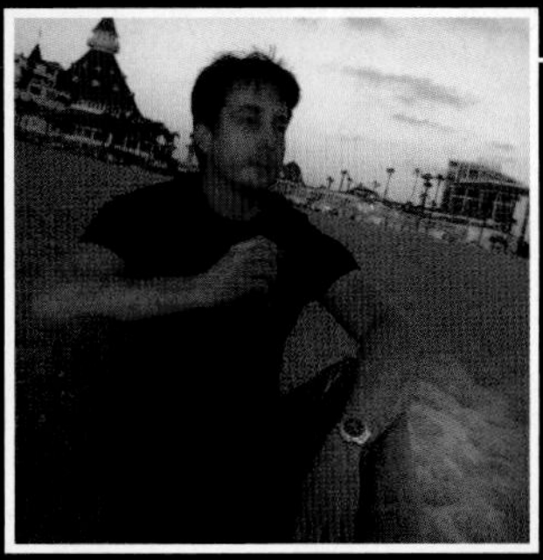

MATT HAWKINS

A veteran of the initial Image Comics launch, Matt started his career in comic book publishing in 1993 and has been working with Image as a creator, writer, and executive for over twenty years. President/ COO of Top Cow since 1998, Matt has created and written over thirty new franchises for Top Cow and Image including *Think Tank, Necromancer, VICE, Lady Pendragon,* and *Aphrodite IX* as well as handling the company's business affairs.

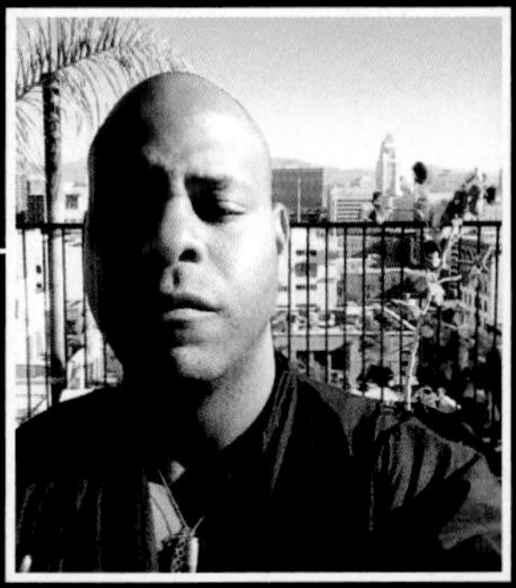

BRYAN HILL

Writes comics, writes movies, and makes films. He lives and works in Los Angeles. @bryanedwardhill | Instagram/bryanehill

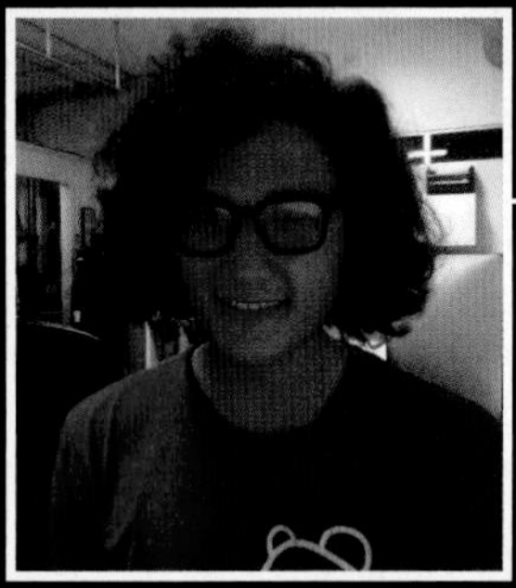

ISAAC GOODHART

A life-long comics fan, Isaac graduated from the School of Visual Arts in New York in 2010. In 2014, he was one of the winners for Top Cow's annual talent hunt. He currently lives in Los Angeles where he storyboards and draws comics.

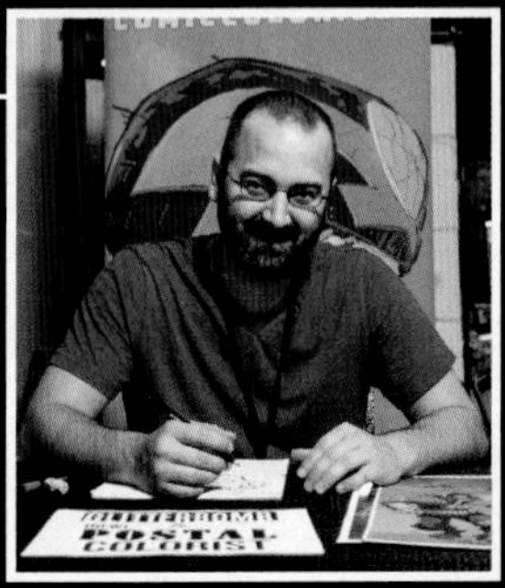

K. MICHAEL RUSSELL

Michael has been working as a comic book color artist since 2011. His credits include the Image series *Glitterbomb* with *Wayward* and *Thunderbolts* writer Jim Zub, *Hack/Slash*, *Judge Dredd*, and the Eisner and Harvey-nominated *In the Dark: A Horror Anthology*. He launched an online comic book coloring course in 2014 at ColoringComics.com and maintains a YouTube channel dedicated to coloring tutorials. He lives on the coast in Long Beach, Mississippi, with his wife of sixteen years, Tina. They have two cats. One is a jerk. @kmichaelrussell

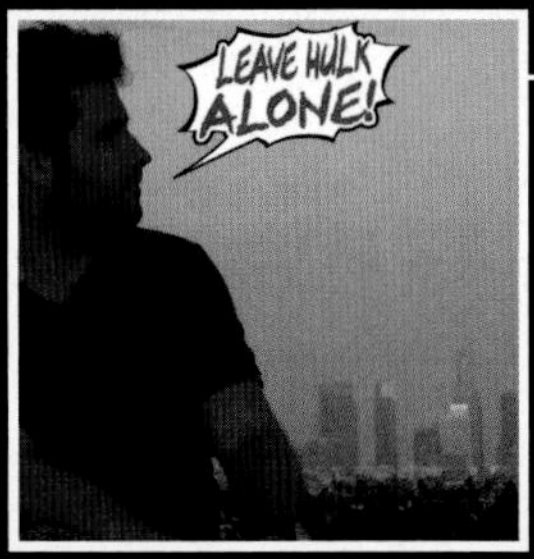
LEAVE HULK ALONE!

TROY PETERI

Starting his career at Comicraft, Troy Peteri lettered titles such as *Iron Man*, *Wolverine*, and *Amazing Spider-Man*, among many others. He's been lettering roughly 97% of all Top Cow titles since 2005. In addition to Top Cow, he currently letters comics from multiple publishers and websites, such as Image Comics, Dynamite, and Archaia. He (along with co-writer Tom Martin and artist Dave Lanphear) is currently writing (and lettering) *Tales of Equinox*, a webcomic of his own creation for www.Thrillbent.com. (Once again, www.Thrillbent.com.) He's still bitter about no longer lettering *The Darkness* and wants it back on stands immediately.

The Top Cow essentials checklist:

For more ISBN and ordering information on our latest collections go to:
www.topcow.com
Ask your retailer about our catalogue of collected editions,
digests, and hard covers or check the listings at:
Barnes and Noble, Amazon.com,
and other fine retailers.

To find your nearest comic shop go to:
www.comicshoplocator.com